WORST CONTACT

BAEN BOOKS EDITED
BY HANK DAVIS

The Human Edge by Gordon R. Dickson

We the Underpeople by Cordwainer Smith
When the People Fell by Cordwainer Smith

The Technic Civilization Saga
The Van Rijn Method by Poul Anderson
David Falkayn: Star Trader by Poul Anderson
Rise of the Terran Empire by Poul Anderson
Young Flandry by Poul Anderson
Captain Flandry: Defender of the Terran Empire by Poul Anderson
Sir Dominic Flandry: The Last Knight of Terra by Poul Anderson
Flandry's Legacy by Poul Anderson

The Best of the Bolos: Their Finest Hour by Keith Laumer

A Cosmic Christmas
A Cosmic Christmas 2 You
In Space No One Can Hear You Scream
The Baen Big Book of Monsters
As Time Goes By
Future Wars . . . and Other Punchlines
Worst Contact
Things from Outer Space (forthcoming)
If This Goes Wrong . . . (forthcoming)

WORST CONTACT

Edited by
HANK DAVIS

WORST CONTACT

A Baen Book

Baen Publishing Enterprises
P.O. Box 1403
Riverdale, NY 10471

ISBN 13: 978-1-4767-8098-6

Cover art by Stephen Hickman

First Baen printing, January 2016

Distributed by Simon & Schuster
1230 Avenue of the Americas
New York, NY 10020

Printed in the United States of America

10 9 8 7 6 5 4 3 2 1

CONTENTS

FROM FIRST TO WORST
Introduction by Hank Davis ✼ 1

PUPPET SHOW by Fredric Brown ✼ 7

CONTACT! by David Drake ✼ 19

THE FLAT-EYED MONSTER by William Tenn ✼ 37

THE POWER by Murray Leinster ✼ 71

EARLY MODEL by Robert Sheckley ✼ 91

HER SISTER'S KEEPER by Sarah A. Hoyt ✼ 113

PLAYTHING by Larry Niven ✼ 127

RANDOM SAMPLE by T. P. Caravan ✼ 133

NO LOVE IN ALL OF DWINGELOO by Tony Daniel ✼ 139

FIRST CONTACT, SORT OF
by Karen Haber and Carol Carr ✼ 159

FORTITUDE by David Brin ✼ 175

THEY'RE MADE OUT OF MEAT by Terry Bisson ✼ 189

ALIEN STONES by Gene Wolfe ✼ 195

PICTURES DON'T LIE by Katherine MacLean ✼ 231

BACKWARDNESS by Poul Anderson ✼ 251

DODGER FAN by Will Stanton ✼ 265

NO SHOULDER TO CRY ON by Hank Davis ✼ 271

HORNETS' NEST by Lloyd Biggle, Jr. ✼ 281

PROTECTED SPECIES by H. B. Fyfe ✼ 295

THE CAGE by A. Bertram Chandler ✼ 309

SHADOW WORLD by Clifford D. Simak ✼ 323

WORST CONTACT

DEDICATION

This one's for my nieces,
Sarah Davis and Jenny Snapp,
with whom I should make contact
more often.

ACKNOWLEDGEMENTS

My thanks to all the contributors (and raise a glass to absent friends), and to those who helped with advice, permissions, contact information, and other kindnesses, including Lara Allen, Katie Shea Boutillier, Hannah Fergesen, Linda Stanton French, Vaughne Hansen, Barry Malzberg, Cameron McClure, Lisa Rodgers, Darrell Schweitzer, John Silbersack, Bud Webster, David Wixon, and Eleanor Wood and probably other kindly carbon-based life forms which my decrepit memory has unforgivably overlooked.

FROM FIRST
TO WORST

Introduction by Hank Davis

"FIRST CONTACT" is, of course, the title of a story that Murray Leinster (the pseudonym of William Fitzgerald Jenkins) published in the May 1945 issue of the field's flagship magazine, *Astounding Science-Fiction*. The editor, John W. Campbell, obviously thought highly of the tale, and made it the cover story, with a painting of the two starships from different planets hovering next to each other in interstellar space. (The cover painting was by William Timmins, a now largely forgotten illustrator.)

I don't know if that was the first time the phrase "first contact" was used in science fiction (first first contact?), but ever since Leinster's classic story, the phrase is often used when humans and extraterrestrials meet for the first time. There were first contact stories prior to Leinster's, such as Stanley G. Weinbaum's celebrated "A Martian Odyssey" and Raymond Z. Gallun's "Old Faithful" (both in 1934, the latter in *Astounding*), but Leinster took a fresh look at the situation. Two starships, one from Earth, the other from parts unknown, encounter each other in the depths of interstellar space— and what do they do next? Neither one can leave, because the other might follow the departing starship back home, discover the location

1

of its home planet, and bring back an attacking fleet. It seems that the only possible out, at least for the human's ship, is to destroy all onboard information that might betray the location of Earth, then either attack the other, or just blow up their own ship and keep the location of the home world secret.

However, neither of those events happen. Leinster gives an ingenious solution to the dilemma which I'm not going to give away here. The result was an instant classic, one of the most repeatedly anthologized stories in SF—editor Ben Bova reprinted it in *two* different anthologies, for example. When the Science Fiction Writers of America took a poll of their members in the late 1960s to determine the best short stories published prior to the 1964 advent of SFWA's Nebula Award, "First Contact" tied with Theodore Sturgeon's "Microcosmic God" for the number four spot, and was included in volume I of *The Science Fiction Hall of Fame*. Later, after Retro-Hugo Awards were inaugurated, it won a Retro-Hugo in 1996. It has been translated into many other languages, it was adapted for radio on both *Dimension X* and *X Minus 1*, and has had the dubious honor of having its famous last line "borrowed" for a comic book story I read in the late 1950s. *Star Trek: The Next Generation*, and a later *Star Trek* movie, both used "First Contact" as a title. (Leinster's estate sued over the movie's title, but lost.) The story is a milestone in science fiction.

There was even a Cold War aspect. In 1958, Russian paleontologist Ivan Yefremov wrote a story whose title, rendered into English, is "The Heart of the Serpent," in which, once again, two ships, one from (of course) a Communist Earth, encounter each other—but there is no possible danger, since for a race to be advanced enough to travel between stars, its society must have inevitably been on The Right Side of History, hence Communist, and therefore peaceful. (Sarcasm? Who, me?) The characters mention Leinster's story, and describe its author as obviously having the evil "heart of a serpent."

When the Russians attack something for impure ideology, it must be famous. (No word, AFAIK, on what the ChiComs thought of it.) But "First Contact" is not in this book. That's because that first contact went well for both parties. Suppose it hadn't?

Murray Leinster was a generally optimistic writer, but not unrealistically so. He wrote other stories of first contact, and in some of them, the ending was far from cheerful. One of them, "The Power," *is* included in this book, along with a number of other writers' stories of *worst* contacts. Sometimes, the humans get the short end of the stick, and sometimes it's the ETs. The results may be tragic or humorous, or a mix. But at least one of the sides involved would greatly prefer that their meeting had never taken place.

There were first contact stories before SF magazines even existed, of course. The label fits both H. G. Wells' *The War of the Worlds* and *The First Men in the Moon*, plus his short story, "The Crystal Egg." If contact with humans in a parallel universe counts, his *Men Like Gods* also qualifies. Except for "The Crystal Egg," none of those human/alien encounters went well—to put it mildly, in *The War of the Worlds*—and the eponymous "egg" is a sort of two-way interplanetary TV camera/viewer (a Mars-Earth reality show?), which limits how badly things can go. Some writer on Wikipedia considers *The Time Machine* to be a first contact story. I don't agree, but if making contact with one's distant descendants counts, then Wells' *The Croquet Player*, going in the other direction, should be added to the list. And maybe his novel *Star-Begotten*, as well.

Nor was Wells the first. In 1752 Voltaire wrote "Micromegas," telling of the visit to Earth of two gigantic aliens, one, from Saturn, who stands 6,000 feet tall and is dwarfed by his companion from a planet circling the star Sirius, who is 20 times as tall. Voltaire's intent is satirical and to make humans appear ridiculous, so it's an early worst contact.

There has been no shortage of first contact stories since Leinster's classic, either, and plenty of those turn out badly for one or both parties. I might have included Damon Knight's classic short story, "To Serve Man" (whose punchline will not be revealed here) if it hadn't already been so frequently reprinted, and even adapted into an episode of the original *Twilight Zone*. But readers definitely should go look it up. Novels, too, such as Larry Niven and Jerry Pournelle's novels *The Mote in God's Eye* (written, according to Niven, to be "the epitome of first contact novels") and *Footfall*. And movies, such as

The Thing from Another World, and *Independence Day*, to name two examples four decades apart. And while this book has (modest cough) a generous selection of very good stories, there were a lot of other good ones I could have used. I regret not being able to include A. E. van Vogt's "The Monster" (also known as "Resurrection"), and would have liked to include a Gordon R. Dickson story, except that I already included my favorites in *The Human Edge*, still available as a Baen e-book. I particularly recommend "On Messenger Mountain" in that collection. Add that to the Knight and van Vogt titles previously cited.

Of course some think any race that doesn't blow itself up and manages to reach the stars will necessarily be peaceful. Carl Sagan argued thus. That's hardly the only major disagreement I have with the late Dr. Sagan, but for a quick thought experiment, imagine that the Nazis developed the A-bomb first, took over the world, then built starships. Peaceful?

Speaking of Carl Sagan, I was surprised to see that a Canadian blogger reviewed my (yikes!) 48-year-old story, included in these pages, and thought I was reacting to Sagan's argument. At the time I wrote the story (summer of 1967), I was aware there was a book, *Intelligent Life in the Universe*, a collaboration between two scientists, a Russian and an American (I. S. Shklovskii and Carl Sagan), which everyone in SF and their cats were raving about, but Sagan's name hadn't stuck in my mind (though, oddly, the Russian's had), and the price of the book put it out of my reach, so Sagan was an unknown to me, along with any of his notions about ETs. The only Sagan I was aware of was named Françoise. In reality, I was thinking of a remark Robert A. Heinlein had made along the lines of "suppose the aliens land and they aren't peaceful and benevolent," and considering doing a switch on the peaceful alien visitors scenario, but more subtly than the old alien invaders shtick. John W. Campbell's alleged insistence for Earthling superiority over aliens, also mentioned by the blogger, may have helped sell the story, but that wasn't on my mind at all. For one thing, I was skeptical about the reality of that insistence, being aware of several stories in *Astounding/Analog* which were counter-examples (though later, I learned that one of those stories, Heinlein's "Goldfish Bowl," might not be a good counter-example after all).

Sagan thought visitors from space would be peaceful, but a considerably higher-ranking scientist, Stephen Hawking, thinks that contact with aliens would be disastrous for Earth. Of course, in the absence of any actual contact with aliens, it's all guesswork. In the meantime, a number of possibilities are entertainingly explored in the following pages. Some of the stories involve Martians, though ETs from inside our Solar System in general, or the Red Planet in particular, are now known to be very unlikely, alas. (We didn't get the Solar System we deserved—whom do I complain to?) My own story was written as a near future tale, and the publisher and I have done some tweaking to keep it still in the future, but my nostalgia for Wells, Burroughs, Brackett, Bradbury and others would be reason enough to leave the Martians alone in those stories by others. Save the Endangered Martians!

And don't forget, "first contact" should not be used as a verb. Nero Wolfe wouldn't approve.

—**Hank Davis**
September, 2015

PUPPET SHOW

by Fredric Brown

Diplomatic dealings with other humans can be complicated enough, but this encounter with the extraterrestrial equivalent was recomplicated and re-recomplicated. And anyone representing the human race should always choose his words very carefully.

⚒ ⚒ ⚒

FREDRIC BROWN *(1906-1972) was a writer with towering reputations in both the science fiction and mystery fields. After writing many short stories for the mystery pulps of the 1940s, he won the Edgar Award of the Mystery Writers of America in 1947 for his first mystery novel,* The Fabulous Clipjoint. *He also wrote many stories for the SF magazines of the 1940s, and was a fixture of* Astounding Science-Fiction's *"Golden Age." He was a master craftsman in both fields, with a wide range of characterization, a lean hard-boiled style, and a sneaky touch of humor. In particular, he was the unchallenged master of the short-short story, a story so short it would take up only one or two pages, yet would have a tightly-controlled plot, and usually a surprise ending— often not a happy one. His sardonic sense of humor was displayed in such SF novels as* What Mad Universe *and* Martians Go Home, *but he also wrote deadly serious novels such as* The Lights in the Sky Are Stars *and* The Mind Thing. *His short story, "Arena," was adapted into one of* Star Trek's *first season episodes (though there was an episode of* The

7

Outer Limits *a couple of years earlier which had a suspicious resemblance to the same story, but didn't acknowledge any debt to Brown). He inserted into a story of more than usual length two lines which have become known as the shortest horror story ever told: "The last man on Earth sat in a room. There was a knock on the door." While this story isn't one of his short-shorts, it concisely tells its tale with brisk economy and makes its concluding point in just a few well-chosen words.*

HORROR CAME TO CHERRYBELL at a little after noon on a blistering hot day in August.

Perhaps that is redundant; any August day in Cherrybell, Arizona, is blistering hot. It is on Highway 89 about forty miles south of Tucson and about thirty miles north of the Mexican border. It consists of two filling stations, one on each side of the road to catch travelers going in both directions, a general store, a beer-and-wine-license-only tavern, a tourist-trap type trading post for tourists who can't wait until they reach the border to start buying serapes and huaraches, a deserted hamburger stand, and a few 'dobe houses inhabited by Mexican-Americans who work in Nogales, the border town to the south, and who, for God knows what reason, prefer to live in Cherrybell and commute, some of them in Model T Fords. The sign on the highway says "Cherrybell, Pop. 42," but the sign exaggerates. Pop died last year—Pop Anders, who ran the now-deserted hamburger stand—and the correct figure is 41.

Horror came to Cherrybell mounted on a burro led by an ancient, dirty and gray bearded desert rat of a prospector who later—nobody got around to asking his name for a while—gave the name of Dade Grant. Horror's name was Garth. He was approximately nine feet tall but so thin, almost a stick-man, that he could not have weighed over a hundred pounds. Old Dade's burro carried him easily, despite the fact that his feet dragged in the sand on either side. Being dragged through the sand for, as it later turned out, well over five miles hadn't caused the slightest wear on the shoes—more like buskins, they were—which constituted all that he wore except for a pair of what could have been swimming trunks, in robin's-egg blue. But it wasn't his dimensions that made him horrible to look upon; it was his *skin*. It looked red, raw. It looked as though he had been skinned alive, and the skin replaced upside down, raw side out. His skull, his face, were equally narrow or elongated; otherwise in every visible way he appeared human—or at least humanoid. Unless you counted such little things as the fact that his hair was a robin's-egg blue to match his trunks, as were his eyes and his boots. Blood red and light blue.

Casey, owner of the tavern was the first one to see them coming across the plain, from the direction of the mountain range to the east. He'd stepped out of the back door of his tavern for a breath of fresh, if hot, air. They were about a hundred yards away at that time, and already he could see the utter alienness of the figure on the lead burro. Just alienness at that distance, the horror came only at closer range. Casey's jaw dropped and stayed down until the strange trio was about fifty yards away, then he started slowly toward them. There are people who run at the sign of the unknown, others who advance to meet it. Casey advanced, however slowly, to meet it.

Still in the wide open, twenty yards from the back of the little tavern, he met them. Dade Grant stopped and dropped the rope by which he was leading the burro. The burro stood still and dropped its head. The stick-man stood up simply by planting his feet solidly and standing, astride the burro. He stepped one leg across it and stood a moment, leaning his weight against his hands on the burro's back, and then sat down in the sand. "High-gravity planet," he said. "Can't stand long."

"Kin I get water for my burro?" the prospector asked Casey. "Must be purty thirsty by now. Hadda leave water bags, some other things, so it could carry—" He jerked a thumb toward the red-and-blue horror.

Casey was just realizing that it *was* a horror. At a distance the color combination seemed a bit *outré*, but close— The skin was rough and seemed to have veins on the outside and looked moist (although it wasn't) and *damn* if it didn't look just like he had his skin peeled off and put back upside down. Or just peeled off, period. Casey had never seen anything like it and hoped he wouldn't ever see anything like it again.

Casey felt something behind him and looked over his shoulder. Others had seen now and were coming, but the nearest of them, a pair of boys, were ten yards behind him. "*Muchachos,*" he called out. "*Aqua por el burro. Un pazal. Pronto.*"

He looked back and said, "What—? Who—?"

"Name's Dade Grant," said the prospector, putting out a hand, which Casey took absently. When he let got of it, it jerked back over the desert rat's shoulders, thumb indicating the thing that sat on the sand. "His name's Garth, he tells me. He's an extra something or other, and he's some kind of minister."

Casey nodded at the stick-man and was glad to get a nod in return instead of an extended hand. "I'm Manuel Casey," he said. "What does he mean, an extra something?"

The stick-man's voice was unexpectedly deep and vibrant. "I am an extraterrestrial. And a minister plenipotentiary."

Surprisingly, Casey was a moderately well-educated man and knew both of those phrases; he was probably the only person in Cherrybell who would have known the second one. Less surprisingly, considering the speaker's appearance, he believed both of them. "What can I do for you, sir?" he asked. "But first, why not come in out of the sun?"

"No, thank you. It's a bit cooler here than they told me it would be, but I'm quite comfortable. This is equivalent to a cool spring evening on my planet. And as to what you can do for me, you can notify your authorities of my presence. I believe they will be interested."

Well, Casey thought, by blind luck he's hit the best man for his purpose within at least twenty miles. Manuel Casey was half-Irish, half-Mexican. He had a half brother who was half-Irish and half-assorted American, and the half brother was a bird colonel at Davis Monthan Air Force Base in Tucson. He said, "Just a minute, Mr. Garth. I'll telephone. You, Mr. Grant, would you want to come inside?"

"Naw, I don't mind sun. Out in it all day every day. An' Garth here, he ast me if I'd stick with him till he was finished with what he's gotta do here. Said he'd gimme something purty vallable if I did. Something'—a 'lectronic—"

"An electronic battery-operated portable ore indicator," Garth said. "A simple little device, indicates presence of a concentration of ore up to two miles, indicates kind, grade, quantity and depth."

Casey gulped, excused himself, and pushed throught the gathering crowd into his tavern. He had Colonel Casey on the phone in one minute, but it took him another four minutes to convince the colonel that he was neither drunk not joking.

Twenty-five minutes after that there was a noise in the sky, a noise that swelled and then died as a four-man helicopter sat down and shut off its rotors a dozen yards from an extraterrestrial, two men and a burro. Casey alone had had the courage to rejoin the trio from the desert; there were other spectators, but they still held well back.

Colonel Casey, a major, a captain and a lieutenant who was the helicopter's pilot all came out and ran over. The stick-man stood up, all nine feet of him; from the effort it cost him to stand, you could tell that he was used to a much lighter gravity than Earth's. He bowed, repeated his name and identification of himself as an extraterrestrial and a minister plenipotentiary. Then he apologized for sitting down again, explained why it was necessary, and sat down.

The colonel introduced himself and the three who had come with him. "And now, sir, what can we do for you?"

The stick-man made a grimace that was probably intended as a smile. His teeth were the same light blue as his hair and eyes. "You have a cliché, 'take me to your leader.' I do not ask that. In fact, I *must* remain here. Nor do I ask that any of your leaders be brought here to me. That would be impolite. I am perfectly willing for you to represent them, to talk to you and let you questions me. But I do ask one thing.

"You have tape recorders. I ask that, before I talk or answer questions, you have one brought. I want to be sure that the message your leaders eventually receive is full and accurate."

"Fine," the colonel said. He turned to the pilot. "Lieutenant, get on the radio in the whirlybird and tell them to get us a tape recorder faster than possible. It can be dropped by para— No, that'd take longer, rigging it for a drop. Have them send it by another helicopter." The lieutenant turned to go. "Hey," the colonel said. "Also fifty yards of extension cord. We'll have to plug it in inside Manny's tavern."

The lieutenant sprinted for the helicopter.

The others sat and sweated a moment and then Manuel Casey stood up. "That's a half an hour wait," he said, "and if we're going to sit here in the sun, who's for a bottle of cold beer? You, Mr. Garth?"

"It is a cold beverage, is it not? I am a bit chilly. If you have something hot—?"

"Coffee, coming up. Can I bring you a blanket?"

"No, thank you. It will not be necessary."

Casey left and shortly returned with a tray with half a dozen bottles of cold beer and a cup of steaming coffee. The lieutenant was back by then. Casey put down the tray and first served the stick-man, who sipped the coffee and said, "It is delicious."

Colonel Casey cleared his throat. "Serve our prospector friend next, Manny. As for us—well, drinking is forbidden on duty, but it was a hundred and twelve in the shade in Tucson, and this is hotter and also is not in the shade. Gentlemen, consider yourselves on official leave for as long as it takes you to drink one bottle of beer, or until the tape recorder arrives, whichever comes first."

The beer was finished first, but by the time the last of it had vanished, the second helicopter was within sight and sound. Casey asked the stick-man if he wanted more coffee. The offer was politely declined. Casey looked at Dade Grant and winked and the desert rat winked back, so Casey went in for two more bottles, one apiece for the civilian terrestrials. Coming back he met the lieutenant coming with the extension cord and returned as far as the doorway to show him where to plug it in.

When he came back, he saw that the second helicopter had brought its full complement of four, besides the tape recorder. There were, besides the pilot who had flown it, a technical sergeant who was skilled in the operation of the tape recorder and who was now making adjustments on it, and a lieutenant-colonel and a warrant officer who had come along for the ride or because they had been made curious by the request for a tape recorder to be rushed to Cherrybell, Arizona, by air. They were standing gaping at the stick-man and whispered conversations were going on.

The colonel said, "Attention" quietly, but it brought complete silence. "Please sit down, gentlemen. In a rough circle. Sergeant, if you rig your mike in the center of the circle, will it pick up clearly what any one of us may say?"

"Yes, sir. I'm almost ready."

Ten men and one extraterrestrial humanoid sat in a rough circle, with the microphone hanging from a small tripod in the approximate center. The humans were sweating profusely; the humanoid shivered slightly. Just outside the circle, the burro stood dejectedly, its head low. Edging closer, but still about five yards away, spread out now in a semicircle, was the entire population of Cherrybell who had been at home at the time; the stores and the filling stations were deserted.

The technical sergeant pushed a button and the tape recorder's reel started to turn. "Testing . . . testing," he said. He held down the rewind button for a second and then pushed the playback button. "Testing . . . testing," said the recorder's speaker. Loud and clear. The sergeant pushed the rewind button, then the erase one to clear the tape. Then the stop button. "When I push the next button, sir," he said to the colonel, "we'll be recording."

The colonel looked at the tall extraterrestrial, who nodded and then the colonel nodded at the sergeant. The sergeant pushed the recording button.

"My name is Garth," said the stick-man, slowly and clearly. "I am from a planet of a star which is not listed in your star catalogs, although the globular cluster in which it is one of ninety thousand stars, is known to you. It is, from here, in the direction of the center of the galaxy at a distance of a little over four thousand light-years.

"However, I am not here as a representative of my planet or my people, but as minister plenipotentiary of the Galactic Union, a federation of the enlightened civilizations of the galaxy, for the good of all. It is my assignment to visit you and decide, here and now, whether or not you are to be welcomed to join our federation.

"You may now ask questions freely. However, I reserve the right to postpone answering some of them until my decision has been made.

If the decision is favorable, I will then answer all questions, including the ones I have postponed answering meanwhile. Is that satisfactory?"

"Yes," said the colonel. "How did you come here? A spaceship?"

"Correct. It is overhead right now, in orbit twenty-two thousand miles out, so it revolves with the Earth and stays over this one spot. I am under observation from it, which is one reason I prefer to remain here in the open. I am to signal it when I want it to come down to pick me up."

"How do you know our language so fluently? Are you telepathic?"

"No, I am not. And nowhere in the galaxy is any race telepathic except among its own members. I was taught your language, for this purpose. We have had observers among you for many centuries—by *we*, I mean the Galactic Union, of course. Quite obviously I could not pass as an Earthman, but there are other races who can. Incidentally, they are not spies, or agents; they have in no way tried to affect you; they are observers and that is all."

"What benefits do we get from joining your union, if we are asked and if we accept?"

"First, a quick course in the fundamental social sciences which will end your tendency to fight among yourselves and end or at least control your aggressions. After we are satisfied that you have accomplished that and it is safe for you to do so, you will be given space travel, and many other things, as rapidly as you are able to assimilate them."

"And if we are not asked, or refuse?"

"Nothing. You will be left alone; even our observers will be withdrawn. You will work out your own fate—either you will render your planet uninhabited and uninhabitable within the next century, or you will master social science yourselves and again be candidates for membership and again be offered membership. We will check from time to time and if and when it appears certain that you are not going to destroy yourselves, you will again be approached."

"Why the hurry, now that you're here? Why can't you stay long enough for our leaders, as you call them, to talk to you in person?"

"Postponed. The reason is not important but it is complicated, and I simply do not wish to waste time explaining."

"Assuming your decision is favorable, how will we get in touch with you to let you know *our* decision? You know enough about us, obviously, to know that I can't make it."

"We will know your decision through our observers. One condition of acceptance is full and uncensored publication in your newspapers of this interview, verbatim from the tape we are now using to record it. Also of all deliberations and decisions of your government."

"And other governments? We can't decide unilaterally for the world."

"Your government has been chosen for a start. If you accept we shall furnish the techniques that will cause the others to fall in line quickly—and these techniques do not involve force or the threat of force."

"They must be *some* techniques," said the colonel wryly, "if they'll make one certain country I don't have to name fall into line quickly, without even a threat."

"Sometimes the offer of reward is more significant than the use of threat. Do you think the country you do not wish to name would like your country colonizing planets of far stars before they even reach Mars? But that is a minor point, relatively. You may trust the techniques."

"It sounds almost too good to be true. But you said that you are to decide, here and now, whether or not we are to be invited to join. May I ask on what factors you will base your decision?"

"One is that I am—was, since I already have—to check your degree of xenophobia. In the loose sense in which you use it, that means fear of strangers. We have a word that has no counterpart in your vocabulary: it means fear of and revulsion toward *aliens*. I—or at least a member of my race—was chosen to make the first overt contact with you. Because I am what you could call roughly humanoid—as you are what I would call roughly humanoid—I am probably more horrible, more repulsive to you than many completely different species would be. Because to you, I am a caricature of a human being, I am more horrible to you than a being who bears no remote resemblance to you.

"You may think you *do* feel horror at me, and revulsion, but believe me, you have passed that test. There *are* races in the galaxy who can never be members of the federation, no matter how they advance otherwise, because they are violently and incurably xenophobic; they could never face or talk to an alien of any species. They would either run screaming from him or try to kill him instantly. From watching you and these people"—he waved a long arm at the civilian population of Cherrybell not far outside the circle of the conference—"I know you feel revulsion at the sight of me, but believe me it is relatively slight and certainly curable. You have passed that test satisfactorily."

"And are there other tests?"

"One other. But I think it is time that I—" Instead of finishing the sentence, the stick-man lay back flat on the sand and closed his eyes.

The colonel started to his feet. "What in *hell*?" he said. He walked quickly around the mike's tripod and bent over the recumbent extraterrestrial, put an ear to the bloody-appearing chest.

As he raised his head, Dade Grant, the grizzled prospector, chuckled. "No heartbeat, Colonel, because no heart. But I may leave him as a souvenir for you and you'll find much more interesting things inside than heart and guts. Yes, he is a puppet whom I have been operating—as your Edgar Bergen operated his—what's his name?—oh yes, Charlie McCarthy. Now that he has served his purpose, he is deactivated. You can go back to your place, Colonel."

Colonel Casey moved back slowly. "Why?" he asked.

Dade Grant was peeling off his beard and wig. He rubbed a cloth across his face to remove makeup and was revealed as a handsome young man. He said, "what he told you, or what you were told through him, was true as far as it went. He is only a simulacrum, yes, but he is an exact duplicate of a member or one of the intelligent races of the galaxy, the one toward whom you would be disposed—if you were violently and incurably xenophobic—to be most horrified by, according to our psychologists. But we did not bring a real member of his species to make first contact because they have a phobia of their own, agoraphobia—fear of space. They are highly civilized and members in good standing of the federation, but they never leave their own planet.

"Our observers assure us you don't have *that* phobia. But they were unable to judge in advance the degree of your xenophobia and the only way to test it was to bring along something in lieu of someone to test it against, and presumably to let him make the initial contact."

The colonel sighed audibly. "I can't say this doesn't relieve me in one way. We could get along with humanoids, yes, and will when we have to. But I'll admit it's a relief to hear that the master race of the galaxy is, after all, human instead of only humanoid. What is the second test?"

"You are undergoing it now. Call me—" He snapped his fingers. "What's the name of Bergen's second-string puppet, after Charlie McCarthy?"

The colonel hesitated, but the tech sergeant supplied the answer, "Mortimer Snerd."

"Right. So call me Mortimer Snerd, and now I think it is time that I—" He lay back flat on the sand and closed his eyes just as the stickman had done a few minutes before.

The burro raised its head and put it into the circle over the shoulder of the tech sergeant. "That takes care of the puppets, Colonel," it said. "And now what's this bit about it being important that the master race be human or at least humanoid? What is a master race?"

CONTACT!

by David Drake

Making contact with an extraterrestrial would surely be the most significant event in human history, and nothing could be more important. Really? Think again.

※ ※ ※

DAVID DRAKE, author of the best-selling Hammer's Slammers future mercenary series, is often referred to as the Dean of military science fiction, but is much more versatile than that label might suggest, as shown by his epic fantasy series that began with Lord of the Isles *(Tor), and his equally popular Republic of Cinnabar Navy series (Baen) starring the indefatigable team of Leary and Mundy. He lives near Chapel Hill, NC, with his family.*

SOMETHING SHRIEKED over the firebase without dipping below the gray clouds. It was low and fast and sounded so much like an incoming rocket that even the man on Golf Company's portable latrine flattened instantly. Captain Holtz had knocked over the card table when he hit the dirt. He raised his head above the wreckage in time to see a bright blue flash in the far distance. The crash that rattled the jungle moments later sent everyone scrabbling again.

"Sonic boom," Major Hegsley, the fat operations officer, pontificated as he levered himself erect.

"The hell you say," Holtz muttered, poised and listening. "Paider, Bayes," he grunted at the two platoon leaders starting to pick up their bridge hands, "get to your tracks."

Then the Klaxon on the tactical operations center blatted and everyone knew Holtz had been right again. The captain kicked aside a lawn chair blocking his way to his command vehicle. The radioman scuttled forward to give his powerful commander room in front of the bank of radios. "Battle six, Battle four-six," the tanker snapped as he keyed the microphone. "Shoot." Thirty seconds of concentrated information spat out of the speaker while Holtz crayoned grid coordinates in on an acetate-covered map. "Roger, we'll get 'em." Turning to the radioman he ordered, "Second platoon stays for security here—get first and third lined up at the gate and tell Speed I'll be with him on five-two." While the enlisted man relayed the orders on the company frequency, Holtz scooped up a holstered .45 and his chicken vest and ran for his tank.

Golf Company was already moving. Most of the drivers had cranked up as soon as they heard the explosion. Within thirty seconds of the Klaxon, the diesels of all nine operable tracks were turning over while the air still slapped with closing breechblocks. Tank 52 jingled as Hauley, its driver, braked the right tread and threw the left in reverse to swing the heavy war machine out of its ready position. Holtz ran up to the left side, snapping his vest closed at the shoulder. He was one of the few men in the squadron who wore a porcelain-armored chicken vest without discomfort, despite its considerably greater weight than the usual nylon flak jacket. In fact, Holtz was built much like one of his tanks. Though he was taller than average, his breadth made him look stocky at a distance and simply gigantic close up. He wore his black hair cropped short, but a thick growth curled down his forearms and up the backs of his hands.

Speed, a weedy, freckled staff sergeant with three years' combat behind him, grasped his captain by the wrist and helped him swing up on five-two's battered fender. As frail as he looked, Speed was probably the best track commander in the company. He was due to rotate home for discharge in three days and would normally have been sent to the rear for stand-down a week before. Holtz liked working with an experienced man and had kept him in the field an extra week, but this was Speed's last day. "You wanna load today, Captain?" he asked with an easy smile. He rocked unconcernedly as Hauley put the tank in gear and sent it into line with a jerk.

Holtz smiled back but shook his head. He always rode in the track commander's position, although in a contact he could depend on Speed to fight five-two from the loader's hatch while he directed the company as a whole. Still smiling, the big officer settled heavily onto the hatch cover behind the low-mounted, fifty-caliber machine gun and slipped on his radio helmet.

"OK, listen up," he said on the company frequency, ignoring commo security as he always did when talking to his unit. He had a serene assurance that his gravelly voice was adequate identification— and that his tanks were a certain answer to any dinks who tried to stop him. His boys were as good and as deadly as any outfit in 'Nam. "Air Force claims they zapped a bird at high altitude and it wasn't one of theirs. We're going to see whose it was and keep Charlie away till C-MEC gets a team out here. Four-four leads, west on the hardball to a trail at Yankee Tango five-seven-two, three-seven-nine; flyboys think the bird went down around seventy-forty, but keep your eyes open all the way—Charlie's going to be looking too."

Holtz's track was second in line with the remaining five tanks of the first and third platoons following in single file. As each one nosed out of the firebase its TC flipped a switch. Electric motors whined to rotate the turrets 30 degrees to one side or the other and lower the muzzles of the 90mm main guns. The big cannons were always loaded, but for safety's sake they were pointed up in the air except when the tanks prowled empty countryside. Otherwise, at a twitch of the red handle beside each track commander a wall or a crowd of people would dissolve in shattered ruin.

"Well, you think we're at war with China now?" Holtz shouted to Speed over the high jangle of the treads. "Hell, I told you you didn't want to go home—what do you bet they nuked Oakland five minutes ago?" Both men laughed.

The path from the firebase to the highway was finely divided muck after three days of use. The tanks, each of them burdened with fifty tons of armor and weaponry, wallowed through it. There was nothing laughable in their awkwardness. Rather, they looked as implacably deadly as tyrannosaurs hunting in a pack. On the asphalt hardball, the seven vehicles accelerated to thirty-five miles an hour, stringing out a little. Four-four had all its left-side torsion bars broken and would not steer a straight line. The tank staggered back and forth across the narrow highway in a series of short zigzags. From the engine gratings on its back deck, a boy with a grenade launcher stared miserably back at the CO's track while the rough ride pounded his guts to jelly.

Holtz ignored him, letting his eyes flick through the vegetation to both sides of the roadway. Here along the hardball the land was in rubber, but according to the map they would have to approach the downed aircraft through broken jungle. Not the best terrain for armor, but they'd make do. Normally the tanks would have backed up an air search, but low clouds had washed the sky gray. Occasionally Holtz could hear a chopper thrumming somewhere, above him but always invisible. No air support in a contact, that was what it meant. Maybe no medevac either.

Ahead, four-four slowed. The rest of the column ground to a chattering halt behind it. Unintelligible noises hissed through Holtz's earphones. He cursed and reached down inside the turret to bring his volume up. Noise crackled louder but all sense was smothered out of it by the increased roar of static. Four-four's TC, Greiler, spoke into the ear of his grenadier. The boy nodded and jumped off the tank, running back to five-two. He was a newbie, only a week or two in the field, and young besides. He clambered up the bow slope of the tank and nervously blurted, "Sir, Chick says he thinks this is the turn-off but he isn't sure."

As far as Holtz could tell from the map, the narrow trail beside four-four should be the one they wanted. It led south, at any rate. Hell, if the MiG was what had gone howling over the firebase earlier the flyboys were just guessing for location anyway. The overcast had already been solid and the bird could have fallen anywhere in III Corps for all anybody knew.

"Yeah, we'll try it," Holtz said into his helmet mike. No reaction from four-four. "God damn it!" the captain roared, stabbing his left arm out imperiously. Four-four obediently did a neutral steer on the hardball, rotating 90 degrees to the left as the treads spun in opposite directions. Clods of asphalt boiled up as the road's surface dissolved under incalculable stresses. "Get on the back, son." Holtz growled at the uncertain newbie. "You're our crew for now. Speed!" he demanded, "What's wrong with our goddam radio? It worked OK at the firebase."

"Isn't the radio," Speed reported immediately, speaking into his own helmet microphone. "See, the intercom works, it's something screwing up off the broadcast freeks. Suppose the dinks are jamming?"

"Crap," Holtz said.

The trail was a half-abandoned jeep route, never intended for anything the width of a tank. They could shred their way through saplings and the creepers that had slunk across the trail, of course, and their massive rubber track blocks spewed a salad of torn greenery over their fenders. But full-sized trees with trunks a foot or more thick made even the tanks turn: grunting, clattering; engines slowing, then roaring loudly for torque to slue the heavy vehicles. Holtz glanced back at the newbie to see that he was all right. The boy's steel pot was too large for him. It had tilted forward over his eyebrows, exposing a fuzz of tiny blond hairs on his neck. The kid had to be eighteen or they wouldn't have let him in the country, Holtz thought, but you sure couldn't tell it by looking at him.

A branch whanged against Holtz's own helmet and he turned around. The vegetation itself was a danger as well as a hiding place for unknown numbers of the enemy. More than one tanker had been dusted off with a twig through his eye. There were a lot of nasty surprises for a man rolling through jungle twelve feet in the air. But if you spent all your time watching for branches, you missed the dink crouched in the undergrowth with a rocket launcher—and he'd kill the hell out of you.

Sudden color in the sky ahead. Speed slapped Holtz on the left shoulder, pointing, but the CO had already seen it. The clouds covered the sky in a dismal ceiling no higher than that of a large auditorium. While both men stared, another flash stained the gray momentarily azure. There was no thunder. Too brightly colored for lightning anyway, Holtz thought. The flashes were really blue, not just white reflected from dark clouds.

"That can't be a klick from here, Chief," Speed's voice rattled. Holtz glanced at him. The sergeant's jungle boots rested on the forward rim of his hatch so that his bony knees poked high in the air. Some people let their feet dangle inside the turret, but Speed had been around too long for that. Armor was great so long as nothing penetrated it. When something did—most often a stream of molten metal blasted by the shaped explosive of a B-41 rocket—it splashed around the inner surface of what had been protection. God help the man inside then. 'Nam offered enough ways to die without looking for easy ones.

The officer squinted forward, trying to get a better idea of the brief light's location. Foliage broke the concave mirror of the clouds into a thousand swiftly dancing segments. Five-two was jouncing badly over potholes and major roots that protruded from the coarse, red soil as well.

"Hey," Speed muttered at a sudden thought. Holtz saw him drop down inside the tank. The earphones crackled as the sergeant switched on the main radio he had disconnected when background noise smothered communications. As he did so, another of the blue flashes lit up the sky. Static smashed through Holtz's phones like the main gun going off beside his head.

"Jesus Christ!" the big officer roared into the intercom. "You shorted the goddamn thing!"

White noise disappeared as Speed shut off the set again. "No, man," he protested as he popped his frame, lanky but bulbous in its nylon padding, back through the oval hatch. "That's not me—it's the lightning. All I did was turn the set on."

"That's not lightning," Holtz grunted. He shifted his pistol holster slightly so that the butt was handy for immediate use. "Hauley," he said over the intercom to the driver, "that light's maybe a hair south of the way we're headed. If you catch a trail heading off to the left, hold it up for a minute."

Speed scanned his side of the jungle with a practiced squint. Tendons stood out on his right hand as it gripped the hatch cover against the tank's erratic lurches. "Good thing the intercom's on wires," he remarked. "Otherwise we'd really be up a creek."

Holtz nodded.

On flat concrete, tanks could get up to forty-five miles an hour, though the ride was spine-shattering if any of the torsion bars were broken. Off-road was another matter. This trail was as straight as what was basically a brush cut could be—did it lead to another section on the plantation that flanked the hardball?—but when it meandered around a heavy tree bole the tanks had to slow to a crawl to follow it. Black exhaust boiled out of the deflector plates serving four-four in place of muffler and tail pipe. The overgrown trail could hide a mine, either an old one long forgotten or a sudden improvisation by a tankkiller team that had heard Golf Company moving toward it. The bursts of light and static were certain to attract the attention of all the NVA in the neighborhood.

That was fine with Holtz. He twitched the double handgrips of his cal-fifty to be sure the gun would rotate smoothly. He wouldn't have been in Armor if he'd minded killing.

The flashes were still intermittent but seemed to come more frequently now: one or two a minute. Range was a matter of guesswork, but appreciably more of the sky lighted up at each pulse. They must be getting closer to the source. The trail was taking them straight to it after all. But how did a MiG make the sky light up that way?

Speed lifted his radio helmet to listen intently. "AK fire," he said. "Not far away either." Holtz scowled and raised his own helmet away from his ears. As he did so, the air shuddered with a dull boom that was not thunder. The deliberate bark of an AK-47 chopped out behind it, little muffled by the trees.

Speed slipped the cap from a flare and set it over the primed end of the foot-long tube. "We can't get the others on the horn." he explained. "They'll know what a red flare means."

"Charlie'll see it too," Holtz argued.

"Hell, whoever heard of a tank company sneaking up on anybody?"

The captain shrugged assent. As always before a contact, the sweat filming the inner surface of his chicken vest had chilled suddenly.

Speed rapped the base of the flare on the turret. The rocket streaked upward with a liquid *whoosh!* that took it above the cloud ceiling. Moments later the charge burst and a fierce red ball drifted down against the flickering background. Holtz keyed the scrambler mike, calling, "Battle six, Battle six; Battle four-six calling." He held one of the separate earphones under his radio helmet. The only response from it was a thunder of static and he shut it off again. Remembering the newbie on the back deck, he turned and shouted over the savage rumble of the engine, "Watch it, kid, we'll be in it up to our necks any time now."

In the tight undergrowth, the tracks had closed up to less than a dozen yards between bow slope and the deflector plates of the next ahead. Four-four cornered around a clump of three large trees left standing to the right of the trail. The tank's bent, rusted fender sawed into the bark of the outer tree, then tore free. Hauley swung five-two wider as he followed.

A rocket spurted from a grove of bamboo forty yards away where the trail jogged again. The fireball of the B-41 seemed to hang in the air just above the ground, but it moved fast enough that before Holtz's thumbs could close on his gun's butterfly trigger the rocket had burst on the bow slope of four-four.

A great splash of orange-red flame enveloped the front of the tank momentarily, looking as if a gasoline bomb had gone off. The flash took only a split second but the roar of the explosion echoed and re-echoed in the crash of heavy gunfire. Four-four shuddered to a halt. Holtz raked the bamboo with the cal-fifty, directing the machine gun with his left hand while his right groped for the turret control to swing the main gun. Beside him, Speed's lighter machine gun chewed up undergrowth to the left of the trail. He had no visible targets, but you almost never saw your enemy in the jungle.

The muzzle brake of the 90mm gun, already as low as it could be aimed, rotated onto the bamboo. A burst of light automatic fire glanced off five-two's turret from an unknown location. Holtz ignored it and tripped the red handle. The air split with a sharp crack and a flash of green. The first round was canister and it shotgunned a deadly cone of steel balls toward the unseen rocketeer, exploding bamboo into the air like a tangle of broom straw. Brass clanged in the turret as the cannon's breech sprang open automatically and flung out the empty case. Speed dropped through the reeking white powder smoke evacuated into the hull.

Holtz hadn't a chance to worry about the newbie behind him until he heard the kid's grenade launcher chunk hollowly. Only an instant later its shell burst on a tree limb not thirty feet from the tank. Wood disintegrated in a puff of black and red; dozens of segments of piano wire spanged off the armor, one of them ripping a line down the captain's blue jowl. "Not so goddam close!" Holtz shouted, just as a slap on his thigh told him Speed had reloaded the main gun.

The second rocket hissed from a thicket to the right of five-two, lighting up black-shrouded tree boles from the moment of ignition. Holtz glimpsed the Vietnamese huddled in the brush with the launching tube on his shoulder but there was no time to turn his machine gun before the B-41 exploded. The world shattered. Even the fifty tons of steel under Holtz's feet staggered as the shaped charge detonated against five-two's turret. A pencil stream of vaporized armor plate jetted through the tank. The baggy sateen of the officer's bloused fatigues burst into flame across his left calf where the metal touched it. Outside the tank the air rang with fragments of the rocket's case. Holtz, deafened by the blast, saw the newbie's mouth open to scream as the boy spun away from the jagged impacts sledging him. Somehow he still gripped his grenade launcher, but its fat aluminum barrel had flowered with torn metal as suddenly as red splotches had appeared on his flak jacket.

Holtz's radio helmet was gone, jerked off his head by the blast. Stupid with shock, the burly captain's eyes followed the wires leading down into the interior of the tank. Pooled on the floorplate was all that remained of Speed. The gaseous metal had struck him while his body was bent. The stream had entered above the collarbone and burned an exit hole through the seventh rib near the spine. The sergeant's torso, raised instantly to a temperature of over a thousand degrees, had exploded. Speed's head had not been touched. His face was turned upward, displaying its slight grin, although spatters of blood made him seem more freckled than usual.

The clouds were thickly alive with a shifting pattern of blue fire and the air hummed to a note unconnected to the rattle of gunfire all along the tank column. The third tank in line, four-six, edged forward, trying to pass Holtz's motionless vehicle on the left. A medic hopped off the deck of four-six and knelt beside the newbie's crumpled body, oblivious to the shots singing off nearby armor.

Hauley jumped out of the driver's hatch and climbed back to his commander. "Sir!" he said, gripping Holtz by the left arm.

Holtz shook himself alert. "Get us moving," he ordered in a thin voice he did not recognize. "Give four-six room to get by."

Hauley ducked forward to obey. Holtz glanced down into the interior of the track. In fury he tried to slam his fist against the hatch coaming and found he no longer had feeling in his right arm. Where the sleeve of his fatigue shirt still clung to him, it was black with blood. Nothing spurting or gushing, though. The main charge of shrapnel that should have ripped through Holtz's upper body had impacted numbingly on his chicken vest. Its porcelain plates had turned the fragments, although the outer casing of nylon was clawed to ruin.

Five-two rumbled as Hauley gunned the engine, then jerked into gear. A long burst of AK fire sounded beyond the bamboo from which the first B-41 had come. A muffled swoosh signaled another rocket from the same location. This time the target, too, was hidden in the jungle. Holtz hosed the tall grass on general principles and blamed his shock-sluggish brain for not understanding what the Vietnamese were doing.

With a howl more like an overloaded dynamo than a jet engine, a metallic cigar shape staggered up out of the jungle less than a hundred yards from five-two's bow. It was fifty feet long, blunt-ended and featureless under a cloaking blue nimbus. Flickering subliminally, the light was less bright than intense. Watching it was similar to laying a bead with an arc welder while wearing a mask of thick blue glass instead of the usual murky yellow.

As the cigar hovered, slightly nose down, another rocket streaked up at it from the launcher hidden in the bamboo. The red flare merged with the nimbus but instead of knifing in against the metal, the missile slowed and hung roaring in the air several seconds until its motor burned out. By then the nimbus had paled almost to nonexistence and the ship itself lurched a yard or two downward. Without the blinding glare Holtz could see gashes in the center section of the strange object, the result of a Communist rocket detonating nearby or some bright flyboy's proximity-fused missile. MiG, for Chrissake! Holtz swore to himself.

A brilliant flash leaped from the bow of the hovering craft. In the thunderclap that followed, the whole clump of bamboo blasted skyward as a ball of green pulp.

To Holtz's left, the cupola machine gun of four-six opened fire on the cigar. Either Roosevelt, the third tank's TC, still thought the hovering vessel was Communist or else he simply reacted to the sudden threat of its power. Brass and stripped links bounded toward Holtz's track as the slender black sent a stream of tracers thundering up at a flat angle.

The blue nimbus slashed and paled. Even as he swore, Holtz's left hand hit the lever to bring the muzzle of his main gun up with a whine. The blue-lit cigar shape swung end on to the tanks, hovering in line with the T-shaped muzzle brake of the cannon. Perhaps a hand inside the opaque hull was reaching for its weapons control, but Holtz's fingers closed on the red switch first. The ninety crashed, bucking back against its recoil stop while flame stabbed forward and sideways through the muzzle brake. Whatever the blue glow did to screen the strange craft, it was inadequate to halt the point-blank impact of a shell delivering over a hundred tons of kinetic energy. The nimbus collapsed like a shattered light bulb. For half a heartbeat the ship rocked in the air, undisturbed except for a four-inch hole in the bare metal of its bow.

The stern third of the craft disintegrated with a stunning crack and a shower of white firedrops that trailed smoke as they fell. A sphincter valve rotated in the center of the cigar. It was half opened when a second explosion wracked the vessel. Something pitched out of the opening and fell with the blazing fragments shaken from the hull. Magnesium roared blindingly as the remainder of the ship dropped out of the sky. It must have weighed more than Holtz would have guessed from the way the impact shook the jungle and threw blazing splinters up into the clouds.

The tanks were still firing but the answering chug-chug-chug of AK-47's had ceased. Holtz reached for the microphone key, found it gone with the rest of his radio helmet. His scrambler phone had not been damaged by the shaped charge, however, and the static blanket was gone. "Zipper one-three," he called desperately on the medical evacuation frequency. "Battle four-six. Get me out a dust-off bird. I've got men down. We're at Yankee Tango seven-oh, four-oh. That's Yankee Tango seven-oh, four-oh, near there. There's clear area to land a bird, but watch it, some of the trees are through the clouds."

"Stand by, Battle four-six," an impersonal voice replied. A minute later it continued, "Battle four-six? We can't get a chopper to you now, there's pea soup over the whole region. Sorry, you'll have to use what you've got to get your men to a surgeon."

"Look, we need a bird," Holtz pressed, his voice tight. "Some of these guys won't make it without medevac."

"Sorry, soldier, we're getting satellite reports as quick as they come in. The way it looks now, nobody's going to take off for seven or eight hours."

Holtz keyed off furiously. "Hauley!" he said. "C'mere."

The driver was beside him immediately, a dark-haired Pfc who moved faster than his mild expression indicated. Holtz handed him the phones and mike. "Hold for me. I want to see what's happened."

"Did you tell about the, the . . ." Hauley started. His gesture finished the thought.

"About the hole in the jungle?" Holtz queried sarcastically. "Hell, you better forget about that right now. Whatever it was, there's not enough of it left to light your pipe." His arms levered him out of the hatch with difficulty.

"Can I—" Hauley began.

"Shut up, I can make it," his CO snapped. His left leg was cramped. It almost buckled under him as he leaped to the ground.

Holding himself as erect as possible, Holtz limped over to four-six. Roosevelt hunched questioningly behind his gunshield, then jumped out of his cupola and helped the officer onto the fender.

"Quit shooting," Holtz ordered irritably as the loader sprayed a breeze-shaken sapling. "Charlie's gone home for today. Lemme use your commo," he added to the TC, "mine's gone."

He closed his eyes as he fitted on the radio helmet, hoping his double vision would clear. It didn't. Even behind closed eyelids a yellow-tinged multiple afterimage remained. The ringing in his ears was almost as bad as the static had been, but at least he could speak. "Four-six to Battle four," Holtz rasped. "Cease firing unless you've got a target, a real target."

The jungle coughed into silence. "Now, who's hurt? Four-four?"

"Zack's bad, sir." Greiler crackled back immediately. "That rocket burned right through the bow and nigh took his foot off. We got the ankle tied, but he needs a doc quick."

Half to his surprise, Holtz found that four-four's driver and the newbie blown off the back of his own track were the only serious casualties. He ignored his own arm and leg; they seemed to have stopped bleeding. Charlie had been too occupied with the damaged cigar to set a proper ambush. Vaguely, he wondered what the Vietnamese had thought they were shooting at. Borrowing the helmet from four-six's loader, the officer painfully climbed off the tank. His left leg hurt more every minute. Heavily corded muscle lay bare on the calf where the film of blood had cracked off.

Davie Womble, the medic who usually rode the back deck of four-six, was kneeling beside the newbie. He had laid his own flak jacket under the boy's head for a cushion and wrapped his chest in a poncho. "Didn't want to move him," he explained to Holtz, "but that one piece went clean through and was sucking air from both sides. He's really wasted."

The boy's face was a sickly yellow, almost the color of his fine blond hair. A glitter of steel marked the tip of a fragment which had zig-zagged shallowly across his scalp. It was so minor compared to other damage that Womble had not bothered to remove it with tweezers. Holtz said nothing. He stepped toward four-four whose loader and TC clustered around their driver. The loader, his M16 tucked under his right arm, faced out into the jungle and scanned the pulverized portion. "Hey," he said, raising his rifle. "Hey! We got one!"

"Watch it," the bloodied officer called as he drew his .45. He had to force his fingers to close around its square butt. Greiler, the track commander, was back behind his cal-fifty in seconds, leaping straight onto the high fender of his tank and scrambling up into the cupola. The loader continued to edge toward the body he saw huddled on the ground. Twenty yards from the tank he thrust his weapon out and used the flash suppressor to prod the still form.

"He's alive," the loader called. "He's—oh my God, oh my *God!*"

Holtz lumbered forward. Greiler's machine gun was live and the captain's neck crawled to think of it, hoping the TC wouldn't bump the trigger. The man on the ground wore gray coveralls of a slick, rubbery-appearing material. As he breathed, they trembled irregularly and a tear above the collarbone oozed dark fluid. His face was against the ground, hidden in shadow, but there was enough light to show Holtz that the man's outflung hand was blue. "Stretcher!" he shouted as he ran back toward the tracks.

Hauley wore a curious expression as he held out the scrambler phone. Holtz snatched and keyed it without explanation. "Battle six, Battle four-six," he called urgently.

"Battle four-six, this is Blackhorse six," the crisp voice of the regimental commander broke in unexpectedly. "What in hell is going on?"

"Umm, sir, I've got three men for a dust-off and I can't get any action out of the chopper jockeys. My boys aren't going to make it if they ride out of here on a tank. Can you—"

"Captain," the cool voice from Quan Loi interrupted, "it won't do your men any good to have a medevac bird fly into a tree in these clouds. I know how you feel, but the weather is the problem and there's nothing we can do about that. Now, what happened?"

"Look," Holtz blurted, "there's a huge goddamn clearing here. If they cruise at five hundred we can guide them in by—"

"God damn it, man, do you want to tell me what's going on or do you want to be the first captain to spend six months in Long Binh Jail?"

Holtz took a deep breath that squeezed bruised ribs against the tight armored vest. Two troopers were already carrying the blue airman back toward the tanks on a litter made of engineer stakes and a poncho. He turned his attention back to the microphone and, keeping his voice flat, said, "We took a prisoner. He's about four feet tall, light build, with a blue complexion. I guess he was part of the crew of the spaceship the Air Force shot down and we finished off. He's breathing now, but the way he's banged up I don't think he will be long."

Only a hum from the radio. Then, "Four-six, is this some kind of joke?"

"No joke. I'll have the body back at the firebase in four, maybe three hours, and when they get a bird out you can look at him."

"Hold right where you are," the colonel crackled back. "You've got flares?"

"Roger, roger." Holtz's face regained animation and he began daubing at his red cheek with a handkerchief. "Plenty of flares, but the clouds are pretty low. We can set a pattern of trip flares on the ground, though."

"Hold there; I'm going up freek."

It was getting dark very fast. Normally Holtz would have moved his two platoons into the cleared area, but that would have meant shifting the newbie—Christ, he didn't even know the kid's name! If they'd found the captive earlier, a chopper might have already been there. Because of the intelligence value. Christ, how those rear-echelon mothers ate up intelligence value.

"Four-six? Blackhorse six."

"Roger, Blackhorse six." The captain's huge hand clamped hard on the sweat-slippery microphone.

"There'll be a bird over you in one-oh, repeat one-oh, mikes. Put some flares up when you hear it."

"Roger. Battle four-six out." On the company frequency, Holtz ordered, "Listen good, dudes, there's a dust-off bird coming by in ten. Any of you at the tail of the line hear it, don't pop a flare but tell me.

We want it coming down here, not in the middle of the jungle." He took off the helmet, setting it beside him on the turret. His head still buzzed and, though he stared into the jungle over the grips of the cal-fifty, even the front sight was a blur. Ten minutes was a long time.

"I hear it!" Roosevelt called. Without waiting for Holtz's order, he fired the quadrangle of trip flares he had set. They lit brightly the area cleared by the alien's weapon. While those ground flares sizzled to full life, Greiler sent three star clusters streaking into the overcast together. The dust-off slick, casting like a coonhound, paused invisibly. As a great gray shadow it drifted down the line of tanks. Its rotor kicked the mist into billows flashing dimly.

Gracelessly yet without jerking the wounded boy, Womble and a third-platoon tanker pressed into service as stretcher-bearer rose and started toward the bird. As soon as the slick touched down, its blades set to idle, the crew chief with his Red Cross armband jumped out. Holtz and the stretcher with the newbie reached the helicopter an instant after the two nearer stretchers.

"Where's the prisoner?" the crew chief shouted over the high scream of unloaded turbines.

"Get my men aboard first," Holtz ordered briefly.

"Sorry, Captain," the air medic replied, "with our fuel load we only take two this trip and I've got orders to bring the prisoner back for sure."

"Stuff your orders! My men go out first."

The crew chief wiped sweat from the bridge of his nose; more trickled from under his commo helmet. "Sir, there's two generals and a bird colonel waiting on the pad for me; I leave that—" he shook his head at the makeshift stretcher— "that back here and it's a year in LBJ if I'm lucky. I'll take one of your—"

"They're both dying!"

"I'm sorry but . . ." The medic's voice dried up when he saw what Holtz was doing. "You can't threaten me!" he shrilled.

Holtz jacked a shell into the chamber of the .45. None of his men moved to stop him. The medic took one step forward as the big captain fired. The bullet slammed into the alien's forehead, just under the streaky gray bristles of his hairline. Fluid spattered the medic and the side of the helicopter behind him.

"There's no prisoner!" Holtz screamed over the shuddering thunder inside his skull. "There's nothing at all, do you hear? Now get my men to a hospital!"

Hauley tried to catch him as he fell, but the officer's weight pulled them both to the ground together.

The snarl of a laboring diesel brought him out of it. He was on a cot with a rolled flak jacket pillowed under his head. Someone had removed his chicken vest and bathed away the crusts of dried blood.

"Where are we?" Holtz muttered thickly. His vision had cleared and the chipped rubber of the treads beside him stood out in sharp relief.

Hauley handed his CO a paper cup of coffee laced with something bitter. "Here you go. Lieutenant Paider took over and we're gonna set up here for the night. If it clears, we'll get a chopper for you too."

"But that . . . ?" Holtz gestured at the twilit bulk of a tank twenty feet away. It grunted to a halt after neutral steering a full 360 degrees.

"That? Oh, that was four-four," Hauley said in a careless voice. "Greiler wanted to say thanks—getting both his buddies dusted off, you know. But I told him you didn't want to hear about something that didn't happen. And everybody in the company'll swear it didn't happen, whatever some chopper jockey thinks. So Greiler just moved four-four up to where the bird landed and did a neutral steer . . . on nothing at all."

"Nothing at all," Holtz repeated before drifting off. He grinned like a she-tiger gorging on her cubs' first kill.

THE FLAT-EYED MONSTER

by William Tenn

Trapped on an alien planet, surrounded by the obligatory bug-eyed monsters, a lone Earthman must somehow escape and return to Earth. If you think you've already read that story far too many times—not so. And consider just who the monster is here.

※ ※ ※

WILLIAM TENN (1920-2010) was the pen name of Philip Klass (not to be confused with Philip J. Klass, the aerospace writer) who began writing SF and fantasy in the late 1940s, and was one of the brightest writers of the 1950s, particularly with his stories in Galaxy (where this story originally appeared). Along with other irreverent writers (notably Robert Sheckley, Fritz Leiber, and Evelyn E. Smith), Tenn set the tone of Galaxy as a home for wit and satire. During World War II, he served in the U.S. Army as a combat engineer in Europe, and later was a technical editor with the Air Force radar and radio laboratory, though if he was somehow teleported to an alien planet as part of his job, at least he got back all right, or we would have missed a lot of great stories, such as this one. Written during a dire time in the author's life, he wrote it under an editor's instruction to be "very, very funny." Mr. Tenn, you didn't know your own strength!

FOR THE FIRST FEW MOMENTS, Clyde Manship—who up to then had been an assistant professor of Comparative Literature at Kelly University—for the first few moments, Manship tried heroically to convince himself that he was merely having a bad dream. He shut his eyes and told himself chidingly, with a little superior smile playing about his lips, that things as ugly as this just did not occur in real life. No. Definitely a dream.

He had himself half-convinced, until he sneezed. It was too loud and wet a sneeze to be ignored. You didn't sneeze like that in a dream— if you sneezed at all. He gave up. He'd have to open his eyes and take another look. At the thought, his neck muscles went rigid with spasm.

A little while ago, he'd fallen asleep while reading an article he'd written for a scholarly journal. He'd fallen asleep in his own bed in his own apartment in Callahan Hall—"a charming and inexpensive residence for those members of the faculty who are bachelors and desire to live on campus." He'd awakened with a slightly painful tingling sensation in every inch of his body. He felt as if he were being stretched, stretched interminably and—and *loosened*. Then, abruptly, he had floated off the bed and gone through the open window like a rapidly attenuating curl of smoke. He'd gone straight up to the star-drenched sky of night, dwindling in substance until he lost consciousness completely.

And had come to on this enormous flat expanse of white tabletop, with a multi-vaulted ceiling above him and dank, barely breathable air in his lungs. Hanging from the ceiling were quantities and quantities of what was indubitably electronic equipment, but the kind of equipment the boys in the Physics Department might dream up, if the grant they'd just received from the government for military radiation research had been a million times larger than it was, and if Professor Bowles, the department head, had insisted that every gadget be carefully constructed to look substantially different from anything done in electronics to date.

The equipment above him had been rattling and gurgling and whooshing, glowing and blinking and coruscating. Then it had stopped as if someone had been satisfied and had turned off a switch.

So Clyde Manship had sat up to see who had turned it off.

He had seen all right.

He hadn't seen so much *who* as he had seen *what*. And it hadn't been a nice *what*.

In fact, none of the *whats* he had glimpsed in that fast look around had been a bit nice. So he had shut his eyes fast and tried to find another mental way out of the situation.

But now he had to have another look. It might not be so bad the second time. "It's always darkest," he told himself with determined triteness, "before the dawn." And then found himself involuntarily adding, "except on days when there's an eclipse."

But he opened his eyes anyway, wincingly, the way a child opens its mouth for the second spoonful of castor oil.

Yes, they were all as he had remembered them. Pretty awful.

The tabletop was an irregular sort of free-form shape, bordered by thick, round knobs a few inches apart. And perched on these knobs, about six feet to the right of him, were two creatures who looked like black leather suitcases. Instead of handles or straps, however, they sported a profusion of black tentacles, dozens and dozens of tentacles, every second or third one of which ended in a moist turquoise eye shielded by a pair of the sweepingest eyelashes Manship had ever seen outside of a mascara advertisement.

Embedded in the suitcase proper, as if for additional decorative effect, were swarms of other sky-blue eyes, only these, without eyelashes, bulged out in multitudes of tiny, glittering facets like enormous gems. There was no sign of ear, nose or mouth anywhere on the bodies, but there was a kind of slime, a thick, grayish slime, that oozed out of the black bodies and dripped with a steady *splash-splash-splash* to the floor beneath.

On his left, about fifteen feet away, where the tabletop extended a long peninsula, there was another one of the creatures. Its tentacles gripped a pulsating spheroid across the surface of which patches of light constantly appeared and disappeared.

As near as Manship could tell, all the visible eyes of the three were watching him intently. He shivered and tried to pull his shoulders closer together.

"Well, Professor," someone asked suddenly, "what would you say?"

"I'd say this was one hell of a way to wake up," Manship burst out, feelingly. He was about to go on and develop this theme in more colorful detail when two things stopped him.

The first was the problem of who had asked the question. He had seen no other human—no other living creature, in fact—besides the three tentacled suitcases anywhere in that tremendous, moisture-filled room.

The second thing that stopped him was that someone else had begun to answer the question at the same time, cutting across Manship's words and ignoring them completely.

"Well, obviously," this person said, "the experiment is a success. It has completely justified its expense and the long years of research behind it. You can see for yourself, Councilor Glomg, that one-way teleportation is an accomplished fact."

Manship realized that the voices were coming from his right. The wider of the two suitcases—evidently "the professor" to whom the original query had been addressed—was speaking to the narrower one, who had swung most of his stalked eyes away from Manship and had focused them on his companion. Only where in blazes were the voices coming from? Somewhere inside their bodies? There was no sign anywhere of vocal apparatus.

AND HOW COME, Manship's mind suddenly shrieked, THEY TALK ENGLISH?

"I can see that," Councilor Glomg admitted with a blunt honesty that became him well. "It's an accomplished fact, all right, Professor Lirld. Only, *what precisely* has it accomplished?"

Lirld raised some thirty or forty tentacles in what Manship realized fascinatedly was an elaborate and impatient shrug. "The teleportation of a living organism from astronomical unit 649-301-3 without the aid of transmitting apparatus on the planet of origin."

The Councilor swept his eyes back to Manship. "You call that living?" he inquired doubtfully.

"Oh, come now, Councilor," Professor Lirld protested. "Let's not have any flefnomorphism. It is obviously sentient, obviously motile, after a fashion—"

"All right. It's alive. I'll grant that. But sentient? It doesn't even seem to *pmbff* from where I stand. And those horrible lonely eyes! Just two of them—and so *flat!* That dry, dry skin without a trace of slime. I'll admit that—"

"You're not exactly a thing of beauty and a joy forever yourself, you know," Manship, deeply offended, couldn't help throwing out indignantly.

"—I tend to flefnomorphism in my evaluation of alien life-forms," the other went on as if he hadn't spoken. "Well, I'm a flefnobe and proud of it. But after all, Professor Lirld, I have seen some impossible creatures from our neighboring planets that my son and other explorers have brought back. The very strangest of them, the most primitive ones, at least can *pmbff!* But this—this *thing*. Not the smallest, slightest trace of a *pmb* do I see on it! It's eerie, that's what it is—eerie!"

"Not at all," Lirld assured him. "It's merely a scientific anomaly. Possibly in the outer reaches of the galaxy where animals of this sort are frequent, possibly conditions are such that *pmbffing* is unnecessary. A careful examination should tell us a good deal very quickly. Meanwhile, we've proved that life exists in other areas of the galaxy than its sun-packed core. And when the time comes for us to conduct exploratory voyages to these areas, intrepid adventurers like your son will go equipped with information. They will know what to expect."

"Now, listen," Manship began shouting in desperation. "Can you or can you not hear me?"

"You can shut off the power, Srin," Professor Lirld commented. "No sense in wasting it. I believe we have as much of this creature as we need. If any more of it is due to materialize, it will arrive on the residual beam."

The flefnobe on Manship's left rapidly spun the strange spheroid he was holding. A low hum, which had filled the building and had been hardly noticeable before, now died away. As Srin peered intently at the patches of light on the surface of the instrument, Manship suddenly guessed that they were meter readings. Yes, that's exactly what they were—meter readings. *Now, how did I know that?* he wondered.

Obvious. There was only one answer. If they couldn't hear him no matter how loudly he shouted, if they gave no sign that they even knew he *was* shouting, and if, at the same time, they seemed to indulge in the rather improbable feat of talking his native language— they were obviously telepaths. Without anything that looked like ears or mouths.

He listened carefully as Srin asked his superior a question. It seemed to sound in his ears as words, English words in a clear, resonant voice. But there was a difference. There was a quality missing, the kind of realistic bite that fresh fruit has and artificial fruit flavoring doesn't. And behind Srin's words there were low, murmuring bubbles of other words, unorganized sentence fragments which would occasionally become "audible" enough to clarify a subject that was not included in the "conversation." That, Manship realized, was how he had learned that the shifting patches of light on the spheroid were meter readings.

It was also evident that whenever they mentioned something for which no equivalent at all existed in English, his mind supplied him with a nonsense syllable.

So far so good. He'd been plucked out of his warm bed in Callahan Hall by a telepathic suitcase named something like Lirld which was equipped with quantities of eyes and tentacles. He'd been sucked down to some planet in an entirely different system near the center of the galaxy, clad in nothing but apple-green pajamas.

He was on a world of telepaths who couldn't hear him at all, but upon whom he could eavesdrop with ease, his brain evidently being a sufficiently sensitive antenna. He was scheduled shortly to undergo a "careful examination," a prospect he did not relish, the more so as he was evidently looked upon as a sort of monstrous laboratory animal. Finally, he was not thought much of, chiefly because he couldn't *pmbff* worth a damn.

All in all, Clyde Manship decided, it was about time that he made his presence felt. Let them know, so to speak, that he was definitely not a lower form of life, but one of the boys. That he belonged to the mind-over-matter club himself and came of a long line of IQ-fanciers on both sides of his family.

Only *how?*

Vague memories of adventure stories read as a boy drifted back to him. Explorers land on a strange island. Natives, armed with assorted spears, clubs and small boulders, gallop out of the jungle to meet them, their whoops an indisputable prelude to mayhem. Explorers, sweating a bit, as they do not know the language of this particular island, must act quickly. Naturally, they resort to—they resort to—the universal sign language! *Sign* language. Universal!

Still in a sitting position, Clyde Manship raised arms straight up over his head. "Me *friend*," he intoned. "Me come in peace." He didn't expect the dialogue to get across, but it seemed to him that voicing such words might help him psychologically and thus add more sincerity to the gesture.

"—and you might as well turn off the recording apparatus, too," Professor Lirld was instructing his assistant. "From here on out, we'll take everything down on a double memory-fix."

Srin manipulated his spheroid again. "Think I should modulate the dampness, sir? The creature's dry skin seems to argue a desert climate."

"Not at all. I strongly suspect it to be one of those primitive forms which can survive in a variety of environments. The specimen seems to be getting along admirably. I tell you, Srin, we can be very well satisfied with the results of the experiment up to this point."

"Me friend," Manship went on desperately, raising and lowering his arms. "Me intelligent entity. Me have IQ of 140 on the Wechsler-Bellevue scale."

"*You* may be satisfied," Glomg was saying, as Lirld left the table with a light jump and floated, like an oversized dandelion, to a mass of equipment overhead, "but I'm not. I don't like this business one little bit."

"Me friendly *and* intelligent enti—" Manship began. He sneezed again. "Damn this wet air," he muttered morosely.

"What was *that?*" Glomg demanded.

"Nothing very important, Councilor," Srin assured him. "The creature did it before. It is evidently a low-order biological reaction that takes place periodically, possibly a primitive method of imbibing *glrnk*. Not by any stretch of the imagination a means of communication, however."

"I wasn't thinking of communication," Glomg observed testily. "I thought it might be a prelude to aggressive action."

The professor skimmed back to the table, carrying a skein of luminescent wires. "Hardly. What could a creature of this sort be aggressive *with*? I'm afraid you're letting your mistrust of the unknown run away with you, Councilor Glomg."

Manship had crossed his arms across his chest and subsided into a helpless silence. There was evidently no way to make himself understood outside of telepathy. And how do you start transmitting telepathically for the first time? What do you use?

If only his doctoral thesis had been in biology or physiology, he thought wistfully, instead of *The Use of the Second Aorist in the First Three Books of the Iliad*. Oh, well. He was a long way from home. Might as well try.

He closed his eyes, having first ascertained that Professor Lirld did not intend to approach his person with the new piece of equipment. He wrinkled his forehead and leaned forward with an effort of extreme concentration.

Testing, he thought as hard as he could, *testing, testing. One, two, three, four—testing, testing. Can you hear me?*

"I just don't like it," Glomg announced again. "I don't like what we're doing here. Call it a presentiment, call it what you will, but I feel we are tampering with the infinite—and we shouldn't."

I'm testing, Manship ideated frantically. *Mary had a little lamb. Testing, testing. I'm the alien creature and I'm trying to communicate with you. Come in, please.*

"Now, Councilor," Lirld protested irritably. "Let's have none of that. This is a scientific experiment."

"That's all very well. But I believe there are mysteries that flefnobe was never meant to examine. Monsters as awful-looking as this—no slime on the skin, only two eyes and both of them flat, unable or unwilling to *pmbff,* an almost-complete absence of tentacles—a creature of this sort should have been left undisturbed on its own hellish planet. There are limits to science, my learned friend—or there should be. One should not seek to know the unknowable!"

Can't you hear me? Manship begged. *Alien entity to Srin, Lirld and Glomg: This is an attempt at a telepathic connection. Come in, please, someone. Anyone.* He considered for a moment, then added: *Roger. Over.*

"I don't recognize such limitations, Councilor. My curiosity is as vast as the universe."

"That may be," Glomg rejoined portentously. "But there are more things in *Tiz* and *Tetzbah,* Professor Lirld, than are dreamed of in your philosophy."

"My philosophy—" Lirld began, and broke off to announce— "Here's your son. Why don't you ask him? Without the benefit of half a dozen scientific investigations that people like you have wanted to call off time after time, none of his heroic achievements in interplanetary discovery would be possible."

Thoroughly defeated, but still curious, Manship opened his eyes in time to see an extremely narrow black suitcase swarm up to the tabletop in a spaghetti-cluster of tentacles.

"What is—*that?*" the newcomer inquired, curling a bunch of supercilious eye-stalks over Manship's head. "It looks like a *yurd* with a bad case of *hipplestatck.*" He considered for a moment, then added, "Galloping *hipplestatck.*"

"It's a creature from astronomical unit 649-301-3 that I've just succeeded in teleporting to our planet," Lirld told him proudly. "Mind you, Rabd, without a transmitting outfit on the other end! I admit I don't know why it worked this time and never before—but that's a matter for further research. A beautiful specimen, though, Rabd. And as near as we can tell, in perfect condition. You can put it away now, Srin."

"Oh, no you don't, Srin—" Manship had barely started to announce when a great rectangle of some pliable material fell from the ceiling and covered him. A moment later, the tabletop on which he'd been sitting seemed to drop away and the ends of the material were gathered in underneath him and fastened with a click by a scuttling individual whom he took to be the assistant. Then, before he had time to so much as wave his arms, the tabletop shot up with an abruptness that he found twice as painful as it was disconcerting.

And there he was, packaged as thoroughly as a birthday present. All in all, things were not improving, he decided. Well, at least they seemed disposed to leave him alone now. And as yet they showed no tendency to shove him up on a laboratory shelf along with dusty jars of flefnobe fetuses pickled in alcohol.

The fact that he was probably the first human being in history to make contact with an extraterrestrial race failed to cheer Clyde Manship in the slightest.

First, he reflected, the contact had been on a distinctly minor key—the sort that an oddly colored moth makes with a collector's bottle rather than a momentous meeting between the proud representatives of two different civilizations.

Second, and much more important, this sort of hands-across-the-cosmos affair was more likely to enthuse an astronomer, a sociologist or even a physicist than an assistant professor of Comparative Literature.

He'd had fantastic daydreams aplenty in his lifetime. But they concerned being present at the premiere of *Macbeth*, for example, and watching a sweating Shakespeare implore Burbage not to shout out the "Tomorrow and Tomorrow and Tomorrow" speech in the last act: "For God's sake, Dick, your wife just died and you're about to lose your kingdom and your life—don't let it sound like Meg at the Mermaid screaming for a dozen of ale. *Philosophical*, Dick, that's the idea, slow, mournful and philosophical. And just a little bewildered."

Or he'd imagined being one of the company at that moment sometime before 700 B.C. when a blind poet rose and intoned for the first time: "Anger, *extreme* anger, that is my tale . . ."

Or being a house guest at Yasnaya Polyana when Tolstoy wandered in from the garden with an abstracted look on his face and muttered: "Just got an idea for a terrific yarn about the Napoleonic invasion of Russia. And what a title! *War and Peace*. Nothing pretentious, nothing complicated. Just simply *War and Peace*. It'll knock them dead in St. Petersburg, I tell you. Of course, it's just a bare little short story at the moment, but I'll probably think of a couple of incidents to pad it out."

Travel to the Moon and the other planets of the solar system, let alone a voyage to the center of the galaxy—in his pajamas? No, that was definitely not a menu calculated to make Clyde Manship salivate. In this respect, he had wisted no farther afield than a glimpse, say, of Victor Hugo's sky-high balcony in St. Germain des Prés or the isles of Greece where burning Sappho loved and, from time to time as it occurred to her, sang.

Professor Bowles, now, Bowles or any of the other slipstick-sniffers in the Physics Department—what those boys would give to be in his position! To be the subject of an actual experiment far beyond the dreams of even theory on Earth, to be exposed to a technology that was patently so much more advanced than theirs—why, they would probably consider that, in exchange for all this, the vivisection that Manship was morosely certain would end the evening's festivities was an excellent bargain and verged on privilege. The Physics Department . . .

Manship suddenly recalled the intricately weird tower, studded with gray dipoles, that the Physics Department had been erecting in Murphy Field. He'd watched the government-subsidized project in radiation research going up from his window in Callahan Hall.

Only the evening before, when it had reached the height of his window, he'd reflected that it looked more like a medieval siege engine designed to bring down walled cities than a modern communicative device.

But now, with Lirld's comment about one-way teleportation never having worked before, he found himself wondering whether the uncompleted tower, poking a ragged section of electronic superstructure at his bedroom window, had been partially responsible for this veritable puree-of-nightmare he'd been wading through.

Had it provided a necessary extra link with Lirld's machine, sort of an aerial connection or grounding wire or whatever? If only he knew a little physics! Eight years of higher education were inadequate to suggest the barest aye or nay.

He gnashed his teeth, went too far and bit his tongue—and was forced to suspend mental operations until the pain died away and the tears dribbled out of his eyes.

What if he knew for certain that the tower had played a potent, though passive, part in his removal through interstellar space? What if he knew the exact part it had played in terms of megavolts and amperages and so forth—would the knowledge be the slightest use to him in this impossible situation?

No, he'd still be a hideous flat-eyed, non-intelligent monster plucked pretty much at random from the outer reaches of the universe, surrounded by creatures to whose minds his substantial knowledge of the many literatures of astronomical unit 649-301-3 would probably come across, allowing even for the miracle of translation, as so much schizophrenic word-salad.

In his despair, he plucked hopelessly at the material in which he'd been wrapped. Two small sections came away in his fingers.

There wasn't enough light to examine them, but the feel was unmistakable. Paper. He was wrapped in an oversized sheet of something very much like paper.

It made sense, he thought, it made sense in its own weird way. Since the appendages of the flefnobes he had seen to date consisted of nothing more than slender tentacles ending in either eyes or tapered points, and since they seemed to need knoblike protuberances on the laboratory table in order to perch beside him, a cage of paper was pretty much escape-proof from their point of view. There was nothing for their tentacles to grip—and they evidently didn't have the musculature to punch their way through.

Well, he did. Athletically, he had never amounted to much, but he believed, given enough of an emergency, in his ability to fight his way out of a paper bag. It was a comforting thought, but, at the moment, only slightly more useful than the nugget about the tower in Murphy Field.

If only there were some way of transmitting *that* bit of information to Lirld's little group: maybe they'd realize that the current flefnobe version of *The Mindless Horror from Hyperspace* had a few redeeming intellectual qualities, and maybe they could work out a method of sending him back. If they wanted to.

Only he couldn't transmit information. All he could do, for some reason peculiar to the widely separate evolutionary paths of man and flefnobe, was receive. So former Assistant Professor Clyde Manship sighed heavily, slumped his shoulders yet a further slump—and stolidly set himself to receive.

He also straightened his pajamas about him tenderly, not so much from latent sartorial ambition as because of agonizing twinges of nostalgia: he had suddenly realized that the inexpensive green garment with its heavily standardized cut was the only artifact he retained of his own world. It was the single souvenir, so to speak, that he possessed of the civilization which had produced both Tamerlane and *terza rima;* the pajamas were, in fact, outside of his physical body, his last link with Earth.

"So far as I'm concerned," Glomg's explorer son was commenting— it was obvious that the argument had been breezing right along and that the papery barrier didn't affect Manship's "hearing" in the slightest—"I can take these alien monsters or leave them alone. When they get as downright disgusting as this, of course, I'd rather leave them alone. But what I mean—I'm not afraid of tampering with the infinite, like Pop here, and on the other side, I can't believe that what you're doing, Professor Lirld, will ever lead to anything really important."

He paused, then went on. "I hope I haven't hurt your feelings, sir, but that's what I honestly think. I'm a practical flefnobe, and I believe in practical things."

"How can you say—nothing really important?" In spite of Rabd's apology, the professor's mental "voice" as it registered on Manship's brain positively undulated with indignation. "Why, the greatest concern of flefnobe science at the moment is to achieve a voyage to some part of the outer galaxy where the distances between stars are prodigious compared to their relative denseness here at the galactic center.

"We can travel at will between the fifty-four planets of our system and we have recently achieved flight to several of our neighboring suns, but going so far as even the middle areas of the galaxy, where this specimen originates, remains as visionary a project today as it was before the dawn of extra-atmospheric flight over two centuries ago."

"Right!" Rabd broke in sharply. "And why? Because we don't have the ships capable of making the journey? Not on your *semble-swol*, Professor! Why, since the development of the *Bulvonn* Drive, any ship in the flefnobe navy or merchant marine, down to my little three-jet runabout, could scoot out to a place as far as astronomical unit 649-301-3—to name just one example—and back without even hotting up her engines. But we don't. And for a very good reason."

Clyde Manship was now listening—or receiving—so hard that the two halves of his brain seemed to grind against each other. He was very much interested in astronomical unit 649-301-3 and anything that made travel to it easier or more difficult, however exotic the method of transportation employed might be by prevailing terrestrial standards.

"And the reason, of course," the young explorer went on, "is a practical one. Mental dwindle. Good old mental dwindle. In two hundred years of solving every problem connected with space travel, we haven't so much as *pmbffed* the surface of *that* one. All we have to do is go a measly twenty light-years from the surface of our home planet and mental dwindle sets in with a bang. The brightest crews start acting like retarded children and, if they don't turn back right away, their minds go out like so many lights: they've dwindled mentally smack down to zero."

It figured, Manship decided excitedly, it figured. A telepathic race like the flefnobes . . . why, of course! Accustomed since earliest infancy to having the mental aura of the entire species about them at all times, dependent completely on telepathy for communication since there had never been a need for developing any other method, what loneliness, what ultimate magnification of loneliness, must they not feel once their ships had reached a point too far from their world to maintain contact!

And their education now—Manship could only guess at the educational system of a creature so different from himself, but surely it must be a kind of high-order and continual mental osmosis, a mutual mental osmosis. However it worked, their educational system probably accentuated the involvement of the individual with the group. Once the feeling of involvement became too tenuous, because of intervening barrier or overpowering stellar distance, the flefnobe's psychological disintegration was inevitable.

But all this was unimportant. There were interstellar spaceships in existence! There were vehicles that could take Clyde Manship back to Earth, back to Kelly University and the work-in-progress he hoped would eventually win him a full professorship in Comparative Literature: *Style vs. Content in Fifteen Representative Corporation Reports to Minority Stockholders for the Period 1919-1931.*

For the first time, hope sprang within his breast. A moment later, it was lying on its back and massaging a twisted knee. Because assume, just assume for the sake of argument, his native intelligence told him, that he could somehow get out of this place and pick his way about what was, by every indication, a complete oddity of a world, until he found the spaceships Rabd had mentioned—could it ever be believed by any imagination no matter how wild or fevered, his native intelligence continued, that he, Clyde Manship, whose fingers were all thumbs and whose thumbs were all knuckles, whose mechanical abilities would have made Swanscombe Man sneer and *Sinanthropus* snicker, could it ever be believed, his native intelligence inquired sardonically, that he'd be capable of working out the various gadgets of advanced spaceship design, let alone the peculiarities that highly unusual creatures like the flefnobes would inevitably have incorporated into their vessels?

Clyde Manship was forced to admit morosely that the entire project was somewhat less than possible. But he did tell his native intelligence to go straight to hell.

Rabd now, though. *Rabd* could pilot him back to Earth if (a) Rabd found it worthwhile personally and if (b) Rabd could be communicated with. Well, what interested Rabd most? Evidently this Mental Dwindle ranked quite high.

"If you'd come up with an answer to that, Professor," he was expostulating at this point, "I would cheer so hard I'd unship my *glrnk.*

That's what's kept us boxed up here at the center of the galaxy for too many years. That's the *practical* problem. But when you haul this Qrm-forsaken blob of protoplasm out of its hole halfway across the universe and ask me what I think of it, I must tell you the whole business leaves me completely dry. This, to me, is not a practical experiment."

Manship caught the mental ripples of a nod from Rabd's father. "I'm forced to agree with you, son. Impractical and dangerous. And I think I can get the rest of the council to see it my way. Far too much has been spent on this project already."

As the resonance of their thoughts decreased slightly in volume, Manship deduced they were leaving the laboratory.

He heard the beginnings of a desperate, "But—but—" from Lirld. Then, off in the distance, Councilor Glomg, evidently having dismissed the scientist, asked his son a question, "And where is little Tekt? I thought she'd be with you."

"Oh, she's out at the landing field," Rabd answered, "supervising last-minute stuff going into the ship. After all, we begin our mating flight tonight."

"A wonderful female," Glomg told him in a "voice" that was now barely audible. "You're a very lucky flefnobe."

"I know that, Pop," Rabd assured him. "Don't think I don't know that. The most plentiful bunch of eye-ended tentacles this side of *Gansibokkle* and they're mine, all mine!"

"Tekt is a warm and highly intelligent female flefnobe," his father pointed out severely from a great distance. "She has many fine qualities. I don't like you acting as if the mating process were a mere matter of the number of eye-ended tentacles possessed by the female."

"Oh, it isn't, Pop," Rabd assured him. "It isn't at all. The mating process is a grave and—er, a serious matter to me. Full of responsibilities—er, serious responsibilities. Yes, sir. Highly serious. But the fact that Tekt has over a hundred and seventy-six slime-washed tentacles, each topped by a lovely, limpid eye, won't do our relationship a bit of harm. Quite the contrary, Pop, quite the contrary."

"A superstitious old crank and a brash bumpkin," Professor Lirld commented bitterly. "But between them, they can have my appropriation shut off, Srin. They can stop my work. Just when it's showing positive results. We've got to prepare countermeasures!"

Manship was not interested in this all-too-familiar academic despair, however. He was straining desperately after the receding minds of Glomg and Rabd. Not that he was at all intrigued by the elder's advice on How to Have a Sane and Happy Sex Life Though Married.

What had excited him prodigiously was a mental by-product of a much earlier comment. When Rabd had mentioned the last-minute loading of his ship, another part of the flefnobe's mind had, as if stimulated by association, dwelt briefly on the construction of the small vessel, its maintenance and, most important, its operation.

For just a few seconds, there had been a flash of a control panel with varicolored lights going on and off, and the beginnings of long-ago, often-repeated instruction: "To warm up the motors of the *Bulvonn* Drive, first gently rotate the uppermost three cylinders . . . Gently now!"

It was the kind of subliminal thought-picture, Manship realized excitedly, that had emanated from Srin a short while ago, and had enabled him to guess that the shifting light-patterns on the sphere the laboratory assistant held were actually meter readings. Evidently, his sensitivity to the flefnobe brain went deeper than the mental statements that were consciously transmitted by it and penetrated, if not the unconscious mind, at least the less submerged areas of personal awareness and memory.

But this meant—this meant—seated as he was, he still managed to stagger at the concept. A little practice, just a little acquired skill, and he could no doubt pick the brain of every flefnobe on the planet.

He sat and glowed at the thought. An ego that had never been particularly robust had been taking an especially ferocious pounding in the past half-hour under the contemptuous scrutiny of a hundred turquoise eyes and dozens of telepathic gibes.

A personality that had been power-starved most of its adult life abruptly discovered it might well hold the fate of an entire planet in the hollow of its cerebrum.

Yes, this certainly made him feel a lot better. Every bit of information these flefnobes possessed was his for the taking. What, for example, did he feel like taking? For a starter, that is.

Manship remembered. His euphoria dwindled like a spat-upon match. There was only one piece of information he desired, only one thing he wanted to know. How to get home!

One of the few creatures on this planet, possibly the only one for all he knew, whose thoughts were of a type to make this possible, was on his way with his father to some flefnobe equivalent of Tony's Bar and Grill. Rabd had, in fact, to judge from the silence reigning on the subject, just this moment passed out of effective telepathic range.

With a hoarse, anguished, yearning cry, similar to that of a bull who—having got in a juicy lick with his horns and having been carried by the momentum of his rush the full length of the bull-ring—turns, only to see the attendants dragging the wounded matador out of the arena . . . with precisely that sort of thoroughly dismayed bellow, Clyde Manship reached up, tore the surrounding material apart with one mighty two-handed gesture, and leaped to his feet on the in-and-out curving tabletop.

". . . And seven or eight charts in full color, representing the history of teleportation prior to this experiment," Lirld was telling his assistant at that moment. "In fact, Srin, if you have time to make *three-dimensional* charts, the Council is even more likely to be impressed. We're in a fight, Srin, and we've got to use every—"

His thoughts broke off as an eyestalk curled around and regarded Manship. A moment later his entire complement of eyestalks as well as those of his assistant swished about and stopped, quivering, with their focus on the erect, emergent human.

"Holy, concentrated *Qrm*," the professor's mind barely transmitted the quavering thought. "The flat-eyed monster. It's broken loose!"

"Out of a cage of solid paper!" Srin added in awe.

Lirld came to a decision. "The blaster," he ordered peremptorily. "Tentacle me the blaster, Srin. Appropriation or no appropriation, we don't dare take chances with a creature like this. We're in a crowded city. Once it got out on a rampage—" He shuddered the entire black suitcase length of him. He made a rapid adjustment in the curlicued instrument that Srin had given him. He pointed it at Manship.

Having actually fought his way out of the paper bag, Manship had paused, irresolute, on the tabletop. Far from being a man of action in any sense, he now found himself distinctly puzzled as to just which way to act. He had no idea of the direction taken by Glomg *père* and *fils;* furthermore he was at a loss as he looked around for anything that in any way resembled a door. He regretted very much that he had not noticed through which aperture Rabd had entered the room when the younger flefnobe had joined their jolly little circle.

He had just about made up his mind to look into a series of zigzag indentations in the opposite wall when he observed Lirld pointing the blaster at him with determined if unprofessional tremulousness. His mind, which had been filing the recent conversation between professor and assistant in an uninterested back portion, suddenly informed him that he was about to become the first, and probably unrecorded victim, in a War of Worlds.

"Hey!" he yelped, entirely forgetting his meager powers of communication. "I just want to look up Rabd. I'm not going on any ramp—"

Lirld did something to the curlicued instrument that seemed like winding a clock, but was probably more equivalent to the pressing of a trigger. He simultaneously shut all of his eyes—no mean feat in itself.

That, Clyde Manship reflected later—when there was time and space to reflect—was the only thing which saved his life. That and the prodigious sideways broad-jump he made as millions of crackling red dots ripped out of the instrument toward him.

The red dots sped past his pajama top and into one of the lower vaults that made up the ceiling. Without a sound, a hole some ten feet in circumference appeared in the masonry. The hole was deep enough—some three or four feet—to let the night sky of the planet show through. A heavy haze of white powder drifted down like the dust from a well-beaten rug.

Staring at it, Manship felt the roll of tiny glaciers toward his heart. His stomach flattened out against its abdominal wall and tried to skulk quietly around his ribs. He had never felt so completely frightened in his life. "Hey-y-y—" he began.

"A little too much power, Professor," Srin observed judiciously from where he rested easily with tentacles outspread against the wall. "A little too much power and not enough *glrnk*. Try a little more *glrnk* and see what happens."

"Thank you," Lirld told him gratefully. "Like this, you mean?" He raised and pointed the instrument again.

"Hey-y-y!" Manship continued in the same vein as before, not so much because he felt the results of such a statement would be particularly rewarding as because he lacked, at the moment, the creative faculties for another, more elaborate comment. "Hey-y-y-y!" he repeated between chattering teeth, staring at Lirld out of eyes no longer entirely flat.

He held up a shaking, admonishing hand. Fear was gibbering through him like the news of panic through a nation of monkeys. He watched the flefnobe make the peculiar winding trigger adjustment again. His thoughts came to a stop and every muscle in his body seemed to tense unendurably.

Suddenly, Lirld shook. He slid backward along the tabletop. The weapon dropped out of stiffened tentacles and smashed into bunches of circular wires that rolled in all directions. "Srin!" his mind whimpered. "Srin! The monster—Do—do you see what's coming out of his eyes? He's—he's—"

His body cracked open and a pale, blue goo poured out. Tentacles dropped off him like so many long leaves in a brisk autumn wind. The eyes that studded his surface turned from turquoise to a dull brown. "*Srin!*" he begged in a tiny, faraway thought. "Help me—the flat-eyed monster is—help—help!"

And then he dissolved. Where he had been, there was nothing but a dark liquid, streaked with blue, that flowed and bubbled and dripped off the curving edge of the table.

Manship stared at it uncomprehendingly, realizing only one thing fully—he was still alive.

A flicker of absolutely mad, stampeding fear reached him from Srin's mind. The laboratory assistant jumped from the wall against which he'd been standing, skidded across the tabletop with thrashing tentacles, paused for a moment at the knobs that lined its edge to get the necessary traction—and then leaped in an enormous arc to the far wall of the building. The zigzag indentations widened in a sort of lightning flash to let his body through.

So that *had* been a door after all. Manship found himself feeling rather smug at the deduction. With so little to go on—pretty smart, *pretty* smart.

And then the various parts of his brain caught up with current events and he began trembling from the reaction. He should be dead, a thing of shredded flesh and powdered bone. What had happened?

Lirld had fired the weapon at him and missed the first time. Just as he was about to fire again, something had struck the flefnobe about as hard as it had the Assyrian back in the days when the latter was in the habit of coming down like the wolf on the fold. *What?* Manship had been using no weapon of his own. He had, so far as he knew, no ally on this world. He looked about the huge, vaulted room. Silence. There was nothing else, nobody else in the place.

What was it the professor had screamed telepathically before he turned into soup? Something about Manship's eyes? Something *coming* out of the Earthman's eyes?

Still intensely puzzled—and despite his relief at having survived the last few minutes—Manship could not help regretting Lirld's extinction. Possibly because of his somewhat similar occupational status, the flefnobe had been the only creature of his type toward whom Manship felt any sympathy. He felt a little lonelier now—and, obscurely, a little guilty.

The different thoughts which had been mashing themselves to and fro in his mind abruptly disappeared, to be replaced by a highly important observation.

The zigzag doorway through which Srin had fled was closing, was coming together! And, as far as Manship knew, it was the only way out of the place!

Manship bounced off the huge tabletop in a jump that for the second time in ten minutes did great credit to a few semester-hours of gym some six years ago. He reached the narrowing gap, prepared to claw his way through the solid stone if necessary.

He was determined not to be trapped in this place when the flefnobe police closed in with whatever they used in place of tear gas and machine guns. He had also not forgotten the need to catch up to Rabd and get two or three more driving lessons.

To his intense relief, the aperture dilated again as he was about to hit it. Some sort of photoelectric gadget, he wondered, or was it just sensitive to the approach of a body?

He charged through, and for the first time found himself on the surface of the planet with the night sky all around him.

The view of the sky almost took his breath away and made him forget, temporarily, the utterly strange city of the flefnobes that stretched away in every direction.

There were so many stars! It was as if these stellar bodies were so much confectioner's sugar and someone had tossed a bagful at the heavens. They glowed with enough luminosity to maintain a three-quarters twilight. There was no moon, but its lack was not felt; rather it seemed that half a dozen moons had been broken up into quadrillions of tiny white dots.

It would be impossible, in this plenty, to trace out a single constellation. It would be necessary, instead, Manship guessed, to speak of a third brightest patch, a fifth largest sector. Truly, here in the center of the galaxy, one did not merely see the stars—one lived amongst them!

He noticed his feet were wet. Glancing down, he saw he was standing in a very shallow stream of some reddish liquid that flowed between the rounded flefnobe buildings. Sewage disposal? Water supply? Probably neither, probably something else completely out of the range of human needs. For there were other colored streams flowing parallel to it, Manship saw now—green ones, mauve ones, bright pink ones. At a street intersection a few yards from him, the reddish stream flowed away by itself down a sort of alley, while a few new colored ribbons joined the main body.

Well, he wasn't here to work out problems in extraterrestrial sociology. He already had the sniffling intimation of a bad head cold. Not only his feet were wet in this spongelike atmosphere; his pajamas clung to his skin in dampest companionship and, every once in a while, his eyes got blurry with the moisture and he had to brush them dry with the back of a hand.

Furthermore, while he was not hungry, he had not only seen nothing resembling human-type victuals since his arrival, but also no evidence to suggest that the flefnobes had stomachs, let alone mouths.

Maybe they took in nourishment through the skin, soaked it up, say, from those differently colored streams that ran through their city. Red might be meat, green could be vegetables, white for dessert—

He clenched his fists and shook himself. *I've no time for any of this philosophic badminton,* he told himself fiercely. *In just a few hours, I'm going to be extremely hungry and thirsty. I'm also going to be extremely hunted. I'd better get moving—work out some solutions!*

Only where? Fortunately, the street outside Lirld's laboratory seemed deserted. Maybe the flefnobes were afraid of the dark? Maybe they were all good, respectable homebodies and everyone, without exception, toddled into his bed at night to sleep the darkness through? Maybe—

Rabd. He had to find Rabd. That was the beginning and the end of the only solution to his problems he had come even close to, since his materialization on Professor Lirld's lab table.

Rabd.

He tried "listening" with his mind. All kinds of drifting, miscellaneous thoughts were sloshing around in his brain, from the nearer inhabitants of the city.

"All right, darling, all right. If you don't want to *gadl,* you don't have to *gadl.* We'll do something else . . ."

"That smart-aleck Bohrg! Will I fix him properly tomorrow . . ."

"Do you have three *zamshkins* for a *plet?* I want to make a long-distance send . . ."

"Bohrg will roll in tomorrow morning, thinking everything is the same as it's always been. Is he going to be surprised . . ."

"I like you, Nernt, I like you a lot. And that's why I feel it's my duty to tell you, strictly as a friend, you understand . . ."

"No, darling, I didn't mean that *I* didn't want to *gadl.* I thought *you* didn't want to; I was trying to be considerate like you always tell me to be. *Of course* I want to *gadl.* Now please don't look at me like that . . ."

"Listen here. I can lick any flefnobe in the place . . ."

"To tell you the truth, Nernt, I think you're the only one who doesn't know. Everybody else . . ."

"So you're all scared, huh? All right, I'll take you on two at a time. Come on, *come on . . .*"

But no hint of Rabd. Manship began to walk cautiously down the stone-paved streets, sloshing through the little rivulets.

He stepped too close to the wall of the dark buildings. Immediately, a zigzag doorway opened its jagged invitation. He hesitated for a moment, then stepped through.

Nobody here either. Did the flefnobes sleep in some central building, dormitory fashion? Did they sleep at all? He must remember to tune in on some likely mind and investigate. The information might be useful.

This building seemed to be a warehouse; it was filled with shelves. The walls were bare, however—there seemed to be some flefnobe inhibition against putting objects against the walls. The shelves rose in tall tiers—again free-form shapes—from the center of the floor.

Manship strolled over to the shelving that was the height of his chest. Dozens of fat green balls rested in white porcelain cups. Food? Could be. They looked distinctly edible, like melons.

He reached out and picked one up. It immediately spread wings and flew away to the ceiling. Every one of the other green balls, on all the shelves, spread a similar set of multiple, tiny wings and flew upward, like so many spherical birds whose nests have been disturbed. When they reached the domed ceiling, they seemed to disappear.

Manship backed out of the place hurriedly through the jagged aperture. He seemed to be setting off alarms wherever he went!

Once out in the street, he sensed a new feeling. There was a sensation of bubbling excitement everywhere, a tense waiting. Very few individual thoughts were coming through.

Suddenly the restlessness coalesced into an enormous mental shout that almost deafened him.

"Good evening!" it said. "Please stand by for an emergency news bulletin. This is Pukr, the son of Kimp, coming to you on a planetwide, mind-to-mind hookup. Here is the latest on the flat-eyed monster:

"At forty-three *skims* past *bebblewort,* tonight, this creature was materialized by Professor Lirld from astronomical unit 649-301-3 as part of an experiment in one-way teleportation. Councilor Glomg was present as a witness to the experiment in the course of his official duties and, observing the aggressive way in which the monster comported itself, immediately warned Lirld of the dangers in letting it remain alive.

"Lirld disregarded the warning and, later, after Councilor Glomg had departed with his son, Rabd, the well-known interplanetary explorer and flefnobe-about-town, the monster ran amuck. Having fought its way out of a cage of solid paper, it attacked the professor with an unknown type of high-frequency mental beam that seems to emanate from its unbelievably flat eyes. This beam seems to be similar, in effect, to that thrown out by second-order *grepsas* when all fuses have blown. Our best psycho-physicists are, at this very moment, working feverishly on that aspect of the problem.

"But Professor Lirld paid with his life for his scientific curiosity and for disregarding the warnings of Councilor Glomg's experience. Despite the best efforts of Srin, Lirld's laboratory assistant, who fought a desperate and courageous diversionary action in an attempt to save the old scientist, Lirld perished horribly before the monster's ferocious onslaught. With his superior dead, Srin retreated tentacle by tentacle, fighting all the way, barely managing to make his escape in time.

"This alien monster with its incredible powers is now loose in our city! All citizens are urged to remain calm, not to panic. Rest assured that as soon as the authorities know what to do, they will do it. Remember—above all—stay calm!

"Meanwhile, Rabd, the son of Glomg, has postponed his mating flight which was to have begun tonight. He is mating, as you all know, with Tekt, the daughter of Hilp—Tekt being the well-known star of *fnesh* and *blelg* from the southern continent. Rabd is leading a troop of volunteer flefnobes to the scientific quarters of the city, where the monster was last seen, in an attempt to exterminate it with already-existing, conventional weapons before the creature starts to reproduce. I will return with more bulletins when they are available. That is all for now."

That was more than enough, Manship felt. Now there wasn't any hope that he could work out some method of communication with these creatures and sit down for a little quiet conversation on ways and means of getting himself home—which seemed to be a conclusion earnestly desired by all. From now on the watchword was going to be *Get That Manship!*

He didn't like that at all.

On the other hand, he didn't have to wander after Rabd. If Manship can't get to the flefnobe, the flefnobe will come to Manship. Heavily armed, however, and with homicidal intent . . .

He decided he had better hide. He stepped up to a building and wandered along a wall until the doorway opened. He walked through and watched it close behind him, then looked around.

To his relief, it seemed like an excellent place to hide. There were quantities of large, heavy objects in the center of the place, none of them, so far as he could tell, alive, and all of them satisfactorily opaque. He wedged himself between two of these, which looked like stored tabletops, and hoped wistfully that the flefnobe sensory apparatus did not boast any more detective mechanisms than he had already experienced.

What he wouldn't give to be an assistant professor in Kelly University again instead of a flat-eyed monster ravening, all unwittingly, through an alien metropolis!

He found himself wondering about the strange powers he was supposed to possess. What was all this nonsense about a high-frequency mental beam emanating from his eyes? He hadn't noticed anything coming out—and he should have noticed if anyone did, he felt. Yet Lirld had made some comment to that effect just before he dissolved.

Was it possible that there was some by-product of the human brain that was only visible to flefnobes and was highly deleterious to them?

After all, he could tune in on the flefnobes' minds and they couldn't tune in on his. Maybe the only way he could make his mental presence felt to them was in some prodigious blast of thought which literally ripped them apart.

But he apparently couldn't turn it on and off at will—he hadn't caused the slightest alteration in Lirld, the first time the professor had fired.

There were ripples of new, excited thoughts reaching him suddenly. They were coming from somewhere in the street outside.

Rabd had arrived with his posse.

"Three of you move down that way," the young flefnobe ordered. "I want two each to cover the side streets. Don't spend too much time searching through the buildings. I'm positive we'll find this monster skulking somewhere in the dark streets, looking for new victims. Tanj, Zogt and Lewv—come with me. And keep on your tentacle-tips, everybody—this thing is crazy dangerous. But remember, we've got to blast it before it starts reproducing. Imagine what this planet would be like with a couple of hundred of these flat-eyed monsters running around!"

Manship let out a long, slow sigh of relief. If they hoped to find him on the streets, he might have a little time.

He let his mind follow that of Rabd. It wasn't too hard—just a matter of concentration—and you pretty much blocked out the thoughts of the other individuals. *Follow Rabd's mind, Rabd's thoughts. Now block out most of Rabd's conscious thoughts. There. The subliminal layer, the memory patterns. No, not the stuff about that female flefnobe last month, all eyes and soft tentacles, dammit!*

The memory patterns, the older ones. "When landing on a C-12 type planet . . ." *No, not that one. A little further. There!* "Having fired the forward jet to clear it, gently depress the . . ."

Manship combed through the operational instructions in Rabd's mind, pausing every once in a while to clear up a concept peculiar to flefnobe terminology, stopping now and then as a grinning thought about Tekt wandered in and threw everything out of focus.

He noticed that whatever information he absorbed in this fashion, he seemed to absorb permanently; there was no need to go back to previous data. Probably left a permanent print on his mind, he concluded.

He had it all now, at least as much about running the ship as it was possible to understand. In the last few moments, he had been operating the ship—and operating the ship for years and years—at least through Rabd's memories. For the first time, Manship began to feel a little confident.

But how was he to find the little spaceship in the streets of this utterly strange city? He clasped his hands in perspired bafflement. After all this—

Then he had the answer. He'd get the directions from Rabd's mind. Of course. Good old encyclopedia Rabd! *He'd* certainly remember where he parked the vessel.

And he did. With a skill that seemed to have come from ages of practice, Clyde Manship riffled through the flefnobe's thoughts, discarding this one, absorbing that one—". . . the indigo stream for five blocks. Then take the first merging red one and . . ."—until he had as thorough and as permanent a picture of the route to Rabd's three-jet runabout as if he'd been studying the subject in graduate school for six months.

Pretty good going for a stodgy young assistant professor of Comparative Literature who up to this night had about as much experience with telepathy as African lion-hunting! But perhaps— perhaps it had been a matter of *conscious* experience of telepathy; perhaps the human mind was accustomed to a sort of regular, deep-in-the-brain, unconscious telepathy from infancy and being exposed to creatures so easy to receive from as flefnobes had brought the latently exercised powers to the surface.

That would explain the quickly acquired skill that felt so much like the sudden surprising ability to type whole words and sentences after months of practicing nothing but meaningless combinations of letters in certain set alphabetical patterns.

Well, it might be interesting, but that particular speculation was not his field of research and not his problem. Not for tonight, anyway.

Right now, what he had to do was somehow slip out of the building unobserved by the crowd of flefnobe vigilantes outside, and get on his way fast. After all, it might not be long before the militia was called out to deal with something as viciously destructive as himself . . .

He slipped out of his hiding place and made for the wall. The zigzag doorway opened. He stepped through—and bowled over a tentacled black suitcase who'd apparently been coming in.

The flefnobe recovered fast. He pointed his spirally weapon at Manship from where he lay and began winding it. Once more, the Earthman went rigid with fright; he'd seen what that thing could do. To be killed now, after all he'd gone through . . .

And once more, there was a quiver and a mental scream of distress from the flefnobe: "The flat-eyed monster—I've found him—his eyes—his eyes. Zogt, Rabd, help! His *eyes*—"

There was nothing left but a twitching tentacle or two and a puddle of liquid rippling back and forth in a little hollow near the building wall. Without looking back, Manship fled.

A stream of red dots chattered over his shoulder and dissolved a domed roof directly ahead of him. Then he had turned the corner and was picking up speed. From the dwindling telepathic shouts behind him, he deduced with relief that feet moved faster than tentacles.

He found the correct colored streams and began to work his way in the direction of Rabd's spaceship. Only once or twice did he come across a flefnobe. And none of them seemed to be armed.

At sight of him, these passersby wound their tentacles about their bodies, huddled against the nearest wall, and, after a few dismal mutters to the effect of "*Qrm* save me, *Qrm* save me," seemed to pass out.

He was grateful for the absence of heavy traffic, but wondered why it should be so, especially since he was now moving through the residential quarters of the city according to the mental map he had purloined from Rabd.

Another overpowering roar in his mind gave him the answer.

"This is Pukr, the son of Kimp, returning to you with more news of the flat-eyed monster. First, the Council wishes me to notify all who have not already been informed through their *blelg* service that a state of martial law has been proclaimed in the city.

"Repeat: a state of martial law has been proclaimed in the city! All citizens are to stay off the streets until further notice. Units of the army and space fleet as well as heavy *maizeltoovers* are being moved in hurriedly. Don't get in their way! Stay off the streets!

"The flat-eyed monster has struck again. Just ten short *skims* ago, it struck down Lewv, the son of Yifg, in a running battle outside the College of Advanced *Turkaslerg,* almost trampling Rabd, the son of Glomg, who courageously hurled himself in its path in a valiant attempt to delay the monster's flight. Rabd, however, believes he seriously wounded it with a well-placed bolt from his blaster. The monster's weapon was the high-frequency beam from its eyes—

"Shortly before this battle, the flat-eyed horror from the outer galactic wastes had evidently wandered into a museum where it completely destroyed a valuable collection of green *fermfnaks.* They were found in a useless winged condition. Why did it do this? Pure viciousness? Some scientists believe that this act indicates intelligence of a very high order indeed, and that this intelligence, together with the fantastic powers already in evidence, will make the killing of the monster a much more difficult task than the local authorities expect.

"Professor Wuvb is one of these scientists. He feels that only through a correct psycho-sociological evaluation of the monster and an understanding of the peculiar cultural milieu from which it evidently derives will we be able to work out adequate countermeasures and save the planet. Therefore, in the interests of flefnobe survival, we have brought the professor here tonight to give you his views. The next mind you hear will be that of Professor Wuvb."

Just as the newcomer began portentously, "To understand any given cultural milieu, we must first ask ourselves what we mean by culture. Do we mean, for example—" Manship reached the landing field.

He came out upon it near the corner on which Rabd's three-jet runabout was parked between an enormous interplanetary vessel being loaded with freight and what Manship would have been certain was a warehouse, if he hadn't learned so thoroughly how wrong he could be about flefnobe equivalents of human activities.

There seemed to be no guards about, the landing field was not particularly well-lit, and most of the individuals in the neighborhood were concentrated around the freighter.

He took a deep breath and ran for the comparatively tiny, spherical ship with the deep hollow in the top and bottom, something like an oversized metallic apple. He reached it, ran around the side until he came to the zigzag line that indicated an entrance and squeezed through.

As far as he could tell, he hadn't been observed. Outside of the mutter of loading and stowage instructions coming from the larger ship, there were only Professor Wuvb's louder thoughts weaving their intricate sociophilosophical web: ". . . So we may conclude that in this respect, at least, the flat-eyed monster does not show the typical basic personality pattern of an illiterate. But then, if we attempt to relate the characteristics of a preliterate urban cultural configuration . . ."

Manship waited for the doorway to contract, then made his way hand over hand up a narrow, twisting ladderlike affair to the control room of the vessel. He seated himself uncomfortably before the main instrument panel and went to work.

It was difficult using fingers on gadgets which had been designed for tentacles, but he had no choice. *"To warm up the motors of the* Bulvonn *Drive—"* Gently, very gently, he rotated the uppermost three cylinders a complete turn each. Then, when the rectangular plate on his left began to show an even succession of red and white stripes across its face, he pulled on the large black knob protruding from the floor. A yowling roar of jets started from outside. He worked almost without conscious effort, letting memory take over. It was as if Rabd himself were getting the spaceship into operation.

A few seconds later, he was off the planet and in deep space.

He switched to interstellar operation, set the directional indicator for astronomical unit 649-301-3—and sat back. There was nothing else for him to do until the time came for landing. He was a little apprehensive about that part, but things had gone so well up to this point that he felt quite the interstellar daredevil. "Old Rocketfingers Manship," he grinned to himself smugly.

According to Rabd's subliminal calculations, he should be arriving on Earth—given the maximum output of the *Bulvonn* Drive which he was using—in ten to twelve hours. He was going to be more than a bit hungry and thirsty, but—What a sensation he was going to make! Even more of a sensation than he had left behind him. The flat-eyed monster with a high-frequency mental beam coming out of its eyes . . .

What *had* that been? All that had happened to him, each time a flefnobe dissolved before his stare, was a good deal of fear. He had been terribly frightened that he was going to be blasted into tiny pieces and had, somewhere in the process of being frightened, evidently been able to throw out something pretty tremendous—to judge from results.

Possibly the abnormally high secretion of adrenalin in the human system at moments of stress was basically inimical to flefnobe body structure. Or maybe there was an entirely mental reaction in Man's brain at such times whose emanations caused the flefnobes to literally fall apart. It made sense.

If he was so sensitive to their thoughts, they should be sensitive to him in some way. And obviously, when he was very much afraid, that sensitivity showed up with a vengeance.

He put his hands behind his head and glanced up to check his meters. Everything was working satisfactorily. The brown circles were expanding and contracting on the *sekkel* board, as Rabd's mind had said they should; the little serrations on the edge of the control panel were moving along at a uniform rate, the visiscreen showed—*the visiscreen!*

Manship leaped to his feet. The visiscreen showed what seemed to be every vessel in the flefnobe army and space fleet—not to mention the heavy *maizeltoovers*—in hot pursuit of him. And getting closer.

There was one large spacecraft that had almost caught up and was beginning to exude a series of bright rays that, Manship remembered from Rabd's recollections, were grapples.

What could have caused all this commotion—the theft of a single jet runabout? The fear that he might steal the secrets of flefnobe science? They should have been so glad to get rid of him, especially before he started reproducing hundreds of himself all over the planet!

And then a persistent thought ripple from inside his own ship—

a thought ripple which he had been disregarding all the time he had been concentrating on the unfamiliar problems of deep-space navigation—gave him a clue.

He had taken off with someone—or something—else in the ship!

Clyde Manship scurried down the twisting ladder to the main cabin. As he approached, the thoughts became clearer and he realized, even before the cabin aperture dilated to let him through, exactly whom he would find.

Tekt.

The well-known female star of *fnesh* and *blelg* from the southern continent and Rabd's about-to-be bride cowered in a far corner; all of her tentacles—including the hundred and seventy-six slime-washed ones that were topped by limpid eyes—twisted about her tiny black body in the most complicated series of knots Manship had ever seen.

"Oo-ooh!" her mind moaned. *"Qrm! Qrm!* Now it's going to happen! That awful, horrible thing! It's going to happen to me! It's coming closer—closer—"

"Look, lady, I'm not even slightly interested in you," Manship began, before he remembered that he'd never been able to communicate with any flefnobe before, let alone a hysterical female one.

He felt the ship shudder as the grapples touched it. *Well, here I go again,* he thought. In a moment there would be boarders and he'd have to turn them into bluish soup.

Evidently, Tekt had been sleeping aboard the vessel when he took off. She'd been waiting for Rabd to return and begin their mating flight. And she was obviously a sufficiently important figure to have every last reserve called up.

His mind caught the sensation of someone entering the ship. Rabd. From what Manship could tell, he was alone, carrying his trusty blaster—and determined to die fighting.

Well, that's exactly what he'd have to do. Clyde Manship was a fairly considerate individual and heartily disliked the idea of disintegrating a bridegroom on what was to have been his honeymoon. But, since he had found no way of communicating his pacific intentions, he had no choice.

"Tekt!" Rabd telepathed softly. "Are you all right?"

"Murder!" Tekt screamed. "Help-help-help-help . . ." Her thoughts abruptly disappeared; she had fainted.

The zigzag aperture widened and Rabd bounced into the cabin, looking like a series of long balloons in his spacesuit. He glanced at the recumbent Tekt and then turned desperately, pointing his curlicued blaster at Manship.

"Poor guy," Manship was thinking. "Poor, dumb, narrow-minded hero type. In just a second, you'll be nothing but goo." He waited, full of confidence.

He was so full of confidence, in fact, that he wasn't a bit frightened.

So nothing came out of his eyes, nothing but a certain condescending sympathy.

So Rabd blasted the ugly, obscene, horrible, flat-eyed thing down where it stood. And scooped up his bride with loving tentacles. And went back home to a hero's reception.

THE POWER

by Murray Leinster

Murray Leinster was, of course, the author of the classic story "First Contact," but it should be remembered that he wrote several stories of first contact between humans and aliens—possibly enough to fill a book by themselves—and while "First Contact" showed the optimistic side of Leinster's thought, he knew his fellow humans too well to think that such contact would always work out for the best, as in this human-alien encounter.

✖ ✖ ✖

WILLIAM FITZGERALD JENKINS *(1896-1975) was a prolific and successful writer, selling stories to magazines of all sorts, from pulps like* Argosy *to the higher-paying slicks such as* Collier's *and* The Saturday Evening Post, *writing stories ranging from westerns, to mysteries, to science fiction. However, for SF he usually used the pen name of* **MURRAY LEINSTER,** *and he used it often. Even though SF was a less lucrative field than other categories of fiction, he enjoyed writing it (fortunately for SF readers everywhere) and wrote a great deal of it, including such classics as (to repeat myself) "First Contact," "Sidewise in Time," and "A Logic Named Joe," the last being a story you should keep in mind the next time someone repeats the canard that sf never predicted the home computer or the internet. Leinster did it (though under his real name, this time) in* Astounding Science-Fiction *in 1946!*

His first SF story was "The Runaway Skyscraper," published in 1919, and his last was the third of three novelizations of the Land of the Giants *TV show. For the length of his career, his prolificity, and his introduction of original concepts into SF, fans in the 1940s began calling him the Dean of science fiction, a title he richly deserved.*

Memorandum from Professor Charles,
Latin Department, Haverford University,
to Professor McFarland, the same faculty:

Dear Professor McFarland:

In a recent batch of fifteenth-century Latin documents from abroad, we found three which seem to fit together. Our interest is in the Latin of the period, but their contents seem to bear upon your line. I send them to you with a free translation. Would you let me know your reaction?

Charles.

To Johannus Hartmannus,
Licentiate in Philosophy,
Living at the house of the Goldsmith Grote,
Lane of the Dyed Fleece, Leyden, the Low Countries:

Friend Johannus:

I write this from the Goth's Head Inn, in Padua, the second day after Michaelmas, Anno Domini 1482. I write in haste because a worthy Hollander here journeys homeward and has promised to carry mails for me. He is an amiable lout, but ignorant. Do not speak to him of mysteries. He knows nothing. Less than nothing. Thank him, give him a drink, and speak of me as a pious and worthy student. Then forget him.

I leave Padua tomorrow for the realization of all my hopes and yours. This time I am sure. I came here to purchase perfumes and mandragora and the other necessities for an Operation of the utmost imaginable importance, which I will conduct five nights hence upon a certain hilltop near the village of Montevecchio. I have found a Word and a Name of incalculable power, which in the place that I know of must open to me knowledge of all mysteries. When you read this, I shall possess powers of which Hermes Trismegistus only guessed, and which Albertus Magnus could speak of only by hearsay. I have been deceived before, but this time I am sure. I have seen proofs!

I tremble with agitation as I write to you. I will be brief. I came upon these proofs and the Word and the Name in the village of Montevecchio. I rode into the village at nightfall, disconsolate because I had wasted a month searching for a learned man of whom I had heard great things. Then I found him—and he was but a silly antiquary with no knowledge of mysteries! So riding upon my way I came to Montevecchio, and there they told me of a man dying even then because he had worked wonders. He had entered the village on foot only the day before. He was clad in rich garments, yet he spoke like a peasant. At first he was mild and humble, but he paid for food and wine with a gold piece, and villagers fawned upon him and asked for alms. He flung them a handful of gold pieces and when the news spread the whole village went mad with greed. They clustered about him, shrieking pleas, and thronging ever the more urgently as he strove to satisfy them. It is said that he grew frightened and would have fled because of their thrusting against him. But they plucked at his garments, screaming of their poverty, until suddenly his rich clothing vanished in the twinkling of an eye and he was but another ragged peasant like themselves and the purse from which he had scattered gold became a mere coarse bag filled with ashes.

This had happened but the day before my arrival, and the man was yet alive, though barely so because the villagers had cried witchcraft and beset him with flails and stones and then dragged him to the village priest to be exorcised.

I saw the man and spoke to him, Johannus, by representing myself to the priest as a pious student of the snares Satan has set in the form of witchcraft. He barely breathed, what with broken bones and pitchfork wounds. He was a native of the district, who until now had seemed a simple ordinary soul. To secure my intercession with the priest to shrive him ere he died, the man told me all. And it was much!

Upon this certain hillside where I shall perform the Operation five nights hence, he had dozed at midday. Then a Power appeared to him and offered to instruct him in mysteries. The peasant was stupid. He asked for riches instead. So the Power gave him rich garments and a purse which would never empty so long—said the Power—as it came not near a certain metal which destroys all things of mystery. And the Power warned that this was payment that he might send a learned man to learn what he had offered the peasant, because he saw that peasants had no understanding. Thereupon I told the peasant that I would go and greet this Power and fulfill his desires, and he told me the Name and the Word which would call him, and also the Place, begging me to intercede for him with the priest.

The priest showed me a single gold piece which remained of that which the peasant had distributed. It was of the age of Antoninus Pius, yet bright and new as if fresh-minted. It had the weight and feel of true gold. But the priest, wryly, laid upon it the crucifix he wears upon a small iron chain about his waist, instantly it vanished, leaving behind a speck of glowing coal which cooled and was a morsel of ash.

This I saw, Johannus! So I came speedily here to Padua, to purchase perfumes and mandragora and the other necessities for an Operation to pay great honor to this Power whom I shall call up five nights hence. He offered wisdom to the peasant, who desired only gold. But I desire wisdom more than gold, and surely I am learned concerning mysteries and Powers! I do not know any but yourself who surpasses me in true knowledge of secret things. And when you read this, Johannus, I shall surpass even you! But it may be that I will gain knowledge so that I can transport myself by a mystery to your attic, and there inform you myself, in advance of this letter, of the results of this surpassing good fortune which causes me to shake with agitation whenever I think of it.

> Your friend Carolus,
> at the Goth's Head Inn in Padua.

. . . Fortunate, perhaps, that an opportunity has come to send a second missive to you, through a crippled man-at-arms who has been discharged from a mercenary band and travels homeward to sit in the sun henceforth. I have given him one gold piece and promised that you would give him another on receipt of this message. You will keep that promise or not, as pleases you, but there is at least the value of a gold piece in a bit of parchment with strange symbols upon it which I enclose for you.

Item: I am in daily communication with the Power of which I wrote you, and daily learn great mysteries.

Item: Already I perform marvels such as men have never before accomplished, by means of certain sigils or talismans the Power has prepared for me.

Item: Resolutely the Power refuses to yield to me the Names or the incantations by which these things are done so that I can prepare such sigils for myself. Instead, he instructs me in divers subjects which have no bearing on the accomplishment of wonders, to my bitter impatience which I yet dissemble.

Item: Within this packet there is a bit of parchment. Go to a remote place and there tear it and throw it upon the ground. Instantly, all about you, there will appear a fair garden with marvelous fruits, statuary, and pavilions. You may use this garden as you will, save that if any person enter it, or you yourself, carrying a sword or dagger or any object however small made of iron, the said garden will disappear immediately and nevermore return.

This you may verify when you please. For the rest, I am like a person trembling at the very door of Paradise, barred from entering beyond the antechamber by the fact of the Power withholding from me the true essentials of mystery, and granting me only crumbs— which, however, are greater marvels than any known certainly to have been practiced before. For example, the parchment I send you. This art I have proven many times. I have in my scrip many such sigils, made for me by the Power at my entreaty. But when I have secretly taken other parchments and copied upon them the very symbols to the utmost exactitude, they are valueless. There are words or formulas to be spoken over them or—I think more likely—a greater sigil which gives the parchments their magic property. I begin to make a plan—a very daring plan—to acquire even this sigil.

But you will wish to know of the Operation and its results. I returned to Montevecchio from Padua, reaching it in three days. The peasant who had worked wonders was dead, the villagers having grown more fearful and beat out his brains with hammers. This pleased me, because I had feared he would tell another the Word and Name he had told me. I spoke to the priest, and told him that I had been to Padua and secured advice from high dignitaries concerning the wonder-working, and had been sent back with special commands to seek out and exorcise the foul fiend who had taught the peasant such marvels.

The next day—the priest himself aiding me!—I took up to the hilltop the perfumes and wax tapers and other things needed for the Operation. The priest trembled, but he would have remained had I not sent him away. And night fell, and I drew the magic circle and the pentacle, with the Signs in their proper places. And when the new moon rose, I lighted the perfumes and the fine candles and began the Operation. I have had many failures, as you know, but this time I knew confidence and perfect certainty. When it came time to use the Name and the Word, I called them both loudly, thrice, and waited.

Upon this hilltop there were many grayish stones. At the third calling of the Name, one of the stones shivered and was not. Then a voice said dryly:

"Ah! So that is the reason for this stinking stuff! My messenger sent you here?"

There was a shadow where the stone had been and I could not see clearly. But I bowed low in that direction:

"Most Potent Power," I said, my voice trembling because the Operation was a success, "a peasant working wonders told me that you desired speech with a learned man. Beside your Potency I am ignorant indeed, but I have given my whole life to the study of mysteries. Therefore I have come to offer worship or such other compact as you may desire in exchange for wisdom."

There was a stirring in the shadow, and the Power came forth. His appearance was that of a creature not more than an ell and a half in height, and his expression in the moonlight was that of sardonic impatience. The fragrant smoke seemed to cling about him, to make a cloudiness close about his form.

"I think," said the dry voice, "that you are as great a fool as the peasant I spoke to. What do you think I am?"

"A Prince of Celestial Race, your Potency," I said, my voice shaking.

There was a pause. The Power said as if wearily:

"Men! Fools forever! Oh, Man, I am simply the last of a number of my kind who traveled in a fleet from another star. This small planet of yours has a core of the accursed metal, which is fatal to the devices of my race. A few of our ships came too close. Others strove to aid them, and shared their fate. Many, many years since, we descended from the skies and could never rise again. Now I alone am left."

Speaking of the world as a planet was an absurdity, of course. The planets arc wanderers among the stars, traveling in their cycles and epicycles as explained by Ptolemy a thousand years since. But I saw at once that he would test me. So I grew bold and said:

"Lord, I am not fearful. It is not needful to cozen me. Do I not know of those who were cast out of Heaven for rebellion? Shall I write the name of your leader?"

He said "Eh?" for all the world like an elderly man. So, smiling, I wrote on the earth the true name of Him whom the vulgar call Lucifer. He regarded the markings on the earth and said:

"Bah! It is meaningless. More of your legendry! Look you, Man, soon I shall die. For more years than you are like to believe I have hid from your race and its accursed metal. I have watched men, and despised them. But—I die. And it is not good that knowledge should perish. It is my desire to impart to men the knowledge which else would die with me. It can do no harm to my own kind, and may bring the race of men to some degree of civilization in the course of ages."

I bowed to the earth before him. I was aflame with eagerness.

"Most Potent One," I said joyfully, "I am to be trusted. I will guard your secrets fully. Not one jot nor tittle shall ever be divulged!"

Again his voice was annoyed and dry.

"I desire that this knowledge be spread abroad so that all may learn it." Then he made a sound which I do not understand, save that it seemed to be derisive. "But what I have to say may serve, even garbled and twisted. And I do not think you will keep secrets inviolate! Have you pen and parchment?"

"Nay, Lord!"

"You will come again, then, prepared to write what I shall tell you."

But he remained, regarding me. He asked me questions, and I answered eagerly. Presently he spoke in a meditative voice, and I listened eagerly. His speech bore an odd similarity to that of a lonely man who dwelt much on the past, but soon I realized that he spoke in ciphers, in allegory, from which now and again the truth peered out. As one who speaks for the sake of remembering, he spoke of the home of his race upon what he said was a fair planet so far distant that to speak of leagues and even the span of continents would be useless to convey the distance. He told of cities in which his fellows dwelt—here, of course, I understood his meaning perfectly—and told of great fleets of flying things rising from those cities to go to other fair cities, and of music which was in the very air so that any person, anywhere upon the planet, could hear sweet sounds or wise discourse at will. In this matter there was no metaphor, because the perpetual sweet sounds in Heaven are matters of common knowledge. But he added a metaphor immediately after, because he smiled at me and observed that the music was not created by a mystery, but by waves like those of light, only longer. And this was plainly a cipher, because light is an impalpable fluid without length and surely without waves!

Then he spoke of flying through the emptiness of the empyrean, which again is not clear, because all can see that the heavens are fairly crowded with stars, and he spoke of many suns and other worlds, some frozen and some merely barren rock. The obscurity of such things is patent. And he spoke of drawing near to this world which is ours, and of an error made as if it were in mathematics—instead of in rebellion—so that they drew too close to Earth as Icarus to the sun.

Then again he spoke in metaphors, because he referred to engines, which are things to cast stones against walls, and in a larger sense for grinding corn and pumping water. But he spoke of engines growing hot because of the accursed metal in the core of Earth, and of the inability of his kind to resist Earth's pull—more metaphor—and then he spoke of a screaming descent from the skies. And all of this, plainly, is a metaphorical account of the casting of the Rebels out of Heaven, and an acknowledgment that he is one of the said Rebels.

When he paused, I begged humbly that he would show me a mystery, and of his grace give me protection in case my converse with him became known.

"What happened to my messenger?" asked the Power.

I told him, and he listened without stirring. I was careful to tell him exactly, because, of course, he would know that—as all else—by his powers of mystery, and the question was but another test. Indeed, I felt sure that the messenger and all that had taken place had been contrived by him to bring me, a learned student of mysteries, to converse with him in this place.

"Men!" he said bitterly at last. Then he added coldly, "Nay! I can give you no protection. My kind is without protection upon this earth. If you would learn what I can teach you, you must risk the fury of your fellow countrymen."

But then, abruptly, he wrote upon parchment and pressed the parchment to some object at his side. He threw it upon the ground.

"If men beset you," he said scornfully, "tear this parchment and cast it from you. If you have none of the accursed metal about you, it may distract them while you flee. But a dagger will cause it all to come to naught!"

Then he walked away. He vanished. And I stood shivering for a very long time before I remembered me of the formula given by Apollonius of Tyana for the dismissal of evil spirits. I ventured from the magic circle. No evil befell me. I picked up the parchment and examined it in the moonlight. The symbols upon it were meaningless, even to one like myself who has studied all that is known of mysteries. I returned to the village, pondering.

I have told you so much at length, because you will observe that this Power did not speak with the pride or the menace of which most authors on mysteries and Operations speak. It is often said that an adept must conduct himself with great firmness during an Operation, lest the Powers he has called up overawe him. Yet this Power spoke wearily, with irony, like one approaching death. And he had spoken of death, also. Which were, of course, a test and a deception, because are not the Principalities and Powers of Darkness immortal? He had some design it was not his will that I should know. So I saw that I must walk warily in this priceless opportunity.

In the village I told the priest that I had had encounter with a foul fiend, who begged that I not exorcise him, promising to reveal certain hidden treasures once belonging to the Church, which he could not touch or reveal to evil men because they were holy, but could describe the location of to me. And I procured parchment, and pens, and ink, and the next day I went alone to the hilltop. It was empty, and I made sure I was unwatched and—leaving my dagger behind me—I tore the parchment and flung it to the ground.

As it touched, there appeared such a treasure of gold and jewels as truly would have driven any man mad with greed. There were bags and chests and boxes filled with gold and precious stones, which had burst with the weight and spilled out upon the ground. There were gems glittering in the late sunlight, and rings and necklaces set with brilliants, and such monstrous hoards of golden coins of every antique pattern.

Johannus, even I went almost mad! I leaped forward like one dreaming to plunge my hands into the gold. Slavering, I filled my garments with rubies and ropes of pearls, and stuffed my script with gold pieces, laughing crazily to myself. I rolled in the riches. I wallowed in them, flinging the golden coins into the air and letting them fall upon me. I laughed and sang to myself.

Then I heard a sound. On the instant I was filled with terror for the treasure. I leaped to my dagger and snarled, ready to defend my riches to the death.

Then a dry voice said:

"Truly you care naught for riches!"

It was savage mockery. The Power stood regarding me. I saw him clearly now, yet not clearly because there was a cloudiness which clung closely to his body. He was, as I said, an ell and a half in height, and from his forehead there protruded knobby feelers which were not horns but had somewhat the look save for bulbs upon their ends. His head was large and—But I will not attempt to describe him, because he could assume any of a thousand forms, no doubt, so what does it matter?

Then I grew terrified because I had no Circle or Pentacle to protect me. But the Power made no menacing move.

"It is real, that riches," he said dryly. "It has color and weight and the feel of substance. But your dagger will destroy it all."

Didyas of Corinth has said that treasure of mystery must be fixed by a special Operation before it becomes permanent and free of the power of Those who brought it. They can transmute it back to leaves or other rubbish, if it be not fixed.

"Touch it with your dagger," said the Power.

I obeyed, sweating in fear. And as the metal iron touched a great piled heap of gold, there was a sudden shifting and then a little flare of heat about me. And the treasure—all, to the veriest crumb of a seed-pearl!—vanished before my eyes. The bit of parchment reappeared, smoking. It turned to ashes. My dagger scorched my fingers. It had grown hot.

"Ah yes," said the Power, nodding. "The force-field has energy. When the iron absorbs it, there is heat." Then he looked at me in a not unfriendly way. "You have brought pens and parchment," he said, "and at least you did not use the sigil to astonish your fellows. Also you had the good sense to make no more perfumish stinks. It may be that there is a grain of wisdom in you. I will bear with you yet a while. Be seated and take parchment and pen. Stay! Let us be comfortable. Sheathe your dagger, or better cast it from you."

I put it in my bosom. And it was as if he thought, and touched something at his side, and instantly there was a fair pavilion about us, with soft cushions and a gently playing fountain.

"Sit," said the Power. "I learned that men like such things as this from a man I once befriended. He had been wounded and stripped by robbers, so that he had not so much as a scrap of accursed metal about him, and I could aid him. I learned to speak the language men use nowadays from him. But to the end he believed me an evil spirit and tried valorously to hate me."

My hands shook with my agitation that the treasure had departed from me. Truly it was a treasure of such riches as no King has ever possessed, Johannus! My very soul lusted after that treasure! The golden coins alone would fill your attic solidly, but the floor would break under their weight, and the jewels would fill hogsheads. Ah, Johannus! That treasure!

"What I will have you write," said the Power, "at first will mean little. I shall give facts and theories first, because they are easiest to remember. Then I will give the applications of the theories. Then you men will have the beginning of such civilization as can exist in the neighborhood of the accursed metal."

"Your Potency!" I begged abjectly. "You will give me another sigil of treasure?"

"Write!" he commanded.

I wrote. And, Johannus, I cannot tell you myself what it is that I wrote. He spoke words, and they were in such obscure cipher that they have no meaning as I con them over. Hark you to this, and seek wisdom for the performance of mysteries in it! "The civilization of my race is based upon fields of force which have the property of acting in all essentials as substance. A lodestone is surrounded by a field of force which is invisible and impalpable. But the fields used by my people for dwellings, tools, vehicles, and even machinery are perceptible to the senses and act physically as solids. More, we are able to form these fields in latent fashion; and to fix them to organic objects as permanent fields which require no energy for their maintenance, just as magnetic fields require no energy supply to continue. Our fields, too, maybe projected as three-dimensional solids which assume any desired form and have every property of substance except chemical affinity."

Johannus! Is it not unbelievable that words could be put together, dealing with mysteries, which are so devoid of any clue to their true mystic meaning? I write and I write in desperate hope that he will eventually give me the key, but my brain reels at the difficulty of extracting the directions for Operations which such ciphers must conceal! I give you another instance: "When a force-field generator has been built as above, it will be found that the pulsatory fields which are consciousness serve perfectly as controls. One has but to visualize the object desired, turn on the generators auxiliary control, and the generator will pattern its output upon the pulsatory consciousness-field—"

Upon this first day of writing, the Power spoke for hours, and I wrote until my hand ached. From time to time, resting, I read back to him the words that I had written. He listened, satisfied.

"Lord!" I said shakenly. "Mighty lord! Your Potency! These mysteries you bid me write—they are beyond comprehension!"

But he said scornfully:

"Write! Some will be clear to someone. And I will explain it a little by a little until even you can comprehend the beginning." Then he added: "You grow weary. You wish a toy. Well! I will make you a sigil which will make again that treasure you played with. I will add a sigil which will make a boat for you, with an engine drawing power from the sea to carry you wheresoever you wish without need of wind or tide. I will make others so you may create a palace where you will, and fair gardens as you please—"

These things he has done, Johannus. It seems to amuse him to write upon scraps of parchment, and think, and then press them against his side before he lays them upon the ground for me to pick up. He has explained amusedly that the wonder in the sigil is complete, yet latent, and is released by the tearing of the parchment, but absorbed and destroyed by iron. In such fashions he speaks in ciphers, but otherwise sometimes he jests!

It is strange to think of it, that I have come a little by little to accept this Power as a person. It is not in accord with the laws of mystery. I feel that he is lonely. He seems to find satisfaction in speech with me. Yet he is a Power, one of the Rebels who was flung to earth from Heaven! He speaks of that only in vague, metaphorical terms, as if he had come from another world like *the* world, save much larger. He refers to himself as a voyager of space, and speaks of his race with affection, and of Heaven—at any rate the city from which he comes, because there must be many great cities there—with a strange and prideful affection. If it were not for his powers, which are of mystery, I would find it possible to believe that he was a lonely member of a strange race, exiled forever in a strange place, and grown friendly with a man because of his loneliness. But how could there be such as he and not a Power? How could there be another world?

This strange converse has now gone on for ten days or more. I have filled sheets upon sheets of parchment with writing. The same metaphors occur again and again. "Force-fields"—a term without literal meaning—occurs often. There are other metaphors such as "coils" and "primary" and "secondary" which are placed in context with mention of wires of copper metal. There are careful descriptions, as if in the plainest of language, of sheets of dissimilar metals which are to be placed in acid, and other descriptions of plates of similar metal which are to be separated by layers of air or wax of certain thickness, with the plates of certain areas! And there is an explanation of the means by which he lives. "I, being accustomed to an atmosphere much more dense than that on Earth, am forced to keep about myself a field of force which maintains an air density near that of my home planet for my breathing. This field is transparent, but because it must shift constantly to change and refresh the air I breathe, it causes a certain cloudiness of outline next my body. It is maintained by the generator I wear at my side, which at the same time provides energy for such other force-field artifacts as I may find convenient." Ah, Johannus! I grow mad with impatience! Did I not anticipate that he would someday give me the key to this metaphorical speech, so that from it may be extracted the Names and the Words which cause his wonders, I would give over in despair.

Yet he has grown genial with me. He has given me such sigils as I have asked him, and I have tried them many times. The sigil which will make you a fair garden is one of many. He says that he desires to give to man the knowledge he possesses, and then bids me write ciphered speech without meaning, such as: "The drive of a ship for flight beyond the speed of light is adapted from the simple-drive generator already described, simply by altering its constants so that it cannot generate in normal space and must create an abnormal space by tension. The process is—" Or else—I choose at random, Johannus—"The accursed metal, iron, must be eliminated not only from all circuits but from nearness to apparatus using high-frequency oscillations, since it absorbs their energy and prevents the functioning—"

I am like a man trembling upon the threshold of Paradise, yet unable to enter because the key is withheld. "Speed of light!" What could it mean in metaphor? In common parlance, as well speak of the speed of weather or of granite! Daily I beg him for the key to his speech. Yet even now, in the sigils he makes for me is greater power than any man has ever known before!

But it is not enough. The Power speaks as if he were lonely beyond compare; the last member of a strange race upon Earth; as if he took a strange, companionlike pleasure in merely talking to me. When I beg him for a Name or a Word which would give me power beyond such as he doles out in sigils, he is amused and calls me fool, yet kindly. And he speaks more of his metaphorical speech about forces of nature and fields of force—and gives me a sigil which should I use it will create a palace with walls of gold and pillars of emerald! And then he amusedly reminds me that one greedy looter with an ax or hoe of iron would cause it to vanish utterly!

I go almost mad, Johannus! But there is certainly wisdom unutterable to be had from him. Gradually, cautiously, I have come to act as if we were merely friends, of different race and he vastly the wiser, but friends rather than Prince and subject. Yet I remember the warnings of the most authoritative authors that one must be ever on guard against Powers called up in an Operation.

I have a plan. It is dangerous, I well know, but I grow desperate. To stand quivering upon the threshold of such wisdom and power as no man has ever dreamed of before, and then be denied—

The mercenary who will carry this to you leaves tomorrow. He is a cripple, and may be months upon the way. All will be decided ere you receive this. I know you wish me well.

Was there ever a student of mystery in so saddening a predicament, with all knowledge in his grasp yet not quite his?

Your friend,

Carolus.

Written in the very bad inn in Montevecchio—

★★★

Johannus! A courier goes to Ghent for My Lord of Brabant and I have opportunity to send you mail. I think I go mad, Johannus! I have power such as no man ever possessed before, and I am fevered with bitterness. Hear me!

For three weeks I did repair daily to the hilltop beyond Montevecchio and take down the ciphered speech of which I wrote you. My scrip was stuffed with sigils, but I had not one Word of Power or Name of Authority. The Power grew mocking, yet it seemed sadly mocking. He insisted that his words held no cipher and needed but to be read. Some of them he phrased over and over again until they were but instructions for putting bits of metal together, mechanicwise. Then he made me follow those instructions. But there was no Word, no Name—nothing save bits of metal put together cunningly. And how could inanimate metal, not imbued with power of mystery by Names or Words or incantations, have power to work mystery?

At long last I became convinced that he would never reveal the wisdom he had promised. And I had come to such familiarity with this Power that I could dare to rebel, and even to believe that I had chance of success. There was the cloudiness about his form, which was maintained by a sigil he wore at his side and called a "generator." Were that cloudiness destroyed, he could not live, or so he had told me. It was for that reason that he, in person, dared not touch anything of iron. This was the basis of my plan.

I feigned illness, and said that I would rest at a peasant's thatched hut, no longer inhabited, at the foot of the hill on which the Power lived. There was surely no nail of iron in so crude a dwelling. If he felt for me the affection he protested, he would grant me leave to be absent in my illness. If his affection was great, he might even come and speak to me there. I would be alone in the hope that his friendship might go so far.

Strange words for a man to use to Power! But I had talked daily with him for three weeks. I lay groaning in the hut, alone. On the second day he came. I affected great rejoicing, and made shift to light a fire from a taper I had kept burning. He thought it a mark of honor, but it was actually a signal. And then, as he talked to me in what he thought my illness, there came a cry from without the hut. It was the village priest, a simple man but very brave in his fashion. On the signal of smoke from the peasant's hut, he had crept near and drawn all about it an iron chain that he had muffled with cloth so that it would make no sound. And now he stood before the hut door with his crucifix upraised, chanting exorcisms. A very brave man, that priest, because I had pictured the Power as a foul fiend indeed.

The Power turned and looked at me, and I held my dagger firmly.

"I hold the accursed metal," I told him fiercely. "There is a ring of it about this house. Tell me now, quickly, the Words and the Names which make the sigils operate! Tell me the secret of the cipher you had me write! Do this and I will slay this priest and draw away the chain and you may go hence unharmed. But be quick, or—"

The Power cast a sigil upon the ground. When the parchment struck earth, there was an instant's cloudiness as if some dread thing had begun to form. But then the parchment smoked and turned to ash. The ring of iron about the hut had destroyed its power when it was used. The Power knew that I spoke truth.

"Ah!" said the Power dryly. "Men! And I thought one was my friend!" He put his hand to his side. "To be sure! I should have known. Iron rings me about. My engine heats—"

He looked at me. I held up the dagger, fiercely unyielding.

"The Names!" I cried. "The Words! Give me power of my own and I will slay the priest!"

"I tried," said the Power quietly, "to give you wisdom. And you will stab me with the accursed metal if I do not tell you things which do not exist. But you need not. I cannot live long in a ring of iron. My engine will burn out; my force-field will fail. I will stifle in the thin air which is dense enough for you. Will not that satisfy you? Must you stab me also?"

I sprang from my pallet of straw to threaten him more fiercely. It was madness, was it not? But I was mad, Johannus!

"Forbear," said the Power. "I could kill you now, with me! But I thought you my friend. I will go out and see your priest. I would prefer to die at his hand. He is perhaps only a fool."

He walked steadily toward the doorway. As he stepped over the iron chain, I thought I saw a wisp of smoke begin, but he touched the thing at his side. The cloudiness about his person vanished. There was a puffing sound, and his garments jerked as if in a gust of wind. He staggered. But he went on, and touched his side again and the cloudiness returned and he walked more strongly. He did not try to turn aside. He walked directly toward the priest, and even I could see that he walked with a bitter dignity.

And—I saw the priest's eyes grow wide with horror. Because he saw the Power for the first time, and the Power was an ell and a half high, with a large head and knobbed feelers projecting from his forehead, and the priest knew instantly that he was not of any race of men but was a Power and one of those Rebels who were flung out from Heaven.

I heard the Power speak to the priest, with dignity. I did not hear what he said. I raged in my disappointment. But the priest did not waver. As the Power moved toward him, the priest moved toward the Power. His face was filled with horror, but it was resolute. He reached forward with the crucifix he wore always attached to an iron chain about his waist. He thrust it to touch the Power, crying, *"In nomine Patri—"*

Then there was smoke. It came from a spot at the Power's side where was the engine to which he touched the sigils he had made, to imbue them with the power of mystery. And then—

I was blinded. There was a flare of monstrous, bluish light, like a lightning stroke from Heaven. After, there was a ball of fierce yellow flame which gave off a cloud of black smoke. There was a monstrous, outraged bellow of thunder.

Then there was nothing save the priest standing there, his face ashen, his eyes resolute, his eyebrows singed, chanting psalms in a shaking voice.

I have come to Venice. My scrip is filled with sigils with which I can work wonders. No men can work such wonders as I can. But I use them not. I labor daily, nightly, hourly, minute by minute, trying to find the key to the cipher which will yield the wisdom the Power possessed and desired to give to men. Ah, Johannus! I have those sigils and I can work wonders, but when I have used them they will be gone and I shall be powerless. I had such a chance at wisdom as never man possessed before, and it is gone! Yet I shall spend years—aye!—all the rest of my life, seeking the true meaning of what the Power spoke! I am the only man in all the world who ever spoke daily, for weeks on end, with a Prince of Powers of Darkness, and was accepted by him as a friend to such a degree as to encompass his own destruction. It must be true that I have wisdom written down! But how shall I find instructions for mystery in such metaphors as—to choose a fragment by chance—"Plates of two dissimilar metals, immersed in an acid, generate a force for which men have not yet a name, yet which is the basis of true civilization. Such plates—"

I grow mad with disappointment, Johannus! Why did he not speak clearly? Yet I will find out the secret.

Memorandum from Professor McFarland,
Physics Department, Haverford University,
to Professor Charles, Latin, the same faculty:

Dear Professor Charles:

My reaction is, Damnation! Where is the rest of this stuff??

McFarland.

EARLY MODEL

by Robert Sheckley

Not only did the planetary scout have the job of making friendly contact with low-tech but intelligent aliens, he had also been picked to test a new device. In many space opera yarns, new devices often work perfectly as soon as a technical genius throws them together. But this is a Robert Sheckley story and it ain't gonna happen like that.

※ ※ ※

__Robert Sheckley__ (1928-2005) seemed to explode into print in the early 1950s with stories in nearly every science fiction magazine on the newsstands. Actually, the explosion was bigger than most realized, since he was simultaneously writing even more stories under a number of pseudonyms. His forte was humor, wild and unpredictable, often absurdist, much like the work of Douglas Adams three decades later. His work has been compared to the Marx Brothers by Harlan Ellison®, to Voltaire by both Brian W. Aldiss and J.G. Ballard, and Neil Gaiman has called Sheckley "Probably the best short-story writer during the 50s to the mid-1960s working in any field." Several of his stories sardonically dealt with the topic of first contact between humans and aliens, so I had to do some serious mulling before picking this one, which I encountered while still a rotten teenager, and is still remembered fondly now that I'm a rotten old geezer.

⊕ ⊕ ⊕

THE LANDING was almost a catastrophe. Bentley knew his coordination was impaired by the bulky weight on his back; he didn't realize how much until, at a crucial moment, he stabbed the wrong button. The ship began to drop like a stone. At the last moment, he overcompensated, scorching a black hole into the plain below him. His ship touched, teetered for a moment, then sickeningly came to rest.

Bentley had effected mankind's first landing on Tels IV.

His immediate reaction was to pour himself a sizable drink of strictly medicinal scotch.

When that was out of the way, he turned on his radio. The receiver was imbedded in his ear, where it itched, and the microphone was a surgically implanted lump in his throat. The portable sub-space set was self-tuning, which was all to the good, since Bentley knew nothing about narrowcasting on so tight a beam over so great a distance.

"All's well," he told Professor Sliggert over the radio. "It's an Earthtype planet, just as the survey reports said. The ship is intact. And I'm happy to report that I did not break my neck in the landing."

"Of course not," Sliggert said, his voice thin and emotionless through the tiny receiver. "What about the Protec? How does it feel? Have you become used to it yet?"

Bentley said, "Nope. It still feels like a monkey on my back."

"Well, you'll adjust," Sliggert assured him. "The Institute sends its congratulations and I believe the government is awarding you a medal of some sort. Remember, the thing now is to fraternize with the aborigines, and if possible to establish a trade agreement of some sort, any sort. As a precedent. We need this planet, Bentley."

"I know."

"Good luck. Report whenever you have a chance."

"I'll do that," Bentley promised and signed off.

He tried to stand up, but didn't make it on the first attempt. Then, using the handholds that had been conveniently spaced above the control board, he managed to stagger erect. Now he appreciated the toll that no-weight extracts from a man's muscles. He wished he had done his exercises more faithfully on the long trip out from Earth.

Bentley was a big, jaunty young man, over six feet tall, widely and solidly constructed. On Earth, he had weighed two hundred pounds and had moved with an athlete's grace. But ever since leaving Earth, he'd had the added encumbrance of seventy-three pounds strapped irrevocably and immovably to his back. Under the circumstances, his movements resembled those of a very old elephant wearing tight shoes.

He moved his shoulders under the wide plastic straps, grimaced, and walked to a starboard porthole. In the distance, perhaps half a mile away, he could see a village, low and brown on the horizon. There were dots on the plain moving toward him. The villagers apparently had decided to discover what strange object had fallen from the skies breathing fire and making an uncanny noise.

"Good show," Bentley said to himself. Contact would have been difficult, if these aliens had shown no curiosity. This eventuality had been considered by the Earth Interstellar Exploration Institute, but no solution had been found. Therefore it had been struck from the list of possibilities.

The villagers were drawing closer. Bentley decided it was time to get ready. He opened a locker and took out his linguascene, which, with some difficulty, he strapped to his chest. On one hip, he fastened a large canteen of water. On the other hip went a package of concentrated food. Across his stomach, he put a package of assorted tools. Strapped to one leg was the radio. Strapped to the other was a medicine kit.

Thus equipped, Bentley was carrying a total of one hundred forty-eight pounds, every ounce of it declared essential for an extraterrestrial explorer.

The fact that he lurched rather than walked was considered unimportant.

The natives had reached the ship now and were gathering around it, commenting disparagingly. They were bipeds. They had short thick tails and their features were human, but nightmare human. Their coloring was a vivid orange.

Bentley also noticed that they were armed. He could see knives, spears, lances, stone hammers, and flint axes. At the sight of this armament, a satisfied smile broke over his face. Here was the justification for his discomfort, the reason for the unwieldy seventy-three pounds which had remained on his back ever since leaving Earth.

It didn't matter what weapons these aboriginals had, right up to the nuclear level. They couldn't hurt him.

That's what Professor Sliggert, head of the Institute, inventor of the Protec, had told him.

Bentley opened the port. A cry of astonishment came from the Telians. His linguascene, after a few seconds' initial hesitation, translated the cries as, "Oh! Ah! How strange! Unbelievable! Ridiculous! Shockingly improper!"

Bentley descended the ladder on the ship's side, carefully balancing his one hundred forty-eight pounds of excess weight. The natives formed a semicircle around him, their weapons ready.

He advanced on them. They shrank back. Smiling pleasantly, he said, "I come as a friend." The linguascene barked out the harsh consonants of the Telian language.

They didn't seem to believe him. Spears were poised and one Telian, larger than the others and wearing a colorful headdress, held a hatchet in readiness.

Bentley felt the slightest tremor run through him. He was invulnerable, of course. There was nothing they could do to him as long as he wore the Protec. Nothing! Professor Sliggert had been certain of it.

Before takeoff, Professor Sliggert had strapped the Protec to Bentley's back, adjusted the straps and stepped back to admire his brainchild.

"Perfect," he had announced with quiet pride.

Bentley had shrugged his shoulders under the weight. "Kind of heavy, isn't it?"

"But what can we do?" Sliggert asked him. "This is the first of its kind, the prototype. I have used every weight-saving device possible—transistors, light alloys, printed circuits, pencil-power packs, and all the rest. Unfortunately, early models of any invention are invariably bulky."

"Seems as though you could have streamlined it a bit," Bentley objected, peering over his shoulder.

"Streamlining comes much later. First must be concentration, then compaction, then group-function, and finally styling. It's always been that way and it will always be. Take the typewriter. Now it is simply a keyboard, almost as flat as a briefcase. But the prototype typewriter worked with foot pedals and required the combined strength of several men to lift. Take the hearing aid, which actually shrank pounds through the various stages of its development. Take the linguascene, which began as a very massive, complicated electronic calculator weighing several tons—"

"Okay," Bentley broke in. "If this is the best you could make it, good enough. How do I get out of it?"

Professor Sliggert smiled.

Bentley reached around. He couldn't find a buckle. He pulled ineffectually at the shoulder straps, but could find no way of undoing them. Nor could he squirm out. It was like being in a new and fiendishly efficient straitjacket.

"Come on, Professor, how do I get it off?"

"I'm not going to tell you."

"Huh?"

"The Protec is uncomfortable, is it not?" Sliggert asked. "You would rather not wear it?"

"You're damned right."

"Of course. Did you know that in wartime, on the battlefield, soldiers have a habit of discarding essential equipment because it is bulky or uncomfortable? But we can't take chances on you. You are going to an alien planet, Mr. Bentley. You will be exposed to wholly unknown dangers. It is necessary that you be protected at all times."

"I know that," Bentley said. "I've got enough sense to figure out when to wear this thing."

"But do you? We selected you for attributes such as resourcefulness, stamina, physical strength—and, of course, a certain amount of intelligence. But—"

"Thanks!"

"But those qualities do not make you prone to caution. Suppose you found the natives seemingly friendly and decided to discard the heavy, uncomfortable Protec? What would happen if you had misjudged their attitude? This is very easy to do on Earth; think how much easier it will be on an alien planet!"

"I can take care of myself," Bentley said.

Sliggert nodded grimly. "That is what Atwood said when he left for Durabella II and we have never heard from him again. Nor have we heard from Blake, or Smythe, or Korishell. Can you turn a knife-thrust from the rear? Have you *eyes* in the back of your head? No, Mr. Bentley, you haven't—*but the Protec has!*"

"Look," Bentley had said, "believe it or not, I'm a responsible adult. I will wear the Protec at all times when on the surface of an alien planet. Now tell me how to get it off."

"You don't seem to realize something, Bentley. If only your life were at stake, we would let you take what risks seemed reasonable to you. But we are also risking several billion dollars' worth of spaceship and equipment. Moreover, this is the Protec's field test. The only way to be sure of the results is to have you wear it all the time. The only way to ensure *that* is by not telling you how to remove it. We want results. You are going to stay alive whether you like it or not."

Bentley had thought it over and agreed grudgingly. "I guess I might be tempted to take it off, if the natives were really friendly."

"You will be spared that temptation. Now do you understand how it works?"

"Sure," Bentley said. "But will it really do all you say?"

"It passed the lab tests perfectly."

"I'd hate to have some little thing go wrong. Suppose it pops a fuse or blows a wire?"

"That is one of the reasons for its bulk," Sliggert explained patiently. "Triple everything. We are taking no chance of mechanical failure."

"And the power supply?"

"Good for a century or better at full load. The Protec is perfect,

Bentley! After this field test, I have no doubt it will become standard equipment for all extraterrestrial explorers." Professor Sliggert permitted himself a faint smile of pride.

"All right," Bentley had said, moving his shoulders under the wide plastic straps. "I'll get used to it."

But he hadn't. A man just doesn't get used to a seventy three-pound monkey on his back.

The Telians didn't know what to make of Bentley. They argued for several minutes, while the explorer kept a strained smile on his face. Then one Telian stepped forward. He was taller than the others and wore a distinctive headdress made of glass, bones and bits of rather garishly painted wood.

"My friends," the Telian said, "there is an evil here which I, Rinek, can sense."

Another Telian wearing a similar headdress stepped forward and said, "It is not well for a ghost doctor to speak of such things."

"Of course not," Rinek admitted. "It is not well to speak of evil in the presence of evil, for evil then grows strong. But a ghost doctor's work is the detection and avoidance of evil. In this work, we must persevere, no matter what the risk."

Several other men in the distinctive headdress, the ghost doctors, had come forward now. Bentley decided that they were the Telian equivalent of priests and probably wielded considerable political power as well.

"I don't think he's evil," a young and cheerful-looking ghost doctor named Huascl said.

"Of course he is. Just look at him."

"Appearances prove nothing, as we know from the time the good spirit Ahut M'Kandi appeared in the form of a—"

"No lectures, Huascl. All of us know the parables of Lalland. The point is, can we take a chance?"

Huascl turned to Bentley. "Are you evil?" the Telian asked earnestly.

"No," Bentley said. He had been puzzled at first by the Telians' intense preoccupation with his spiritual status. They hadn't even asked him where he'd come from, or how, or why. But then, it was not so strange. If an alien had landed on Earth during certain periods of religious zeal, the first question asked might have been, "Are you a creature of God or of Satan?"

"He says he's not evil," Huascl said.

"How would he know?"

"If he doesn't, who does?"

"Once the great spirit G'tal presented a wise man with three kdal and said to him—"

And on it went. Bentley found his legs beginning to bend under the weight of all his equipment. The linguascene was no longer able to keep pace with the shrill theological discussion that raged around him. His status seemed to depend upon two or three disputed points, none of which the ghost doctors wanted to talk about, since to talk about evil was in itself dangerous.

To make matters more complicated, there was a schism over the concept of the penetrability of evil, the younger ghost doctors holding to one side, the older to the other. The factions accused each other of rankest heresy, but Bentley couldn't figure out who believed what or which interpretation aided him.

When the sun drooped low over the grassy plain, the battle still raged. Then, suddenly, the ghost doctors reached an agreement, although Bentley couldn't decide why or on what basis.

Huascl stepped forward as spokesman for the younger ghost doctors.

"Stranger," he declared, "we have decided not to kill you."

Bentley suppressed a smile. That was just like a primitive people, granting life to an invulnerable being!

"Not yet, anyhow," Huascl amended quickly, catching a frown upon Rinek and the older ghost doctors. "It depends entirely upon you. We will go to the village and purify ourselves and we will feast. Then we will initiate you into the society of ghost doctors. No evil thing can become a ghost doctor; it is expressly forbidden. In this manner, we will detect your true nature."

"I am deeply grateful," Bentley said.

"But if you *are* evil, we are pledged to destroy evil. And if we must, we can!"

The assembled Telians cheered his speech and began at once the mile trek to the village. Now that a status had been assigned Bentley, even tentatively, the natives were completely friendly. They chatted amiably with him about crops, droughts, and famines.

Bentley staggered along under his equipment, tired, but inwardly elated. This was really a coup! As an initiate, a priest, he would have an unsurpassed opportunity to gather anthropological data, to establish trade, to pave the way for the future development of Tels IV.

All he had to do was pass the initiation tests. And not get killed, of course, he reminded himself, smiling.

It was funny how positive the ghost doctors had been that they *could* kill him.

The village consisted of two dozen huts arranged in a rough circle. Beside each mud-and-thatch hut was a small vegetable garden, and sometimes a pen for the Telian version of cattle. There were small green-furred animals roaming between the huts, which the Telians treated as pets. The grassy central area was common ground. Here was the community well and here were the shrines to various gods and devils. In this area, lighted by a great bonfire, a feast had been laid out by the village women.

Bentley arrived at the feast in a state of near-exhaustion, stooped beneath his essential equipment. Gratefully, he sank to the ground with the villagers and the celebration began.

First the village women danced a welcoming for him. They made a pretty sight, their orange skin glinting in the firelight, their tails swinging gracefully in unison. Then a village dignitary named Occip came over to him, bearing a full bowl.

"Stranger," Occip said, "you are from a distant land and your ways are not our ways. Yet let us be brothers! Partake, therefore, of this food to seal the bond between us, and in the name of all sanctity!"

Bowing low, he offered the bowl.

It was an important moment, one of those pivotal occasions that can seal forever the friendship between races or make them eternal enemies. But Bentley was not able to take advantage of it. As tactfully as he could, he refused the symbolic food.

"But it is purified!" Occip said.

Bentley explained that, because of a tribal taboo, he could eat only his own food. Occip could not understand that different species have different dietary requirements. For example, Bentley pointed out, the staff of life on Tels IV might well be some strychnine compound. But he did not add that even if he wanted to take the chance, his Protec would never allow it.

Nonetheless, his refusal alarmed the village. There were hurried conferences among the ghost doctors. Then Rinek came over and sat beside him.

"Tell me," Rinek inquired after a while, "what do you think of evil?"

"Evil is not good," Bentley said solemnly.

"Ah!" The ghost doctor pondered that, his tail flicking nervously over the grass. A small green-furred pet, a mog, began to play with his tail. Rinek pushed him away and said, "So you do not like evil."

"No."

"And you would permit no evil influence around you?"

"Certainly not," Bentley said, stifling a yawn. He was growing bored with the ghost doctor's tortuous examining.

"In that case, you would have no objection to receiving the sacred and very holy spear that Kran K'leu brought down from the abode of the Small Gods, the brandishing of which confers good upon a man."

"I would be pleased to receive it," said Bentley, heavy-eyed, hoping this would be the last ceremony of the evening.

Rinek grunted his approval and moved away. The women's dances came to an end. The ghost doctors began to chant in deep, impressive voices. The bonfire flared high.

Huascl came forward. His face was now painted in thin black and white stripes. He carried an ancient spear of black wood, its head of shaped volcanic glass, its length intricately although primitively carved.

Holding the spear aloft, Huascl said, "O Stranger from the Skies, accept from us this spear of sanctity! Kran K'leu gave this lance to

Trin, our first father, and bestowed upon it a magical nature and caused it to be a vessel of the spirits of the good. Evil cannot abide the presence of this spear! Take, then, our blessings with it."

Bentley heaved himself to his feet. He understood the value of a ceremony like this. His acceptance of the spear should end, once and for all, any doubts as to his spiritual status. Reverently he inclined his head, Huascl came forward, held out the spear and—

The Protec snapped into action.

Its operation was simple, in common with many great inventions. When its calculator-component received a danger cue, the Protec threw a force-field around its operator. This field rendered him invulnerable, for it was completely and absolutely impenetrable. But there were certain unavoidable disadvantages.

If Bentley had had a weak heart, the Protec might have killed him there and then, for its action was electronically sudden, completely unexpected and physically wrenching. One moment, he was standing in front of the great bonfire, his hand held out for the sacred spear. In the next moment, he was plunged into darkness.

As usual, he felt as though he had been catapulted into a musty, lightless closet, with rubbery walls pressing close on all sides. He cursed the machine's super-efficiency. The spear had not been a threat; it was part of an important ceremony. But the Protec, with its literal senses, had interpreted it as a possible danger.

Now, in the darkness, Bentley fumbled for the controls that would release the field. As usual, the force field interfered with his positional sense, a condition that seemed to grow worse with each subsequent use. Carefully he felt his way along his chest, where the button should have been, and located it at last under his right armpit, where it had twisted around to. He released the field.

The feast had ended abruptly. The natives were standing close together for protection, weapons ready, tails stretched stiffly out. Huascl, caught in the force-field's range, had been flung twenty feet and was slowly picking himself up.

The ghost doctors began to chant a purification dirge, for protection against evil spirits. Bentley couldn't blame them.

When a Protec force-field goes on, it appears as an opaque black sphere, some ten feet in diameter. If it is struck, it repels with a force equal to the impact. White lines appear in the sphere's surface, swirl, coalesce, vanish. And as the sphere spins, it screams in a thin, high-pitched wail.

All in all, it was a sight hardly calculated to win the confidence of a primitive and superstitious people.

"Sorry," Bentley said, with a weak smile. There hardly seemed anything else to say.

Huascl limped back, but kept his distance. "You cannot accept the sacred spear," he stated.

"Well, it's not exactly that," said Bentley. "It's just—well, I've got this protective device, kind of like a shield, you know? It doesn't like spears. Couldn't you offer me a sacred gourd?"

"Don't be ridiculous," Huascl said. "Who ever heard of a sacred gourd?"

"No, I guess not. But please take my word for it—I'm not evil. Really I'm not. I've just got a taboo about spears."

The ghost doctors talked among themselves too rapidly for the linguascene to interpret it. It caught only the words "evil", "destroy", and "purification." Bentley decided his forecast didn't look too favorable.

After the conference, Huascl came over to him and said, "Some of the others feel that you should be killed at once, before you bring some great unhappiness upon the village. I told them, however, that you cannot be blamed for the many taboos that restrict you. We will pray for you through the night. And perhaps, in the morning, the initiation will be possible."

Bentley thanked him. He was shown to a hut and then the Telians left him as quickly as possible. There was an ominous hush over the village; from his doorway, Bentley could see little groups of natives talking earnestly and glancing covertly in his direction.

It was a poor beginning for cooperation between two races.

He immediately contacted Professor Sliggert and told him what had happened.

"Unfortunate," the professor said. "But primitive people are notoriously treacherous. They might have meant to kill you with the spear instead of actually handing it to you. Let you have it, that is, in the most literal sense."

"I'm positive there was no such intention," Bentley said. "After all, you have to start trusting people sometime."

"Not with a billion dollars' worth of equipment in your charge."

"But I'm not going to be able to *do* anything!" Bentley shouted. "Don't you understand? They're suspicious of me already. I wasn't able to accept their sacred spear. That means I'm very possibly evil. Now what if I can't pass the initiation ceremony tomorrow? Suppose some idiot starts to pick his teeth with a knife and the Protec saves me? All the favorable first impressions I built up will be lost."

"Good will can be regained," Professor Sliggert said sententiously. "But a billion dollars' worth of equipment—"

"—can be salvaged by the next expedition. Look, Professor, give me a break. Isn't there some way I can control this thing manually?"

"No way at all," Sliggert replied. "That would defeat the entire purpose of the machine. You might just as well not be wearing it if you're allowed to rely on your own reflexes rather than electronic impulses."

"Then tell me how to take it off."

"The same argument holds true—you wouldn't be protected at all times."

"Look," Bentley protested, "you chose me as a competent explorer. I'm the guy on the spot. I know what the conditions are here. Tell me how to get it off."

"No! The Protec must have a full field test. And we want you to come back alive."

"That's another thing," Bentley said. "These people seem kind of sure they can kill me."

"Primitive peoples always overestimate the potency of their strength, weapons, and magic."

"I know, I know. But you're certain there's no way they can get through the field? Poison, maybe?"

"Nothing can get through the field," Sliggert said patiently. "Not even light rays can penetrate. Not even gamma radiation. You are wearing an impregnable fortress, Mr. Bentley. Why can't you manage to have a little faith in it?"

"Early models of inventions sometimes need a lot of ironing out," Bentley grumbled. "But have it your way. Won't you tell me how to take it off, though, just in case something goes wrong?"

"I wish you would stop asking me that, Mr. Bentley. You were chosen to give Protec a *full* field test. That's just what you are going to do."

When Bentley signed off, it was deep twilight outside and the villagers had returned to their huts. Campfires burned low and he could hear the call of night creatures.

At that moment, Bentley felt very alien and exceedingly homesick.

He was tired almost to the point of unconsciousness, but he forced himself to eat some concentrated food and drink a little water. Then he unstrapped the tool kit, the radio, and the canteen, tugged defeatedly at the Protec, and lay down to sleep.

Just as he dozed off, the Protec went violently into action, nearly snapping his neck out of joint.

Wearily he fumbled for the controls, located them near his stomach, and turned off the field.

The hut looked exactly the same. He could find no source of attack.

Was the Protec losing its grip on reality, he wondered, or had a Telian tried to spear him through the window?

Then Bentley saw a tiny mog puppy scuttling away frantically, its legs churning up clouds of dust.

The little beast probably just wanted to get warm, Bentley thought. But of course it was alien. Its potential for danger could not be overlooked by the ever-wary Protec.

He fell asleep again and immediately began to dream that he was locked in a prison of bright red sponge rubber. He could push the walls out and out and out, but they never yielded, and at last he would have to let go and be gently shoved back to the center of the prison. Over and over, this happened, until suddenly he felt his back wrenched and awoke within the Protec's lightless field.

This time he had real difficulty finding the controls. He hunted desperately by feel until the bad air made him gasp in panic. He located the controls at last under his chin, released the field, and began to search groggily for the source of the new attack.

He found it. A twig had fallen from the thatch roof and had tried to land on him. The Protec, of course, had not allowed it.

"Aw, come on now," Bentley groaned aloud. "Let's use a little judgment."

But he was really too tired to care. Fortunately, there were no more assaults that night.

Huascl came to Bentley's hut in the morning, looking very solemn and considerably disturbed.

"There were great sounds from your hut during the night," the ghost doctor said, "Sounds of torment, as though you were wrestling with a devil."

"I'm just a restless sleeper," Bentley explained.

Huascl smiled to show that he appreciated the joke. "My friend, did you pray for purification last night and for release from evil?"

"I certainly did."

"And was your prayer granted?"

"It was," Bentley said hopefully. "There's no evil around me. Not a bit."

Huascl looked dubious. "But can you be sure? Perhaps you should depart from us in peace. If you cannot be initiated, we shall have to destroy you—"

"Don't worry about it," Bentley told him. "Let's get started."

"Very well," Huascl said, and together they left the hut.

The initiation was to be held in front of the great bonfire in the village square. Messengers had been sent out during the night and ghost doctors from many villages were there. Some had come as far as twenty miles to take part in the rites and to see the alien with their own eyes. The ceremonial drum had been taken from its secret hiding place and was now booming solemnly. The villagers watched, chattered together, laughed. But Bentley could detect an undercurrent of nervousness and strain.

There was a long series of dances. Bentley twitched worriedly when the last figure started, for the leading dancer was swinging a glass-studded club around his head. Nearer and nearer the dancer whirled, now only a few feet away from him, his club a dazzling streak.

The villagers watched, fascinated. Bentley shut his eyes, expecting to be plunged momentarily into the darkness of the force-field.

But the dancer moved away at last and the dance ended with a roar of approval from the villagers.

Huascl began to speak. Bentley realized with a thrill of relief that this was the end of the ceremony.

"O brothers," Huascl said, "this alien has come across the great emptiness to be our brother. Many of his ways are strange and around him there seems to hang a strange hint of evil. And yet who can doubt that he means well? Who can doubt that he is, in essence, a good and honorable person? With this initiation, we purge him of evil and make him one of us."

There was dead silence as Huascl walked up to Bentley. "Now," Huascl said, "you are a ghost doctor and indeed one of us." He held out his hand.

Bentley felt his heart leap within him. He had won! He had been accepted! He reached out and clasped Huascl's hand.

Or tried to. He didn't quite make it, for the Protec, ever alert, saved him from the possibly dangerous contact.

"You damned idiotic gadget!" Bentley bellowed, quickly finding the control and releasing the field.

He saw at once that the fat was in the fire.

"Evil!" shrieked the Telians, frenziedly waving their weapons.

"Evil!" screamed the ghost doctors.

Bentley turned despairingly to Huascl.

"Yes," the young ghost doctor said sadly, "it is true. We had hoped to cure the evil by our ancient ceremonial. But it could not be. This evil must be destroyed! *Kill the devil!*"

A shower of spears came at Bentley. The Protec responded instantly.

Soon it was apparent that an impasse had been reached. Bentley would remain for a few minutes in the field, then override the controls. The Telians, seeing him still unharmed, would renew their barrage and the Protec would instantly go back into action.

Bentley tried to walk back to his ship. But the Protec went on again each time he shut it off. It would take him a month or two to cover a mile, at that rate, so he stopped trying. He would simply wait the attackers out. After a while, they would find out they couldn't hurt him and the two races would finally get down to business.

He tried to relax within the field, but found it impossible. He was hungry and extremely thirsty. And his air was starting to grow stale.

Then Bentley remembered, with a sense of shock, that air had not gone through the surrounding field the night before. Naturally— nothing could get through. If he wasn't careful, he could be asphyxiated.

Even an impregnable fortress could fall, he knew, if the defenders were starved or suffocated out.

He began to think furiously. How long could the Telians keep up the attack? They would have to grow tired sooner or later, wouldn't they?

Or would they?

He waited as long as he could, until the air was all but unbreathable, then overrode the controls. The Telians were sitting on the ground around him. Fires had been lighted and food was cooking. Rinek lazily threw a spear at him and the field went on.

So, Bentley thought, they had learned. They were going to starve him out.

He tried to think, but the walls of his dark closet seemed to be pressing against him. He was growing claustrophobic and already his air was stale again.

He thought for a moment, then overrode the controls. The Telians looked at him coolly. One of them reached for a spear.

"Wait!" Bentley shouted. At the same moment, he turned on his radio.

"What do you want?" Rinek asked.

"Listen to me! It isn't fair to trap me in the Protec like this!"

"Eh? What's going on?" Professor Sliggert asked, through the ear receiver.

"You Telians know—" Bentley said hoarsely—"you know that you can destroy me by continually activating the Protec. I can't turn it off! I can't get out of it!"

"Ah," said Professor Sliggert. "I see the difficulty. Yes."

"We are sorry," Huascl apologized. "But evil must be destroyed."

"Of course it must," Bentley said desperately. "But not me. Give me a chance. *Professor!*"

"This is indeed a flaw," Professor Sliggert mused, "and a serious one. Strange, but things like this, of course, can't show up in the lab, only in a full-scale field test. The fault will be rectified in the new models."

"Great! But I'm here now! How do I get this thing off?"

"I *am* sorry," Sliggert said. "I honestly never thought the need would arise. To tell the truth, I designed the harness so that you could not get out of it under any circumstances."

"Why, you lousy—"

"Please!" Sliggert said sternly. "Let's keep our heads. If you can hold out for a few months, we might be able—"

"I can't! The air! Water!"

"Fire!" cried Rinek, his face contorted. "By fire, we will chain the demon!"

And the Protec snapped on.

Bentley tried to think things out carefully in the darkness. He would have to get out of the Protec. But how? There was a knife in his tool kit. Could he cut through the tough plastic straps? He would have to!

But what then? Even if he emerged from his fortress, the ship was a mile away. Without the Protec, they could kill him with a single spear thrust. And they were pledged to, for he had been declared irrevocably evil.

But if he ran, he at least had a chance. And it was better to die of a spear thrust than to strangle slowly in absolute darkness.

Bentley turned off the field. The Telians were surrounding him with campfires, closing off his retreat with a wall of flame.

He hacked frantically at the plastic web. The knife slithered and slipped along the strap. And he was back in Protec.

When he came out again, the circle of fire was complete. The Telians were cautiously pushing the fires toward him, lessening the circumference of his circle.

Bentley felt his heart sink. Once the fires were close enough, the Protec would go on and stay on. He would not be able to override a continuous danger signal. He would be trapped within the field for as long as they fed the flames.

And considering how primitive people felt about devils, it was just possible that they would keep the fire going for a century or two.

He dropped the knife, used side-cutters on the plastic strap and succeeded in ripping it halfway through.

He was in Protec again.

Bentley was dizzy, half-fainting from fatigue, gasping great mouthfuls of foul air. With an effort, he pulled himself together. He couldn't drop now. That would be the end.

He found the controls, overrode them. The fires were very near him now. He could feel their warmth against his face. He snipped viciously at the strap and felt it give.

He slipped out of the Protec just as the field activated again. The force of it threw him into the fire. But he fell feet first and jumped out of the flames without getting burned.

The villagers roared. Bentley sprinted away; as he ran, he dumped the linguascene, the tool kit, the radio, the concentrated food and the canteen. He glanced back once and saw that the Telians were after him.

But he was holding his own. His tortured heart seemed to be pounding his chest apart and his lungs threatened to collapse at any moment. But now the spaceship was before him, looming great and friendly on the flat plain.

He was going to just make it. Another twenty yards . . .

Something green flashed in front of him. It was a small, green-furred mog puppy. The clumsy beast was trying to get out of his way.

He swerved to avoid crushing it and realized too late that he should never have broken stride. A rock turned under his foot and he sprawled forward.

He heard the pounding feet of the Telians corning toward him and managed to climb on one knee.

Then somebody threw a club and it landed neatly on his forehead.

"Ar gwy dril?" a voice asked incomprehensibly from far off.

Bentley opened his eyes and saw Huascl bending over him. He was in a hut, back in the village. Several armed ghost doctors were at the doorway, watching.

"Ar dril?" Huascl asked again.

Bentley rolled over and saw, piled neatly beside him, his canteen, concentrated food, tools, radio and linguascene. He took a deep drink of water, then turned on the linguascene.

"I asked if you felt all right," Huascl said.

"Sure, fine," Bentley grunted, feeling his head. "Let's get it over with."

"Over with?"

"You're going to kill me, aren't you? Well, let's not make a production out of it."

"But we didn't want to destroy *you*," Huascl said. "We knew you for a good man. It was the devil we wanted!"

"Eh?" asked Bentley in a blank uncomprehending voice.

"Come, look."

The ghost doctors helped Bentley to his feet and brought him outside. There, surrounded by lapping flames, was the glowing great black sphere of the Protec.

"You didn't know, of course," Huascl said, "but there was a devil riding upon your back."

"Huh!" gasped Bentley.

"Yes, it is true. We tried to dispossess him by purification, but he was too strong. We had to force you, brother, to face that evil and throw it aside. We knew you would come through. And you did!"

"I see," Bentley said. "A devil on my back. Yes, I guess so."

That was exactly what the Protec would have to be, to them. A heavy, misshapen weight on his shoulders, hurling out a black sphere whenever they tried to purify it. What else could a religious people do but try to free him from its grasp?"

He saw several women of the village bring up baskets of food and throw them into the fire in front of the sphere. He looked inquiringly at Huascl.

"We are propitiating it," Huascl said, "for it is a very strong devil, undoubtedly a miracle-working one. Our village is proud to have such a devil in bondage."

A ghost doctor from a neighboring village stepped up. "Are there more such devils in your homeland? Could you bring us one to worship?"

Several other ghost doctors pressed eagerly forward. Bentley nodded. "It can be arranged," he said.

He knew that the Earth-Tels trade was now begun. And at last a suitable use had been found for Professor Sliggert's Protec.

HER SISTER'S KEEPER

by Sarah A. Hoyt

The aliens claimed they had come in peace, even if their gigantic starship had flattened blocks of a crowded city. Just an accident. Even advanced aliens can make a mistake. Their next mistake was causing a very determined xenolinguist's sister to disappear.

SARAH A. HOYT *won the Prometheus Award for her novel* Darkship Thieves, *published by Baen, and since has authored* Darkship Renegades, A Few Good Men, *and the forthcoming* Through Fire, *more novels set in the same universe. She has written numerous short stories and novels in a number of genres, science fiction, fantasy, mystery, historical novels and historical mysteries, some under a number of pseudonyms, and has been published—among other places—in* Analog, Asimov's *and* Amazing. *For Baen, she has also written three books in her popular shape-shifter urban fantasy series,* Draw One in the Dark, Gentleman Takes a Chance, *and* Noah's Boy. *Her* According to Hoyt *is one of the most interesting blogs on the internet. Originally from Portugal, she lives in Colorado with her husband, two sons and the surfeit of cats necessary to a die-hard Heinlein fan.*

"LILLIAN, what do you think you're doing?" Xavier asked.

What I was doing was looking for a pair of night vision goggles someone had requisitioned to look at alien writing—piles and piles of thin, metallike material inscribed in increasingly-more-decipherable squiggles—which had been turned over to the newly founded Bureau of Alien Contact, after a ten-block wide alien spaceship had flattened the Denver capitol and everything around it for . . . well, ten blocks.

No one had any idea why they'd wanted the night vision goggles, but they'd also wanted to look at it in various color lights. It had revealed nothing more than what could be seen in daylight. But the goggles were still around, and I wanted them.

Xavier was my boss and here, where he won't read, I can admit he had also been my crush since college.

He'd been one of very few people on Earth—twenty-three to be precise and one had died of old age three days before the landing—who had devoted their lives to studying the possibility of xenolinguistics. A subject without an object, it would seem, for all this time, save for the exchange of papers, speculation and discussion on what an alien language would look like and what we'd do to recognize it when we found it.

That last turned out not to be necessary, after all, but never mind. He'd devoted his entire life—well, to the age of forty-five—and obsessed every day on the possibility that there was another intelligent race out there in the universe and that it would try to communicate with us someday. He'd hoped it would happen when he was alive, but he'd left a lot of documents explaining precisely what he'd thought and done and calculated, so that even if he should be long dead people still alive could follow his reasoning and perhaps be there in his name to greet what he referred to apparently without irony as *our brothers from the stars.*

His brilliant melding of mathematical and psychological principles, his study of the most obscure languages and extrapolations to other, more obscure, methods of signaling between intelligent species, even his daring studies of other terrestrial species and their means of communication: all of it had attracted me to the study of xenolinguistics and brought me here, to be his assistant.

Here, where he was glaring at me from the door, his dark eyes intent and worried under dark eyebrows.

I sighed. At least he hadn't seen me secrete into my pocket the gun I knew I shouldn't have had in my desk at work. Honestly, I didn't even know why I had it, except that there was this sense of looming danger.

"It's Cressy," I'd said.

"Cressy?" He lowered his eyebrows and shook his head. "Who is Cressy?"

"My sister," I said. "My baby sister, only that seems funny to say now she's thirty. You see, she was born when I was eight."

"What on Earth," he said, giving me the once over, "can your sister, thirty or not, have to do with your being here, in the middle of the night, dressed in black and grabbing night goggles?"

"It's the aliens," I said.

This time his eyebrows rose and I realized that for a linguist I was making a fine mull of telling him anything that mattered. This of course made perfect sense, since I've always thought xenolinguistics should cover the communications between human sexes, too. I sighed at his expression and said, "Cressy was very excited about the aliens landing, see?"

He shook his head. "I don't see. Everyone, us included, has been very excited for the last three weeks. I mean, the news can't talk about anything else. And it's right, of course. All these millennia we've been living alone in the universe. How are we to know what we've learned and what we've done is for the best, or even if it makes any sense without anyone else to compare it to? We were like—"

"Orphans locked in a darkened room," I said, tartly. "Yes, I've read the poet laureate, too." It was churlish of me to say it. Because Xavier was not one of the talking heads prattling on endlessly about nothing much. He was genuinely interested, for genuine reasons. "But you don't know Cressy."

He came into the room and sat on my desk, facing me. "All right. Tell me about Cressy then, and why you think you need to break into a spaceship because of your sister."

"When Mom disappeared—"

"Disappeared?"

"Oh, probably died. She was a landscape photographer, and did many of her trips on small, privately leased planes. She was taking pictures of a storm off the East coast of the US—"

He made a sound deep in his throat and I said, "Yes, there. Anyway, she disappeared. It's presumed she crashed and the plane went down somewhere where it was never found, but no one knows. And I was ten, and Cressy was two and someone had to look after her."

"You don't have a father?"

"My father . . . Hey, you took math in undergrad, and Farewell is not that common a name. You've probably heard of him? Doctor Ignatius Farewell?"

"Your father?"

"Yes, and don't get me wrong, wonderful man. But he doesn't have a connection to reality at the best of times, and even as a child I kind of got that. We had sitters and nannies, but . . . Cressy is pretty, you see?" He raised an eyebrow, as though doubting it. "No, really. We don't look anything alike. I look just like Dad, but she looks like Mom. Now she's this beautiful, Scandinavian looking blond goddess, but when she was little, she was small and chubby, with a round face and enormous blue eyes that melted the heart of all our caretakers. Which means they all treated her as if she were an angel. And of course, she isn't." I tried to explain, "You see, I tried to get her to study and to work, but she . . . she could get away just sliding through life with a smile and a thank you, so she never worked a day in her life. Which means. . . . Well, she dropped out of high school and started a feng shui business. Then she set up as an astrologer, but she couldn't hack the math. The last thing she was working at, and I use working loosely, because without dad and I making her an allowance she would starve, is astral massage, whatever the heck that means."

He was looking amused. "I see, and what does this have to do with aliens?"

"Well. The last time I saw her, she was waving her hands and talking ten to the dozen about the brotherhood of sentient beings and how these star creatures had come to Earth to show us the error of our ways, and how now we'd have peace and justice and all that . . ." I trailed off before saying "all that rot," because I realized at the last minute, Xavier who'd been indefatigably working so we could talk with these beings and the greater brotherhood and all that, probably believed in it too.

But he sighed and said, "I've never understood people—and they've always been around, long before this—who think the possession of a star drive means that aliens are a sort of angel, with all the fine qualities we don't have. It's just as likely that they consider everything we find despicable a virtue, and that mass cannibalism is the top of their attainment."

I looked at him, stunned, because I'd always assumed he was the prototype of scientist idealist, somewhere between my father and my sister. He sighed again, this time more deeply. "That's why I came in after hours, Lil. Because I think there is something wrong in those documents they gave us. It's like they carefully censored the entire history of their star travel device. They have FTL, clearly, but they're not willing to share. Now, to an extent I understand it, of course—"

"Perhaps we have to develop our own drive before—"

"Being admitted to the federation of star-traveling beings. Too much science fiction, my girl. No, I can see them not wanting naked apes in the stars," he said, and smiled a little, because the aliens looked like those spider-monkey dolls, very fuzzy, about a meter and a half tall. "But all the same, some of what they censored is the history of the drive, which wouldn't tell us how to use it. Also . . ." He shrugged. "I know they're talking peace and brotherhood, and our lovely president and politicians are swallowing it but two things stand out. First, they knew precisely what they were doing when they landed in the middle of a crowded city. Yes, I know they said it was an emergency, but how hard would it be for a starship to aim slightly away and land in an area in Colorado where they'd not hurt any humans? The second part is that in our own history, when a civilization with the means to travel establishes trade relations with a civilization without such means, the civilization that can't travel always ends up with the short end of the stick. It can be colonization or . . . or glass beads for their most valuable resources." He frowned. "Oh, there is a third lesson. I get the feeling these documents have been purged for the eyes of Earthlings, which means this is not an unexpected landing, with no previous contact. I think . . . well. There is a good chance these things have been the UFOs people have been talking about for centuries."

"Mass delusion," I said.

"Maybe, but what if not? What if all those kidnapped people really were kidnapped? It doesn't give you the best view of them, does it?"

I shook my head and he said, "What I still don't understand, is why you think, excited or not, your sister would be inside the alien ship. I mean, the world must have fifty million chowderheads like Cressy, but how would she have made it past their sentinels, or even our sentinels, to be inside the ship."

"But that's just it," I said. "You don't understand. Remember when I told you I was my sister's keeper, since she was very little? Well, I developed a sense for where she was likely to be. And my sense tells me she's in the ship. No, don't ask me how. I don't even know how to get in."

"Well, as to that," he said. He pursed his lips in a silent whistle. "Well, as I said, I've been suspecting something is wrong there, and I'm not alone, whatever the president—" he spat out the word "—thinks, or emotes, or feels, so I have been collecting data. We all have. So I have some idea how to get in, but that ship is a small city. How do you plan to find your sister, even supposing she's in there?"

"I don't know," I said. "Except for using my sense of where she's supposed to be."

"You do realize this is coming dangerously close to telepathy or a woman's way of knowing, or other claptrap like that?"

"Yeah, I do, but . . ."

"But what if not?" he said. "Right. Okay. Tell you what, let's go and take a gander."

"We?" I said, aghast, as he stood up, off the desk and gave me a grin that can only be described as piratical. "Lil, my dear friend, you're not going to keep me out of this one."

I tried to talk him out of it, but he was as stubborn as I was, and twice as misguided. His view was that if I felt responsible for Cressy, he felt responsible for me, and therefore he would do his best to keep me safe.

Okay, so he surprised me even more by actually having guns in his desk—not one but two—even though I was absolutely sure it was against policy. They looked like antique pistols, with tooled grips, and were probably inherited from the Spanish ancestor after whom he was named. He also knew where to find another pair of night vision goggles. I started wondering if perhaps he was different than I'd imagined him, not so naïve as I'd been told.

We planned the raid accordingly to his knowledge of the terrain. He said the place where the ship's main entry faced had more sentinels, so we'd go around the backside. I drove my beat-up Accord near the barricade that surrounded the spaceship where it'd landed, just about crushing the Denver Capitol. He'd double-talked the human guard into letting us through the barricade, which walled off about three blocks of the city in every direction of the destroyed government building and the circular, grey spaceship squatting atop of it.

That is perhaps something that no one who hadn't seen it up close and personal will believe. Yes, I know there were pictures of the spaceship, and of the aliens, all fuzzy gold and with a face that looked like it was made for hugs and to be cuddled by a child. I know you heard them talk of the peace of civilized races, and also saw them meeting the president, right in front of their ship.

And I know that in these pictures, the ship looked high tech but not threatening.

Up close and personal, where we got, when Xavier had convinced the sentinel put there by our own government that we were just there to get some documents to translate, the ship looked wrong.

There's nothing I can put my finger on, mind. It looked like glistening silver metal, and it felt body-temperature to the touch, which was the first thing that was wrong, but after that it looked pretty familiar: there were guarded doors, there was a cargo hold, there were stairs and ramps. If I hadn't known it moved to space, it would have looked much like a no-frills municipal building. But it still felt wrong. It was I think a combination of a lot of little things. For instance there were no rivets visible anywhere in the not-metal. And no sign of joining. It was as though this blocks-wide structure had been made in a single piece. And then there were other, more subtle tells. Like what human would make stairs with each step a different height?

At the door to the ship there was another sentinel. Theirs. He was a golden spider monkey who looked less friendly than the ones on the news due to glowing red eyes. I wondered why we hadn't seen any of those before, just as he made a guttural sound and advanced towards us. Xavier raised his arm high and hit him. The golden spider monkey sighed and fell, in a heap.

I was so shocked, I stood, paralyzed, wondering what he'd done and why—until Xavier got me by the arm and pulled me into the ship. He had his finger to his lips, so I had no idea how he apparently cold-cocked another alien who approached unexpectedly from our side.

I'd have asked, but he kept taking his finger to his lips, commanding silence, and I suppose it made sense. The aliens were not deaf.

We walked along dark corridors so long that I started wondering if I'd been crazy to come here, and also realizing that this was a fool's errand and Xavier had been right. This was like searching a small town—the ship had at least three vertical floors, spread over the area of ten city blocks which it had crushed on landing.

But then I stopped being an idiot and started "feeling" for Cressy. Look, I can't explain it, but ever since mom disappeared and I became responsible for her, I'd been able to find Cressy by going with my gut feeling of what she was doing. And also of whether she was in trouble. Which, all things considered, was a lot of the time.

So I took the lead, taking Xavier down two flights of uneven stairs, where we almost broke our necks, and towards the center of the ship, where Xavier'd cold cocked two more aliens, and then on towards . . .

A huge red-glowing door. My first thought was to kick it down, then I realized there was a plaque on the wall. It warned against unauthorized access. This was the engine room and only engineers— or as they called them keeper of the machine spirits—were allowed in.

Xavier whispered in my ear then, his breath ticklish and warm, "Are you sure we need to go in there?"

I nodded. Then I turned back and whispered into his ear, smelling his shampoo, feeling more intimate than I ever had with him, "Cressy is in there."

He gave me a look, and I gave one back, and he nodded, as if that solved it. He raised his hand for me to stay, disappeared briefly down a hallway and came back with a necklace which held a softly-glowing green-gem pendant, which he applied to the middle of the glow on the door. The glow went down, the doors slid open and we entered . . .

I don't think I can fully describe it, partly because it was in darkness. There were two . . . for lack of a better word, work stations, at which sat—no, *knelt*, two spider monkey aliens, looking into monitors covered with strange symbols. There were also vertical cylinders, and something that looked like it was a large tube made of glass and filled with varying light. If you looked at that light too long, you saw faces in it, not all of them human or spider-monkey.

But all these impressions were received, as it were, at the periphery of my vision, because what I was concentrating on were the three circles and the people on them.

Imagine, if you will, embroidery hoops eight feet across, made of glowing silver metal. Onto these, strapped with what looked like an intricate silver web which ran all along the sides, were three humans.

Two of them were young men, one looking respectable and like he wore what remained of a business suit, somewhat tattered and torn, the other looking like he'd been picked up on his way to the bong shop, with long hair, pajama pants and a yellow T-shirt with a smiley face.

The remaining one held Cressy, who looked like she was concentrating very hard on something and wore the dress I'd seen her wearing: a creamy lace thing, with all sorts of dips and ruffles that could only look good on someone who resembled a living China doll.

She was awake, and saw me, and opened her mouth and tried to say something. No sound came out.

The spider monkey aliens got up and advanced towards us. Fortunately they got to Xavier first. This time I saw where he hit them, with the butt of his gun, and had only to follow suit.

"How did you know where to hit them?" I said, as I looked around for instructions on how to release people from the embroidery hoops from hell.

"They gave us what I think are their secondary education books.

One of them was an anatomy manual. Hitting them where we did should concuss them but not kill them. They'll be fine when they awake."

"Is that how you learned that the necklace thing would open doors?" I asked, and he nodded.

We'd continued looking for instructions, while Cressy tried to mouth something at me, and so did the guy in the remains of the suit. The other guy looked thoroughly spaced-out and I wasn't sure he even knew we were there.

It was infuriating. There were no affixed instructions to anything, in this room. But there were, against the far wall, a series of plaques, and Xavier called me over with a strangled sort of voice, like someone who just found a bunch of spiders crawling on his breakfast cereal.

I went around the embroidery hoops to where he stood, facing a wall of plaques. There were pictures on the plaques. Not all of them human. One of the pictures was of my mother. I traced the wording next to it, engraved deep in the shiny golden metal in alien characters I'd learned to parse out. "To Maureen Farewell, who gave her"—spider-monkey word that we'd determined could be mind, but also essence or all—"to reach the stars."

There were hundreds of plaques. I looked at Xavier and he at me. I wondered if the aliens imagined these people had been volunteers. I looked back at the hoops. What a strange way to do this. "The instructions are probably in the computers," he said.

"Yes," I said. "But it is only in movies that humans instinctively know how to program alien machines."

"True, so what do you propose?"

I reached into my pocket and got a gun. "Brute force. Smash enough and they'll be free."

"Okay," he said. "But if we smash machinery, it might kill them."

"So, we smash the hoops," I said.

We did, starting at the bottom, using the butt of our guns. Halfway through breaking the hoop, which was stronger than it looked, alarms started up. I beat the hoop that held Cressy faster. And suddenly, without warning, there was a yellow glow, and she fell, as did the stoner guy, whom Xavier had been freeing.

She fell straight down, all of a heap on the floor, and I thought she would start yelling at me, as soon as she was done taking deep breaths and looking like she'd been starved of oxygen for days, but meanwhile Xavier and I had started on the hoop that held the businessman and hammered on it with a will, until he also dropped.

This was when the lights started flickering madly, and Xavier was doing something on one of the two work stations. I didn't know what and couldn't see the screen, but stoner-boy and Cressy were on their—shaky—feet and I helped businessman up and told all of them, "Any minute now, they're going to come check what's going on," this is when the power on the ship went out, and an alarm sounded which made exactly the same sound as a dog baying at the moon, only much louder, like this was a Doberman from hell.

"She's right," Xavier said, somehow audible over the alarm, "Let's get, ladies and gentlemen."

At which point we proceeded to flank the three dazed rescues and lead them in the direction of the hallway and out of the ship, at a trot.

No, we didn't get very far, and I can't say I remember this part very clear. I remember, in the utter darkness, spider monkeys with laser—were they laser? I must remember to ask the researchers going over their equipment—weapons trying to shoot us, and Xavier shooting at them, at first alone, till I joined him. I remember dead spider monkeys underfoot and having to walk on them to try to get out, all the while sure that there were only two of us armed.

And then Cressy had grabbed the high tech weapons of the fallen monkeys and started shooting wildly at them too, which seemed very odd in my sister, who proudly displayed a bumper sticker that said *Arms are for hugging*. I swear she was saying under her breath "die, motherfuckers," and what I could see of her was blood splattered, as she shamelessly grabbed more weapons from the cadavers of the monkeys she'd killed. The two guys belatedly joined in too.

Of course when we reached the exit, it was blocked by a dense crowd of monkeys, a vast enough crowd we could never make our way through them, and they were shooting at us, so we flattened ourselves against the wall of the ship.

For some reason they wouldn't shoot when we were near the walls, and instead started walking towards us.

Stoner boy turned to run, but I grabbed his shirt at the back, and I told Cressy, "Cressy, shoot the wall, that wall. It will lead to the outside."

She turned without a word, and started cutting a rough circle in the wall, in which businessman joined her, and eventually stoner boy did too.

The guard of spider monkeys seeing what we were doing ran towards us and Xavier and I shot them down using all our spare ammo. Just as we ran out, the portion of the ship fell out, and we ran out with spider monkeys in hot pursuit.

Yes, we were arrested. No, the policemen didn't deliver us to the spider monkeys as a matter of course, and instead we were driven to the local police station for questioning. Apparently the police had seen enough weird things in their days of guarding the ship to sense this was not quite the peaceful expedition it depicted itself as. Plus there were many of them who had family die in the obliteration of Capitol Hill.

And in the end, with Xavier, who had a reputation as not just the best linguist on Earth, but the coolest headed one, explaining the lacunae and omissions in the aliens communication, and with my sister explaining that she'd been strapped into their engine, to provide power, somehow, and that those plaques were people—or at least sentient beings of various species—they had killed to power their FTL and their ships, even our president had come around to figuring out that there was something very wrong.

Six months later, the secret of travel to the stars had been figured. And we were never going to do it. At least not while we retained the sense of horror of what had almost been done to us. We couldn't go to the stars, because FTL required—for lack of a better word—the soul of a sentient being to power it.

Maybe someday our scientists will come up with another method, because there are some more things we now know: apparently sentience is rare in the stars, and the spider monkeys have run through all of the easy pickings within reach. The primitive tribes who believe it an honor to be sacrificed to the sky-traversing gods are pretty much all gone. All that is left in their—and our—corner of the sky are technological civilizations, deeply suspicious of sky-gods and ready to kill any of them who try to land.

We were the last one where they might come in pretend peace, and get, perhaps, a delegation of us to go back. And then perhaps "immigrants" under which guise we could provide them fuel for centuries of travel.

Thank heavens for Cressy's innocence and the aliens' greed. There had in fact been a loss of power, their last victim, a Canid from a nearby star, having died unexpectedly. They ran out of power before being able to maneuver to land. So they'd taken Cressy and two other chance-met victims.

Which had allowed us to figure out the whole thing just in time. Now, until and unless we find a way to travel through the stars and clean them out, we're going to have to watch the sky with extreme prejudice, ready to shoot down any so-called friendly alien on a run for souls to power their ships.

Because it turns out the sky isn't filled with angels. At least not angels of the benevolent variety.

In the aftermath of all this, I met with Cressy at a coffee shop, in between one of the presentations Xavier was making and one I was due for. Cressy had cleaned up in the last six months. All the appearances on TV perhaps, or perhaps the fact that her illusions had shattered with a rather loud bang.

She was wearing a skirt-suit in cream-colored silk and looked if anything a little pale and wan, as she toyed with her sandwich and took little sips of her coffee. She'd thanked me for, what I swear was the first time, for rescuing her, and now she cleared her throat. "I'm going to marry him, of course."

"Him?" I said.

"Joe," she said.

And since the idea of my sister marrying was wholly alien, but if she were getting married I thought I knew her taste, I said, "Stoner boy?"

She grinned. "That's Malachy. He's not a stoner. In fact, he owns one of those Aspen ski resorts, you know? Entrepreneur, fabulously rich." She sighed.

"But he didn't propose?"

"Oh, no, he did, but he's . . . you know, peace and harmony and blah, blah, blah. I think . . . I don't know, Lillian, I think this whole thing made me tougher. Harder, you know. And Joe has been teaching me to shoot." She brightened up. "He owns a used book store. It will be a little tight, but we're going to get married and see what we can make of this." She smiled happily. "And you? Are you going to get married?"

"We did," I said. "When they let us out of custody. You see . . . you see . . . If we have to keep watch and if we're going to find a way to get to the stars and stop them, we're going to need a new generation."

"Yes," she said. "We do. And besides, we'll need lots of bright people to figure out how to get to the stars without this horrible trade off. Because you know, some humans—"

"You mean the less conscience-impaired regimes will go to the stars anyway? And kill people to do it?" I shuddered. "If one of these ships lands in North Korea, or if they steal our research—"

"That," she said. "So we're doing our best to marry and raise children who will come up with a solution to the problem and preserve the future for free… sentients who will not kill others for their benefit." And she smiled as though she knew very well that wasn't why I'd got married.

PLAYTHING

by Larry Niven

There is a frequently reiterated refrain about how adults are the ones who have messed up the world, and children, on the other hand, are uncorrupted, wiser, and more understanding. The people who write things like that must not know many children—human that is. And how about the extraterrestrial equivalent?

⚒ ⚒ ⚒

LARRY NIVEN is renowned for his ingenious science fiction stories which are solidly based on authentic science, often of the cutting edge variety. His Known Space series is one of the most popular "future history" sagas in SF and includes Ringworld, *one of the few novels to have won both the Hugo and Nebula awards, as well as the Locus and Ditmar awards, and which is recognized as a milestone in modern science fiction. Four of his shorter works have also won Hugos. Most recently, the Science Fiction and Fantasy Writers of America have presented him with the Damon Knight Memorial Grand Master Award, given for lifetime achievement in the field. Lest this all sounds too serious, it should be remembered that one of his most memorable short works is "Man of Steel, Woman of Kleenex," a not-quite serious essay on Superman and the problems of his having a sex life. Niven has also demonstrated a talent for creating memorable aliens, beginning with his first novel,* World of Ptaavs, *in 1966. A possible reason for this, Niven writes, is that, "I grew up with dogs. I live with a cat, and borrow dogs to hike with. I have passing acquaintance with raccoons and ferrets. Associating with nonhumans has certainly gained me insight into alien intelligences." His insight and ingenuity are on full display in this hilarious example of a less than optimal first contact.*

THE CHILDREN WERE PLAYING six-point Overlord, hopping from point to point over a hexagonal diagram drawn in the sand, when the probe broke atmosphere over their heads. They might have sensed it then, for it was heating fast as it entered atmosphere; but nobody happened to look up.

Seconds later the retrorocket fired. A gentle rain of infrared light bathed the limonite sands. Over hundreds of square miles of orange martian desert, wide-spaced clumps of black grass uncurled their leaves to catch and hoard the heat. Tiny sessile things buried beneath the sand raised fan-shaped probes.

The children hadn't noticed yet, but their ears were stirring. Their ears sensed heat rather than sound; and unless they were listening to some heat source, they usually remained folded like silver flowers against the children's heads. Now they uncurled, flowers blooming, showing black centers; now they twitched and turned, seeking. One turned and saw it.

A point of white light high in the east, slowly setting.

The children talked to each other in coded pulses of heat, opening and closing their mouths to show the warm interiors.

Hey!

What is it?

Let's go see!

They hopped off across the limonite sand, forgetting the Overlord game, racing to meet the falling thing.

It was down when they got there and still shouting-hot. The probe was big, as big as a dwelling, a fat cylinder with a rounded roof above and a great hot mouth beneath. Black and white paint in a checkerboard pattern gave it the look of a giant's toy. It rested on three comically splayed metal legs with wide, circular feet.

The children began rubbing against the metal skin, flashing pulses of contentment as they absorbed the heat.

The probe trembled. Motion inside. The children jumped back, stood looking at each other, each ready to run if the others did. None wanted to be first. Suddenly it was too late. One whole curved wall of the probe dropped outward and thudded to the sand.

A child crawled out from underneath, rubbing his head and flashing heat from his mouth: words he shouldn't have learned yet. The wound in his scalp steamed briefly before the edges pulled shut.

The small, intense white sun, halfway down the sky, cast opaque black shadow across the opening in the probe. In the shadow something stirred.

The children watched, awed.

ABEL paused in the opening, then rolled out, using the slab of reentry shielding as a ramp. ABEL was a cluster of plastic and metal widgetry mounted on a low platform slung between six balloon tires. When it reached the sand it hesitated as if uncertain, then rolled out onto Mars, jerkily, feeling its way.

The child who'd been bumped by the ramp hopped over to lick the moving thing. ABEL stopped at once. The child shied back.

Suddenly an adult stood among them.

WHAT ARE YOU DOING?

Nothing, one answered.

Just playing, said another.

WELL, BE CAREFUL WITH IT. The adult looked like the twin of any of the six children. The roof of his mouth was warmer than theirs—but the authority in his voice was due to more than mere loudness. *SOMEONE MAY HAVE GONE TO GREAT TROUBLE TO BUILD THIS OBJECT.*

Yes sir.

Somewhat subdued, the children gathered around the Automated Biological Laboratory. They watched a door open in the side of the drum-shaped container that made up half of ABEL's body. A gun inside the door fired a weighted line high into the air.

That thing almost hit me.

Serves you right.

The line, coated with sand and dust, came slithering back into ABEL's side. One of the children licked it and found it covered with something sticky and tasteless.

Two children climbed onto the slow-moving platform, then up onto the cylinder. They stood up and waved their arms, balancing precariously on flat triangular feet. ABEL swerved toward a clump of black grass, and both children toppled to the sand. One picked himself up and ran to climb on again.

The adult watched it all dubiously.

A second adult appeared beside him.

YOU ARE LATE. WE HAD AN APPOINTMENT TO XAT BNORNEN CHIP. HAD YOU FORGOTTEN?

I HAD. THE CHILDREN HAVE FOUND SOMETHING.

SO THEY HAVE. WHAT IS IT DOING?

IT WAS TAKING SOIL SAMPLES AND PERHAPS TRYING TO COLLECT SPORES. NOW IT SHOWS AN INTEREST IN GRASS. I WONDER HOW ACCURATE ITS INSTRUMENTS ARE.

IF IT WERE SENTIENT IT WOULD SHOW INTEREST IN THE CHILDREN.

PERHAPS.

ABEL stopped. A box at the front lifted on a telescoping leg and began a slow pan of the landscape. From the low dark line of the Mare Acidalium highlands on the northeastern horizon, it swung around until its lens faced straight backward at the empty orange desert of Tracus Albus. At this point the lens was eye to eye with the hitchhiking child. The child flapped his ears, made idiot faces, shouted nonsense words, and flicked at the lens with his long tongue.

THAT SHOULD GIVE THEM SOMETHING TO THINK ABOUT.

WHO WOULD YOU SAY SENT IT?

EARTH, I WOULD THINK. NOTICE THE SILICATE DISC IN THE CAMERA, TRANSPARENT TO THE FREQUENCIES OF LIGHT MOST LIKELY TO PENETRATE THAT PLANET'S THICK ATMOSPHERE.

AGREEMENT.

The gun fired again, into the black grass, and the line began to reel back. Another box retracted its curved lid. The hitchhiker peered into it, while the other children watched admiringly from below.

One of the adults shouted, *GET BACK, YOU YOUNG PLANT-BRAIN!*

The child turned to flap his ears at him. At that moment ABEL flashed a tight ruby beam of laser light just past his ear. For an instant it showed, an infinite length of neon tubing against the navy blue sky.

The child scrambled down and ran for his life.

EARTH IS NOT IN THAT DIRECTION, an adult observed.

YET THE BEAM MUST HAVE BEEN A MESSAGE. SOMETHING IN ORBIT, PERHAPS?

The adults looked skyward. Presently their eyes adjusted.

ON THE INNER MOON. DO YOU SEE IT?

YES. QUITE LARGE . . . AND WHAT ARE THOSE MIDGES IN MOTION ABOUT IT? THAT IS NO AUTOMATED PROBE, BUT A VEHICLE. I THINK WE MUST EXPECT VISITORS SOON.

WE SHOULD HAVE INFORMED THEM OF OUR PRESENCE LONG AGO. A LARGE RADIO-FREQUENCY LASER WOULD HAVE DONE IT.

WHY SHOULD WE DO ALL THE WORK WHEN THEY HAVE ALL THE METALS, THE SUNLIGHT, THE RESOURCES?

Having finished with the clump of grass, ABEL lurched into motion and rolled toward a dark line of eroded ring wall. The children swarmed after it. The lab fired off another sticky string, let it fall, and started to reel it back. A child picked it up and pulled. Lab and martian engaged in a tug of war which ended when the string broke. Another child poked a long, fragile finger into the cavity and withdrew it covered with something wet. Before it could boil away, he put the finger in his mouth. He sent out a pulse of pleasure and stuck his tongue in the hole, into the broth intended for growing Martian microorganisms.

STOP THAT! THAT IS NOT YOUR PROPERTY!

The adult voice was ignored. The child left his tongue in the broth, running alongside the lab to keep up. Presently the others discovered that if they stood in front of ABEL it would change course to crawl around the "obstruction."

PERHAPS THE ALIENS WILL BE SATISFIED TO RETURN HOME WITH THE INFORMATION GATHERED BY THE PROBE.

NONSENSE. THE CAMERAS HAVE SEEN THE CHILDREN. NOW THEY KNOW THAT WE EXIST.

WOULD THEY RISK THEIR LIVES TO LAND, MERELY BECAUSE THEY HAVE SEEN DITHTA? DITHTA IS A HOMELY CHILD, EVEN TO MY OWN EYE, AND I AM PERHAPS HIS PARENT.

LOOK WHAT THEY ARE DOING NOW.

By moving to left and right of the lab, by forming moving "obstructions," the children were steering ABEL toward a cliff. One still rode high on top, pretending to steer by kicking the metal flanks.

WE MUST STOP THEM. THEY WILL BREAK IT.

YES . . . DO YOU REALLY EXPECT THAT THE ALIENS WILL LAND A MANNED VEHICLE?

IT IS THE OBVIOUS NEXT STEP.

WE MUST HOPE THAT THE CHILDREN WILL NOT GET HOLD OF IT.

RANDOM SAMPLE

by T. P. Caravan

Larry Niven's Martian children may have been a disaster in progress, but I'm sure that the human children of Earth could give them a run for their money . . . at least, for a time.

⚒ ⚒ ⚒

T. P. CARAVAN *was the alias under which* **CHARLES C. MUNOZ,** *according to the Internet Speculative Fiction Database, wrote 17 short stories for a number of science fiction magazines beginning with "Happy Solution" in the January 1952* Other Worlds Science Stories, *and apparently ending with "Blind Date" in the April 1965* Magazine of Fantasy and Science Fiction, *the same magazine where "Random Sample" appeared in the April 1953 issue. Other stories appeared in* Science Stories *and* Universe, *like* Other Worlds, *magazines edited by the, ah,* flamboyant *Ray Palmer, of Shaver Mystery fame and Bea Mahaffey (mention of whose considerable pulchritude recently threw the PC goose steppers of the Science Fiction and Fantasy Writers of America into a demented frenzy). His "Evil Old Professor" series of stories in* Other Worlds *showed his gift for humor, though there are too few of the stories to collect in a book, and the later stories lacked the ingenuity of the initial installment. And that, alas, is all I can say about Mr. Munoz/Caravan. He has no listing in either the Clute-Nicholls or Gunn SF encyclopedias, and an online search only turned up mentions* *of stories published. I would like to know more about the creator of the Evil Old Professor, and of the starkly unsentimental narrator of the brief tale which follows.*

IF YOU DON'T GIVE ME another piece of candy I'll cry. You'd be surprised how loud I can cry. Mother wouldn't like that.

Thank you. I just love candy.

I'm very polite for my age; everybody says so. I can get more candy that way. Old ladies are best. I'm also a very intelligent little girl, but I suppose you found that out from your tests. They gave me the same kind of tests, but they didn't give me any candy, so I was bad and didn't answer anything right.

Thank you. I'll take two this time. Do you have any hard candies? The heat's melted these chocolates a little.

My father says to get all I can out of you, because all you Viennese head-thumpers are quacks. He says you cost an awful lot of money. He says only an old fraud would have a beard like a billy goat. He says . . .

Are you getting angry?

All right, then, if you give me just one more piece of candy, I'll tell you all about it.

Merci. That's French, you know.

My brother Johnny and I were out in the back yard, stomping ants, when the space ship came down. It's fun sometimes watching ants, they run around so hopefully going about their business, carrying little bits of twigs and things in their mouths, and they don'e even seem to know you're there until your foot just about touches them. Then they run away, waving their feelers before they squish. But the big red ants are the really good ones. You can jump right spang on them and they don't even seem to notice it. I guess they sink into the ground a little ways, because if you pound one between two rocks he squishes without any trouble. They taste funny. Once Johnny saw a red one fighting a black one and they kept right on fighting until he burned them both up with his magnifying glass.

Will you buy me a magnifying glass if I tell you about it? I'd just love to have a magnifying glass. I bet the ant thinks the sun is spread out over the whole sky. I bet he thinks the whole world is burning up. I bet it hurts. I bet I could burn up more ants than Johnny can, even though I'm a whole year younger. He's ten.

Please, can I have a magnifying glass? Please? Please? Can I? Can I? I'll cry.

When can I have it?

Thank you.

It was his birthday so I let him take the ones near the ant hill. I'm really very generous at times. You let them get almost down the hole before you jump on them. That's the most fun. I was watching one I'd pulled the legs off, waiting to see if the others would eat it, when Johnny yelled for me to come quick and I went running over. He showed me one ant carrying another on its back, trying to get it down into the ant hill before we squished it. We were just about to stomp on its little head when we heard the noise in the sky. It was the kind of skreeky sound I make when I pull my fingernail along the blackboard in school and make old Miss Cooper get the shivers. I hate Miss Cooper. She doesn't give me any candy—thank you—and I never answer any questions for her.

We looked up and saw the rocket ship coming down for a landing in the woods. It didn't look like a ship to me, but that's what Johnny says it was. It looked like a big washing machine to me. Father says it was a hallucination—I like big words—but he didn't even see it, so how could he know?

Sometimes I hate Father. Are you writing that down? Was that the right thing to say? Can I have some more candy?

Thank you.

This is very good, even if it is melted. I should think you could afford to have your office air conditioned, then the candy wouldn't melt at all. If you were smart you'd think of these things.

What happened? I've told it over and over but nobody believes me. Isn't that sad? I don't think I'll tell anybody else about it.

The whole box? For me? Thank you. I just love chocolates.

Your beard isn't really much like a billy goat's.

We saw it come down in the woods and we ran over to the place. Nobody else was there. The grass and underbrush was burning a little but they were putting it out, and when they saw us they stopped still and made little noises to each other. I held up my hand and I said, "I'm queen here. You must all bow down." And Johnny held up his hand and said, "I'm king." He never thinks of anything for himself.

I hate them. They didn't bow down to me. One of them picked up a squirrel that had been burned a little when they landed, and he was petting it and putting something on the burned place, ahd he didn't pay any attention to me. I hated him most of all, so I went over and kicked him. He was smaller than Johnny, so Johnny kicked him too. I kicked him first, though, and he was just my size.

What did they look like? They didn't look like old billy goats.

They took us inside their space ship, and they started to give us some tests like the one you gave me. They were very simple tests, but I didn't like them so I got them all wrong. Johnny got them all wrong too, because I told him I'd scratch his eyes out if he didn't. I remember some of them. They drew little triangles with boxes on two of the sides and then they gave me the pen and waited to see what I'd do. I fooled them. I took the pen and threw ink all over them. It wasn't a pen, exactly, but it was like one. Then they held up one little block, then two, then three, then four. They did this a few times, and then they held up one block, then two. Then they waited for me to pick up three. I picked up all the blocks and hit them over the head with them. I had a lot of fun. I was very bad.

They got Johnny off in a corner, and before you could say "boo!" he was telling them about all the people he'd killed in the war. He wasn't really in the war, of course, but he likes to pretend he was. He likes television best when they kill lots of people. I don't think they really knew what he was talking about, but they looked as if they did. He's a very good actor.

I suppose they thought we were grownups; they were pretty much the same size we are. Anyway, they paid a lot of attention to him, so I went over and punched him a couple of times. I'm afraid we broke up the insides of their space ship a little.

They looked pretty mad. I guess they were disgusted with Johnny, a lot of people are. I always try tomake a good impression on strangers, even when they don't give me any candy, so I took some of them outside and showed them how to stomp ants. It was very funny. One of them got sick. Johnny and I were still jumping up and down, stomping ants, when they took off. I hated them. They were nasty; they didn't bow down to me.

That's all. Nothing else happened.

Father says not to take up too much of your expensive old time. He says no honest man could afford a penthouse for his office. You have a very nice view, don't you? You can see all over the city from here.

My, isn't it hot? I wish I had a refrigerator to keep my candy in.

Look there. Look at the fires springing up across the river. Aren't they pretty? Look. Look. And some on this side.

Take me away from here. It's too hot.

Look at the sun. Look at it. It's spreading out over the whole sky. It's burning up the city. Billy goat, help me! Save me! I'm sorry I was bad.

NO LOVE IN ALL OF DWINGELOO

by Tony Daniel

The aliens called geists weren't malevolent—but they were very good at business. They had an unsettling way of communicating, and might be able to show someone their future. And that was not necessarily a good thing . . .

※ ※ ※

TONY DANIEL *is the author of seven science fiction books, the latest of which is* Guardian of Night, *as well as an award-winning short story collection,* The Robot's Twilight Companion. *He also collaborated with David Drake on the novel* The Heretic, *and its sequel,* The Savior, *new novels in the popular military science fiction series,* The General. *His story "Life on the Moon," was a Hugo finalist and also won the Asimov's Reader's Choice Award. Daniel's short fiction has been much anthologized and has been collected in multiple year's best anthologies. Daniel has also co-written screen plays for SyFy Channel horror movies, and during the early 2000s was the writer and director of numerous audio dramas for critically-acclaimed SCIFI.COM's Seeing Ear Theater. Born in Alabama, Daniel has lived in St. Louis, Los Angeles, Seattle, Prague, and New York City. He is now an editor at Baen Books and lives in Wake Forest, North Carolina with his wife and two children.*

AFRICA WAS BURNING when the first *geists* appeared on Kokopelli Station. The aliens could have picked a better time in human history to contact us. The cable lift from Nairobi was, without clearance, shooting up to us double runs, a few thousand souls crammed into wagons meant to hold only a few hundred. I was placed in charge of shuffling the refugees over to other cables. All of them had some degree of old-fashioned radiation poisoning. Many of them were seething with retroflux, and an epidemic of the plague on a space station would be horrific. Most of the others were hungry, and would have gutted the station if they got loose (and who could blame them?). As for the others, the Broker Guild's unofficial insurrection front was recruiting, and refugees were prime targets.

So the transfer was very exciting, and demanded all of my attention, and when the first reports of the geists started coming in, they didn't particularly register with me. I believe there was a bit of fanfare for them at the very beginning, but I was entirely preoccupied, and missed it. There was the problem of where in the world to send the African refugees. The St. Louis lift was restricted to visiting traders down Earthside, and *they* had to live in quarantine in East St. Louis and Cahokia. Buenos Aires agreed to several shipments, but the Eugenistas had control of the seaboard, and, after seeing some Link of the New Mandate Barrios in Rio, I was wondering just what they intended to *do* with several thousand Africans. Nevertheless, the diplomatic situation demanded that I send some their way, poor souls.

As usual, Amsterdam needed working bodies—anybody—to shovel fill and hold back the rising sea, so we dropped over half there. Tibet agreed to take about a quarter for prisoner swaps with NAGAN in Libya. Theirs would not be a happy life, but at least it would be a life. And the other quarter we ended up freezing and orbiting, hoping for better days. There was a glitch with a pod of about three hundred, and for a time the night sky over the Pacific archipelago was lit by African meteors. There were reports on the Link that some even made it through the atmosphere and splashed, iridescent, into the sea.

Then the first wagon full of the dead came up. Each body was carefully beheaded. The next wagon contained severed heads—whether they belonged to the bodies or not, we didn't try to ascertain. And so they alternated, another and another, until we shut the lift down manually, and lost all contact with the central continent.

I had just stepped off a rimshot, and was on my way to my office in the Third Dictate Magistracy when I saw my first alien. I thought for an instant that it was a breach in the hull and I prepared myself for death. But there was no sucking wind, and, as my heart stilled, the geist approached me. It was like a floating nanoscreen, but it was as amorphous as a giant amoeba. It seemed to be infinitely deep when looked at head-on, but when you passed it, there were no sides, and when you turned around to look at it, it was gone. In fact, you could walk through it from behind and feel nothing, then turn around, and there it would be. For me, they had no discernible smell, although others had reported a faint stench, or the tang of ionized air. Inside the geists were colors, textures and—

Humans. Your friends and relatives. And these friends and relatives would talk to you. But all a little *wrong*. Your mother was young, perhaps, but she wore clothes that were in fashion now. Or your friend from childhood might be an old man. Or she might be a three-year-old who could barely speak. These images, these visages, shifted constantly. Each would say a word, several words, and then the channel would change, the frequency shift, and another would take their place. In this way, the aliens spoke to us in our native languages. Since their selection was limited, it was, unfortunately, a speech riddled with clichés and catch-phrases, yet meant with completely serious intent.

For the first few people with whom the geists spoke, the experience was unsettling, and it drove at least one man to insanity. Most people could not get used to it at all. Getting over the emotional response to the visages, the voices, was the difficult part. And the way to do that was to realize that the aliens absolutely did not comprehend or care about the tide of feelings their method of communication unleashed in listeners.

As for me, the adjustment was minimal. It is not, I like to think, that I have no feelings, just that I had no family and few friends. The geist that I first met used the history teacher from DePaul University who was also my academic advisor and mentor as its first image, alternated with a prostitute from Bangkok (where I am originally from) with whom I'd thought I was in love, and my brother, whose face I only knew from some damaged sculptagraphs. For a moment I was startled, for I thought it was, instead, a reflection of me.

"Hello, Haliman Yorasi," said Dr. Myers. "We were informed that you will make significant contributions to—"

"—some people who are coming tomorrow—" spoke Mala, my beautiful, doomed fancy of youth.

"—to a meeting to make a deal with the whites," my brother said.

"The whites?" I asked, surprised by my brother's resemblance to me and his words.

"Excuse me, I misspoke," Dr. Myers replied. "I should have said, 'the geists.' Ourselves, I mean."

I will spare you a description of the alternations henceforth, but, as I say, they ceased to have much meaning for me after a few similar discussions, and I began to think of the alien itself as the speaker who addressed me.

"I'm sorry, but you must be mistaken," I said.

The geist said nothing for a long moment, and, as I thought it was done speaking with me, I made to go on my way, but as I took a step, it moved backward with me, and stayed in front of me. As I later discovered, I could move briskly down a hall and the geist would match my every move.

"Are you not on the Ethics Committee of the Interlocking Finance Directorate?" asked the geist.

"Well. Yes," I replied. I stopped walking, out of respect, but of course this meant nothing to the geist. "But that committee is not of much importance. In fact, I don't believe we ever met. . . ."

"Unless we are very much mistaken, and certainly that is not the case, the Ethics Committee has the hot potato in this regard and will make initial policy."

I considered what the geist said. Its statement did follow the unofficial axiom of all public service positions. As my mentor, Dr. Myers used to tell me—

"Even in space, shit flows downhill," said Myers-geist.

"Well, what can I do for you? Should we find a more convenient place to talk?"

"Sorry, my dear?"

"Some place private?"

"Are you planning to lie?"

"Of course not."

"Then here is fine."

"Fine."

"Fine." Since we were in a cylindrical hallway, there was no convenient corner to step into. I did stand somewhat to the side of the corridor, although the exchange drew curious glances from all who passed by.

"We wish to ease the business process along by whatever means necessary, and in that regard we would like to grease the wheels at this point as regards your participation."

"Come again?" I couldn't believe what I was hearing. I mean, it is common, even customary, for Kokopelli officials to supplement their service income with various gratuities and unofficial fees, but I had never been approached in so blatant a manner. And then the geist went even further.

"Here is a bribe." For a brief instant, the amoeba expanded, filled the entire hallway. And then, it contracted, as a pricked muscle will in reflex. Directly in front of the geist, and between it and myself, a disk appeared—a metallic disk. It fell to the floor, bounced against the molefoam carpeting, and settled at my feet.

"My dear, er, friend, I don't know what to say. This is highly unusual."

"But heartfelt," said the geist.

"What, I say, what is your name?"

There was another pause. This time I stood my ground and waited the geist out.

"You may call me The Dwingeloo Time and Life Company," said the geist. "It is a pleasure doing business with you, Haliman Yorasi."

And with that, the geist blinked out of my existence. I picked up the metallic disk, and went about my duties.

★★★

Dwingeloo, as most humans were destined to learn, was our own name for a galaxy in the Milky Way's local cluster. About ten million light-years from here, it is obscured by the dust and gas at our galaxy's center, and only visible by radio telescope. It was discovered two centuries ago using such a telescope located at Dwingeloo in the old Netherlands. The aliens were "from" Dwingeloo only in a manner of speaking—in the same way you and I are "from" the Pangaeia supercontinent.

The Secretary and General Board of Trade had a great many problems on its hands at the particular moment the geists chose to show up, and, as some of us were shortly to surmise, the geists had planned it this way. There was fighting in the East Rim, where the Broker Guild had their strongest support from the free traders and the franchise networks. Although we were kept from officially confirming this, it was a *de facto* civil war. Strange how humanity had been waiting centuries for contact with another sentient species, and when they came we relegated them to a third-tier committee in the provisional government of a space station.

But the geists chose *us*—Kokopelli Station—as their contact point. Nobody really knew why, and I heard through the grapevine that the Secretary grew quite incensed when he learned that he couldn't pass this particular problem along to some other potentate. Not that anyone on Earth was in a better condition to welcome the aliens.

After my encounter with my first geist, I spent a grueling day at the office, mopping up the African operation. I took a rimshot home to the Brown and Green District, where I lived. It was a nice neighborhood; the apartments had good views and there were parks and good people, most of whom were middle managers and professionals, like myself. What we lacked in great culture, we made up for with an effective local government—I was a council member—and relative safety, when compared with both the richer and poorer districts.

My apartment was spare by any standards, I must admit. I ordered up dinner—pasta with alfredo sauce—and sat down in the living room to join the Link. In the evenings I liked to lie back and let the couch massage me while I caught up with the day's polling and news. The metallic disk that the alien had given me was in my pocket and as I reclined, I felt it cool against my thigh. I know it sounds strange, but events had overtaken me, and I had completely forgotten about the disk.

I took it from my pocket. The disk was the size of a large coin, and gold, with a silvery tint when held to the light. One side was utterly smooth. It had virtually no thickness. I turned it over. There were two indentations on the other side, like two crescent moons, or two thumbnail prints, each turned with their curving sides toward one another and toward the center of the disk. I ran my finger over the marks.

What could the alien have been thinking? Even if the disk were pure platinum, it would not be worth enough to influence a major policy decision. In fact, I *could* take the pettiness of the bribe as an insult, were I so inclined. Perhaps there was more to the disk—some inactivated nano, or interior circuitry. I twisted on it slightly, to see if there were any give to it—

—*I was drinking orange juice, while Bina got ready for work. She had to go in early today to prepare to present a paper in conference, and she'd awakened jittery and frightened. We'd made love while I was half-unconscious, and she seemed to draw my calm and untroubled sleep into herself, even as it left me and I awoke to her skin and kisses and sighs. Now she was humming softly as she clasped her bra and moistened her brown skin with lotion—*

Stunned, I let go my pressure on the disk—and the world returned. What startled me was not the realism of the vision I'd had. The nano ensconced in my head, in practically everyone's head, could interact with the Link feed and provide as real an experience as one could want. There were madmen and criminals who were perpetually linked and never knew. But this vision was different. It took me a moment to realize why.

Memories.

Feelings that were mine, but feelings that I'd never had before. Associations, likes, dislikes that were *true*—as true as any I had in this, my other life. The vision was *real*. As real as here and now. As true as life. And love. There was a woman named Bina whom I loved with all my heart.

I twisted the disk back to that vision.

We lived in a small space—smaller than my apartment in the Brown and Green—but still on Kokopelli Station. There were more people living up-cable, thousands and thousands more. Still, this was just a trickle of refugees compared with the billions who had died below. Earth was horribly worse, and it was then that I realized I was seeing the *future*.

The squabbles and wars of the present had played themselves out and we'd done it, we'd ruined the planet. The seas were biohazard cauldrons, seething with an ecology of war viruses. The land was haunted by nanoplasms, the primal form that life had taken, been reduced to. Sea and land were at war—over nothing, any longer—just a meaningless perpetual struggle between viral life and nano algorithms caught in a perpetual loop. Those who crafted the weaponry were dead.

A few million humans survived on the coasts, in the land between the warring elements. They were temporarily immune to the nano, but none could say for how long, since the nano evolved, its sole purpose finding ways to beat back the living, zombie sea—and, incidentally, to remake whatever people remained into a substance that could not wield a gun and could not think to use one.

Yet I found myself completely, unshakably content. Kokopelli was safe. We had severed all but one cablelift, and created defenses that kept the muck below at bay. In fact, Bina had been one of those responsible for our salvation. I didn't understand how it worked, and I didn't want to. I had my job and I had my love.

She was unlike me in so many ways—impetuous, severe with herself, angry at the world. When we first met, I was a kind of respite for her, a sanctuary. She'd spent ten years in a hurtful marriage to a theoretical physicist who grew jealous and sought to limit her work when she began to eclipse him. In many ways, I was her reaction against that man. But I didn't care. And, in time, she grew to depend upon me in other ways. *Grew,* Bina herself said, as a vine.

"You are like a trellis to me, Haliman," Bina told me. "You seem ordinary enough—"

"I am," I said.

"Yes, you are then. But you are constant. I wind around you and through you"—here she placed a finger to my lips, touched the sides of my face with her cool, brown hands—"I would collapse into a tangled mess without you. You're always there, beneath every thought I have."

And I depended upon her. Before Bina, I had had only my job, and the faint satisfaction of doing adequate work in a difficult situation. Now there was waking up to her caress in the morning, feeling her absence all day long as a sweet bitterness that evening would wash away—and there were the nights.

Bina brought her day home with her—her frustrations, her triumphs—and transformed them into passion. She looked somewhat like the fantasy of my youth, the Bangkok prostitute, and so there was always something salacious, something forbidden about entering her, even wanting her. I could not grow bored.

Yet there was so much more. Bina held nothing back, neither her mind nor her heart. She led me to such places as I would never have found on my own, or with anyone else. Places, feelings—I cannot say, cannot explain.

She emerged from the bedroom wearing only pants and a bra, glistening still from the lotion she'd applied.

"Do you think the paper will go well?" she asked me. This was a ritual, but she never tired of it.

"Didn't the last one go well?"

"Yes," she said, her voice small, her eyes sparkling. "Because you said it would, it did."

I put down my orange juice, pulled her to me. The fragrance of lotion, and beneath that, the faint trace of young leaves in spring, Bina's natural smell.

"Well then," I said, "I declare that you will do extraordinarily well today, better than you ever have before." I kissed the curve of her stomach, rubbed my stubbly face against her side. This tickled her, and she laughed, and then kept on laughing after I'd stopped, until I'd pulled her into my lap and kissed her. After a moment, she kissed back, hard and deep. She nibbled on my neck.

"Bina, you wanted to go in early. . . ."

"No." She pulled open my shirt and kissed a shoulder.

"Yes, you said so last night."

"I was too sleepy to know what I was saying."

"I think you were wide awake."

But we had passed the point of reason. Her hands were on my chest, on my pants. I unclasped her bra and suckled at her breasts.

We stumbled together to our little bedroom, folded down the bed, and fell on it, and upon each other. As we made love, as I nudged and rubbed into the curves and spaces of her body, the leafy, budding smell rose from her, more and more intense. On Kokopelli, there were no seasons, but every time we made love it was the spring—the spring that would never come again. It was always the same, yet always new and growing, living forth. We redeemed what we could of Earth's life. I spent myself in her like the April rain; she came around me with the swelling bloom of May.

After this, my day at work was a pale shadow existence, and coming home meant coming back to life.

Or emptiness. I untwisted the disk and was alone in my apartment. I'd never known how lonely I was until this moment, and now there was no way I could ever forget. I could never forget Bina.

I'm afraid I quite neglected my job over the next few shifts. There was much extra work to do, too, and I risked having my subordinates claim much of the credit and overstep me in advancement. When this had occurred before, it irked me considerably. I'd lain awake tallying my mistakes and resolving never to let such a thing happen again. Now I did not care whether I were promoted or not. For the first time in years, I worked only my required hours. I spent all my leisure time in the vision provided by the disk. Of course I questioned this, thinking that I was under the influence of some sort of drug or brainwashing. But there was no coercion, no longing that was not wholly my own natural desire.

And I knew that if the aliens demanded the disk back, I could and would give it to them. I had not forgotten my place or the position I was in. If they had thought to buy me with such a gift, they had miscalculated. Using the disk—living in that world—concentrated and enhanced my judgment. I felt a whole man when I was in the vision, and the effect lingered, for a while at least, when I was not. I resolved, however, to make as much use of the disk as possible, so that I could always remember, should they reclaim it.

In due time, the Ethics Committee on which I sat convened to listen to the geists' proposal. We met on the other side of the station, and I had to take a rimshot around half the perimeter to get there. There was only one Link analyst outside the meeting, and he contented himself with asking us to respond to the latest poll results concerning the aliens. Since nobody really knew what the geists wanted, the numbers meant little, and I said as much.

The meeting room was nondescript. There was a round table with closely spaced Link pads. A geist glowed somberly near the table, and we took seats around it. Our committee chair was Esmerelda Hillyer-Ortega, who held a position comparable to mine in the Second Dictate. Several members were late in arriving, and Hillyer-Ortega apologized to the geist. It replied using images of dark-haired people and one woman who was very light and blonde. Hillyer-Ortega seemed a bit shaken by the blonde woman's appearance.

Then Bina came in.

She was younger. I could tell by looking at her that she was troubled and trying not to show it. This was the way she always looked before a difficult presentation. With her was a tall man with closely cropped hair. Pendergrass, the devil.

I found myself staring, and touched the Link pad. Instantly, the room shrank to a corner icon, and a list of committee members popped up, accompanied by pictures. I selected Bina's image.

"My name is Tabrina Singh," it said. "I'm a research associate in the Bank of Toronto's statistics division, Kokopelli Branch."

Personal information, I shamelessly requested.

My inquiry would be recorded and Bina would get a note saying as much.

"I'm thirty-two years old. I was born on Kokopelli, and grew up in the Khushwant District. I live now in Extension Eight. My parents were from England. We are Pakistani. I went to the University of California in Los Angeles for my undergraduate degree, and completed my Ph.D. at the London School of Economics. I'm married to Dr. Gerald Pendergrass. We have no children."

Complete entry. Inquiry noted. Anything else?

"Let's get underway," said Hillyer-Ortega. I reluctantly exited the Link. She made a speech welcoming the geist.

She turned to the rest of us. "Ordinarily, I would introduce and try to create a context for a guest's appearance before this committee, but, in this case, I am as curious as the rest of you as to what our . . . speaker . . . has to say." She sat down. The alien immediately split into as many geists as there were committee members. The geists were about the size of a desk viewscreen, and each hovered before someone's face.

"To get straight to the point," said my geist, "it is our fervent desire to establish in this system a branch of the Dwingeloo Time and Life Company." The alien was silent for a moment.

"Er, what services does your company provide?" asked Hillyer-Ortega. At the first sound of her voice, all the geists around the table became translucent, and the committee members could see one another through them.

"You may very well wonder what service our company can provide," replied the geist, back to opaque images. "Never fear. It is comprehensible by you and that's why we're here."

The image within my geist, my brother, faded, and was replaced by a picture of a foggy sea of lights, concentrated to a brightness in the very middle. Stars perhaps? A galaxy? Suddenly the core of the lights emitted a pulse of energy that rippled through the other lights, changing their sizes and colors as it progressed. Very pretty. Then back to Dr. Myers.

"Time, as your species has deduced, is not a line. In fact, time has what you may call infinite dimensions. In fact, you might very well say that everything is happening all at once. In fact, you might say that the universe is both moving and being still, that forever is the same as now. What is real to us is what we choose to see."

"Choose?" Bina said. Her husband shot her a petulant glance, as if she'd spoken out of turn. But she was just as much a member of this committee as he was. "We *can't* choose. We are constructed a certain way and we see what we see. This is a crude way of speaking. The mathematics is quite clear, however—"

And the geist cut her off. Did it mean to? There was no way to tell. "Ah yes. Well, no. Actually, if we could just—" My geist flashed a series of equations within itself, their symbology glowing in neon colors.

"And to get right to the point," it continued. "We have some initial investments to make in your system. A virtual immolation energy device, for instance, that should supply your foreseeable needs until the end of time."

"I thought you said time had no end," one of the committee intoned.

"Yes, well, you know what I mean," the geist replied. "In whatever case, this will prepare you for full entry into our local economy, and eventually into the Intergalactic Prosperity Alliance."

"Excuse me," I said.

"Yes, what can we do for you, sir?" said the geist.

"I was just wondering. If you can take care of our energy needs, I assume you and the . . . others . . . are taken care of as well?"

"This is true, and furthermore—"

"—then there *is* no economy. There is no relative scarcity or abundance. Money is meaningless without them."

"Good point," said the geist. "Well taken."

"Yes," Bina said. "So you are giving us some kind of rechargeable black hole. What could we possibly provide you in return?"

"Your future," said the geist.

"Come again?"

"The Dwingeloo Time and Life Company deals in futures," it said. "As a matter of common knowledge, futures are the monetary unit of the local cluster. An option is what one future is called. Like a yen or dollar. At the moment, your system is worth about thirty billion options."

The geist went on at some length, explaining how the universal economy worked. It was similar, in some ways, to the Hindu concept of karma, only with no moral component whatsoever. All of the choices that we *don't* make, both as individuals and as larger groups, are tallied in a kind of possibility bank. For us, the bank is like a piggy bank that we drop coins into, but which we can never open. The geists had a way of cracking it open. And with that *fund* of coins we'd saved—with those unused options—we could *invest*. Others could use our options, and pay us interest, in the form of more options, for the service. Also, we could borrow, the alien mentioned in passing.

But we could not only use options that we hadn't taken in the past. We could invest our *future options* as well. In fact, past options were merely nickels and dimes compared with the futures. The marketplace for futures *was* the universal economy, and, in a sense, we carried the past around in our pockets as mere change.

Bina closely questioned the geist on the mathematics of this point, and she seemed satisfied with the answers, but I must confess that the discussion was far over my head. Oh, I understood the concept well enough. And the disk, my bribe, began to make sense to me. Options let you buy a desirable future life. You could borrow, and buy a better life than was, at least in your perception, possible before. If you invested wisely, then you would produce a future rich in even more options, and you could pay the loan back and have plenty of options to spare. You might even loan some out yourself, and get an even better future for your money.

I waited until Bina was through, then asked another question. "What if someone were to invest poorly, and create a future with only a few options? What if they couldn't pay back Dwingeloo?" I asked.

"Well, then, we would call in whatever we could and write off the loss."

"You would call in whatever they had?"

"Yes, essentially. We zero balance them."

"And they would have no further options?"

"No. That state is impossible."

"But, you just said—"

"They would cease to exist. They would cease to be and cease to *have been.* They wouldn't be missed, because no one would ever have known them. Not even us, by the way. It's a risk we take."

"Very brave of you."

The geist evidently had no concept of sarcasm. "We like to think of it as the cost of doing business."

The committee decided, as was expected, not to decide anything at the moment. This seemed to content the geists, who acted as if they had all the time in the world. As we left the room, Pendergrass and Bina were arguing—well, actually Bina was listening as Pendergrass chided her on several points she'd raised. The gist was, I took it, that she'd awkwardly stated some of the points she made, and the aliens might think us mathematically primitive because of her. I bided my time, and walked out with them.

"I'm going right past Extension Eight on my way home," I said. "Perhaps we could share a ride?" Ah, what stupidity, I immediately thought. How could I know where they lived?

Pendergrass stared at me for a moment. "Oh yes, you were the contentious gentleman on the committee," he said. "Well, we *are* going that way—"

"Splendid. I'll order a rimshot." I stepped over to a Link pad on the corridor wall. What was I doing? This could only lead to no good. But I called up the capsule.

Note: Inquiry into Level One Personal Information was initiated by Tabrina Singh 421050432 at 1348.24 KST, Access provided. Trace code available upon request, the Link informed me. So, Bina had asked about me, too.

We had a good twenty-minute ride ahead of us. Of course, the trip only took me further out of my way home, but that was unimportant. I wanted to spend at least a few moments of my real life—the life I was in now—with Bina.

Once we were inside, Bina immediately addressed me as if I were a friend with whom formalities could be dropped. This seemed to bother Pendergrass, but I paid him no mind.

"Did they give you one of these?" asked Bina. She pulled a metallic disk identical to mine from her pocket.

"Yes," I said.

"We've discussed that," said Pendergrass. "Those are merely a way of overawing us with their technical superiority. Obviously, it is some kind of fantasy, wish-fulfilling device, a fancy drug if you like." He took the disk from Bina, turned it in his fingers, tossed it back. "That offer they made . . . unlimited energy. Does anyone but me realize how incredible it is?"

"I do," I said. "I believe I realize many things."

"This is an option," Bina said, fingering the disk. "I'm sure of it."

"It's a hundred-thousand-option note," I said. "Perhaps more."

"What are we to make of this? What could they want from us that is worth this much . . . money?"

"Nothing," said Pendergrass. "You're jumping to conclusions, as usual, my dear. And what if it *is* valuable in the larger scheme of things? Why, then, we're rich—for all the good it will do us." He chuckled. "I'm not planning on buying a *star* any time soon. What would I do with it?"

"What he said is true," I replied. "*Nothing* is what they want."

"We are the ones who asked the questions, you and I," said Bina.

"You are the only person on the committee who really understands the technical side of what is going on."

"I beg your pardon," Pendergrass cut in. "I'm perfectly aware of the implications of what was discussed."

I looked at Pendergrass coolly. "Yes," I said. "Pardon me."

"So all we have to do is keep our mouths shut and let them go about business as usual," Bina said. "Let them set up their bank, or whatever."

"Then we deposit our funds."

"And the future . . . happens. The one we want; the one we pay for." Bina looked at me, looked me over, as if she were drinking me in. As if this were the last chance she'd ever have to be with me. She's seen the same vision as I have, I thought. She has loved me in another life.

"I wonder how much thirty billion options is in real money," she said. "I wonder who will decide how to invest it."

"Oh, I think this is too important a matter for our little committee," said Pendergrass. "We'll have to kick this one upstairs."

"That's what I'm afraid of," Bina said. "That's what I'm afraid of."

She rubbed her hands together, the way she did when she was truly worried. "I want to clean them," she once told me. "The more stress I'm under, the dirtier they feel to me."

"A power source that cannot be depleted, powering a war that never ends," I said. "Seems like a good way to keep generating a few options. Maybe not many. But what a safe bet, eh? Like buying bonds."

When she looked up at me, tears were in her eyes. "Did you see it, too?"

"Stuff and nonsense," said Pendergrass.

"I saw it," I said. "And I saw other things."

Now she was crying outright. Pendergrass huffed. I reached over, touched her hand. "Bina, we were so happy. Anything else would—"

"It can't be," she said. She took my hand, turned it over and ran her finger along my palm.

"I say!" Pendergrass exclaimed.

"Oh, Haliman," she said. "When you *know* the future, there are some things that must cancel each other out, and some things *must* be. It's in the math, in the logic. If we take the bribe, the horror we saw will happen."

"Precisely because we've taken the bribe."

"Yes," she replied, and let go my hand. "In the future."

We parted at the Extension Eight transfer. She held out her small hand. I did not shake it. I could not. And then I watched her walk away—watched her light and beautiful gait, the sway of her shoulders and hips. It was all so familiar. Never was. She turned a corner. Never will be.

I took the next rimshot and flew around Planet Earth three times before I finally returned to my apartment. Why not? I was a rich man, after all.

The Dwingeloo Time and Life Company established a branch office within days of gaining permission from the Ethics Committee. I have no idea if the vote were close, or what the discussion was. I attended no more meetings.

But I was first in line when the geists opened up. The office was a

simple room, with a chair for me. A geist hung in the air before me—
a geist phalange, actually, poking through my reality like a fingertip,
radiating from one of the central beings, who were as invisible as time
to us.

"Dwingeloo wants to be your neighborhood bank," said the geist.
"Here at Dwingeloo, we operate on a handshake, so to speak, and our
good faith in one another."

"That is acceptable," I said. I took the metallic disk from my
pocket. "I have two transactions to make."

"You wish to cash in your options," the geist replied. "We will be
pleased to serve you."

"No."

"Bring it back again? You wish to borrow more, then? Well, seeing
as you're a good customer—"

"I want to make an investment," I said. "I wish to place half the
amount of this note in a high-yield account. I will accept whatever
risk applies, of course. Do you have anything like that?"

The geist was silent. The phalange was integrating with the parent
being, getting its order on how to proceed. I waited.

"Well, according to Intergalactic Accord, I am compelled to
inform you of the investment instruments we offer," it finally said.
"But I should also warn you that it is possible to lose more than the
amount you invest. In that case, we would be forced to call in your
other options."

"As I stated, I'm prepared to take that risk."

"Very well." The disk flashed in my hands, and then disappeared.
"And how do you wish to handle the other two million options,
Haliman Yorasi?"

"I want to bribe you with it," I said.

"Come again a second time?"

"I am tired of working for Kokopelli Station. I want a change. I
want a position with Dwingeloo. Middle management will be fine."

"Haliman Yorasi, surely you cannot—" But this time the parent
being pulled the phalange back to *it*. All of this would one day be
utterly familiar to me. It was gone a long while. I waited. I had plenty
of time and nothing better to do.

The geist blinked back into existence. "Sure thing," it said. "When do you want to start?"

After five years, I have been kicked upstairs. Now I am on my way to a new position at headquarters. I am on my way to Dwingeloo. I travel—although that is not quite the word for it—in an invisible capsule of events that did not happen. Mutual exclusion powers the stardrive.

I did quite well for Earth, I must say, even at the risk of appearing to gloat. I took on our systemic account, after about a year of learning the ropes, and turned it around. It had fallen into a sorry state under geist management, whether deliberate or not. I find that the geists and I have a lot in common, actually. They are not evil; they are just good business people. When I showed them that Earth could turn a tidy profit without war and ruin, they were quick to come around and do things my way. In fact, the home office decided it needed more go-getters like me in upper management.

So now, fair Dwingeloo lies before me. The Milky Way glows fiercely behind me, but I have taken my last backward glance. I will never see Bina again. What is the use? And if we did meet in some secret way, and lived in some hidden room the life that might have been, would we not run the risk of making it actually so? When you know the future, there are some things that cancel one another out, some things that must not be.

And so I ride to the corporate office in a ship of lost loves, broken promises, and stifled passion. Oh yes, out here among the stars, it's business as usual. And there is no love in all of Dwingeloo.

FIRST CONTACT, SORT OF

by Karen Haber and Carol Carr

- -

The alien from Rigel 9 thought that humans having fingers was absolutely great, but otherwise they were primitive wimps, with weak minds easy to control Too bad the creature had never read The Exorcist. *Or even seen the movie.*

❊ ❊ ❊

KAREN HABER is the author of nine novels including Star Trek Voyager: Bless the Beasts, *and co-author of* Science of the X-Men. *She is a Hugo Award nominee, nominated for* Meditations on Middle Earth, *an essay collection celebrating J.R.R. Tolkien that she edited. Her recent work includes the short story collection* The Sweet Taste Of Regret. *Other publications:* The Mutant Season *series, the* Woman Without A Shadow *series,* Masters of Science Fiction and Fantasy Art, Crossing Infinity, Exploring the Matrix, *and* Transitions: Todd Lockwood. *Her short fiction has appeared in* Asimov's Science Fiction Magazine, The Magazine of Fantasy and Science Fiction, *and many anthologies including* The Madness of Cthulhu *and* Zombies! Zombies! Zombies! *She reviews art books for* Locus *Magazine. She lives in Oakland, California with her spouse, Robert Silverberg, and three cats.*
WEBSITE: http://karenhaber.com/

CAROL CARR was born in Brooklyn, New York, discovered Greenwich Village at age 15 and was immediately told by her friends that she would "never be one of us" again. Thus pulled untimely from her roots, she turned leftwardly political at Brooklyn College before finding herself trapped by circumstances in the early 1960s in the dubious world of science fiction, where she knew everybody and everybody knew her, and from which she has never completely escaped. While trapped there, she became known for writing hilarious pieces for fanzines, plus short science fiction stories for more professional venues. She moved to California in 1972, when home ownership was affordable, and is now retired in the East Bay hills with her husband and a series of repair people who come around every week to remove her dying trees, and replace her rotten siding and rusty plumbing. She has always been a writer who dabbled in this and that and, recently, emails. She stubbornly refuses to dabble in Facebook or Twitter. She recently published a selection of essays, evocative stories, and poems in the book, Carol Carr: The Collected Writings, *a book highly recommended by yr. hmbl. editor.*

THE TERRAN WAS IN A TELEPHONE BOOTH on Telegraph Avenue when the invisible alien scout from Rigel 9 wafted along on a breeze and noticed him.

A likely prospect, thought the alien. It pulled in its pseudowing, settled to the pavement, and turned up the amplifier on its transspecies transponder.

"No, no, no," the Earthling squealed in its peculiar dialect. It was speaking into a quaint audio transmitter which it held in front of its mouth with clever pink articulated front paws. "I lost a quarter. Q-U-A-R-T-E-R. What I want from you is simple, Operator, so simple that a child could do it. Perhaps you could find a child for me? No? Well, would you like *me* to find a child? Then perhaps it could ask you for my money back. I don't care that you don't believe me. If you won't give me a quarter, how about a dime? A nickel? Hello? Hello?"

The alien padded closer on soft, mutable pseudofeet.

If it had had lips it would have smacked them. Yes—yes. This creature was the one. The perfect sample. Probe the enemy for weaknesses, that was the Rigelian's mission. And here was this nice little Earthling all alone in its box. Even more important, its mind was as chaotic and closed a system as the alien had ever scanned. It would never know what had hit it.

With a sound halfway between a purr and a sob the alien slipped on the earthling. *Ah*, thought the alien. *Almost a perfect fit.*

Such cunning little fingers: almost as nice as that otter in Monterey. But this creature didn't seem to think as well as a sea mammal. Fast, but not well. Maybe it was the lack of salt water.

Not a bad body, really. Surprising upper torso strength and nice stretchy muscles. All the necessary parts seemed to be present. The alien scanned the external area as well. The Terran seemed to have little awareness of its outer aura. Perhaps this was a potential weakness to be exploited. How pliable was this species? Investigate. Probe. Learn. The alien directed the earthling to return to its nest.

The dual-lobed brain was a bit slow in processing the order: there seemed to be a great deal of peripheral noise and interference.

Inside the phone booth Wendell Davis was on hold, waiting for the supervisor of Information. As the seconds ticked away he had mentally redesigned the booth to include a little toilet complete with bidet and modesty panel, expanded the concept to provide miniature living quarters for the homeless, added wheels and a motor and . . .

. . . he couldn't understand why he felt such an overwhelming compulsion to go back to his apartment.

I just got out here, Wendell thought. *I haven't even had a decaf cappuccino yet.*

But he couldn't shake the sudden yen for his own four walls. *Okay,* he thought. *Okay. I'm going, I'm going. Jeez.* He hung up and slammed open the door of the booth.

It was about 2:30 on a cold post-Christmas day and the sky over Berkeley was a glorious canopy of bruises. Wendell was immediately cheered by the sight and considered stopping in to see Verna and

Henry, but changed his mind when he remembered that he had borrowed Henry's portable television and accidentally dropped it to death and Henry didn't know yet. Besides, he was going home.

He caught the very next bus with none of his usual arguments, detours, or complications. *Sometimes you just have to get on the bus and go home,* Wendell thought. He liked the phrase. It had simplicity. Directness. He decided to adopt it as his new mantra.

His door was still unlocked because he had not yet found his key but nothing inside was missing—at least nothing Wendell noticed.

He took off his jacket and started to drop it on the floor. Suddenly, his arm twitched, he spun around, opened the closet, and pulled out a wire hanger. His eyes bugging out of his head, Wendell neatly hung the jacket in the closet and closed the door. His mouth was dry.

I need something to drink, he thought. *Right now.*

Somewhere in the room the phone began to ring.

Don't answer it, Wendell thought. *You don't even know where the phone is.*

The phone rang again.

He scanned the mounds on the floor but didn't see anything that looked remotely like a telephone, just bunches of dark clothing, the tools he used for fixing things when they didn't act right, parts of radios and sandwiches.

Geological, he thought. *I never have to wonder what I was doing yesterday. Yesterday is the top layer of the heap.* Speaking of which, hadn't Susan left her pregnant calico cat here yesterday when she had stopped by?

Wendell managed to find the phone on the third ring, right next to Susan's cat, who hissed at him, gave an odd twitch, and begin to extrude a shiny pink ratlike kitten.

Emergency mantra: just deliver the kittens.

By the time Wendell had midwived all five births, put together a makeshift crib from an old shoebox from which he dumped half a lifetime's accumulated yellowed check stubs and two mattress tags, and placed the newborns in eight new homes, (some of his friends would only agree to shared custody), he was weary and sweaty and still extremely thirsty.

He shambled into the kitchen, turned on the faucet, cupped his hand under it and slurped. In mid-slurp a wave of dizziness sent him reeling against the counter. *Damned water additives*, he thought. *Probably all that fluoride.*

Wendell felt peculiar, almost as if he were standing across the room watching himself. He did a quick mental inventory. Arms, legs, nose— yes, everything was still attached, still in place on his body, and he was still inside of it. His skin itched like a thousand ants were commuting across him to the breadbox. He scratched madly without relief.

But the itching was nothing compared to the odd compulsion he suddenly felt. Eerie. Not like him at all, not a bit. He felt the urge—a ravening need—to clean.

Under the sink he found a rotting pair of once-green rubber gloves with four fingers left on one hand and three (with tooth marks) on the other. Wendell pulled them on, grabbed the half-full container of cleanser, and upended it over the sink. A few flakes drifted down. He rapped the can hard against the counter. The top fell off and the remaining cleanser fell into the sink. He grunted and turned on the water.

Long after the gloves had fallen away from his hands, his fingertips had shriveled, and the hot water had turned tepid, Wendell was still scrubbing. He had moved on from the dishes to the large appliances and was now on his hands and knees in that no-man's-land between the refrigerator and the counter. He was tired, he was hungry, and he had to go to the bathroom. But every time he tried to concentrate on anything other than cleaning his thoughts skipped back to it like a needle caught in the groove of an old long-playing record album.

What's happening to me? he wondered.

Was it something he had eaten? Sugar in the granola or too much caffeine? He had heard about people getting stuck on dangerous cleaning jags and waking up three days later to discover that they had been washing the ceiling, stacking the dog food cans by color, or retyping the phone book according to assonance.

He didn't even like cleaning. But he couldn't make himself stop. He was tired but even worse, he was frightened because this mind that he had lived with for thirty-two years had suddenly narrowed down into one infinitely exhausting, unremitting track. Where was his creativity, his sidelights and highlights, his familiar digressions and enticing permutations? He couldn't even think of a new mantra to make sense of his confusion and calm himself. Still, his arm scrubbed on.

Wendell moved from the kitchen to the rest of the apartment, dusting, polishing, vacuuming. It was three a.m. before he had finished and he was worn beyond a frazzle.

When he awoke, ten hours later, his bed felt unfamiliar. The sheets were crisp, smooth, firmly tucked in place, and—he opened his eyes— oh God, they were even clean.

The sun poured through the window onto the brown rug. Wendell sat up in bed. Yes, it was brown. He remembered.

He felt a driving need to take a shower. To shave. To wash and rebraid his long greying hair. He itched in a thousand places. But when he opened the door to the bathroom, he froze.

The room was spotless. It smelled fresh and minty. The blue (ah, blue!) towels were folded neatly over the towel rack. The pale pink (pink!) shower curtain was tucked inside the tub. The sink was white. He could see his reflection in the chrome faucet.

Wendell began to gulp air. *Calm*, he thought. *I am completely calm. I have never been calmer. It's my new mantra.*

He stepped inside the bathroom. He might even have made it all the way to the toilet. But he noticed the grout, and that was his undoing.

Even the damned grout was clean.

Mantra forgotten, Wendell sank to his knees on the green threadbare rug and sobbed his heart out for the death of his old self, a self that never, in a zillion millennia, would have had it together enough to clean the mildewed yards of purple-splotched grout in his bathroom until they shined with the fervid whiteness of a public monument in a fascist state.

When he had emptied his tear ducts, panic took over and shook him like a slab of landfill in an earthquake.

The Rigelian awoke to the myriad sensations the human body afforded. Distracted by various reports from the nerve relays, the pores, the aural levels, the vascular pressure, all the workings of the basic human machine, the alien did not at first notice the earthling's dismay. But it soon became apparent that something was seriously wrong.

The alien peeked out of the earthling's eyes and saw the small room that the human had cleaned before going to sleep. Something about it seemed to be troubling the human, and the resultant respiratory and digestive distress made him uncomfortable to reside in. The alien groped around inside its host, trying to find a way to reassure him.

It hit the adrenaline trigger. No, that only seemed to intensify the agitation. The human shook harder.

Next it fiddled with the serotonin levels.

The human burst into tears yet again.

The Rigelian sighed and reached for the endorphin controls.

Ah, much better. The earthling relaxed, smiled, and emptied his bladder into the water-filled receptacle called a toilet. The alien nearly swooned with the pleasurable sensation. It tried to get the human to do it again, but apparently there was some restriction on the number of times this function could be repeated. Well, the alien could wait.

The earthling turned on the water sprayer in the enclosure next to the toilet, took off his sleep costume, and got under the spray. The Rigelian felt the delightful bombardment of a thousand tiny watery collisions with epidermis. *No wonder this human being was in such mental disarray,* it thought. With such a distracting variety of sensual input, each day must be too full of pleasure to allow much concentration on anything else.

The Rigelian was tempted to stay in the shower for several awareness periods. But it reminded itself that it was here for a purpose, and as pleasant as this water spray might be, it was time to get down to the serious business of testing the enemy. Investigate the target population's psychological tolerance for foreign matrices. There would be time enough for bladder-emptying and other delights once the Earth had been conquered.

Wendell felt peculiarly cheerful as he stepped out of the shower. He toweled off, dressed in his cleanest jeans and shirt, and decided to organize his paperwork.

He had never done anything like this before. "Don't think," he told himself. "Just do." Situational mantras seemed like a good improvisation. But once he lit into the job, he didn't have time to think, even about not thinking.

Three days later, Wendell sat upright in a straight-backed chair, surveying his domain.

The place was spotless. His papers were alphabetized and color-coded; his clothing had been washed, dried, folded, or hung. He didn't owe anybody any money. His apartment key was in plain sight. The kittens had all been given away and their mother returned to Susan. He had gotten a haircut and bought a pair of slacks. He was thinking of looking for a job. He was terrified.

He needed a friend, and in a hurry.

Emergency mantra time. "Find a friend," he intoned. "Just find a friend."

"Susan," he said, staring at the back of her head, which was bent over her keyboard. "You've got to help me."

"What's happening?" she mumbled, not turning around, not even looking up.

"Nothing. Everything."

"Beg pardon?"

"My grout is spotless, Susan." Wendell paused meaningfully. Surely she would intuit the problem.

"Wish I could say the same."

"You don't understand."

She sighed and turned to him. Her blue eyes were bloodshot and her short dark hair was frazzled. "Wendell, are you getting weird on me?"

"No. Yes. I mean, I don't know."

"Well, look. I've got a really gnarly deadline here. Since we can't seem to find anything wrong with you, or your grout, why don't we just agree that you're okay. Want to go to a movie next week? I'll call you."

Wendell found her patronizing attitude offensive, told her so, and left, pausing only to insult her cat.

He went back to his apartment, but the sight of it—neat, clean, *finished*—unnerved him. He needed fresh air, fast.

Out on the street, between the Palm Reader's bay window and the Sierra Club picket line in front of the Whole Bark pet supply store, Wendell bumped into a street person. The street person's hair might once have been blond but it was now a strange beige mat that sat high upon his head at an angle like a beret. He was wearing a purple shower curtain and pulling a shopping cart along behind him.

Wendell admired the shower curtain but thought that it needed several pockets and at least one zippered compartment with expandable accordion pleats.

"Goddadolla?" said the street person.

"Yeah." Wendell felt around in his pants and, with a familiar sense of apprehension, found a wad of neatly folded bills. He peeled one off. "Here."

"Thanks." The man put the money into an aperture in his curtain and leaned closer. His stench was amazing, like barbequed sneakers. Old ones. "End times are near."

"Oh, sure," Wendell said. But he couldn't help wondering if that was the reason why things—his life in particular—felt so peculiar, suddenly.

The street person nodded. "Be ready. They're coming."

Wendell wanted to walk away but he couldn't help asking, "Who?"

"The ones from up there." The bum pointed to the sulphurous five o'clock sky.

"Pilots?" Wendell said.

"Angels, you jerk. They'll eat our brains, spit out what they don't need like peach pits. Already eaten mine."

"They have?" Wendell stared at him. Just because the guy was crazy didn't mean that he was wrong.

"Yeah. So be careful. Get straight with Him-or-Her-or-Whatever." The street person paused, scratched his head as though he had lost his place, shrugged, and said, "Goddadolla?"

But Wendell was no longer listening. The idea of making peace with Him-or-Her-or-Whatever was suddenly very appealing. Compelling, even. There was just one problem. Wendell was sort of secular and eclectic and heavily nondenominational. He didn't particularly believe in one—or even several gods—although he hoped that his nonbelief wouldn't offend any or all of the theoretically omnipotent beings who might or might not take notice of it.

"Find a religious person," Wendell thought aloud, mantra-like. "Find a seriously religious person." And he began walking swiftly uphill toward the University's seminary complex.

A young blond man in a red and white rugby shirt was wedged furtively between two rose bushes outside the Albert Schweitzer cafeteria. He was puffing on a cigarette and, when Wendell walked by, apologized profusely for any smoke that might have drifted into Wendell's lungs. Wendell assured him that he was okay. Well, sort of okay, except for this spiritual problem he was having.

The young man, a seminary student named Jason, listened raptly, nodding between puffs.

"Grout?" he asked.

"Grout," Wendell said.

"Okay," Jason said, when Wendell had finished. "I think I know what's wrong with you."

"You do?" Hoped leaped in Wendell's stomach like a hungry puppy.

Jason smiled cheerfully. "Sure. You're possessed. There's a lot of that going around right now."

"Possessed? You mean by some sort of demon?" Wendell hadn't really considered the option.

"Demon, dybbuk, spirit," Jason said, and shrugged. "It all depends on your outlook. I can't say what it is for certain on such short observation."

"Well, what should I do?" Wendell asked.

Jason admitted that although his church was very strict about exorcisms, he personally was fascinated by Wendell's case and wouldn't mind a little field experience.

The alien noted the Earthling's dawning awareness of and pathetic attempts to cope with the foreign consciousness in its body. If the Rigelian had had a sense of humor it would have been amused. As it was, the alien merely added the datum to its already copious file and continued to observe. Of course the Terran would fail in its investigations. It was hopelessly primitive and its powers of concentration were minimal at best. In the Rigelian's opinion, the Terran race would be vastly improved by accepting the rule of superior beings with an evolved sense of organization.

The next morning, Jason the seminarian arrived at Wendell's apartment. In his arms were a three-foot white candle in the shape of a cross ("I got it from a vendor on Telegraph"), a jar of pickled garlic ("We can always eat it."), the Bible, and a dogeared paper-back copy of *The Exorcist*.

"Have you ever done this before?" Wendell asked.

"Oh, no. But I've talked about it a lot with my roommates after lights-out, and I'm a big movie fan. Is it all right with you if I run out for a smoke before we begin? Is there anywhere I won't be seen?"

Wendell gave him a saucer and planted him on the fire escape. When the seminarian came back inside a few minutes later his breath alone could have exorcised demons.

Jason cleared his throat a few times and they got down to business. Wendell sat in a chair in the middle of the room. Jason lit the cross-candle and raised it over his head three times. He picked up the Bible and put it in Wendell's lap. For good measure he put the jar of pickled garlic on top of it. Now he flipped through *The Exorcist*, pausing at one of the red-flagged pages.

"God and lord of all creation," he intoned, "let your mighty hand cast out this cruel demon from your servant, Wendell."

He slapped his own slightly clammy nicotine-stained hand over Wendell's forehead. "It is He who commands you, oh fetid and evil one, tremble in fear, Oh Prince of Evil, and begone! Come forth, yield the . . ."

"Mustard plaster," said a high, quavering voice.

"What?" said Wendell and Jason together.

"Use a mustard plaster. Or Ben Gay, that's good too."

The voice was familiar. "Mom!" Wendell cried.

"Wendell, you remember me!"

"Of course I do," he said, feeling insulted. "But mom, you're dead."

"It's not so bad, honey. Could be worse. Listen, Wendell, I know you think there's some demon or something possessing you, but I've looked around and I don't see anybody in here besides me. You're probably just overstimulated. Did you have any sugar? You know how you get with glucose."

Wendell sighed. "No, mom."

"Well, all right. If you really think there's somebody or thing here, just tell it to leave. Go on, dear, speak up for yourself. Be mommy's great big man."

Wendell opened his mouth to defend his masculinity, when to his horror he recognized the earnest baritone of his high school history teacher, Mr. Severinson.

"Have you been reading trash again, Wendell? I told you . . ."

Jason had picked up the cross again and was intoning, "It is He who commands you, He who expels you, He who . . ."

". . . not to hang out with these hippie types and learn to direct your energy."

A new voice, flat and nasal, chimed in. "A personality change is often the first sign of the fragmentation of the already fragile ego."

Wendell allowed himself a tiny smile. It was the voice of his first—and favorite—psychiatrist, tiny Dr. Gow. The one who had arranged his permanent disability status.

"Hey, you quack," cried Wendell's mother. "Get away from my precious boy or I'll fragment you."

". . . Lord grant that this vileness be gone . . ."

"It's always hippie trash and garbage."

Wendell squirmed as the voices of three long-dead great-aunts whom he'd dubbed "The Harpy Trio" chimed in. And above them in the background, was that the trilling laugh of crazy Marsha, his second cousin-by-marriage? And behind her, the whispered suggestions of a stranger who had once tried to pick him up at a movie? Lecturing, declaiming, chiding, urging, while in the background, like a mad leitmotif played much too fast, ran the theme song to a cartoon show he had watched every Saturday morning when he was nine.

He struggled to free himself from the chair and the voices, the snakepit of the past. His head was beginning to feel very noisy and crowded but not in any good way.

The Rigelian had been relaxing for a moment, contemplating the coming invasion. It would be a snap. Such confused, chaotic animals, humans. So easily dominated and organized.

The swarm was poised on Rigel 9 awaiting the scout's signal. Soon the attack forces would be launched across the dark vastness of space and nothing would be able to stop them.

"Excuse me."

The alien stared in amazement at the short, round, neatly coiffed, impeccably attired female human addressing him. She was unmistakeably noncorporeal, an interesting fact. The alien had thought that Homo sapiens were only able to communicate while in the body. Obviously, this was not always the case.

"Would you mind telling me just what you think you're doing inside my son's head?"

Other post-life incarnations began to manifest themselves.

"What's the matter, you don't have your own head to hang around in?"

"Unhand this young man."

"You leave Wendell alone. He's a nice boy."

"Very sensitive."

"Sweet."

The alien tried to defend itself. It feinted with its jagged pseudohorns. It gnashed its long and pointed pseudoteeth. All to no effect. Never had it encountered anything like this . . . this collective energy.

Wendell's mother raised her wide leatherette purse and whirled it on its chain strap around her head like a lariat.

Mr. Severinson pulled a sleek can of mace from the pocket of his tweed jacket. Dr. Gow brandished *The Ego and The Id* in his left hand and *Beyond the Pleasure Principle* in his right. Crazy Marsha whipped out a set of steaming orange hair rollers.

The alien screamed and ran toward the deepest recesses of Wendell's mind. But Wendell's posse of spirits pursued it relentlessly.

"Get out of here!"

"Beat it."

"Hit the road, Jack!"

They showed it terrible things: failed exams, late-night lectures, fumbling sexual encounters, toilet training.

The alien reeled under the onslaught, sustaining lacerating bruises to its psychological matrices.

I must get away, it thought. *Back to safety, back to Rigel 9. Must warn the others. The humans have a secret weapon lodged in their brains. Memories capable of triggering the emotions. Oh, awful, horrendous, unthinkable. How do they bear the pain? I must flee. Nothing is worth this. Not even fingers.*

Meanwhile, outside, in Wendell's living room, Jason droned on, improvising, "Ad hominum, donutum, inadvertum." In the middle of a particularly intense excoriation he was overtaken by a sputum-spraying coughing fit.

"Yuck," said the phantom mob behind Wendell's forehead.

There was a scurrying, a great whoosh and gabble, tinny giggles, and a wheezing bagpipe arpeggio which slowly died away to silence.

The Rigelian wandered over the streets of Berkeley, a transparent wisp sailing on its pseudowing. *I must go home*, it thought. *Yes, quickly now, I must tell them, warn them, before it's too late.*

But slowly, horrifyingly, the alien realized that in the turmoil of escaping from the earthling's brain and in the agony of its injuries it had somehow forgotten the all-important command for intersystem transport.

I had it here a minute ago, it thought. *Was it on a slip of paper? Perhaps I wrote it on my pseudofoot. Didn't there used to be a pile of stuff here? Maybe the cat ate it. Or gave it to Susan. I could call her, she's a programmer, she could look for it with a search program. No, better yet, I'll call Information. No, they take too long. Maybe Jason stays up all night. I'll bet he knows . . .*

Wendell leaned against the cushions of his old flowered sofa and took a deep, careful breath. He felt purged, as though he'd just had a really good rolfing. And he was blessedly alone. Jason had taken his cigarettes, his pickled garlic, his cough, and gone. The apartment was silent, no voices, no memories, no cats or kittens. It was almost holy.

The stillness was a perfect repository for thought. Wendell sat, comfortably at one with his mind. *Just think*, he mused, *something or other was inside my head with me, trying to eat my brain. Seriously weird. But it's gone. Jason and my personal demons sent it packing, and now I'm okay.*

He opened his eyes, stretched luxuriously, and looked around. The saucer that Jason had used for an ashtray was sitting, abandoned, on the windowsill. Grey and white ashes had coagulated in its center declivity.

Wendell stared at it. He shut his eyes. He opened them and looked at the ashes, hard.

He didn't feel the slightest urge to pick the saucer up, to dump its contents in the garbage, to rinse it off, dry it, or put it away in the cupboard.

Really okay.

He was free. The exorcism, or whatever, had worked. No boojums or dybbuks or Republican cleaning fascists were playing hide-and-go-seek inside his cerebellum. He felt sure of it.

He kicked off his shoes and left them in the middle of the living room floor. He unbraided his hair and, giggling with relief, shook his head. He pulled off his socks, rolled them into a ball, and bowled them down the hallway. As he watched them roll to a stop he pounded his hands against the cushions with glee.

The phone rang. But Wendell was too busy thinking to answer it. There was work to be done. The apartment really needed shaping up. For starters, a pulley system from the pantry to the living room, yes, wall to wall. He would devise a clip that would roll along the tiger tail wire and hold chip bags at the same time, and maybe an insulated noose to carry soda cans and keep them cold . . .

As Wendell planned he intoned his new mantra: "I think therefore I am and I am because I think."

Nodding, he extended his long pointed pseudotail and scratched his back contentedly.

FORTITUDE

by David Brin

Humans were delighted to have encountered another, more advanced intelligent race. But the aliens were thinking, "Well, there goes the neighborhood!" Fortunately, Earthlings discovered they had a card trick to play . . . what might be called a royal flush.

⚹ ⚹ ⚹

DAVID BRIN's roster of accomplishments might run longer than his story here awaiting the reader's attention, but here goes . . . He is a scientist (Ph.D. in physics from the University of California at San Diego), speaker, technical consultant and world-known author. His novels have been New York Times *bestsellers, winning multiple Hugo, Nebula and other awards. At least a dozen have been translated into more than twenty languages. His 1989 ecological thriller,* Earth, *foreshadowed global warming, cyberwarfare and near-future trends such as the World Wide Web. His 2012 novel* Existence *extends this type of daring, near future extrapolation by exploring bio-engineering, intelligence and how to maintain an open-creative civilization. His post-apocalyptic novel,* The Postman, *became a 1998 movie, directed by Kevin Costner. Brin serves on advisory committees dealing with subjects as diverse as national defense and homeland security, astronomy and space exploration, SETI and nanotechnology, future/prediction and philanthropy. He has served since 2010 on the council of external advisers for NASA's Innovative and Advanced*

Concepts group (NIAC), which supports the most inventive and potentially ground-breaking new endeavors. In 2013 David Brin helped to establish the Arthur C. Clarke Center for Human Imagination at UCSD, where he was honored as a "distinguished alumnus" and where he was thereafter a Visiting Scholar in Residence. He has had other visiting scholar positions including one at Bard College, in 2015. His non-fiction book—The Transparent Society: Will Technology Force Us to Choose Between Freedom and Privacy?—deals with secrecy in the modern world. It won the Freedom of Speech Prize from the American Library Association. As a public "scientist/futurist" David appears frequently on TV, including, most recently, on many episodes of "The Universe" and on the History Channel's best-watched show (ever) "Life After People." David's science fictional Uplift Universe series explores a future when humans genetically engineer higher animals like dolphins to become equal members of our civilization. He also recently tied up the loose ends left behind by the late Isaac Asimov. Foundation's Triumph brings to a grand finale Asimov's famed Foundation Universe. As a speaker and on television, he shares unique insights—serious and humorous—about ways that changing technology may affect our future lives. Brin lives in San Diego County with his wife, three children, and a hundred very demanding trees. And for more, much more, go to http://www.davidbrin.com/about.html

THE ALIENS seemed especially concerned over matters of genealogy.

"It is the only way we can be sure with whom we are dealing," said the spokes-being for the Galactic Federation. Terran-Esperanto words emerged through a translator device affixed to the creature's speaking-vent, between purple, compound eyes. "Citizen species of the Federation will have nothing to do with you humans. Not until you can be properly introduced."

"But *you're* speakin' to us, right now!" Jane Fingal protested. "You're not makin' bugger-all sense, mate."

Jane was our astronomer aboard the *Straits of Magellan*. She had first spotted the wake of the N'Gorm ship as it raced by, far swifter than any Earth vessel, and it had been Jane's idea to pulse our engines, giving off weak gravity waves to attract their attention. For several days she had labored to help solve the language problem, until a meeting could be arranged between our puny ETS survey probe and the mighty N'Gorm craft.

Still, I was surprised when Kwenzi Mobutu, the Zairean anthropologist, did not object to Jane's presence in the docking bubble, along with our official contact team. Kwenzi seldom missed a chance to play up tension between Earth's two greatest powers— Royal Africa and the Australian Imperium—even during this historic first encounter with a majestic alien civilization.

The alien slurped mucousy sounds into its mouthpiece, and out came more computer-generated words.

"You misunderstand. I am merely a convenience, a construct-entity, fashioned to be as much like you as possible, thereby to facilitate your evaluation. I have no name, and will return to the vats when this is done."

Fashioned to be like us? I must have stared. (Everyone else did.) The being in front of us was bipedal and had two arms. On top were objects and organs we had tentatively named ears and a mouth. Beyond that, he (She? It?) seemed about as alien as could be.

"Yipes!" Jane commented. "I'd hate to meet your *boss* in a dark alley, if you're the handsomest bloke they could come up with."

I saw Mobutu, the African aristocrat, smile. That's when I realized why he had not vetoed Jane's presence, but relished it. *He knows this meeting is being recorded for posterity. If she makes a fool of herself here, at the most solemn meeting of races, it could win points against Australians back home.*

"As I have tried to explain," the alien reiterated. "You will not meet my 'boss' or any other citizen entity. Not until we are satisfied that your lineage is worthy."

While our Israeli and Tahitian xenobiologists conferred over this surprising development, our Patagonian captain stared out through the docking bubble at the Federation ship whose great flanks arched away, gleaming, in all directions. Clearly, he yearned to bring these advanced technologies home to the famed shipyards of Tierra del Fuego.

"Perhaps I can be helpful in this matter," Kwenzi Mobutu offered confidently. "I have some small expertise. When it comes to tracking one's family tree, I doubt any other human aboard can match my own genealogy."

His smile was a gleaming white contrast against gorgeously-perfect black skin, the sort of rich complexion that the trendy people from pole to pole had been using chemicals to emulate, when we left home.

"Even before the golden placards of Abijian were discovered, my family line could be traced back to the great medieval households of Ghana. But since the recovery of those sacred records, it has been absolutely verified that my lineage goes all the way to the black pharaohs of the XXth Dynasty—an unbroken chain of four thousand years."

Mobutu's satisfaction faded when the alien replied with a dismissive wave.

"That interval is far too brief. Nor are we interested in the time-thread of mere individuals. Larger groups concern us."

Jane Fingal chuckled, and Mobutu whirled on her angrily.

"Your attitude suits a mongrel nation whose ancestors were criminal transportees, and whose 'emperor' is chosen at a *rugby match*!"

"Hey. Our king'd whip yours any day, even half-drunk and with 'is arse in a sling."

"Colleagues!" I hastened to interrupt. "These are serious matters. A little decorum, if you please?"

The two shared another moment's hot enmity, until Nechemia Meyers spoke up.

"Perhaps they refer to *cultural* continuity. If we can demonstrate that one of our social traditions has a long history, stretching back—"

"—five thousand years?" inserted Mohandas Nayyal, our linguist from Delhi Commune. "Of course the Hindi tradition, as carried by the Vedas, goes back easily that far."

"*Actually*," Meyers continued, a bit miffed. "I was thinking more along the lines of *six* thousand—"

He cut short as the alien let out a warbling sigh, waving both "hands."

"Once again, you misconstrue. The genealogy we seek *is* genetic, but a few thousand of your years is wholly inadequate."

Jane muttered— "Bugger! It's like dickering with a Pattie over the price of a bleeding iceberg . . . no offense, Skipper."

The captain returned a soft smile. Patagonians are an easy-going lot, til you get down to business.

"Well then," Mobutu resumed, nodding happily. "I think we can satisfy our alien friends, and win Federation membership, on a purely *biochemical* basis. For many years now, the Great Temple in Abijian has gathered DNA samples from every sub-race on Earth, correlating and sorting to trace out our genetic relationships. Naturally, African bloodlines were found to be the least mutated from the central line of inheritance—"

Jane groaned again, but this time Kwenzi ignored her.

"—stretching back to our fundamental common ancestor, that beautiful, dark ancestress of all human beings, the one variously called Eva, or M'tum, who dwelled on the eastern fringes of what is now the Zairean Kingdom, over *three million years ago!*"

So impressive was Mobutu's dramatic delivery that even the least sanguine of our crew felt stirred, fascinated and somewhat awed. But then the N'Gorm servant-entity vented another of its frustrated sighs.

"I perceive that I am failing in my mission to communicate with lesser beings. Please allow me to try once again.

"We in the Federation are constantly being plagued by young, upstart species, rising out of planetary nurseries and immediately yammering for attention, claiming rights of citizenship in our ancient culture. At times, it has been suggested that we should routinely sterilize such places—filthy little worlds—or at least eliminate noisy, adolescent infestations by targeting their early stages with radio-seeking drones. But the *Kutathi*, who serve as judges and law-givers in the Federation, have ruled this impermissible. There are few crimes worse than meddling in the natural progress of a nursery world. All we can do is snub the newcomers, and restrict them to their home systems until they have matured enough for decent company."

"That's *all*?" The Captain spoke for the first time, aghast at what this meant—an end to the Earth's bold ventures with interstellar travel. Crude our ships might be, by galactic standards, but humanity was proud of them. They were a unifying force, binding fractious nations in a common cause. It was awful to imagine that our expedition might be the last.

The translator apparently failed to convey the Captain's sarcasm. The alien envoy-entity nodded in solemn agreement.

"Yes, that is all. So you may rejoice, in your own pathetic way, that your world is safe for you to use up or destroy any way you see fit, since that is the typical way most puerile species finish their brief lifespans. If, by some chance, you escape this fate, you will eventually be allowed to send forth *your* best and brightest to serve in carefully chosen roles, earning eventual acceptance on the lowest rungs of proper society."

Jane Fingal growled. "Why you puffed-up pack of pseudo-pommie bast—"

I cut in with urgent speed. "Excuse me, but there is one thing I fail to understand. You spoke earlier of an 'evaluation.' Does this mean that our fate is *not* automatic?"

The alien emissary regarded me for a long time, as if pondering whether I deserved an answer, Finally, it must have decided I was not that much lower than my crewmates, anyway. It acknowledged my query with a nod.

"There *is* an exception—if you can prove a relationship with a citizen race. To determine that possibility was the purpose of my query about species-lineage."

"Ah, now it becomes clear," Mohandas Nayyal said. "You want to know if we are *genetically related* to one of your high-born castes. Does this imply that those legends may be true? That star beings have descended, from time to time, to engage in sexual congress with our ancestors? By co-mingling their seed with ours, they meant to generously endow and improve our . . ."

He trailed off as we all saw the N'Gorm quiver. Somehow, disgust was conveyed quite efficiently across its expressive "face."

"Please, do not be repulsive in your bizarre fantasies. The behavior you describe is beyond contemplation, even by the mentally ill. Not only is it physically and biologically absurd, but it assumes the high-born might *wish* to improve the stock of bestial nuisances. Why in the universe would they want to do such a thing?"

Ignoring the bald insult, Meyers, the exobiologist added—

"It's unlikely for another reason. Human DNA has been probed and analyzed for three centuries. We have a pretty good idea where most of it came from. We're creatures of the Earth, no doubt about it."

When he saw members of the contact team glaring at him, Meyers shrugged. "Oh, it would all come out in time, anyway. Don't you think they'd analyze any claim we made?"

"Correct," buzzed the translator. "And we would bill you for the effort."

"Well, I'm still confused," claimed our Uzbecki memeticist. "You make it sound as if there is no way we could be related to one of your citizen-races, so why this grilling about our genealogy?"

"A formality, required by law. In times past, a few exceptional cases won status by showing that they possessed common genes with highborn ones."

"And how did these commonalities come about?" Mobutu asked, still miffed over the rejection of his earlier claims.

The N'Gorm whistled yet another sigh. "Not all individuals of every species behave circumspectly. Some, of noble birth, have been known to go down to planets, seeking thrills, or testing their mettle to endure filth and heavy gravity."

"In other words, they go slumming!" Jane Fingal laughed. "Now *those* are the only blokes I'd care to meet, in your whole damn Federation."

I caught Jane's eye, gesturing for restraint. She needn't make things worse than they already were. The whole of Earth would watch recordings of what passed here today.

Nechemia Meyers shook his head. "I can see where all this is leading. When galactics go *slumming*, as Jane colorfully put it, they risk unleashing alien genes into the ecosystem of a nursery world. This is forbidden interference in the natural development of such planets. It *also* makes possible a genetic link that could prove embarrassing later, when that world spawns a star-travelling race."

The translator buzzed gratification. "At last, I have succeeded in conveying the basic generalities. Now, before we take your ship in tow, and begin the quarantine of your wretched home system, I am required by law to offer you a chance. Do you wish formally to claim such a genetic link to one of our citizen races? Remember that we will investigate in detail, at your expense."

A pall seemed to settle over the assembled humans. This was not as horrible as some of the worst literary fantasies about alien contact, but it was pretty bad. Apparently, the galaxy was ruled by an aristocracy of age and precedence. One that jealously guarded its status behind a veneer of hypocritical law.

"How can we *know* whether or not to make such a claim!" Kwenzi Mobutu protested. "Unless we meet your high castes for ourselves."

"That will not happen. Not unless your claim is upheld."

"But—"

"It hardly matters," inserted Nechemia, glumly.

We turned and the Captain asked— "What do you mean?"

"I mean that we cannot make such a claim. The evidence refutes it. All we need is to look at the history of life on Earth.

"Consider, friends. Why did we think for so long that we were alone in the cosmos? It wasn't just that our radio searches for intelligent life turned up nothing, decade after decade. Aliens *could* have efficient technologies that make them abandon radio, the way we gave up signal-drums. This is exactly what we found to be the case.

"No, a much stronger argument for our uniqueness lay in the sedimentary rocks of our own world.

"If intelligent life was plentiful, someone would invent starships and travel. Simple calculations showed that just one such outbreak, if it flourished, could fill the galaxy with its descendants in less than fifty million years . . . and that assumed ship technology far cruder than this N'Gorm dreadnought hovering nearby."

He gestured at the sleek, gleaming hull outside, that had accelerated so nimbly in response to Jane Fingal's hail.

"Imagine such a life-swarm, sweeping across the galaxy, settling every habitable world in sight. It's what we *humans* thought we'd do, once we escaped Earth's bonds, according to most science fiction tales. A prairie fire of colonization that radically changes every world it touches, forever mixing and re-shuffling each planet's genetic heritage."

The emissary conceded. "It is illegal, but it has happened, from time to time."

Meyers nodded. "Maybe it occurred elsewhere, but not on Earth."

"How can you be sure?" I asked.

"Because we can read Earth's biography in her rocks. For more than two billion years, our world was 'prime real estate,' as one great 20th century writer once put it. It had oceans and a decent atmosphere, but no living residents higher than crude, prokaryotes—bacteria and algae—simmering in the sea. In all that time, until the Eukaryotic Explosion half a billion years ago, any alien interference would have profoundly changed the course of life on our world."

Jane Fingal edged forward. "This 'explosion' you spoke of. What was that?"

"The *Eukaryotic Explosion*," Meyers explained, "occurred about 560 million years ago, when there evolved nucleated cells, crammed with sophisticated organelles. Soon after, there arose multi-celled organisms, invertebrates, vertebrates, fishes, dinosaurs, and primates. But the important datum is the two billion years before that, when even the most careful of colonizations would have utterly changed Earth's ecology, by infecting it with advanced alien organisms we would later see in sediments. Even visitors who flushed their *toilets* carelessly . . ."

Meyers trailed off as our astronomer made choking sounds, covering her mouth. Finally, Jane burst out with deep guffaws, laughing so hard that she nearly doubled over. We waited until finally Jane wiped her eyes and explained.

"Sorry, mates. It's just that . . . well, somethin' hit me when Nechemia mentioned holy altars."

I checked my memory files and recalled the euphemism, popular in Australian English. Every Aussie home is said to contain at least one porcelain "altar," where adults who have over-indulged with food or drink often kneel and pray for relief, invoking the beer deities, "Ralph" or "Ruth." On weekdays, these altars have other, more mundane uses.

Kwenzi Mobutu seemed torn between outrage over Jane's behavior and delight that it was all being recorded.

"And what insight did this offer you?" He asked with a tightly controlled voice.

"Oh, with your interest in genealogy you'll love this, Kwenzi," Jane assured, in a friendly tone. She turned to Nechemia. "You say there couldn't have been any alien interference before the Eukaryotic Explosion, and after that, everything on Earth seems to be part of the same tree of life, right? Neither of those long periods seems to show any trace of outside interference."

The Israeli nodded, and Jane smiled.

"But what about the explosion, *itself*? Isn't that *just* the sort of sudden event you say would be visible in rocks, if alien toilets ever ever got dumped on Earth?"

Meyers frowned, knotting his brow. "Well . . . ye-e-e-es. Off hand, I cannot think of any perfect refutation, providing you start out assuming a general similarity in amino and nucleic acid coding . . . and compatible protein structures. That's not too far-fetched. From that point on, prokaryotic and early eukaryotic genes mixed, but the eukaryote seed stock *might* have come, quite suddenly —"

A short squeal escaped the alien emissary.

"This is true? Your life history manifested such a sudden transformation on so basic a level? From un-nucleated to fully competent multicellular organisms? How rapid was this change?"

Meyers shook his head. "No one has been able to parse the boundary thinly enough to tell. But clearly it was on the order of a million years, or less. Some hypothesize a chain of fluke mutations, leveraging on each other rapidly. But that explanation *did* always seem a bit too pat. There are just too many sudden, revolutionary traits to explain . . ."

He looked up at Jane, with a new light in his eyes. "You aren't joking about this, are you? I mean, we could be onto something! I wonder why this never occurred to us before?"

The Captain uttered a short laugh. "Trust an Australian to think of it. They don't give a damn *what* you think about their ancestors."

A flurry of motion drew our eyes to the tunnel leading to the N'Gorm ship, just in time to catch sight of the envoy-entity, fleeing our presence in a state of clear panic. A seal hissed shut and vibrations warned that the huge vessel was about to detach. We made our own prudent exit, hurrying back to our ship.

Last to re-board was Kwenzi Mobutu, wearing a bleak look on his face, paler than I had ever seen him. The African aristocrat winced as Jane Fingal offered a heartfelt, Australian prayer of benediction, aimed at the retreating N'Gorm frigate.

"May Ruth follow you everywhere, mates, and keep you busy at her altar."

Jane laughed again, and finished with a slurpy, *flushing* sound.

Many years have passed since that epiphany on the spacelanes. Of all of the humans present when we held the fateful meeting, only I, made of durable silicon and brass, still live to tell an eyewitness-tale.

By the laws of Earth, I am equal to any biological human being, despite galactic rules that would have me enslaved. No noble genes lurk in *my* cells. No remnants of ruffians who went *slumming* long ago, on a planet whose only life forms merged in scummy mats at the fringes of a tepid sea. I carry no DNA from those alien rapscallions, those high-born ones who carelessly gave Earth an outlawed gift, a helpful push. But my kind was *designed* by the heirs of that little indiscretion, so I can share the poignant satisfaction brought by recent events.

For decade after decade, ever since that fateful meeting between the stars, we have chased Federation ships, who always fled like scoundrels evading a subpoena. Sometimes our explorers would arrive at one of their habitat clusters, only to find vast empty cities, abandoned in frantic haste to avoid meeting us, or to prevent our emissaries from uttering one terrible word—*Cousin*!

It did them no good in the long run. Eventually, we made contact with the august, honest *Kutathi*, the judges, who admitted our petition before them.

The galactic equivalent of a cosmo-biological paternity suit.

And now, the ruling has come down at last, leaving Earth's accountants to scratch their heads in awe over the damages we have been awarded, and the official status we have won.

As for our unofficial *social position*, that is another matter. Our having the right to vote in high councils will not keep most of the haughty aliens from snubbing Earthlings for a long time to come. (Would *we* behave any better, if a strain of our intestinal flora suddenly began demanding a place at the banquet table? I hope so, but you can never tell until you face the situation for yourself.)

None of that matters as much as the freedom—to come and go as we please. To buy and sell technologies. To learn . . . and eventually to teach.

The Kutathi judges kindly told our emissaries that humans seem to have a knack, a talent, for *the law*. Perhaps it will be our calling, the Kutathi said. It makes an odd kind of sense, given the jokes people have long told about the genetic nature of lawyers.

Well, so be it.

Among humans of all races and nations, there is agreement. There is common cause. Something has to change. The snooty ways of high-born clans must give way, and we are just the ones to help make it happen. We'll find *other* loopholes in this rigid, inane class system, other ways to help spring more young races out of quarantine, until at last the stodgy old order crumbles.

Anyway, who cares what aristocrats think of us, their illegitimate cousins, the long-fermented fruit of their bowels?

Jane Fingal wrote our anthem, long ago. It is a stirring song, hauntingly kindred to *Waltzing Matilda*, full of verve, gumption, and a spirit of rebellion. Like the *1812 Overture*, it can't properly be played without an added instrument. Only in this case, the guest soloist plays no cannon, but a porcelain *altar*, one that swishes, churns and gurgles with the soulful strains of destiny.

THEY'RE MADE OUT OF MEAT

by Terry Bisson

Those poor, pathetic humans are more to be pitied than scorned (not that any self-respecting extraterrestrial would associate with them). They can't help it—it's in their makeup.

❊ ❊ ❊

TERRY BALLANTINE BISSON a native of Kentucky, a resident of New York City for "some thirty years," now residing on the west coast, has worked as an auto mechanic and as a magazine and book editor. Though good auto mechanics are in short supply, we should all be grateful that he published his first novel in 1981, and has been a working science fiction writer ever since. Politically he was part of the New Left, associated with the John Brown Anti-Klan Ctte and the May 19 Communist Organization. His novels include Wyrldmaker, Talking Man, Fire on the Mountain, Voyage to the Red Planet, Pirates of the Universe, The Pickup Artist, Numbers Don't Lie, *and* Any Day Now. *His short fiction has appeared in* Playboy, *Asimov's,* Omni, Fantasy & Science Fiction, Harper's, Socialism & Democracy, *Tor.com,* Southern Exposure, Infinite Matrix, *and* Flurb. *His story collections include* Bears Discover Fire, In the Upper Room and Other Unlikely Stories, Greetings, Billy's Book, *and* TVA Baby. *His short story, "Bears Discover Fire" won the Nebula and Hugo awards, the Theodore Sturgeon short fiction award, and the* Asimov's *and* Locus *readers' awards. Other awards and honors he has received are the Phoenix Award, France's Gran Prix de l'Imaginaire, a second Nebula for his short story, "macs," a Fellowship in Screenwriting and Playwriting by the New York Foundation for the Arts, and his induction into the Owensboro, Kentucky Hall of Fame. He was selected by the estate of Walter M. Miller, Jr. to complete Miller's* Saint Leibowitz and the Wild Horse Woman, *the unfinished sequel to the SF classic,* A Canticle for Leibowitz. *He is the editor of PM Press's Outspoken Author series which features such SF icons as Michael Moorcock, Ursula K. LeGuin, Rudy Rucker, Cory Doctorow and Kim Stanley Robinson. In his copious spare time, Bisson hosts an author reading series, SFinSF, in San Franscisco. The superhumanly busy Mr. Bisson lives in Oakland, California with his companion of 40 years, Judy Jensen. For much more about him, including his nonfiction, screenwriting, novelizations, scripting for comics, etc., etc., including the stage and film adaptations of the brilliant short story which follows, visit terrybisson.com.*

"They're made out of meat."

"Meat?"

"Meat. They're made out of meat."

"Meat?"

"There's no doubt about it. We picked up several from different parts of the planet, took them aboard our recon vessels, and probed them all the way through. They're completely meat."

"That's impossible. What about the radio signals? The messages to the stars?"

"They use the radio waves to talk, but the signals don't come from them. The signals come from machines."

"So who made the machines? That's who we want to contact."

"*They* made the machines. That's what I'm trying to tell you. Meat made the machines."

"That's ridiculous. How can meat make a machine? You're asking me to believe in sentient meat."

"I'm not asking you, I'm telling you. These creatures are the only sentient race in that sector and they're made out of meat."

"Maybe they're like the orfolei. You know, a carbon-based intelligence that goes through a meat stage."

"Nope. They're born meat and they die meat. We studied them for several of their life spans, which didn't take long. Do you have any idea what's the life span of meat?"

"Spare me. Okay, maybe they're only part meat. You know, like the weddilei. A meat head with an electron plasma brain inside."

"Nope. We thought of that, since they do have meat heads, like the weddilei. But I told you, we probed them. They're meat all the way through."

"No brain?"

"Oh, there's a brain all right. It's just that the brain is *made out of meat*! That's what I've been trying to tell you."

"So . . . what does the thinking?"

"You're not understanding, are you? You're refusing to deal with what I'm telling you. The brain does the thinking. The meat."

"Thinking meat! You're asking me to believe in thinking meat!"

"Yes, thinking meat! Conscious meat! Loving meat. Dreaming meat. The meat is the whole deal! Are you beginning to get the picture or do I have to start all over?"

"Omigod. You're serious then. They're made out of meat."

"Thank you. Finally. Yes. They are indeed made out of meat. And they've been trying to get in touch with us for almost a hundred of their years."

"Omigod. So what does this meat have in mind?"

"First it wants to talk to us. Then I imagine it wants to explore the Universe, contact other sentiences, swap ideas and information. The usual."

"We're supposed to talk to meat."

"That's the idea. That's the message they're sending out by radio. 'Hello. Anyone out there. Anybody home.' That sort of thing."

"They actually do talk, then. They use words, ideas, concepts?"

"Oh, yes. Except they do it with meat."

"I thought you just told me they used radio."

"They do, but what do you think is *on* the radio? Meat sounds. You know how when you slap or flap meat, it makes a noise? They talk by flapping their meat at each other. They can even sing by squirting air through their meat."

"Omigod. Singing meat. This is altogether too much. So what do you advise?"

"Officially or unofficially?"

"Both."

"Officially, we are required to contact, welcome and log in any and all sentient races or multibeings in this quadrant of the Universe, without prejudice, fear or favor. Unofficially, I advise that we erase the records and forget the whole thing."

"I was hoping you would say that."

"It seems harsh, but there is a limit. Do we really want to make contact with meat?"

"I agree one hundred percent. What's there to say? 'Hello, meat. How's it going?' But will this work? How many planets are we dealing with here?"

"Just one. They can travel to other planets in special meat containers, but they can't live on them. And being meat, they can only travel through C space. Which limits them to the speed of light and makes the possibility of their ever making contact pretty slim. Infinitesimal, in fact."

"So we just pretend there's no one home in the Universe."

"That's it."

"Cruel. But you said it yourself, who wants to meet meat? And the ones who have been aboard our vessels, the ones you probed? You're sure they won't remember?"

"They'll be considered crackpots if they do. We went into their heads and smoothed out their meat so that we're just a dream to them."

"A dream to meat! How strangely appropriate, that we should be meat's dream."

"And we marked the entire sector *unoccupied*."

"Good. Agreed, officially and unofficially. Case closed. Any others? Anyone interesting on that side of the galaxy?"

"Yes, a rather shy but sweet hydrogen core cluster intelligence in a class nine star in G445 zone. Was in contact two galactic rotations ago, wants to be friendly again."

"They always come around."

"And why not? Imagine how unbearably, how unutterably cold the Universe would be if one were all alone . . ."

ALIEN STONES

by Gene Wolfe

The starship had encountered a gigantic alien ship drifting between the stars, apparently abandoned with no beings aboard—until one of the humans exploring the alien vessel's interior mysteriously disappeared.

※ ※ ※

GENE WOLFE *is one of, if not* the *most critically-praised and award-winningest writers in science fiction and fantasy (if he sees a difference; he has been quoted as saying that "All novels are fantasy. Some are more honest about it."). He has received two Nebula Awards, four World Fantasy Awards, a John W. Campbell Memorial Award, an August Derleth Award, a British SF Association Award, a Rhysling Award, seven Locus Awards, and has been nominated for a Hugo Award eight times, but with no wins, which is . . . interesting . . . in view of some of the specimens of thin gruel that have lately won that tarnished rocket. And when it comes to lifetime achievement, he has received the World Fantasy Award and the Science Fiction Writers of America's awards for just that. In 2007, he was inducted into the Science Fiction Hall of Fame. All that, and, according to Wikipedia, in his other life as an engineer, he contributed to the machine used to make Pringle's Potato Chips. Of such things is immortality made. Ursula K. LeGuin has stated, "Wolfe is our Melville." I don't recall his writing about pursuit of great white whales so far, or even of scriveners, but the millennium is still young. In the* *meantime, go read this enigmatic, multi-layered yarn about another kind of pursuit. Or pursuits.*

"HEADING UNCHANGED," Gladiator said. "Speed unchanged." She flashed figures on the cathode-ray-tube terminal at the command console to substantiate it.

Daw nodded. Twenty-eight firing studs stretched along the mid-band of the console. They would permit him, Daw, alone on the bridge (as he liked it) to launch every missile aboard the ship; even if Gladiator's central processing unit were knocked out or under system overload, there would be strike vectors from the independent minicomputers that clung, embryonic self-brains, to the walls of the missile foramens.

But there was no need for the minis. His ship was untouched; he could order Gladiator herself to do the shooting. Instead he asked, "Drive?"

And Gladiator answered: "No indication of drive in use."

"Okay."

"Shall present course be maintained? Present course is a collision course in point three one hours."

"Match their velocity and lay us alongside. How long?"

"One point forty-four hours."

"Do it. Meantime maintain battle stations." Daw flipped on his console mike without touching the switch that would have put his own image on the terminals in every compartment of the ship. Naval tradition decreed that when the captain spoke he should be seen as well as heard, but Daw had watched tapes of his own long, brown face as he announced, in what he felt to be unbearably stiff fashion, various unimportances, and he found it impossible to believe that his crew, seeing the same stretched cheeks and preposterous jaw, would not snicker.

"This is your captain. The ship sighted last night is still on her course." Daw chewed his lower lip for a moment, trying to decide just what to say next. The crew must be alerted, but it would be best if they were not alarmed. "There is no indication, I repeat, no indication, that she is aware of our presence. Possibly she doesn't want to scare us off—she may want peace, or she may just have something up her sleeve. Possibly something's wrong with her sensors. My own guess—which isn't worth any more than yours—is that she's a derelict; there's no sign of drive, and we haven't been able to reach her on any frequency. But we have to stay sharp. Battle conditions until further notice."

He flicked off the mike switch. Several como lights were blinking and he selected one: the reactor module. Mike switch again. "What is it, Neal?"

"Captain, if you could give me a breakdown on the radiation they're putting out, it might be possible for me to work up an estimate of how long it's been since they've used their drive."

"I'm happy to hear that you know their engineering," Daw said. "Especially since Gladiator's been unable to identify even the ship type."

Neal's face, seen in the CRT, flushed. He was a handsome, slightly dissipated-looking man whose high forehead seemed still higher under a thick crest of dark hair. "I would assume their drives are about the same as ours, sir," he said.

"I've done that. On that basis they shut down only an hour before we picked them up. But I'm not sure I believe it." He cut Neal off and scanned the rest of the lights. One was from the ship's cybernetics compartment; but Polk, the cyberneticist, was bunking with the systems analyst this trip. Daw pushed the light and a woman's face appeared on the screen. It was framed in honey-toned hair, a face with skin like a confection and classic planes that might have shamed a fashion model. And a smile. He had seen that smile often before— though as seldom, he told himself, as he decently could.

"Yes, Mrs. Youngmeadow?"

"*Helen,* please. I can't see you, Captain. The screen is blank."

"There's some minor repair work to be done on the camera here," Daw lied. "It's not important, so we've given it low priority."

"But you can see me?"

"Yes." He felt the blood rising in his cheeks.

"About this ship, Captain . . ." Helen Youngmeadow paused, and Daw noticed that her husband was standing behind her, beyond the plane of focus. "Captain, everyone on the ship can hear me—can't they?"

"I can cut them out of the circuit if you prefer."

"No—Captain, may I come up there?"

"To the bridge? Yes, if you like. It's a long way."

Another como light. This time the alternate bridge module—in appearance much like his, but lacking the battered Old and New Testaments bound in steel and magnetically latched to the console. "Hello, Wad," Daw said gently.

Wad made a half-salute. His young, dark-complexioned face showed plainly the strain of two years' involvement in a hell that demanded night and day a continual flow of deductions, inferences, and decisions—all without effect. Looking at Daw significantly, he drew a finger across his throat, and Daw gave him the private circuit he had offered Mrs. Youngmeadow.

"Thanks, Skipper. I've got something I thought you ought to know about."

Daw nodded.

"I've been running an artifact correlation on the visual image of that ship."

"So have I. Electronic and structural."

"I know, I got your print-out. But my own analysis was bionic."

"You think that's valid?"

Wad shrugged. "I don't know, but it's interesting. You know what the biologists say. Man has reached the stage where he evolves through his machines. The earliest spacecraft resembled single-celled animals—pond life. The dilettante intellectuals of the time tried to give them a sexual significance—that was the only thing they knew—but they were really much closer to the things you find in a drop of pond water than to anything else."

"And what does your analysis say about this ship?"

"No correlation at all. Nothing higher than a tenth."

Daw nodded again. "You think the lack of correlation is significant?"

"It suggests to me that it may have originated somewhere where life forms are quite different from what we are accustomed to."

"Mankind has colonized some queer places."

With heavy significance Wad said, "Would it *have* to be mankind, Captain?" He was speaking, Daw knew, not to him but to his instructors back home. If his guess were correct he would, presumably, be given some small number of points; if not, he would lose ground. In time he would, or would not, be given his own command. The whole thing embarrassed Daw and made him feel somehow wretched, but he could not really blame Wad. He was Wad. To keep the ball rolling—mostly because he did not want to answer the other como lights—he said, "Men have spread their seed a long way across the galaxy Wad. We've seen a lot of strange ships, but they've always turned out to be of human origin."

"The part of the galaxy we know about is tiny compared to the vastness we don't know. And there are other galaxies!"

Daw said, "I've been thinking about the stranger's build myself, as I told you. He looks like a crystal to me—modules ranged in a three-dimensional rectangular array."

"What do you think that means?"

"Comes from a world where they've discovered radio."

Wad broke the connection; Daw grinned but found he didn't much blame him for it.

Daw wondered what Gladiator's bionic correlation program would say about Gladiator herself. Perhaps liken her to the armor of a caddis-fly larva—an empty cylinder of odds and ends. Caddis-fly armor exploded. The interior of his helmet held the familiar smells of fine lubricating oil, sweat, and the goo he sometimes used on his hair; he kicked down and the soles of his boots clinked home on the hull of the bridge module.

Above him and around him Gladiator flung her shining threads, the stars a dust of ice seen through the interstices, the connecting tubes like spider web—half-glittering, half-drowned in inky shadow.

Still ten thousand miles off, the other ship was, under the immense lasers Gladiator directed toward it, another star; but one that winked and twinkled as its structure surged and twisted to the urgings of accelerations long departed.

A hatch at Daw's feet opened and a metal-clad figure he knew to be Helen Youngmeadow rose, caught his hand, and stood beside him. Like his own, her faceplate was set for full transparency; her beautiful face, thus naked to the darkness of a billion suns, seemed to him to hold a hideous vulnerability. In his earphones her voice asked: "Do you know this is the first time I've been out? It's lovely."

"Yes," Daw said.

"And all this is Gladiator; she doesn't seem this big when she talks to me in our cabin. Could you show me which one it is? I'm lost."

"Which module?" From his utility belt Daw took a silver rod, then locked the articulations of his suit arm so that he could aim it like a missile projector with the fine adjustment controls. In the clean emptiness no beam showed, but a module miles down the gossamer cylinder of the ship flashed with the light.

"Way down there," the girl said. "It would be a lot more sociable if everyone were quartered together."

"In a warship, the men must be near their duty," Daw explained awkwardly. "And everything has to be decentralized so that if we're blown apart, all the parts can fight. The module you and your husband are in has more of the ship's, central processor than any of the others, but even that is scattered all over."

"And their ship—the ship out there—is modular too."

"Yes," Daw said. He remembered his conversation with Wad. "Ours is a hollow cylinder, theirs a filled rectangle. Our modules are different sizes and shapes depending on function; theirs are uniform. You're the empathist—the intercultural psychologist—what do those things tell you?"

"I have been thinking about it," Helen Youngmeadow said, "but I'd like to think some more before I talk, and I'm anxious to fly. Can't we go now?"

"You're sure—?"

"I've had all the training." She relaxed her boots' grip on the steel world beneath her, kicked out, for an instant floated above him, then was gone. Backpack rockets made a scarcely visible flame, and it was several seconds before he could pick out the spark of her progress. He followed, knowing that all around them, invisible and distant by hundreds of miles, the other boarding parties he had dispatched were making for the ship ahead as well.

"I'm an empathist, as you said," the girl's voice continued. "Gladiator is a warship, but my husband and I are here to take the side of the enemy."

"That doesn't bother me."

"Because by taking their side we help you. We give you someone who thinks like them and reacts to *their* needs. In a way we're traitors."

"This is exploration; if we had come just to fight you wouldn't even be on board."

"Because the Navy's afraid we might blow our own vessel up, or induce the crew to mutiny. We humans have such a high empathy coefficient—some of us."

"When you and I reach that ship," Daw said wryly, *"we'll* be the underdogs. Perhaps then you'll empathize with the Navy."

"That's the danger—if I do that I won't be doing my job."

He chuckled.

"Listen, Captain Daw. If I ask you something, will you tell me the truth? Straight?"

"If you'll let me catch up to you, and assuming it's not classified."

"All right, I've cut my jets. I'm—"

"I see you, and I've been ranging you on suit radar. It's just that with more mass to accelerate I can't match you for speed when you're flat out." Ahead of them something had been transformed from a winking star to a tiny scrap of diamond lace. Three thousand miles yet, Daw estimated, and checked his radar for confirmation. Five thousand. That ship was big. He said aloud, "What's the question?"

"Why did you let me come? I want to, and I'm terribly grateful, but while I was going up to the bridge I was sure you'd say no. I was thinking of ways to go without your permission—crazy things like that."

For the second time Daw lied.

***

He held her in space, his hand on her arm, telling her it was a safety precaution. The scrap of lace grew to an immense net and at last acquired a third dimension, so that it was seen as thousands of cubes of void, tubes outlining the edges, spherical modules at the intersections.

"Right angles," Helen Youngmeadow said. "I never knew right angles could be so lovely." Then, a moment later, "This is more beautiful than ours."

Daw felt something he tried to choke down. "More regular, certainly," he admitted. "Less individualized."

"Do you still think it's abandoned?"

"Until they show me otherwise. The question is, which one of these things should we enter?"

"If we *can* enter."

"We can. Mrs. Youngmeadow, you empathize with these people, even though you've never seen anything of theirs except this ship. Where would you put the command module?"

It was a challenge, and she sensed it. "Where would you put it, Captain? As a sailor and a military man?"

"On a corner," Daw said promptly.

"You're right." He saw her helmet swivel as she looked at him. "But how did you know? Are you trained in empathies too?"

"No. But you agree? I thought you were going to say in the center."

"That's what I thought *you* were going to say—but it has to be wrong. The entire ship is a structure of empty cubes, with the edges and corners having the only importance. An outer corner would be the corner of corners—did you feel that?"

"No, but I saw that observation from an interior module would be blocked in every direction, and even on an outside plane the rest of the ship would blot out a hundred and eighty degrees. A corner module has two hundred and seventy degrees of clear field."

They explored the surface of the nearest corner module (Daw estimated its diameter at sixty thousand feet, which would give it a surface area of over three hundred and fifty square miles) until they found a hatch, with what appeared to be a turning bar on the side opposite the hinge.

"How do you know it's not locked?" the girl asked as Daw braced himself to heave at the bar.

"Nobody's worried about burglars out here. But anyone's going to worry about having a crew member outside who has to get in fast." He pulled. The bar moved a fraction of an inch and the hatch a barely visible distance. "I'll give you some more data to empathize on," Daw said. "Whoever built this thing is damn strong."

The girl grasped the other end of the bar, and together they turned it until the hatch stood wide open. Light poured from it into the limitless night of space, and Helen Youngmeadow said softly, "They left everything turned on," and a moment afterward, "No airlock."

"No, they don't mind vacuum." Daw was already climbing into the module. There were no floors and no interior partitions; windowed solids that might have been instruments lined the hull wall; machines the size of buildings, braced with guying cables thousands of feet long, dotted the vast central space.

"It's weird, isn't it?" the girl said. "Like being in a birdcage—only I can't tell which way is up."

"Up is always an illusion on a ship," Daw told her. "Why have illusions?" He was already far over her head, exploring. "No chairs, no beds. I like it."

"You mean they don't rest?" The girl had launched herself toward him now, and she put herself into a slow roll so that, to her eyes, the interior of the module revolved around her.

"No." Daw moved closer to one of the great mechanisms. "Look, on our ship we have couches and chairs with thousands of little suction holes in them, so that when your clothes touch them you stay where you put yourself. But somebody who might have been doing something more valuable had to make every one of those pieces of fancy furniture, and then a hundred times their cost was spent lugging them up out of Earth's gravity well into space. Then their pumps require power, which means waste heat the ship has a hard time getting rid of—and any time we want to go anywhere on reaction drive—all the close-in maneuvers—we have to accelerate their mass, and decelerate it again when we get there. All this to hold you down on a ship that never gets up much over half a G, and in addition to the crash couches on the tenders and lifeboats."

"But we have to lie down to sleep."

"No, you don't; you're simply accustomed to it. All you really have to do is pull your feet off the floor, turn out the lights, and hold onto something—like this guy wire—with one hand. Which is probably what the people who built this ship did. Our ancestors, in case you've forgotten, were a tree-dwelling species; and when we go to sleep with our hands around anything that resembles a limb, we automatically tighten up if it starts to slip out."

"You still think this ship was built by human beings?"

Daw said carefully, "We've never found one that wasn't."

"Until now."

"You don't."

There was no reply. Daw looked at the girl to make certain she was all right, jockeyed himself to within touching distance of the great machine, then repeated, "You don't?"

"People? With no airlock?"

"The hatch we used may not have been intended for use in space. Or there might be safety devices we don't know about, deactivated now."

"There wasn't any atmosphere, even before we opened it; as large as this place is, it would have to discharge for hours, and we'd have felt the push as we came through. There wasn't anything. You said yourself that they didn't mind vacuum."

Daw said, "I was thinking they might use this one for some special purpose, or they might wear suits all the time in here."

"Captain, I love mankind. I know when somebody says that, it's usually just talk; but I mean it. Not just the people who are like me, but all human beings everywhere. And yet I don't like this ship."

"That's funny." Daw swung himself away from the machine he had been examining. "I do. They're better naval engineers—I think—than we are. Do you want to go back?"

"No, of course not. The job is here. What are you going to do now?"

"First check out a few more modules; then have some of our

people land on the opposite corner of this thing with routes mapped out for them that will take at least one man through every module. They can work their way toward us, and I'll take their reports as they come in."

"Are you going into some of the other modules now?"

"Yes."

"Then I'll come with you. I don't like it here."

It was almost ten hours later when the first searchers reached the point where Daw and the girl waited, having traversed the diagonal length of the ship. They came in talking, in threes and fours, having met when their lines of search converged. Daw, who except for one brief return to Gladiator had spent the time studying some of the devices in the corner module and those immediately adjacent, broke up the groups and questioned each man separately, using a private communication frequency. Helen Youngmeadow chatted with those waiting for debriefing and waved to each party going back to the ship.

In time the groups thinned, fewer and fewer men clustered around the girl; and at last the last crewman saluted and departed, and she and Daw were alone again. To make conversation she said, "It always seems so lonely on our ship, but seeing all these men makes me realize how many there are; and there are some I'd swear I've never even met."

"You probably haven't," Daw said. The list Gladiator was flashing on his in-helmet display showed one man still out, and he was not sure the girl was aware of it—or that she was not.

"I've been wondering what they all do. I mean, the ship can almost run itself, can't it?"

"Yes, Gladiator could pretty well take care of herself for a long time, if nothing had to be changed."

"If nothing had to be changed?"

"We have to worry about damage control too, on a warship; but adaptability is the chief justification for a big crew. We can beat our swords into plowshares if we have to, and then our plowshares back into swords; in other words we can re-wire and re-rig as much as we need to—if necessary fit out Gladiator to transport a half-million refugees or turn her into a medical lab or a factory. And when something like this comes up we've got the people. This ship is too big to have every part visited by a specialist in every discipline, but the men I've just sent through her included experts in almost any field you could think of."

She was too far off for him to see the beauty of her smile, but he could feel it. "I think you're proud of your command, Captain."

"I am," Daw said simply. "This was what I wanted to do, and I've done it."

"Captain, who is Wad?"

For an instant the question hung in the nothingness between them; then Daw asked, "How did you meet Wad?"

"I asked the ship something—a few hours ago when we went back—and she referred me to him. He looks like you, only . . ."

"Only much younger."

"And he's wearing some sort of officer's insignia—but I'm certain I've never seen him before, not at mess or anywhere else."

"I didn't think Gladiator would do that," Daw said slowly. "Usually Wad only talks to me—at least that's what I thought."

"But who is he?"

"First I'd like to know what question you had that made the ship turn you over to him—and how he answered it."

"I don't think it was anything important."

"What was it?"

"I think she just felt—you know—that it needed the human touch."

"Which Wad has in plenty."

"Yes." Helen Youngmeadow sounded serious. "He's a very sympathetic, very sensitive young man. Not like an empathist of course, but with some training he could become one. Is he your second in command?"

Daw shook his head, though perhaps she could not see it. "No," he said, "Moke's my second—you've met him." He thought of the times he and Moke had shared a table with Helen Youngmeadow and her husband—Youngmeadow slender and handsome, a bit proud of his blond good looks, intelligent, forceful and eloquent in conversation; Moke's honest, homely face struggling throughout the tasteless and untasted meal to hide the desire Youngmeadow's wife waked in every man, and the shame Moke felt at desiring the wife of so likable a shipmate as Youngmeadow.

"Then who *is* Wad?"

"If I tell you, will you tell me what it was you asked him?"

The girl's shoulders moved, for Daw could see the bulky metal shoulders of her suit move with them. "I suppose so—Gladiator would tell you if you asked."

"Yes, but it wouldn't be the same thing as your telling me, Mrs. Youngmeadow. You see, Wad is me. I suppose you could say, too, that I am Wad, grown up."

"I don't understand."

"Do you know how ship captains are trained?"

"I know an officer's training is very hard—"

"Not officers—captains." Unexpectedly Daw launched himself toward her, his arms outstretched like a bird's wings, dodging the wide-spaced guy wires until, almost beside her, he caught one and swung to a stop.

"That was good," she said. "You're very graceful."

"I like this. I've spent a lot of time in space, and you won't find any of that sucking furniture in my cabin. You can laugh if you like, but I think this is what God intended."

"For us?" He could see the arch of her eyebrows now, through the dark transparency of her faceplate.

"For us. Leaping between the worlds."

"You know, understanding people is supposed to be my profession—but I don't think I really understand you at all, Captain. How *are* captains trained, anyway? Not like other officers?"

"No," Daw said. "We're not just officers who've been promoted, although I know that's what most people think."

"It's what I thought."

"That was the old way. I suppose the British carried it to the ultimate. Around eighteen hundred. Have you ever read about it?"

The girl did not answer.

"They put their future skippers on board warships when they were boys of eight or nine—they were called midshipmen. They were just children, and if they misbehaved they were bent over a gun and whipped, but at the same time they were gentlemen and treated as such. The captain, if he was a good captain, treated them like sons and they got responsibility shoved at them just as fast as they could take it."

"It sounds like a brutal system," Helen Youngmeadow said.

"Not as brutal as losing ship and crew. And it produced some outstanding leaders. Lord Nelson entered the navy at twelve and was posted captain when he was twenty; John Paul Jones started at the same age and was first mate on a slaver when he was nineteen and a captain at twenty-three."

"I'm sorry . . ." The girl's voice was so faint in Daw's earphones that he wondered for a moment if her suit mike was failing. "I've never heard of either of those men. But I'll look them up when we get back to Gladiator."

"Anyway," Daw continued, "it was a good system—for as long as people were willing to send promising boys off to sea almost as soon as we'd send them off to school; but after a while you couldn't count on that anymore. Then they took boys who were almost grown and sent them to special universities first. By the time they were experienced officers they were elderly—and the ships, even though these weren't starships yet, had become so large that their captains hadn't had much real contact with them until they were nearly ready to take command of a ship themselves. After a hundred years or so of that—about the time the emphasis shifted from sea to space—people discovered that this system really didn't work very well. A man who'd spent half his life as a subordinate had been well trained in being a subordinate, but that was all."

The taut cable beneath Daw's suit-glove shook with a nearly undetectable tremor, and he turned to look toward the hatch, aware as he did that the girl, who must have felt the same minute vibration, had turned instead to the mouths of the connecting tubes that led deeper into the ship.

The man coming through the hatch was Polk, the cyberneticist, identifiable not by his face but by the name and number stenciled on his helmet. He saluted, and Daw waved him over.

"Got something for me, Captain?"

"I think so, the big cabinet in the center of this module. It's their computer mainframe, or at least an important part of it."

"Ah," said Polk.

"Wait a minute—" There was an edge of shrillness to Helen Youngmeadow's voice, though it was so slight Daw might easily have missed it. "How can you know that?"

"By looking at the wiring running to it. There are hundreds of thousands of wires—braided together into cables, of course, and very fine; but still separate wires, separate channels for information. Anything that can receive that much and do anything with it is a computer by definition—a data-processing device."

Polk nodded as though to support his captain and began examining the great floating octahedron Daw had pointed out. After a minute had passed the girl said in a flat voice, "Do you think theirs might be better than ours? That would be important, I suppose."

Daw nodded. "Extremely important, but I don't know if it's true. From what I've been able to tell from looking into that thing they're a little behind us, I think. Of course there might be some surprises."

Polk muttered, "What am I looking for, Captain, just their general system?"

"To begin with," Daw said slowly, "I'd like to know what the last numbers in the main registers were."

Polk whistled, tinny-sounding over the headphones.

"What good would that be?" Helen Youngmeadow asked. "Anyway, wouldn't they just print it—" She remembered how much of Gladiator's output came over CRTs and audio, and broke off in midsentence.

Polk said, "Nobody prints much in space, Mrs. Youngmeadow. Printing—well, it eats up a lot of paper, and paper's heavy. It looks to me like they use a system a lot like ours. See this?" He passed a space-gloved hand across the center of one facet of the cabinet, but the girl could see no difference between the area he indicated and the surrounding smooth grey metal. To look more closely she dove across the emptiness much as Daw had a moment before.

"This was one of their terminals," Polk continued. "There are probably thousands scattered all through the ship. And they seem to have been used about the same way ours are, with turnoff after a set period to conserve the phosphors; they go bad if you excite them for too long."

"I've noticed that on Gladiator," the girl said. "If something's written on the screen—when I'm reading, for example—and I don't instruct it to bring up the next page, it fades out after a while. Is that what you mean? It seems remarkable that people as different as these should handle the problem the same way."

Daw said, "Not any more remarkable than that both of us use wires—or handles like the one that opened the hatch outside. Look inside that box, though, at the back of that panel and you'll find something that *is* remarkable. Show her, Polk."

The cyberneticist unlatched the section he had indicated. It swung out smoothly, and the girl saw the display tubes behind it, tubes so flat that each was hardly more than a sheet of glass with a socket at the base. "Vacuum tubes?" she said. "Like a television? Even I know what those are."

Daw grunted. "Vacuum tubes in a vacuum."

"That's right. They shouldn't need anything around them out here, should they?"

"They don't, out here. This ship, or at least parts of it, goes into atmospheres at times. Even though the crew doesn't seem to care whether there's one in here or not."

"Captain," Helen Youngmeadow said suddenly, "where is my husband?"

Hours later Moke's voice (unexpectedly loud and near because Moke had the kind of voice that transmitted well through the phones' medium-range frequencies) asked a similar question: "You find Youngmeadow yet, Skipper?"

"We don't know that he's lost."

"You didn't find him, huh?"

"No, not yet."

"You really think he's alive and just not answering?"

"It could be," Daw said. He did not have to remind Moke, as he had Helen Youngmeadow, that there was no danger of running out of oxygen in a modern spacesuit—each suit being a system as self-sufficient as a planet and its sun; energy from the suit's tiny pile scavenging every molecule of water and whisper of carbon dioxide and making new, fresh food, fresh water, clean air that could be used again, so that once in the suit the occupant might live in plenty until time itself destroyed him. (He had not mentioned that even death would not end the life encysted in that steady protection, since the needs of the bacteria striking in at the now defenseless corpse from the skin, out from the intestines, would be sensed, still, by the faithful, empty suit; and served.)

Daw thought of Youngmeadow dead somewhere in this strange vessel, still secure in his suit, his corpse bloating and stinking while the suit hummed on; and found, startled, that the thought was pleasant—which was absurd, he hardly knew Youngmeadow, and certainly had nothing against the man.

"His wife still out looking for him?" Moke asked.

Daw nodded, though Moke could not see him. "Yes," he said. "So are the other parties. I've got a couple of men with Mrs. Youngmeadow to make sure she comes back all right."

"I was just talking to her," Moke said. "I think she's been talking to Polk, too."

"What about?"

"She said she'd heard you found some maps, Captain. I guess Gladiator told her."

"No reason why she shouldn't, but I found those while she was here—she must have seen them. While we were waiting for the first survey parties to come in."

"You didn't hide them from her, or anything like that?"

"No, of course not. She just didn't show much interest in them." Actually, Daw remembered, he had taken the charts—technically they were star charts rather than maps—to show Helen and had been rather disappointed by her reaction; as an empathist, she had explained, she was much more concerned with things that had *not* been vital to the ship's operations than with the things that had. *"Everyone takes what is necessary, Captain,"* she had said. *"By*

*definition they have to. It's what is taken that could be left behind that
reveals the heart."*

"She wanted to know if any of them showed the inside of the ship,"
Moke said.

Daw felt tired. "I'll talk to her," he said, and cut Moke off.

He started to adjust his communicator for the girl's band, then
thought better of it. His investigation of the command module—if in
fact this was the command module—was nearly complete, and it
served no purpose for him to stand by and watch Polk tinkering with
his instruments. After having Gladiator scan the charts so that
duplicates could be made on board for study, he had replaced the
originals. Now he gathered them again.

It was the first time he had been more than two units away from
the corner module he and Helen had first investigated, and though
he had heard the chambers of the interior modules described by the
men he had sent through them, and had seen the pictures they had
taken, it was a new and a strange experience to plunge through tube
after tube and emerge in chamber after chamber, each so huge it
seemed a sky around him, each seeming without end.

The tubes, like those of his own ship, were circular in section;
but they were dim (as Gladiator's were not) and lined with
shimmering, luminous pastels he felt certain were codes but could
not decipher. His years in space had taught him the trick of creating
the things called *up* and *down* in his mind, changing them when it
suited him, destroying them with the truth of gravitationless reality
when he wished. In the tubes he amused himself with them,
sometimes diving down a pulsing pink well, sometimes rocketing
up a black gun barrel, until at last he found that he was no longer
master of these false perceptions, which came and went without his
volition.

Entering each module was like being flung from a ventilation duct
into the rotunda of some incredible building. The walls of most were
lined with enigmatic machines, the centers cobwebbed with cables
spanning distances that dwarfed the great mechanisms they held.
Light in the modules—at least in most—was like that in the first Daw
had examined—bright, shadowless, and all-surrounding; but some

were dim, and some dark. In these his utility light showed shapes and cables not greatly different from those he had seen in other modules, but in the dancing shadows it cast to the remote walls, it sometimes seemed to Daw that he saw living shapes.

At last, when he had become almost certain he had lost his way and was cursing himself (for his religious beliefs permitted any degree of self-condemnation, though they caviled at the application of the same terms to any soul except his own) for a fool and a damned fool, he saw the flicker of other lights in one of the half-lit modules and was able, a moment later, to pick out Helen Youngmeadow's suit with his own beam and, a half-second afterward, the suits of the sailors he had sent with her. At almost the same instant he heard her voice in his phones: "Captain, is that you?"

"Yes," he said. Now that he had found her, he discovered that he was unwilling to admit that he had come looking for her. Everyone, notoriously, fell in love with empathists—the reason they were invariably assigned as married couples. In retrospect he realized how foolish it had been for him to allow her to accompany him at all, despite the rationalizations with which he had defended the decision to himself; and he found that he was anxious that neither she nor the men with her should think that he had come here for her sake. "I understand you were asking my second about charts, Mrs. Youngmeadow," he said, deliberately bringing his voice to the pitch he used in delivering minor reprimands. "I want to make it clear to you that if you have found any such documents they should be submitted to me for scanning as soon as possible."

"We haven't found any maps," the girl said, "and if we did, of course I'd turn them over to you, though I don't suppose you could read them either."

The fatigue in her voice made Daw despise himself. Softening the question as much as he could, he asked, "Then why were you questioning Mr. Moke?"

"I knew you had found some. I was hoping they showed this ship and could tell us where my husband might be."

"They're star charts, Mrs. Youngmeadow. You saw them when I found them."

"I wasn't paying much attention then. Do you think they're important?"

"Very important," Daw said. "They could easily be the key to understanding—well, the entire system of thought of the people who built this ship. Naturally, Gladiator can't stay here—"

"Can't stay here until my husband's found?"

"We aren't going to abandon your husband, Mrs. Youngmeadow."

"I don't suppose I could stop you if you wanted to."

"We don't."

"But if you do, Captain, you'll have to abandon me too. I'm not going back to our ship until we find out what happened to him, and if he's still alive; you say that a person can live indefinitely in one of these suits—all right, I'm going to do that. Even if your ship leaves they'll still send out another one from Earth to investigate this, with cultural anthropologists and so forth on board; and when they get here they'll find me."

One of the crewmen muttered, "Tell him!" under his breath; Daw wondered if the man realized it had been picked up by his helmet mike. To the girl he said, "They'll find me, too, Mrs. Youngmeadow. This ship is much too valuable a discovery for us to leave before someone else comes—but when they do come—this is what I was trying to say when you interrupted me—we'll have to go. They'll have equipment and experts; we are primarily a fighting ship. But it should be possible for you to arrange a transfer at that time."

"Captain . . ."

After a moment had passed, Daw said, "Yes?"

"Captain, can these men hear us?"

"Of course."

"Would you send them away? Just for a minute?"

"They could still hear us, if we stay on general band. If you have something private you wish to say, switch to my own band."

He watched as she fumbled with the controls on the forearm of her suit. One of the crewmen glided skillfully toward her to help, but she waved him away. Her voice came again. "Have I got you, Captain?"

"Yes."

"I just wanted to tell you that I'm sorry I said what I did. You've been a friend to my husband and me, I know. I'm very tired."

Daw said, "I understand."

"Captain, I've been thinking. Will you mind if I ask some questions? I realize it may be silly, but if I don't at least try—"

"Certainly."

"That cyberneticist—Lieutenant Polk. You asked him to find out—" She hesitated. Then, "I'm sorry, I can't think of the words."

"I asked him to find out for me what the numbers in the operating registers of this ship's computer were. To put it another way, I asked him to find out the answer—in raw form at least—of the last computation they performed."

"Is that possible? I would think their numbers would be all different—like Roman numbers or something, or worse. I asked him about it—a few hours ago when you went back to Gladiator—and he explained to me that whatever he found would just be ones and zeros—"

"Binary notation," Daw said.

"Yes, binary notation, because it isn't *really* numbers, you can't have real numbers inside a machine because they're not physical, but just things turned on or off; but I don't see what good knowing it— just one, one, one, zero, zero, zero, like that—will do you if you don't know how they'd be used when they came out of the machine. Captain, I know you must think I don't know what I'm talking about, but I did have to take some mathematics . . . even if I wasn't very good at it." The transmission ended in a whisper of despair.

"I know you're worried about your husband," Daw said. "We're looking for him, as you know. I've got parties out. I shouldn't have included him among the searchers—that was a mistake, and I'm—"

"No!" Helen Youngmeadow jerked at the cable she was holding, swinging herself toward him until their faceplates touched and he could hear her voice, conducted through the metal, like an echo to the sound in his earphones. "You should have sent him. That's just it. At first, when we were waiting and waiting and the others came back, I talked to them and listened to them, and, my God, they didn't know anything, they hadn't seen anything, and I thought just wait, just wait,

Mr. Captain Daw, my man will show you what an empathist can do! Then when he didn't come I started to blame you, but that isn't right. *I'm* an empathist, my profession is supposed to be understanding cultures—every culture, when most people don't even comprehend their own. Now you've got these men staying with me to watch out for me—to watch out for me!—and do you know what they are? I asked them, and one is a plastics engineer and the other's a pharmacist's mate."

"They're good men," Daw said. "That's why I sent them with you, not because I thought they could assist you professionally."

"Well, you were wrong," the girl said in a much calmer voice. "We found a dingus of some sort floating loose in that last module we were in, and your plastics engineer looked at it for a while and then told us what he thought it was and how it had been made. He said they had used a four-part mold, and showed me where they had squirted in the melted stuff. So he understands his part of them, you see, but I don't understand mine. Now you're implying that you understand their math, or at least something about it. Can't you explain it to me?"

"Certainly," Daw said, "if you're interested. I'm afraid, though, that I don't see that it has any immediate bearing on locating your husband."

"A computer will answer anyone, won't it? I mean normally."

"Unless some sort of privacy provision has been made in the program."

"But there isn't much chance they'd do that on a ship like this; you said when we opened the hatch to get in that no one worried about burglars in space, so I doubt if they'd be worried about snoopers aboard their own ship either. And if their computer is like Gladiator, meant to run everything, it will know where my husband is—all we have to do is learn how to turn it on and ask it."

"I see what you mean," Daw told her, "but I'm afraid that's going to be a good deal more complicated than what I've got Polk trying to do."

"But it's the first step. Show me."

Moved by some democratic impulse he did not bother to analyze, Daw switched back to the general communication band before spreading one of the charts—without gravity or air currents it hung like smoke in the emptiness—to illustrate what he was about to say; then for the benefit of the crewmen he explained: "This is one of their star charts—we found it in the first module we entered. In a rough way you could consider it a map of this part of the galaxy, as seen from above."

The girl said: "I don't understand how you can talk about seeing a galaxy from above or from below, except by convention—or how you know those dots on the chart are stars at all without being able to read the language. And if they are stars, how do you know they represent the region we're in? Or is that just a guess?" Her voice was as controlled as it might have been during a dinner-table discussion on board Gladiator, but Daw sensed tension that held her at the edge of hysteria.

"To begin with," he said, "the galaxy's not a shapeless cloud of stars—it is disk-shaped, and it seems pretty obvious that anyone mapping any sizable portion of it would choose to look at things from one face or the other. Which face is chosen is strictly a matter of convention, but there are only two choices. And we're pretty certain these things are star charts, because Gladiator measured the positions of the dots and ran a regression analysis between them and the known positions of the stars. The agreement was so good that we can feel pretty sure of the identities of most of the dots. What's more, if you'll look at the chart closely you'll see that our friends have used three sizes of dots."

Daw paused and one of the crewmen asked, "Magnitude, Captain?"

"That's what we thought at first, but actually the three sizes seem to symbolize the principal wavelengths radiated—small dots for the blue end of the spectrum, medium for yellow stars like Sol, and large for the red giants and the dark stars."

Helen Youngmeadow said, "I don't see how that can help you read the numbers."

"Well, you'll notice faint lines running from star to star, with symbols printed along them; it seems reasonable to assume that these are distances, and of course we know the actual distances."

"But you don't know what sort of squiggle they use for each number, or what units the distances are given in."

"Worse than that," Daw admitted, "we don't—or at least we didn't—know whether they ran their figures from left to right or from right to left—or whether they were using positional notation at all. And of course we didn't know what base they were using, either. Or which symbol took the place of our decimal point."

"But you were able to find all that out, just from the chart?"

"Yes. The base was fairly easy. You probably remember from your own math that the number of numerals a system needs is equal to the number of the base. Our decimal notation, for example, uses ten—zero through nine. If you'll look at these numbers you'll see that a total of thirteen symbols are used—"

"Base thirteen?"

Daw shook his head. "We doubt it very much. Thirteen is a prime number, divisible only by one and itself, and as such an almost impossible base. But if we assume that one of the symbols is a position indicator like our decimal point, that leaves twelve; and twelve is a very practical base. So the question was which symbol divided the wholes—of whatever unit they were using—from the fractional parts."

Helen Youngmeadow leaned toward the chart, and Daw sensed, with a happiness he had hardly known himself capable of, that some portion of her despair was fading. "You could try them one by one," she said. "After all, there are only thirteen."

"We could have, but there turned out to be a much quicker way. Remember, these numbers represent stellar distances, and we felt that we knew what most of the stars were. So we programmed a search routine to look for a star whose distance from one of the base stars on the chart was twelve times that of some other, closer star. In positional notation—and we had to assume for the time being that they were using a positional notation, since if they weren't they wouldn't need an analogue to the decimal point—when you shift the symbol, or group of symbols, at the front of a number up by one position, it has the effect, roughly, of multiplying the number by the base. So we had our program determine the ratio nearest twelve, the closer the better; and when we had located our stars we looked for a symbol that hadn't changed position in the larger number. Here"—he indicated two lines of print on the chart—"see what I mean?"

"No," the girl said after a moment. "No, I don't. There are eight symbols in one expression and nine in the other, but the one on the right looks like an equation—the thing like a fish with a spear through it is equal to one group minus another."

"Yes, it does," Daw admitted, "but the thing that resembles an equals sign is their mark for seven, and the 'minus' is a one. The vertical mark that looks like our one is their decimal point, and the numbers are read from right to left instead of left to right."

"How did you get the values of the numerals?"

"Do you really want to hear about all this?"

"Yes, I do, but I don't know why. Captain, is there actually a chance we might be able to get the computer on this ship working, and ask it where my husband is? And it would answer—just like that? That's what I'm trying to believe, but sometimes it slips. Maybe I'm just interested because you are, and I empathize; it's a fault of mine."

Daw was suddenly embarrassed, and conscious as he had not been for some time of the empty ship around him. "Gladiator could explain this as well as I could," he said. "Better."

"I could guess some of them myself, I think. You've already told me that the horizontal mark is a one, so since the equals sign isn't two it must be the S-shaped thing."

"You're right," Daw said, "how did you know?"

"Because it looks like our two, only backward; and ours is a cursive mark for what used to be two horizontal lines—it used to look like a '2'. From the shape of their 'S' sign I'd say it started out as two lines slanted." She smiled.

"It is interesting, isn't it?" Daw said.

"Very interesting. But now will you tell me what you're going to learn when you can read whatever number the people who built this place left in their computer?"

"We don't know, really, but from the nature of the number we may be able to guess what it was. What I'm hoping for is the heading they took when they abandoned the ship."

"Did they abandon this ship?"

Daw was nonplussed. "We've been all through it."

"Even through the path assigned my husband?"

"Of course; the first thing I did when he failed to return was to send a party to retrace his route."

"And they did it?"

"Yes."

"And came back and reported?"

"Yes."

"Captain Daw, could *we* do it? I mean, I know you're needed to direct things, even if I'm not, but could we do it? I don't have your logical mind, but I have a feeling for situations, it's part of my stock-in-trade. And I think the two of us might find something where no one else would."

Daw thought for a moment. "Good administrative practice," he said. "I see what you mean."

"Then tell me, because I don't myself."

"Just that since this is our biggest problem I should give it my personal attention; and you should come too, because you are the one who wants it settled most and will have the greatest dedication to the job. You realize though, don't you, that you are—we are—almost in the center of your husband's route now."

Even as he made this last small protest, Daw felt himself carried away by the attraction of the idea. He would lose a certain amount of face with the men he had assigned to guard Helen, but, as he told himself, he could afford to lose some face. Addressing them, he said: "Mrs. Youngmeadow and I are going to retrace her husband's search path through this vessel in person. You may return to your duty."

The two saluted, and Daw saw—incredibly—a new respect in

their expressions, and something like envy as well. "Dismissed!" he snapped.

When they had gone Helen Youngmeadow said: "You really like it, don't you, going off by yourself? I should have known when we went alone to board this ship."

"No," Daw said. "I should be on Gladiator."

"That's the voice of conscience. But this is what you like." The girl launched herself from the cable she had been holding and gave half-power to her backpack rockets, doing a lazy wingover to avoid the next wire.

"Where are you going?" Daw called.

"Well, we're going to retrace the way my husband came, in the same direction he did, aren't we? So there's no use going back to the beginning that way; but if we take the modules next to his we might find something."

"Do you think your husband would have deviated from the assigned route?"

"He might have," said Helen's voice in Daw's ear. He could see her now, far ahead in the dimness, ready to dive into the pale, circular, lime-green immensity of a tube. "He was a funny person, and I guess maybe I may not have known him as well as I thought I did."

Daw put on a burst of speed and was up with her before she had gone a thousand yards into the tube. "You're right," he said, "this is what I like."

"I do too—maybe my husband liked it too much. That would be in harmony with his personality profile, I think." Daw did not answer, and a few seconds later she asked in a different tone, "Do you know what I was thinking of, while you were telling me about those charts? Stones. Little pebbles. Do you get it?"

"No," Daw said. The tube was bent just enough here for the ends to be invisible to them. They sailed through a nothingness of pale green light.

"Well, I may not know a lot of math but I know some etymology. You were talking about calculations, and that word comes from the Latin for a stone: *calculus*. That was the way they used to count—one stone for one sheep or one ox. And later they had a thing like an abacus except that instead of rods for the counters it had a board with cup-shaped holes to put stones in. Those numbers you figured out were little stones from a world we've never seen."

Daw said, "I think I understand." He could make out the end of the tube now, a region of brighter light where vague shapes floated.

"The thing I wonder about is where are they now, those first stones? Ground to powder? Or just kicking around Italy or Egypt somewhere, little round stones that nobody pays any attention to. I don't really think anything would happen if they were destroyed— not really—but I've been wondering about it."

"Your sense of history is too strong," Daw told her. He nearly added, *"Like Wad's,"* but thought better of it and said instead, "For some reason that reminds me—you were going to tell me why you were talking to Wad, but you never did."

"Wad is the boy that looks like you? I said I would if you'd tell me about him."

"That's right," Daw said, "I didn't finish." They were leaving the tube now, thrown like the debris from an explosion through an emptiness whose miles-distant walls seemed at first merely roughened, but whose roughness resolved into closely packed machines, a spinniness of shafts and great gears and tilted beams—all motionless.

"You told me about the midshipmen," Helen reminded him. "I think I can guess the rest, except that I don't know how it's done."

"And what's your guess?"

"You said that you were Wad—at least in a sense. In some way you're training yourself."

"Time travel? No."

"What then?"

"Future captains are selected by psychological testing when, as cadets, they have completed their courses in basic science. Then instead of being sent to space as junior officers, they go as observers on a two-year simulated flight—all right on Earth. The advantage is that they see more action in the two years of simulation than they'd get in twenty of actual service. They go through every type of emergency that's ever come up at least once, and some more than once—with variations."

"That's interesting; but it doesn't explain Wad."

"They have to get the material for the simulations somewhere. Sure, in most of it the midshipman just views, but you don't want to train him to be a detached observer and nothing else. He has to be able to talk to the people on shipboard, and especially the captain, and get meaningful, typical replies. To get material for those conversations, a computer on every navy ship simulates a midshipman whom the captain and crew must treat as an individual."

"Do they all look like you?"

"They have to look like someone, so they're made to look—and talk and act—as the captain himself did during his midshipman days. It's important, as I said, that the captain treat his midshipman as a son, and that way there's more—" Daw paused.

"Empathy?" He could hear the fragile smile.

"That's your word. Sympathy."

"Before it was corrupted by association with pity; that used to mean what empathy does now."

A new voice rang in Daw's headphones" *"Captain! Captain!"*

"Yes, here."

"This is Polk, Captain. We didn't want to bother you, sir, but we've got the numbers from the central registers in that corner module, and from the form—well, we think you're right. It's a bearing."

"You've got duplicates of the charts, don't you?" Where were they going?"

"What star, you mean, sir?"

"Yes, of course."

"It doesn't seem to be a bearing for any star, Captain. Not on their charts or ours either."

Helen Youngmeadow interrupted to say: "But it has to point to some star! There are millions of them out there."

Daw said, "There are billions—each so remote that for most purposes it can be treated as a nondimensional point."

"The closest star to the bearing's about a quarter degree off," Polk told her. "And a quarter of a degree is, well ma'am, a hell of a long way in astrogation."

"Perhaps it isn't a bearing then," the girl said.

Daw asked, "What does it point to?"

"Well, sir—"

"When I asked you a minute ago what the bearing indicated, you asked if I meant what star. So it does point to something, or you think it does. What is it?"

"Sir, Wad said we should ask Gladiator what was on the line of the bearing at various times in the recent past. I guess he thought it might be a comet or something. It turned out that it's pointing right to where our ship was while we were making our approach to this one, sir."

Unexpectedly, Daw laughed. (Helen Youngmeadow tried to remember if she had ever heard him laugh before, and decided she had not.)

"Anything else to report, Polk?"

"No, sir."

She asked, "Why did you laugh, Captain?"

"We're still on general band," Daw said. "What do you say we switch over to private?"

His own dials bobbed and jittered as the girl adjusted her controls.

"I laughed because I was thinking of the old chimpanzee experiment; you've probably read about it. One of the first scientists to study the psychology of the nonhuman primates locked a chimp in a room full of ladders and boxes and so on—"

"And then peeked through the keyhole to see what he did, and saw the chimpanzee's eye looking back at him." Now Helen laughed too. "I see what you mean. You worked so hard to see what they had been looking at—and they were looking at us."

"Yes," said Daw.

"But that doesn't tell you where they went, does it?"

Daw said, "Yes, it does."

"I don't understand."

"They were still here when we sighted them, because we changed course to approach this ship."

"Then they abandoned the ship because we came, but that still doesn't tell you where they went."

"It tells me where they are now. If they didn't leave before we had them in detection range, they didn't leave at all—we would have seen them. If they didn't leave at all, they are still on board."

"They can't be."

"They can be and they are. Think of how thinly we're scattered on Gladiator. Would anyone be able to find us if we didn't want to be found?"

Far ahead in the dimness her utility light answered him. He saw it wink on and dart from shadow to shadow, then back at him, then to the shadows again. "We're in no more danger than we were before," he said.

"They have my husband. Why are they hiding, and who are they?"

"I don't know; I don't even know that they are hiding. There may be very few of them—they may find it hard to make us notice them. I don't know."

The girl was slowing, cutting her jets. He cut his own, letting himself drift up to her. When he was beside her she said: "Don't you know anything about them? Anything?"

"When we first sighted this ship I ran an electronic and structural correlation on its form. Wad ran a bionic one. You wouldn't have heard us talking about them because we were on a private circuit."

"No." The girl's voice was barely audible. "No, I didn't."

"Wad got nothing on his bionic correlation. I got two things out of mine. As a structure this ship resembles certain kinds of crystals. Or you could say that it looks like the core stack in an old-fashioned computer—cores in rectangular arrays with three wires running through the center of each. Later, because of what Wad had said, I started thinking of Gladiator; so while we were more or less cooling our heels and hoping your husband would come in, I did what Wad had and ran a bionic correlation on her." He fell silent.

"Yes?"

"There were vertebrates—creatures with spinal columns—before there were any with brains; did you know that? The first brains were little thickenings at the end of the spinal nerves nearest the sense organs. That's what Gladiator resembles—that first thin layer of extra neurons that was . . . the primitive cortex. This ship is different."

"Yes," the girl said again.

"More like an artificial intelligence—the computer core stack of course, but the crystals too; the early computers, the ones just beyond the first vacuum-tube stage, used crystalline materials for transducers: germanium and that kind of thing. It was before Ovshinsky came up with ovonic switches of amorphous materials."

"What are you saying? That the ship is the entity? That the crew are robots?"

"I told you I don't know," Daw said. "I doubt if our terms are applicable to them."

"But what can we do?"

"Get in touch with them. Let them know we're here, that we're friendly and want to talk." He swung away from her—up, in his current orientation, up six miles sheer before coming to rest like a bat against the ceiling, then revolving the ship in his mind until the ceiling became a floor. The girl hovered five hundred feet above his head as he inspected the machines.

"I see," she said, "you're going to break something."

"No," Daw said slowly, "I'm going to find something to repair or improve—if I can."

Several hours passed while he traced the dysfunction that held the equipment around him immobile. From the module where he had begun he followed it to the next, where he found broken connections and fused elements; another hour while he made the connections again, and found, in cabinets not wholly like any he had seen built by men, parts to replace those the overloads had destroyed. When he had finished his work, three lights came on in distant parts of the module; and far away some great machine breathed a sigh that traveled through the metal floor to the soles of his boots, though Helen, still floating above him, did not hear it. "Do you think they'll come now?" she asked when the lights gleamed. "Will they give him back to us?"

Daw did not answer. A shape—a human shape—was emerging from the mouth of a distant tube. It was a half-mile away, but he had seen it as the girl spoke, a mere speck, but a speck with arms and legs and a head that was a recognizable helmet. In a moment she had followed his eyes. "Darling," she said. "Darling." Daw watched. A voice, resonant yet empty, said, "Helen."

"Darling," the girl said again.

The empty voice said: "I am not your husband. I know what you believe."

Daw saw it as the figure came down beside him. He thought the girl would not see it, but she said, "Who are you?"

Through the clear faceplate Daw could see Youngmeadow's face. The lips shaped: "Not your husband. You would call me a simulation of him. Something that can talk to you; they cannot, or will not, do that directly." It seemed to Daw that the face, so like Youngmeadow's, was in some deeper way not like Youngmeadow's at all, or anyone's—as though, perhaps, those moving lips concealed organs of sight in the recesses of the mouth, and the voice, the sound he heard, poured forth from the nose and ears.

"Where is my husband?"

"I cannot answer that."

"Cannot," Daw asked, "or will not?"

"There are four words, and all are difficult. What is meant by *is*? By *husband*? I can ask, but you could only answer in further words, further concepts we could not define."

"You are a simulation of him?"

"I said, 'You would call me a simulation of him.' "

Helen asked suddenly, "What have you come to tell us?"

"That with this"—the figure that looked like Youngmeadow gestured toward the repairs Daw had made—"there has been enough. You have seen something of us; we, now, of you. There cannot be more, now. We both must think."

"Are you trying to tell us," Daw asked, "that we could not have worked out a philosophy for dealing with your culture until we made this contact?"

"I can answer few questions. We must think. You too."

"But you want us to leave your ship. Are we friends?"

"We are not," the simulation answered carefully, "not-friends." He lifted off as a man would have, and in a few seconds was gone.

"He wasn't your husband," Daw said.

"I know it."

"Do you trust me, Helen? Will you take my word for something?"

She nodded.

"Your husband is dead. It's over."

"You know."

Daw thought of the scattered bits of rag and vacuum-shriveled flesh he had seen—and not mentioned to the girl overhead—while making the repairs. "I know," he said.

He lifted off, and she flew beside him for a time, silently. There was a dysfunction in his headphones so that he heard, constantly, a sound like the noise of the wind. It was not unpleasant, except that it was a dysfunction. At last she said, "Was he ever alive, Captain? Do you know what I've been thinking? That perhaps he never was. The cabins, you know."

"What about them?" Daw asked.

"They're only supposed to be for one person, but you had two of us in there. Because everybody knows empathists have to be married . . . and there's Wad—he really wasn't on the ship either. Are you sure my husband existed, Captain? That he wasn't just something implanted in our minds before we left Earth? I can remember the way he held me, but not one thing he said, not word for word. Can you?"

"He was real," Daw said, "and he's dead. You'll feel better when you've seen the medics and had some rest."

"Captain . . ."

"He came in here," Daw said, "and somehow he realized the truth, that the crew of this ship—whatever you want to call them—was still on board. Then he thought the same thing you did: that he would break something and make them notice him. His empathy was all for people, not for things. He broke something and they noticed him, and he's dead."

"Only people are important," the girl said.

"To other people," Daw answered, "sometimes."

On board Gladiator she said: "I never told you what it was I asked Wad, did I? I was asking about you—what your childhood was like."

In Daw's mind a voice more insistent than hers quoted: *"At the resurrection, therefore, of which of the seven will she be the wife? For they all had her."* But Jesus answered and said to them, *"You err because you know neither the Scriptures nor the power of God. For at the resurrection they will neither marry nor be given in marriage . . ."*

Aloud he said, "I hope Wad told you the truth."

"When you were in training—I mean, like he is now—you were watching a simulated captain, weren't you? Was it yourself you saw there, only older?"

"I don't think so," Daw said. "A real captain. He was a crusty bastard, but he generally knew what he was doing."

PICTURES DON'T LIE

by Katherine MacLean

The alien ship, crewed by beings of good will, was ready to land and greet the Earthlings. What could possibly go wrong?

⌗ ⌗ ⌗

KATHERINE MacLEAN'S first written story (though while she was revising it to John W. Campbell's editorial request, a couple of her other stories got into print before it), "Incommunicado," dealing with a crisis on a space station which is solved by communication theory, appeared in the June 1950 issue of Astounding Science-Fiction *and made her reputation instantly—and not just among her readers and colleagues in science fiction. When she tried to sneak into an invitation-only science conference, and the gatekeeper asked her name, she was suddenly surrounded by the legitimate attendees who had read "Incommunicado" and were eager to meet its author. (Incidentally, "Incommunicado" is my favorite MacLean story, though "Fearhound" is close behind.) She won a Nebula Award for her novella, "The Missing Man" (later incorporated in her novel with the same title) and was named an SFWA Author Emeritus by the Science Fiction Writers of America in 2003. Her story collections* The Diploids *and* The Trouble with You Earth People *are both out of print (which is unforgiveable in the age of e-books), but are certainly worth seeking out in used copies. And, if I may wax politically incorrect for a moment, the next time you hear someone claiming that there were no women writing SF before the 1970s (or the 1980s, or the 1990s—the purveyors of this nonsense keep moving the chronological goalposts), remember the date of her first published story, "Defense Mechanism": 1949. As writer, editor, and critic Damon Knight once commented, "As a science fiction writer, she has few peers . . ." Still very true.*

THE MAN FROM THE *NEWS* ASKED, "What do you think of the aliens, Mr. Nathen? Are they friendly? Do they look human?"

"Very human," said the thin young man.

Outside, rain sleeted across the big windows with a steady, faint drumming, blurring and dimming the view of the airfield where *They* would arrive. On the concrete runways the puddles were pockmarked with rain, and the grass growing untouched between the runways of the unused field glistened wetly, bending before gusts of wind.

Back at a respectful distance from the place where the huge spaceship would land were the gray shapes of trucks, where TV camera crews huddled inside their mobile units, waiting. Farther back in the deserted, sandy landscape, behind distant sandy hills, artillery was ringed in a great circle, and in the distance across the horizon bombers stood ready at airfields, guarding the world against possible treachery from the first alien ship ever to land from space.

"Do you know anything about their home planet?" asked the man from the *Herald*.

The *Times* man stood with the others, listening absently, thinking of questions but reserving them. Joseph R. Nathen, the thin young man with the straight black hair and the tired lines on his face, was being treated with respect by his interviewers. He was obviously on edge, and they did not want to harry him with too many questions at once. They wanted to keep his good will. Tomorrow he would be one of the biggest celebrities ever to appear in headlines.

"No, nothing directly."

"Any ideas or deductions?" the *Herald* persisted.

"Their world must be Earthlike to them," the weary-looking

young man answered uncertainly. "The environment evolves the animal. But only in relative terms, of course." He looked at them with a quick glance and then looked away evasively, his lank black hair beginning to cling to his forehead with sweat. "That doesn't necessarily mean anything."

"Earthlike," muttered a reporter, writing it down as if he had noticed nothing more in the reply.

The *Times* man glanced at the *Herald,* wondering if he had noticed, and received a quick glance in exchange.

The *Herald* asked Nathen, "You think they are dangerous, then?"

It was the kind of question, assuming much, that usually broke reticence and brought forth quick facts—when it hit the mark. They all knew of the military precautions, although they were not supposed to know.

The question missed. Nathen glanced out the window vaguely. "No I wouldn't say so."

"You think they are friendly, then?" said the *Herald,* equally positive on the opposite tack.

A fleeting smile touched Nathen's lips. "Those I know are."

There was no lead in this direction, and they had to get the basic facts of the story before the ship came. The *Times* asked, "What led up to your contacting them?"

Nathen answered, after a hesitation, "Static. Radio static. The Army told you my job, didn't they?"

The Army had told them nothing at all. The officer who had conducted them in for the interview stood glowering watchfully, as if he objected by instinct to telling anything to the public.

Nathen glanced at him doubtfully. "My job is radio decoder for the Department of Military Intelligence. I use a directional pickup, tune in on foreign bands, record any scrambled or coded messages I hear, and build automatic decoders and descramblers for all the basic scramble patterns."

The officer cleared his throat but said nothing.

The reporters smiled, noting that down.

Security regulations had changed since arms inspection had been legalized by the U.N. Complete information being the only public security against secret rearmament, spying and prying had come to seem a public service. Its aura had changed. It was good public relations to admit to it.

Nathen continued, "In my spare time I started directing the pickup at stars. There's radio noise from stars, you know. Just stuff that sounds like spatter static, and an occasional squawk. People have been listening to it for a long time, and researching, trying to work out why stellar radiation on those bands comes in such jagged bursts. It didn't seem natural."

He paused and smiled uncertainly, aware that the next thing he would say was the thing that would make him famous—an idea that had come to him while he listened, an idea as simple and as perfect as the one that came to Newton when he saw the apple fall.

"I decided it wasn't natural. I tried decoding it."

Hurriedly, he tried to explain it away and make it seem obvious. "You see, there's an old intelligence trick, speeding up a message on a record until it sounds just like that, a short squawk of static, and then broadcasting it. Undergrounds use it. I'd heard that kind of screech before."

"You mean they broadcast at us in code?" asked the *News*.

"It's not exactly code. All you need to do is record it and slow it down. They're not broadcasting at us. If a star has planets, inhabited planets, and there is broadcasting between them, they would send it on a tight beam to save power." He looked for comprehension. "You know, like a spotlight. Theoretically, a tight beam can go on forever without losing power. But aiming would be difficult from planet to planet. You can't expect a beam to stay on target, over such distances, more than a few seconds at a time. So they'd naturally compress each message into a short half-second- or one-second-length package and send it a few hundred times in one long blast to make sure it is picked up during the instant the beam swings across the target."

He was talking slowly and carefully, remembering that this explanation was for the newspapers. "When a stray beam swings through our section of space, there's a sharp peak in noise level from that direction. The beams are swinging to follow their own planets at home, and the distance between there and here exaggerates the speed of swing tremendously, so we wouldn't pick up more than a *bip* as it passes."

"How do you account for the number of squawks coming in?" the *Times* asked. "Do stellar systems rotate on the plane of the Galaxy?" It was a private question; he spoke impulsively from interest and excitement.

The radio decoder grinned, the lines of strain vanishing from his face for a moment. "Maybe we're intercepting everybody's telephone calls, and the whole Galaxy is swarming with races that spend all day yacking at each other over the radio. Maybe the human type is standard model."

"It would take something like that," the *Times* agreed. They smiled at each other.

The *News* asked, "How did you happen to pick up television instead of voices?"

"Not by accident," Nathen explained patiently. "I'd recognized a scanning pattern, and I wanted pictures. Pictures are understandable in any language."

Near the interviewers, a senator paced back and forth, muttering his memorized speech of welcome and nervously glancing out the wide streaming windows into the gray, sleeting rain.

Opposite the windows of the long room was a small raised platform flanked by the tall shapes of TV cameras and sound pickups on booms, and darkened floodlights, arranged and ready for the senator to make his speech of welcome to the aliens and the world. A shabby radio sending set stood beside it without a case to conceal its parts, two cathode television tubes flickering nakedly on one side and the speaker humming on the other. A vertical panel of dials and knobs jutted up before them, and a small hand-mike sat ready on the table before the panel. It was connected to a boxlike, expensively cased piece of equipment with "Radio Lab, U.S. Property" stenciled on it.

"I recorded a couple of package screeches from Sagittarius and began working on them," Nathen added. "It took a couple of months to find the synchronizing signals and set the scanners close enough to the right time to even get a pattern. When I showed the pattern to the

Department, they gave me full time to work on it, and an assistant to help. It took eight months to pick out the color bands and assign them the right colors, to get anything intelligible on the screen."

The shabby-looking mess of exposed parts was the original receiver that they had labored over for ten months, adjusting and readjusting to reduce the maddening rippling plaids of unsynchronized color scanners to some kind of sane picture.

"Trial and error," said Nathen, "but it came out all right. The wide band spread of the squawks had suggested color TV from the beginning."

He walked over and touched the set. The speaker bipped slightly and the gray screen flickered with a flash of color at the touch. The set was awake and sensitive, tuned to receive from the great interstellar spaceship which now circled the atmosphere.

"We wondered why there were so many bands, but when we got the set working and started recording and playing everything that came in, we found we'd tapped something like a lending-library line. It was all fiction, plays."

Between the pauses in Nathen's voice, the *Times* found himself unconsciously listening for the sound of roaring, swiftly approaching rocket jets.

The *Post* asked, "How did you contact the spaceship?"

"I scanned and recorded a film copy of *The Rite of Spring,* the Disney-Stravinsky combination, and sent it back along the same line we were receiving from. Just testing. It wouldn't get there for a good number of years, if it got there at all, but I thought it would please the library to get a new record in.

"Two weeks later, when we caught and slowed a new batch of recordings, we found an answer. It was obviously meant for us. It was a flash of the Disney being played to a large audience, and then the audience sitting and waiting before a blank screen. The signal was very clear and loud. We'd intercepted a spaceship. They were asking for an encore, you see. They liked the film and wanted more . . ."

He smiled at them in sudden thought. "You can see them for yourself. It's all right down the hall where the linguists are working on the automatic translator."

The listening officer frowned and cleared his throat, and the thin young man turned to him quickly. "No security reason why they should not see the broadcasts, is there? Perhaps you should show them." He said to the reporters reassuringly, "It's right down the hall. You will be informed the moment the spaceship approaches."

The interview was very definitely over. The lank-haired, nervous young man turned away and seated himself at the radio set while the officer swallowed his objections and showed them dourly down the hall to a closed door.

They opened it and fumbled into a darkened room crowded with empty folding chairs, dominated by a glowing bright screen. The door closed behind them, bringing total darkness.

There was the sound of reporters fumbling their way into seats around him, but the *Times* man remained standing, aware of an enormous surprise, as if he had been asleep and wakened to find himself in the wrong country.

The bright colors of the double image seemed the only real thing in the darkened room. Even blurred as they were, he could see that the action was subtly different, the shapes subtly not right.

He was looking at aliens.

The impression was of two humans disguised, humans moving oddly, half-dancing, half-crippled. Carefully, afraid the images would go away, he reached up to his breast pocket, took out his polarized glasses, rotated one lens at right angles to the other, and put them on.

Immediately, the two beings came into sharp focus, real and solid, and the screen became a wide, illusively near window through which he watched them.

They were conversing with each other in a gray-walled room, discussing something with restrained excitement. The large man in the green tunic closed his purple eyes for an instant at something the other said and grimaced, making a motion with his fingers as if shoving something away from him.

Mellerdrammer.

The second, smaller, with yellowish-green eyes, stepped closer, talking more rapidly in a lower voice. The first stood very still, not trying to interrupt.

Obviously, the proposal was some advantageous treachery, and he wanted to be persuaded. The *Times* groped for a chair and sat down.

Perhaps gesture is universal; desire and aversion, a leaning forward or a leaning back, tension, relaxation. Perhaps these actors were masters. The scenes changed: a corridor, a parklike place in what he began to realize was a spaceship, a lecture room. There were others talking and working, speaking to the man in the green tunic, and never was it unclear what was happening or how they felt.

They talked a flowing language with many short vowels and shifts of pitch, and they gestured in the heat of talk, their hands moving with an odd lagging difference of motion, not slow, but somehow drifting.

He ignored the language, but after a time the difference in motion began to arouse his interest. Something in the way they walked . . .

With an effort he pulled his mind from the plot and forced his attention to the physical difference. Brown hair in short, silky crew cuts, varied eye colors, the colors showing clearly because their irises were very large, their round eyes set very widely apart in tapering, light-brown faces. Their necks and shoulders were thick in a way that would indicate unusual strength for a human, but their wrists were narrow and their fingers long and thin and delicate.

There seemed to be more than the usual number of fingers.

Since he came in, a machine had been whirring and a voice muttering beside him. He turned from counting their fingers and looked around. Beside him sat an alert-looking man wearing earphones, watching and listening with hawklike concentration. Beside him was a tall streamlined box. From the screen came the sound of the alien language. The man abruptly flipped a switch on the box, muttered a word into a small hand microphone, and flipped the switch back with nervous rapidity.

He reminded the *Times* man of the earphoned interpreters at the U.N. The machine was probably a vocal translator and the mutterer a linguist adding to its vocabulary. Near the screen were two other linguists taking notes.

The *Times* remembered the senator pacing in the observatory room, rehearsing his speech of welcome. The speech would not be just the empty pompous gesture he had expected. It would be translated mechanically and understood by the aliens.

On the other side of the glowing window that was the stereo screen the large protagonist in the green tunic was speaking to a pilot in a gray uniform. They stood in a brightly lit canary-yellow control room in a spaceship.

The *Times* tried to pick up the thread of the plot. Already he was interested in the fate of the hero, and liked him. That was the effect of good acting, probably, for part of the art of acting is to win affection from the audience, and this actor might be the matinee idol of whole Solar Systems.

Controlled tension, betraying itself by a jerk of the hands, a too quick answer to a question. The uniformed one, not suspicious, turned his back, busying himself at some task involving a map lit with glowing red points, his motions sharing the same fluid, dragging grace of the others, as if they were under water or on a slow-motion film. The other was watching a switch, a switch set into a panel, moving closer to it, talking casually—background music coming and rising in thin chords of tension.

There was a close-up of the alien's face watching the switch, and the *Times* noted that his ears were symmetrical half-circles, almost perfect, with no earholes visible. The voice of the uniformed one answered—a brief word in a preoccupied, deep voice. His back was still turned. The other glanced at the switch, moving closer to it, talking casually, the switch coming closer and closer stereoscopically. It was in reach, filling the screen. His hand came into view, darted out, closed over the switch—

There was a sharp clap of sound and his hand opened in a frozen shape of pain. Beyond him, as his gaze swung up, stood the figure of the uniformed officer, unmoving, a weapon rigid in his hand, in the startled position in which he had turned and fired, watching with widening eyes as the man in the green tunic swayed and fell.

The tableau held, the uniformed one drooping, looking down at his hand holding the weapon which had killed, and music began to build in from the background. Just for an instant, the room and the things within it flashed into one of those bewildering color changes that were the bane of color television—to a color negative of itself, a green man standing in a violet control room, looking down at the body of a green man in a red tunic. It held for less than a second; then the color-band alternator fell back into phase and the colors reversed to normal.

Another uniformed man came and took the weapon from the limp hand of the other, who began to explain dejectedly in a low voice while the music mounted and covered his words and the screen slowly went blank, like a window that slowly filmed over with gray fog.

The music faded.

In the dark, someone clapped appreciatively.

The earphoned man beside the *Times* shifted his earphones back from his ears and spoke briskly. "I can't get any more. Either of you want a replay?"

There was a short silence until the linguist nearest the set said, "I guess we've squeezed that one dry. Let's run the tape where Nathen and that ship radio boy are kidding around CQing and tuning their beams in closer. I have a hunch the boy is talking routine ham talk and giving the old radio count—one-two-three-testing."

There was some fumbling in the semi-dark and then the screen came to life again.

It showed a flash of an audience sitting before a screen and gave a clipped chord of some familiar symphony. "Crazy about Stravinsky and Mozart," remarked the earphoned linguist to the *Times,* resettling his earphones. "Can't stand Gershwin. Can you beat that?" He turned his attention back to the screen as the right sequence came on.

The *Post,* who was sitting just in front of him, turned to the *Times* and said, "Funny how much they look like people." He was writing, making notes to telephone his report. "What color hair did that character have?"

"I didn't notice." He wondered if he should remind the reporter that Nathen had said he assigned the color bands on guess, choosing the colors that gave the most plausible images. The guests, when they arrived, could turn out to be bright green with blue hair. Only the gradations of color in the picture were sure, only the similarities and contrasts, the relationship of one color to another.

From the screen came the sound of the alien language again. This race averaged deeper voices than human. He liked deep voices. Could he write that?

No, there was something wrong with that, too. How had Nathen established the right sound-track pitch? Was it a matter of taking the modulation as it came in, or some sort of heterodyning up and down by trial and error? Probably.

It might be safer to assume that Nathen had simply preferred deep voices.

As he sat there, doubting, an uneasiness he had seen in Nathen came back to add to his own uncertainty, and he remembered just how close that uneasiness had come to something that looked like restrained fear.

"What I don't get is why he went to all the trouble of picking up TV shows instead of just contacting them," the *News* complained. "They're good shows, but what's the point?"

"Maybe so we'd get to learn their language, too," said the *Herald*.

On the screen now was the obviously unstaged and genuine scene of a young alien working over a bank of apparatus. He turned and waved and opened his mouth in the comical O shape which the *Times* was beginning to recognize as their equivalent of a smile, then went back to trying to explain something about the equipment, in elaborate, awkward gestures and carefully mouthed words.

The *Times* got up quietly, went out into the bright white stone corridor, and walked back the way he had come, thoughtfully folding his stereo glasses and putting them away.

No one stopped him. Secrecy restrictions were ambiguous here. The reticence of the Army seemed more a matter of habit—mere reflex, from the fact that it had all originated in the Intelligence Department— than any reasoned policy of keeping the landing a secret.

The main room was more crowded than he had left it. The TV camera and sound crew stood near their apparatus, the senator had found a chair and was reading, and at the far end of the room eight men were grouped in a circle of chairs, arguing something with impassioned concentration. The *Times* recognized a few he knew personally, eminent names in science, workers in field theory.

A stray phrase reached him: "—reference to the universal constants as ratio—" It was probably a discussion of ways of converting formulas from one mathematics to another for a rapid exchange of information.

They had reason to be intent, aware of the flood of insights that novel viewpoints could bring, if they could grasp them. He would have liked to go over and listen, but there was too little time left before the spaceship was due, and he had a question to ask.

The hand-rigged transceiver was still humming, tuned to the sending band of the circling ship, and the young man who had started it all was sitting on the edge of the TV platform with his chin resting in one hand. He did not look up as the *Times* approached, but it was the indifference of preoccupation, not discourtesy.

The *Times* sat down on the edge of the platform beside him and took out a pack of cigarettes, then remembered the coming TV broadcast and the ban on smoking. He put them away, thoughtfully watching the diminishing rain spray against the streaming windows.

"What's wrong?" he asked.

Nathen showed that he was aware and friendly by a slight motion of his head.

"*You* tell me."

"Hunch," said the *Times* man. "Sheer hunch. Everything sailing along too smoothly, everyone taking too much for granted."

Nathen relaxed slightly. "I'm still listening."

"Something about the way they move . . ."

Nathen shifted to glance at him.

"That's bothered me, too."

"Are you sure they're adjusted to the right speed?"

Nathen clenched his hands out in front of him and looked at them consideringly. "I don't know. When I turn the tape faster, they're all rushing, and you begin to wonder why their clothes don't stream behind them, why the doors close so quickly and yet you can't hear them slam, why things fall so fast. If I turn it slower, they all seem to be swimming." He gave the *Times* a considering sideways glance. "Didn't catch the name."

Country-bred guy, thought the *Times*. "Jacob Luke, *Times*" he said, extending his hand.

Nathen gave the hand a quick, hard grip, identifying the name. "Sunday Science Section editor. I read it. Surprised to meet you here."

"Likewise." The *Times* smiled. "Look, have you gone into this rationally, with formulas?" He found a pencil in his pocket. "Obviously, there's something wrong with our judgment of their weight-to-speed to momentum ratio. Maybe it's something simple, like low gravity aboard ship, with magnetic shoes. Maybe they *are* floating slightly."

"Why worry?" Nathen cut in. "I don't see any reason to try to figure it out now." He laughed and shoved back his black hair nervously. "We'll see them in twenty minutes."

"Will we?" asked the *Times* slowly.

There was a silence while the senator turned a page of his magazine with a slight crackling of paper and the scientists argued at the other end of the room. Nathen pushed at his lank black hair again, as if it were trying to fall forward in front of his eyes and keep him from seeing.

"Sure." The young man laughed suddenly, talked rapidly. "Sure we'll see them. Why shouldn't we, with all the government ready with welcome speeches, the whole Army turned out and hiding over the hill, reporters all around, newsreel cameras—everything set up to broadcast the landing to the world. The President himself shaking hands with me and waiting in Washington—"

He came to the truth without pausing for breath.

He said, "Hell, no, they won't get here. There's some mistake somewhere. Something's wrong. I should have told the brass hats yesterday when I started adding it up. Don't know why I didn't say anything. Scared, I guess. Too much top rank around here. Lost my nerve."

He clutched the *Times* man's sleeve. "Look. I don't know what—"

A green light flashed on the sending-receiving set. Nathen didn't look at it, but he stopped talking.

The loud-speaker on the set broke into a voice speaking in the aliens' language. The senator started and looked nervously at it, straightening his tie. The voice stopped.

Nathen turned and looked at the loud-speaker. His worry seemed to be gone.

"What is it?" the *Times* asked anxiously.

"He says they've slowed enough to enter the atmosphere now. They'll be here in five to ten minutes, I guess. That's Bud. He's all excited. He says holy smoke, what a murky-looking planet we live on." Nathen smiled. "Kidding."

The *Times* was puzzled. "What does he mean, 'murky'? It can't be raining over much territory on Earth." Outside, the rain was slowing and bright-blue patches of sky were shining through breaks in the cloud blanket, glittering blue light from the drops that ran down the windows. He tried to think of an explanation. "Maybe they're trying to land on Venus." The thought was ridiculous, he knew. The spaceship was following Nathen's sending beam. It couldn't miss Earth. "Bud" had to be kidding.

The green light glowed on the set again, and they stopped speaking, waiting for the message to be recorded, slowed, and replayed. The cathode screen came to life suddenly with a picture of the young man sitting at his sending set, his back turned, watching a screen at one side that showed a glimpse of a huge dark plain approaching. As the ship plunged down toward it, the illusion of solidity melted into a boiling turbulence of black clouds. They expanded in an inky swirl, looked huge for an instant, and then blackness swallowed the screen. The young alien swung around to face the camera, speaking a few words as he moved, made the O of a smile again, then flipped the switch and the screen went gray.

Nathen's voice was suddenly toneless and strained. "He said something like 'break out the drinks, here they come.'"

"The atmosphere doesn't look like that," the *Times* said at random, knowing he was saying something too obvious even to think about. "Not Earth's atmosphere."

Some people drifted up. "What did they say?"

" 'Entering the atmosphere, ought to be landing in five or ten minutes' ," Nathen told them.

A ripple of heightened excitement ran through the room. Cameramen began adjusting the lens angles again, turning on the mike and checking it, turning on the floodlights. The scientists rose and stood near the window, still talking. The reporters trooped in from the hall and went to the windows to watch for the great event. The three linguists came in, trundling a large wheeled box that was the mechanical translator, supervising while it was hitched into the sound-broadcasting system.

"Landing where?" the *Times* asked Nathen brutally. "Why don't you do something?"

"Tell me what to do and I'll do it," Nathen said quietly, not moving.

It was not sarcasm. Jacob Luke of the *Times* looked sideways at the strained whiteness of his face and moderated his tone. "Can't you contact them?"

"Not while they're landing."

"What now?" The *Times* took out a pack of cigarettes, remembered the rule against smoking, and put it back.

"We just wait," Nathen leaned his elbow on one knee and his chin in his hand.

They waited.

All the people in the room were waiting. There was no more conversation. A bald man of the scientist group was automatically buffing his fingernails over and over and inspecting them without seeing them; another absently polished his glasses, held them up to the light, put them on, and then a moment later took them off and began polishing again. The television crew concentrated on their jobs, moving quietly and efficiently, with perfectionist care, minutely arranging things that did not need to be arranged, checking things that had already been checked.

This was to be one of the great moments of human history, and they were all trying to forget that fact and remain impassive and wrapped up in the problems of their jobs, as good specialists should.

After an interminable age the *Times* consulted his watch. Three minutes had passed. He tried holding his breath a moment, listening for a distant approaching thunder of jets. There was no sound.

The sun came out from behind the clouds and lit up the field like a great spotlight on an empty stage.

Abruptly, the green light shone on the set again, indicating that a squawk message had been received. The recorder recorded it, slowed it, and fed it back to the speaker. It clicked and the sound was very loud in the still, tense room.

The screen remained gray, but Bud's voice spoke a few words in the alien language. He stopped, the speaker clicked, and the light went out. When it was plain that nothing more would occur and no announcement was to be made of what was said, the people in the room turned back to the windows and talk picked up again.

Somebody told a joke and laughed alone.

One of the linguists remained turned toward the loud-speaker, then looked at the widening patches of blue sky showing out the window, his expression puzzled. He had understood.

"It's dark," the thin Intelligence Department decoder translated, low-voiced, to the man from the *Times*. "Your atmosphere is *thick!* That's precisely what Bud said."

Another three minutes. The *Times* caught himself about to light a cigarette and swore silently, blowing the match out and putting the cigarette back into its package. He listened for the sound of the rocket jets. It was time for the landing, yet he heard no blasts.

The green light came on in the transceiver.

Message in.

Instinctively, he came to his feet. Nathen abruptly was standing beside him. Then the message came in the voice he was coming to think of as Bud. It spoke and paused. Suddenly the *Times* knew.

"We've landed." Nathen whispered the words.

The wind blew across the open spaces of white concrete and damp soil that was the empty airfield, swaying the wet, shiny grass. The people in the room looked out, listening for the roar of jets, looking for the silver bulk of a spaceship in the sky.

Nathen moved, seating himself at the transmitter, switching it on to warm up, checking and balancing dials. Jacob Luke of the *Times* moved softly to stand behind his right shoulder, hoping he could be useful. Nathen made a half-motion of his head, as if to glance back at him, unhooked two of the earphone sets hanging on the side of the tall streamlined box that was the automatic translator, plugged them in, and handed one back over his shoulder to the *Times* man.

The voice began to come from the speaker again.

Hastily, Jacob Luke fitted the earphones over his ears. He fancied he could hear Bud's voice tremble. For a moment it was just Bud's voice speaking the alien language, and then, very distant and clear in his earphones, he heard the recorded voice of the linguist say an English word, then a mechanical click and another clear word in the voice of one of the other translators, then another as the alien's voice flowed from the loud-speaker, the cool single words barely audible, overlapping and blending like translating thought, skipping unfamiliar words yet quite astonishingly clear.

"Radar shows no buildings or civilization near. The atmosphere around us registers as thick as glue. Tremendous gas pressure, low gravity, no light at all. You didn't describe it like this. Where are you, Joe? This isn't some kind of trick, is it?" Bud hesitated, was prompted by a deeper official voice, and jerked out the words.

"If it is a trick, we are ready to repel attack."

The linguist stood listening. He whitened slowly and beckoned the other linguists over to him and whispered to them.

Joseph Nathen looked at them with unwarranted bitter hostility while he picked up the hand mike, plugging it into the translator. "Joe calling," he said quietly into it in clear, slow English. "No trick. We don't know where you are. I am trying to get a direction fix from your signal. Describe your surroundings to us if at all possible."

Nearby, the floodlights blazed steadily on the television platform, ready for the official welcome of the aliens to Earth. The television channels of the world had been alerted to set aside their scheduled programs for an unscheduled great event. In the long room the people waited, listening for the swelling sound of rocket jets.

This time, after the light came on, there was a long delay. The speaker sputtered and sputtered again, building to a steady scratching through which they could barely hear a dim voice. It came through in a few tiny words and then wavered back to inaudibility. The machine translated in their earphones.

"Tried . . . seemed . . . repair . . ." Suddenly it came in clearly. "Can't tell if the auxiliary blew, too. Will try it. We might pick you up clearly on the next try. I have the volume down. Where is the landing port? Repeat. Where is the landing port? Where are you?"

Nathen put down the hand mike and carefully set a dial on the recording box and flipped a switch, speaking over his shoulder. "This sets it to repeat what I said the last time. It keeps repeating." Then he sat with unnatural stillness, his head still half turned, as if he had suddenly caught a glimpse of answer and was trying with no success whatever to grasp it.

The green warning light cut in, the recording clicked, and the playback of Bud's face and voice appeared on the screen. "We heard a few words, Joe, and then the receiver blew again. We're adjusting a viewing screen to pick up the long waves that go through the murk and convert them to visible light. We'll be able to see out soon. The engineer says that something is wrong with the stern jets, and the captain has had me broadcast a help call to our nearest space base." He made the mouth O of a grin. "The message won't reach it for some years. I trust you, Joe, but get us out of here, will you?—They're buzzing that the screen is finally ready. Hold everything."

The screen went gray and the green light went off.

The *Times* considered the lag required for the help call, the speaking and recording of the message just received, the time needed to reconvert a viewing screen.

"They work fast." He shifted uneasily and added at random, "Something wrong with the time factor. All wrong. They work *too* fast."

The green light came on again immediately. Nathen half-turned to him, sliding his words hastily into the gap of time as the message was recorded and slowed. "They're close enough for our transmission power to blow their receiver."

If it was on Earth, why the darkness around the ship? "Maybe they see in the high ultraviolet—the atmosphere is opaque to that band," the *Times* suggested hastily as the speaker began to talk in the young extra-Terrestrial's voice.

That voice *was* shaking now. "Stand by for the description."

They tensed, waiting. The *Times* brought a map of the state before his mind's eye.

"A half-circle of cliffs around the horizon. A wide muddy lake swarming with swimming things. Huge, strange white foliage all around the ship and incredibly huge, pulpy monsters attacking and eating each other on all sides. We almost landed in the lake, right on the soft edge. The mud can't hold the ship's weight, and we're sinking. The engineer says we might be able to blast free, but the tubes are mud-clogged and might blow up the ship. When can you reach us?"

The *Times* thought vaguely of the Carboniferous Era. Nathen obviously had seen something he had not.

"Where are they?" the *Times* asked him quietly.

Nathen pointed to the antenna position indicators. The *Times* let his eyes follow the converging imaginary lines of focus out the window to the sunlit airfield, the empty airfield, the drying concrete; green waving grass where the lines met.

Where the lines met. The spaceship was there!

The fear of something unknown gripped him suddenly.

The spaceship was broadcasting again. *"Where are you? Answer if possible! We are sinking! Where are you?"*

He saw that Nathen knew. "What is it?" the *Times* asked hoarsely. "Are they in another dimension or the past or on another world or what?"

Nathen was smiling bitterly, and Jacob Luke remembered that the young man had a friend in that spaceship. "My guess is that they evolved on a high-gravity planet with a thin atmosphere, near a blue-white star. Sure, they see in the ultraviolet range. Our sun is abnormally small and dim and yellow. Our atmosphere is so thick it screens out ultraviolet." He laughed harshly. "A good joke on us, the weird place we evolved in, the thing it did to us!"

"Where are you?" called the alien spaceship. "Hurry, please! We're sinking!"

The decoder slowed his tumbled, frightened words and looked up into the *Times* face for understanding. "We'll rescue them," he said quietly. "You were right about the time factor, right about them moving at a different speed. I misunderstood. This business about squawk coding, speeding for better transmission to counteract beam waver—I was wrong."

"What do you mean?"

"They don't speed up their broadcasts."

"They don't—?"

Suddenly, in his mind's eye, the *Times* began to see again the play he had just seen—but the actors were moving at blurring speed, the words jerking out in a fluting, dizzying stream, thoughts and decisions passing with unallowable rapidity, rippling faces in a twisting blur of expressions, doors slamming wildly, shatteringly, as the actors leaped in and out of rooms.

No—faster, faster—he wasn't visualizing it as rapidly as it was, an hour of talk and action in one almost instantaneous "squawk," a narrow peak of "noise" interfering with a single word in an Earth broadcast! Faster—faster—it was impossible. Matter could not stand such stress—inertia—momentum—abrupt weight.

It was insane. "Why?" he asked. "How?"

Nathen laughed again harshly, reaching for the mike. "Get them out? There isn't a lake or river within hundreds of miles from here!" A shiver of unreality went down the *Times* spine. Automatically and inanely, he found himself delving in his pocket for a cigarette while he tried to grasp what had happened. "Where are they, then? Why can't we see their spaceship?"

Nathen switched the microphone on in a gesture that showed the bitterness of his disappointment. "We'll need a magnifying glass for that.

BACKWARDNESS

by Poul Anderson

Earth has been discovered by extraterrestrials who look quite human and seem very friendly. Surely they have a lot to teach us less-advanced humans of Earth. Or maybe we have a few things to teach them . . .

⌘ ⌘ ⌘

POUL ANDERSON (1926-2001) was one of the most prolific and popular writers in science fiction. He won the Hugo Award seven times and the Nebula Award three times, as well as many other awards, notably including the Grand Master Award of the Science Fiction Writers of America for a lifetime of distinguished achievement. With a degree in physics, and a wide knowledge of other fields of science, he was noted for building stories on a solid foundation of real science, as well as for being one of the most skilled creators of fast-paced adventure stories. He was author of over a hundred science fiction and fantasy novels and story collections, and several hundred short stories, as well as historical novels, mysteries and non-fiction books. He wrote several series, notably the Technic Civilization novels and stories, the Psychotechnic League series, the Harvest of Stars novels, and his Time Patrol series. Lest the new reader think that Anderson only wrote series stories and novels, I'll also mention some stand-alone novels such as The High Crusade, The Star Fox, Three Hearts and Three Lions, A Midsummer Tempest, The Enemy Stars, Brain Wave, The Corridors of Time, The Boat of a Million Years, *and many more. I would say, as*

I've said before, that all are worth seeking out, but then, they were written by Poul Anderson, so that really goes without saying. Now, repeat the above remarks for his stand-alone (and standout) stories. Such as this one.

AS A SMALL BOY he wanted to be a rocket pilot—and what boy didn't in those days?—but learned early that he lacked the aptitudes. Later he decided on psychology, and even took a bachelor's degree *cum laude.* Then one thing led to another, and Joe Husting ended up as a confidence man. It wasn't such a bad life; it had challenge and variety as he hunted in New York, and the spoils of a big killing were devoured in Florida, Greenland Resort, or Luna City.

The bar was empty of prospects just now, but he dawdled over his beer and felt no hurry. Spring had reached in and touched even the East Forties. The door stood open to a mild breeze, the long room was cool and dim, a few other men lazed over mid-afternoon drinks and the TV was tuned low. Idly, through cigarette smoke, Joe Husting watched the program.

The Galactics, of course. Their giant spaceship flashed in the screen against wet brown fields a hundred miles from here. Copter view . . . now we pan to a close-up, inside the ring of UN guards, and then back to the sightseers in their thousands. The announcer was talking about how the captain of the ship was at this moment in conference with the Secretary-General, and the crewmen were at liberty on Earth. "They are friendly, folks. I repeat, they are friendly. They will do no harm. They have already exchanged their cargo of U-235 for billions of our own dollars, and they plan to spend those dollars like any friendly tourist. But both the UN Secretariat and the President of the United States have asked us all to remember that these people come from the stars. They have been civilized for a million years. They have powers we haven't dreamed of. Anyone who harms a Galactic can ruin the greatest—"

Husting's mind wandered off. A big thing, yes; maybe the biggest thing in all history. Earth a member planet of the Galactic Federation!

All the stars open to us! It was good to be alive in this year when anything could happen . . . hm. To start with, you could have some rhinestones put in fancy settings and peddle them as gen-yu-wine Tardenoisian sacred flame-rocks, but that was only the beginning

He grew aware that the muted swish of electrocars and hammering of shoes in the street had intensified. From several blocks away came a positive roar of excitement. What the devil? He left his beer and sauntered to the door and looked out. A shabby man was hurrying toward the crowd. Husting buttonholed him. "What's going on, pal?"

"Ain't yuh heard? Galactics! Half a dozen of 'em. Landed in duh street uptown, some kinda flying belt dey got, and went inna Macy's and bought a million bucks' wortha stuff! Now they're strolling down dis-a-way. Lemme go!"

Husting stood for a while, drawing hard on his cigarette. There was a tingle along his spine. Wanderers from the stars, a million-year-old civilization embracing the whole Milky Way! For him actually to see the high ones, maybe even talk to them . . . it would be something to tell his grandchildren about if he ever had any.

He waited, though, till the outer edge of the throng was on him, then pushed with skill and ruthlessness. It took a few sweaty minutes to reach the barrier.

An invisible force-field, holding off New York's myriads—wise precaution. You could be trampled to death by the best-intentioned mob.

There were seven crewmen from the Galactic ship. They were tall, powerful, as handsome as expected: a mixed breed, with dark hair and full lips and thin aristocratic noses. In a million years you'd expect all the human races to blend into one. They wore shimmering blue tunics and buskins, webby metallic belts in which starlike points of light glittered—and jewelry! My God, they must have bought all the gaudiest junk jewelry Macy's had to offer, and hung it on muscular necks and thick wrists. Mink and ermine burdened their shoulders, a young fortune in fur. One of them was carefully counting the money he had left, enough to choke an elephant. The others beamed affably into Earth's milling folk.

Joe Husting hunched his narrow frame against the pressure that was about to flatten him on the force screen. He licked suddenly dry lips, and his heart hammered. Was it possible—could it really happen that *he,* insignificant he, might speak to the gods from the stars?

Elsewhere in the huge building, politicians, specialists, and vips buzzed like angry bees. They should have been conferring with their opposite numbers from the Galactic mission—clearly, the sole proper way to meet the unprecedented is to set up committees and spend six months deciding on an agenda. But the Secretary-General of the United Nations owned certain prerogatives, and this time he had used them. A private face-to-face conference with Captain Hurdgo could accomplish more in half an hour than the councils of the world in a year.

He leaned forward and offered a box of cigars. "I don't know if I should," he added. "Perhaps tobacco doesn't suit your metabolism?"

"My what?" asked the visitor pleasantly. He was a big man, running a little to fat, with distinguished gray at the temples. It was not so odd that the Galactics should shave their chins and cut their hair in the manner of civilized Earth. That was the most convenient style.

"I mean, we smoke this weed, but it may poison you," said Larson. "After all, you're from another planet."

"Oh, that's OK," replied Hurdgo. "Same plants grow on every Earthlike planet, just like the same people and animals. Not much difference. Thanks." He took a cigar and rolled it between his fingers. "Smells nice."

"To me, that is the most astonishing thing about it all. I never expected evolution to work identically throughout the universe. *Why?*"

"Well, it just does." Captain Hurdgo bit the end off of his cigar and spat it out onto the carpet. "Not on different-type planets from this, of course, but on Earth-type it's all the same."

"But why? I mean, what process—it can't be coincidence!"

Hurdgo shrugged. "I don't know. I'm just a practical spaceman.

Never worried about it." He put the cigar in his mouth and touched the bezel of an ornate finger ring to it. Smoke followed the brief, intense spark.

"That's a . . . a most ingenious development," said Larson. Humility, yes, there was the line for a simple Earthman to take. Earth had come late into the cosmos and might as well admit the fact.

"A what?"

"Your ring. That lighter."

"Oh, that. Yep. Little atomic-energy gizmo inside." Hurdgo waved a magnanimous hand. "We'll send some people to show you how to make our stuff. Lend you machinery till you can start your own factories. We'll bring you up to date."

"It—you're incredibly generous," said Larson, happy and incredulous.

"Not much trouble to us, and we can trade with you once you're all set up. The more planets, the better for us."

"But . . . excuse me, sir, but I bear a heavy responsibility. We have to know the legal requirements for membership in the Galactic Federation. We don't know anything about your laws, your customs, your—"

"Nothing much to tell," said Hurdgo. "Every planet can pretty well take care of itself. How the hell you think we could police fifty million Earth-type planets? If you got a gripe, you can take it to the, uh, I dunno what the word would be in English. A board of experts with a computer that handles these things. They'll charge you for the service—no Galactic taxes, you just pay for what you get, and out of the profits they finance free services like this mission of mine."

"I see," nodded Larson. "A Coordinating Council."

"Yeh, I guess that's it."

The Secretary-General shook his head in bewilderment. He had sometimes wondered what civilization would come to be, a million years hence. Now he knew, and it staggered him. An ultimate simplicity, superman disdaining the whole cumbersome apparatus of interstellar government, freed of all restraints save the superman morality, free to think his giant thoughts between the stars!

Hurdgo looked out the window to the arrogant towers of New

York. "Biggest city I ever saw," he remarked, "and I seen a lot of planets. I don't see how you run it. Must be complicated."

"It is, sir." Larson smiled wryly. Of course the Galactics would long ago have passed the stage of needing such a human ant hill. They would have forgotten the skills required to govern one, just as Larson's people had forgotten how to chip flint.

"Well, let's get down to business." Hurdgo sucked on his cigar and smacked his lips. "Here's how it works. We found out a big while back that we can't go letting any new planet bust its way into space with no warning to anybody. Too much danger. So we set up detectors all over the Galaxy. When they spot the, uh, what-you-call-'ems—vibrations, yes, that's it, vibrations—the vibrations of a new star drive, they alert the, uh, Coordinating Council and it sends out a ship to contact the new people and tell 'em the score."

"Ah, indeed. I suspected as much. We have just invented a faster-than-light engine . . . very primitive, of course, compared to yours. It was being tested when—"

"Uh-huh. So me and my boys are supposed to give you the once-over and see if you're all right. Don't want warlike peoples running around loose, you know. Too much danger."

"I assure you—"

"Yes, yes, pal, it's OK. You got a good strong world setup and the computer says you've stopped making war." Hurdgo frowned. "I got to admit, you got some funny habits. I don't really understand everything you do . . . you seem to think funny, not like any other planet I ever heard of. But it's all right. Everybody to his own ways. You get a clean bill of health."

"Suppose . . ." Larson spoke very slowly. "Just suppose we had not been . . . approved—what then? Would you have reformed us?"

"Reformed? Huh? What d'you mean? We'd have sent a police ship and blown every planet in this system to smithereens. Can't have people running loose who might start a war."

Sweat formed under Larson's arms and trickled down his ribs. His mouth felt dry. *Whole planets.*

But in a million years you would learn to think *sub specie aeternitatis*. Five billion warlike Earthlings could annihilate fifty billion peaceful Galactics before they were overcome. It was not for him to judge a superman.

"Hello, there!"

Husting had to yell to be heard above the racket. But the nearest of the spacemen looked at him and smiled.

"Hi," he said.

Incredible! He had greeted little Joe Husting as a friend. Why—? Wait a minute! Perhaps the sheer brass of it had pleased him. Perhaps no one else had dared speak first to the strangers. And when you only said, "Yes, sir," to a man, even to a Galactic, you removed him—you might actually make him feel lonely.

"Uh, like it here?" Husting cursed his tongue, that its glibness should have failed him at this moment of all moments.

"Sure, sure. Biggest city I ever seen. And *draxna,* look at what I got!" The spaceman lifted a necklace of red glass sparklers. "Won't their eyes just bug out when I get home!"

Someone shoved Husting against the barrier so the wind went from him. He gasped and tried to squirm free.

"Say, cut that out. You're hurting the poor guy." One of the Galactics touched a stud on his belt. Gently but inexorably, the field widened, pushing the crowd back . . . and somehow, somehow Husting was inside it with the seven from the stars.

"You OK, pal?" Anxious hands lifted him to his feet.

"I, yeah, sure. Sure, I'm fine!" Husting stood up and grinned at the envious faces ringing him in. "Thanks a lot."

"Glad to help you. My name's Gilgrath. Call me Gil." Strong fingers squeezed Husting's shoulder. "And this here is Bronni, and here's Col, and Jordo, and—"

"Pleased to meet you," whispered Husting inadequately. "I'm Joe."

"Say, this is all right!" said Gil enthusiastically. "I was wondering what was wrong with you folks."

"Wrong?" Husting shook a dazed head, wondering if They were peering into his mind and reading thoughts of which he himself was unaware. Vague memories came back, grave-eyed Anubis weighing the heart of a man.

"You know," said Gil. "Standoffish, like."

"Yeh," added Bronni. "Every other new planet we been to, everybody was coming up and saying hello and buying us drinks and—"

"Parties," reminded Jordo.

"Yeh. Man, remember that wing-ding on Alphaz? Remember those girls?" Col rolled his eyes lickerishly.

"You got a lot of good-looking girls here in New York," complained Gil. "But we got orders not to offend nobody. Say, do you think one of those girls would mind if I said hello to her?"

Husting was scarcely able to think; it was the reflex of many years which now spoke for him, rapidly: "You have us all wrong. We're just scared to talk to you. We thought maybe you didn't want to be bothered."

"And *we* thought *you*—Say!" Gil slapped his thigh and broke into a guffaw. "Now ain't that something? They don't want to bother us and we don't want to bother them!"

"I'll be *rixt!*" bellowed Col. "Well, what do you know about that?"

"Hey, in that case—" began Jordo.

"Wait, wait!" Husting waved his hands. It was still habit which guided him; his mind was only slowly getting back into gear. "Let me get this straight. You want to do the town, right?"

"We sure do," said Col. "It's mighty lonesome out in space."

"Well, look," chattered Husting, "you'll never be free of all these crowds, reporters—" (A flashbulb, the tenth or twelfth in these few minutes, dazzled his eyes.) "You won't be able to let yourselves go while everybody knows you're Galactics."

"On Alphaz—" protested Bronni.

"This isn't Alphaz. Now I've got an idea. Listen." Seven dark heads bent down to hear an urgent whisper. "Can you get us away from here? Fly off invisible or something?"

"Sure," said Gil. "Hey, how'd you know we can do that?"

"Never mind. OK, we'll sneak off to my apartment and send out for some Earthstyle clothes for you, and then—"

John Joseph O'Reilly, Cardinal Archbishop of New York, had

friends in high places as well as in low. He thought it no shame to pull
wires and arrange an interview with the chaplain of the spaceship.
What he could learn might be of vital importance to the Faith. The
priest from the stars arrived, light-screened to evade the curious, and
was received in the living room.

Visible again, Thyrkna proved to be a stocky white-haired man in
the usual blue-kirtled uniform. He smiled and shook hands in quite
an ordinary manner. At least, thought O'Reilly, these Galactics had
during a million years conquered overweening Pride.

"It is an honor to meet you," he said.

"Thanks," nodded Thyrkna. He looked around the room. "Nice
place you got."

"Please be seated. May I offer you a drink?"

"Don't mind if I do."

O'Reilly set forth glasses and a bottle. In a modest way, the
Cardinal was a connoisseur, and had chosen the Chambertin-Clos
carefully. He tasted the ritual few drops. Whatever minor saint, if any,
was concerned with these things had been gracious; the wine was
superb. He filled his guest's glass and then his own.

"Welcome to Earth," he smiled.

"Thanks." The Galactic tossed his drink off at one gulp. "Aaah!
That goes good."

The Cardinal winced, but poured again. You couldn't expect
another civilization to have the same tastes. Chinese liked aged eggs
while despising cheese . . .

He sat down and crossed his legs. "I'm not sure what title to use,"
he said diffidently.

"Title? What's that?"

"I mean, what does your flock call you?"

"My *flock?* Oh, you mean the boys on board? Plain Thyrkna.
That's good enough for me." The visitor finished his second glass and
belched. Well, so would a cultivated Eskimo.

"I understand there was some difficulty in conveying my request,"
said O'Reilly. "Apparently you did not know what our word *chaplain*
means."

"We don't know every word in your lingo," admitted Thyrkna. "It works like this. When we come in toward a new planet, we pick up its radio, see?"

"Oh, yes. Such of it as gets through the ionosphere."

Thyrkna blinked. "Huh? I don't know all the *de*-tails. You'll have to talk to one of our tech . . . technicians. Anyway, we got a machine that analyzes the different languages, figures 'em out. Does it in just a few hours, too. Then it puts us all to sleep and teaches us the languages. When we wake up, we're ready to come down and talk."

The Cardinal laughed. "Pardon me, sir. Frankly, I was wondering why the people of your incredibly high civilization should use our worst street dialects. Now I see the reason. I am afraid our programs are not on a very high level. They aim at mass taste, the lowest common denominator—and please excuse my metaphors. Naturally you—But I assure you, we aren't all that bad. We have hopes for the future. This electronic educator of yours, for instance . . . what it could do to raise the cultural level of the average man surpasses imagination."

Thyrkna looked a trifle dazed. "I never seen anybody what talks like you Earthlings. Don't you ever run out of breath?"

O'Reilly felt himself reproved. Among the Great Galactics, a silence must be as meaningful as a hundred words, and there were a million years of dignity behind them. "I'm sorry," he said.

"Oh, it's all right. I suppose a lot of our ways must look just as funny to you." Thyrkna picked up the bottle and poured himself another glassful.

"What I asked you here for . . . there are many wonderful things you can tell me, but I would like to put you some religious questions."

"Sure, go ahead," said Thyrkna amiably.

"My Church has long speculated about this eventuality. The fact that you, too, are human, albeit more advanced than we, is a miraculous revelation of God's will. But I would like to know something about the precise form of your belief in Him."

"What do you mean?" Thyrkna sounded confused. "I'm a, uh, quartermaster. It's part of my job to kill the rabbits—we can't afford the space for cattle on board a ship. I feed the gods, that's all."

"The *gods!*" The Cardinal's glass crashed on the floor.

"By the way, what's the names of your top gods?" inquired Thyrkna. "Be a good idea to kill them a cow or two, as long as we're here on their planet. Don't wanna take chances on bad luck."

"But . . . you . . . *heathen—*"

Thyrkna looked at the clock. "Say, do you have TV?" he asked. "It's almost time for *John's Other Life.* You got some real good TV on this planet."

By the dawn's early light, Joe Husting opened a bleary eye and wished he hadn't. The apartment was a mess. What happened, anyway?

Oh, yeah . . . those girls they picked up . . . but had they really emptied all those bottles lying on the floor?

He groaned and hung onto his head lest it split open. *Why* had he mixed scotch and stout?

Thunder lanced through his eardrums. He turned on the sofa and saw Gil emerging from the bedroom. The spaceman was thumping his chest and booming out a song learned last night. "Oh, *roly poly—*"

"Cut it out, will you?" groaned Husting.

"Huh? Man, you've had it, ain't you?" Gil clicked his tongue sympathetically. "Here, just a minute." He took a vial from his belt. "Take a few drops of this. It'll fix you up."

Somehow Husting got it down. There was a moment of fire and pinwheels, then—

—he was whole again. It was as if he had just slept ten hours without touching alcohol for the past week.

Gil returned to the bedroom and started pummeling his companions awake. Husting sat by the window, thinking hard. That hangover cure was worth a hundred million if he could only get the exclusive rights. But no, the technical envoys would show Earth how to make it, along with star ships and invisibility screens and so on. Maybe, though, he could hit the Galactics for what they had with them, and peddle it for a hundred dollars a drop before the full-dress mission arrived.

Bronni came in, full of cheer. "Say, you're all right, Joe," he trumpeted. "Ain't had such a good time since I was on Alphaz. What's next, old pal, old pal, old pal?" A meaty hand landed stunningly between Husting's shoulderblades.

"I'll see what I can do," said the Earthman cautiously. "But I'm busy, you know. Got some big deals cooking."

"I know," said Bronni. He winked. "Smart fellow like you. How the hell did you talk that bouncer around? I thought sure he was gonna call the cops."

"Oh, I buttered him up and slipped him a ten-spot. Wasn't hard."

"Man!" Bronni whistled in admiration. "I never heard anybody sling the words like you was doing."

Gil herded the others out and said he wanted breakfast. Husting led them all to the elevator and out into the street. He was rather short-spoken, having much to think about. They were in a ham-and-eggery before he said: "You spacemen must be pretty smart. Smarter than average, right?"

"Right," said Jordo. He winked at the approaching waitress.

"Lotta things a spaceman's got to know," said Col. "The ships do just about run themselves, but still, you can't let just any knucklehead into the crew."

"I see," murmured Husting. "I thought so."

A college education helps the understanding, especially when one is not too blinkered by preconceptions.

Consider one example: Sir Isaac Newton discovered (a) the three laws of motion, (b) the law of gravitation, (c) the differential calculus, (d) the elements of spectroscopy, (e) a good deal about acoustics, and (f) miscellaneous, besides finding time to serve in half a dozen official and honorary positions. A single man! And for a genius, he was not too exceptional; most gifted Earthmen have contributed to several fields.

And yet . . . such supreme intellect is not necessary. The most fundamental advances, fire- and tool-making, language and clothing and social organization, were made by apish dim-bulbs. It simply took a long time between discoveries.

Given a million years, much can happen. Newton founded modern physics in one lifespan. A hundred less talented men, over a thousand-year period, could slowly and painfully have accomplished the same thing.

The IQ of Earth humanity averages about 100. Our highest geniuses may have rated 200; our lowest morons, as stupid as possible without needing institutional care, may go down to 60. It is only some freak of mutation which has made the Earthman so intelligent; he never actually *needed* all that brain.

Now if the Galactic average IQ was around 75, with their very brightest boys going up to, say, 150—

The waitress yipped and jumped into the air; Bronni grinned shamelessly as she turned to confront him.

Joe Husting pacified her. After breakfast he took the Galactic emissaries out and sold them the Brooklyn Bridge.

DODGER FAN

by Will Stanton

As every science fiction fan knows, or think they know, the ideal person
to make first contact with extraterrestrials would be a science fiction
fan. But these ETs found themselves dealing with a fan of something else
entirely.*

⌘ ⌘ ⌘

*WILLIAM FRANK "WILL" STANTON (1918-1996) was a prolific
writer of humorous pieces, both fiction and essays, and a frequent
contributor to* The New Yorker, The Saturday Evening Post, Woman's
Day, Reader's Digest *(for which he was at one time a staff writer)*, Life,
Look, Esquire, Atlantic Monthly, *and other such notable publications.
He wrote four books, one published posthumously, and hundreds of
short stories and articles. One of his most popular articles was "How to
Tell a Democrat from a Republican," in* Ladies' Home Journal, *which
was read into the* Congressional Record *and, along with the poem
"Dandelions," and the science fiction story "Barney," has been included
in anthologies for use in classrooms as a learning tool. Another, "A Good
Word for November," was read for several years every November 1 by
Jim Mader on radio station WIBA in Madison, Wisconsin. Between*

---

* *By "science fiction fan," I mean someone who* reads *science fiction. I'd hate to
see ETs make contact with the Fandom-Is-a-Way-of-Life (FIAWOL) fuggheads.*

1951 and 1963, he contributed eleven stories to The Magazine of Fantasy and Science Fiction, *of which "Dodger Fan" is a sterling and hilarious example.*

"SOME VACATION," Jerome snapped off the TV. "All year I look forward to a little rest and relaxation. And what happens. The first game we lose on an error and a wild pitch—twelve innings. Game two is rained out. Today we get our hits—grand total."

Cleo, his wife, unwrapped a fresh stick of gum. "Five hits," she said. "Campy two, Duke one—"

"Who cares?" He walked to the window and looked out disgustedly. "You call that baseball?" He picked up his hat and headed for the door. "Some vacation."

"Erskine pitches tomorrow," Cleo said.

"Tomorrow the President could pitch," Jerome said. "I wouldn't be watching." He left the apartment and headed down the street. After a couple of blocks he hesitated and then stepped back and looked up at the gold sign. He couldn't remember seeing it before.

WANT TO VISIT MARS? STEP INSIDE.

Jerome stepped inside. He hadn't been going anyplace in particular. The man behind the counter was very friendly.

"Glad to have you aboard," he said. "You're the first to come in all day, and I was beginning to wonder. You see, I took a special course in Earth Psychology, so this is of great interest to me. What prompted you to visit Mars?"

"I just wanted to get out of town," Jerome said. "Detroit, Baltimore, Mars—it don't make any special difference."

"I graduated with honors, you know, from the Academy of Earthly Advertising and Customer Response. I was groomed for this job. So naturally your reaction—"

"If you've got a trip to Philly, I'll take that," Jerome said. "Anything so I don't have to hear about that crummy outfit they call a ball club. Mars is OK."

"I see. You understand the trip would be brief. We must depend on the space-warp continuum, which will be effective for only six more days. We would have to leave at once."

"It's my vacation," Jerome said. "I can do what I want."

When he stepped down on Mars, all of the big wheels were waiting. The Chairman of Lions Interplanetary, the Editor of *Martian Digest*, the head of the Future Voters' League, and others. The welcoming address was delivered by the President of the Solar Council.

"In conclusion," he said, "at this first meeting of the dominant cultures of the planetary system, may I extend to you, Jerome of Earth, the keys to our cities and the hearts of our people, in the fervent hope—"

Jerome had taken a pair of clippers from his pocket and was trimming his nails. "Likewise," he said.

"—in the fervent hope," said the President, "that the civilizations we represent may gain by this association some insight—"

"Looks like a mighty nice little planet you've got here," Jerome said.

After the ceremonies there was a small banquet at the Palace with some informal entertainment, and somewhat later Jerome was installed in the visitor's suite. He slept well.

The next morning he was treated to a gala patio breakfast with the Royal Martian Ballet performing on the terrace below. "You are surprised to feel so much at home," said the President, smiling. "You see, we have been listening to your radio for many years, and so have learned your language, your customs, your likes and dislikes.—"

"I like my eggs over easy," Jerome said. "But these are OK." He poked at them politely with his fork. "Anyhow, it's a change."

"We have planned so long for this occasion," said the President, "to show you our way of life, only to find our time so short—"

"Why don't we just drive around for a while," said Jerome. "If you got a car?"

They visited the Bureau of Statistical Research and Loving Kindness and the Criminal Building, and Jerome left his footprints in concrete at the Santorium of the Daughters of the Martian Revolution.

"Actually," said the President, "the Revolution never amounted to much, but these ladies are the daughters of it, and they're quite well to do. Now this afternoon—"

"As long as it's my vacation," said Jerome, "let's take in a ball game."

"First of all there is the Memorial Service of the Young Republicans' Club and then—" He paused. "A ball game, you say. Yes." He seemed to be thinking. "Very well, then, suppose we begin by having a bite of lunch."

There were fourteen courses, with appropriate wines and Solar Cola, so the luncheon was rather long. Long enough for the Martian Engineers and the Royal Construction Corps to erect a triple-decked stadium, and for two baseball teams to learn the game by means of microwave hypnosis. And for 120,000 volunteer fans to receive a short treatment of mass-suggestion. Jerome and the President arrived at the park and took their seats. The umpire dusted off home plate, the first baseman took a chew of tobacco, the batter knocked the dirt out of his spikes and the game began.

In the first inning there was a triple play and a triple steal. One of the managers was thrown out and the umpire was hit by a pop-bottle. Jerome frowned. "I only wish Cleo was here," he said.

"You miss her a great deal," said the President.

"She never did see an ump get flattened," he said. "Not from this close anyhow."

In the second inning, there was an inside-the-park grand slam home run, the third baseman made a triple error, and Jerome caught a pop foul. "Pretty fair seats," he said.

Returning to the Palace, the President outlined the rest of the day's schedule. "We're having a cocktail party in your honor," he said, "followed by a state dinner and the premiere of a new opera. Then a reception and a masked ball—"

"I thought I'd turn in early tonight," Jerome said. "Have a sandwich and a beer in my room and read the baseball almanac awhile."

"A sandwich and a beer in your room," said the President, "I see. Well, there should be beer in the icebox. If there's any special kind of sandwich you'd like we can stop at a delicatessen—"

"No special kind," Jerome said. The car turned in at the Palace.

The second morning was as busy as the first. The Tri-Centennial Military Review and Air Command Proceedings took up most of it so there was barely time to visit the Museum of Metaphysics and Household Design before lunch.

"This afternoon," said the President over the soup, "we have a program of unusual interest—"

"Who's pitching?" Jerome asked.

The royal construction Corps was forced to call on its civilian reserve to help rebuild the stadium it had torn down the night before. No one on Mars had considered the possibility that anybody would want to see more than one baseball game.

Driving home after the game, the President smiled. "Nothing wrong with a little relaxation, is there? Especially since tomorrow is going to be our big day. Something like your Independence Day: the Annual Opening of the Canals, address by the Philosopher-in-Chief, Dedication of the Five Hundredth Congress of Scientific—"

"Sounds great," said Jerome. "Be playing a double-header, I presume?"

"—of Scientific and Cultural Evalua—" The President paused. "A double-header, you say. Well, yes—naturally. If you'll excuse me a moment I have to make a phone call." He was in time. They had only ripped out the first three rows of seats.

Returning to the Palace the third day, Jerome seemed restless. "Nice of you to ask me up," he said, "and all, but I'd better be getting home."

"There are still two days," the President said. "It will be years before conditions will enable us to communicate with Earth again. There is much we have to give you: a cure for the common cold—the formula for universal peace—plans for a thirty-five inch color TV set the average boy can build for ten dollars—"

"I wouldn't mind staying on," Jerome said, "I'd like to see that little southpaw pitch tomorrow, but I got to get home. I promised Cleo I'd pick up the laundry, for one thing—"

"We had envisioned an exchange program," said the President, "of specialized personnel. Some of us going to Earth—some of you coming here."

"We could use a left-handed pitcher," Jerome said. "Probably we could give you a pretty good third baseman."

The President nodded. "At a moment like this there isn't very much I can say."

The trip to Earth was uneventful. Jerome was glad to be home. He hurried up to the apartment. Cleo was sitting in the same chair, watching the game.

"What inning?" he asked.

"Last of the third, no score," she said. "Been away?"

"Yeah." He settled down on the couch. "Newcombe pitching, huh?"

She nodded. "Got his fast ball working pretty good. Where'd you go—Canarsie?"

"Mars," he said. He started to unlace his shoes. "Campy's thumb bother him any?"

"Still got it taped, but he's swinging OK." She unwrapped a stick of gum. "What's it like up there—nice?

"Yeah," he said. "seemed like a pretty good crowd, what I saw of them. What did Reese do last time up?"

"Grounded to short," she said. "Why don't you come to the meeting Thursday—the Current Events Club? Give a little talk about them?Might be interesting."

Jerome went up to the set and adjusted the dial. "Talk about who?"

"Now you got it too dark," she said. "Talk about these friends you went to see. Up to Mars. They worth while getting to know?"

Jerome shook his head slowly. "Can't hit the curve ball," he said.

NO SHOULDER
TO CRY ON

by Hank Davis

Wouldn't it be simply splendid if someone older and wiser than you could hand you the solution to your problems on a platinum platter (why settle for mere silver?) and then you could live happily ever after. But happiness is relative and other things are, as well.

While it didn't solve any of my problems in 1968 when this story appeared in Analog—*for one thing, I was expecting to be drafted any time, and, a few months later I was—the check from Condé Nast was very welcome, and more important, I had sold a story to John W. Campbell, the man who had practically created the field of modern science fiction before I was even born. I wish that had been the first of other stories for Campbell's magazine, but in three years and two months, his death brought the end of an era. This story, of course, is not in the same league as the Olympian stories he published by Heinlein, Sturgeon, van Vogt, Leinster, Williamson, Asimov, et glorious al., and I would write it differently now, but it did appear in Campbell's magazine, and, barring time travel, they (forgive me, Ira Gershwin) can't take that away from me.*

✖ ✖ ✖

HANK DAVIS *is an editor emeritus at Baen Books. While a naïve* *youth in the early 1950s (yes, he's old!), he was led astray by sf comic books, and then by A. E. van Vogt's* Slan, *which he read in the Summer 1952 issue of* Fantastic Story Quarterly *while in the second grade, sealing his fate. He has had stories published mumble-mumble years ago in* Analog *(the one in this book),* If, F&SF, *and Damon Knight's* Orbit *anthology series. (There was also a story sold to* The Last Dangerous Visions, *but let's not go there.) A native of Kentucky, he currently lives in North Carolina to avoid a long commute to the Baen office.*

THE SHIP PURRED as it bored a tunnel through space; purred like a pampered and petted kitten.

It is, I was thinking, a hell of a noise for a spaceship to make.

A spaceship should roar like all the enraged lions that have ever walked the Earth, roaring *fortissimo* and in unison. It should spew flame burning more brightly than any tiger in any jungle—even Blake's bright burner.

This spaceship, however, spurned the more flamboyant traits of feline heritage and purred like an enormous kitten.

If it weren't for the purring, I thought, I wouldn't know that we were moving—the purring and the violet shift.

My shirt had been white when I left Earth. It now appeared to be a delicate violet hue. The field which allowed the ship to cheat Einstein and cover light-years in a matter of days shifted all light within the ship slightly toward the violet end of the spectrum. During the first few days of flight the shift had been irritating, giving me an irrational feeling that something was wrong with my eyes. I had compulsively rubbed my eyes until they were red and throbbing.

Now I scarcely noticed the shift. But I couldn't get used to the purring.

Maybe I associated it with cats. But that shouldn't have bothered me. Cats to me were like spinach. Some people love the stuff and some people hate it. I'm apathetic.

I'm edgy because of what Arthon said yesterday, I decided. I'm just reading something sinister into what he said. It's silly to get cold feet just as mankind's salvation comes out of the skies at the eleventh hour, I told myself. There's no reason to be afraid. There should be an end to fear now that there will be no atomic doom.

There had been the usual bumper crop of brushfire wars, some smoldering, some flaming brightly, all to the background music of rattling sabers. Dangerous, merrily blazing little brushfire wars in a world of deadly thermonuclear inflammables. There had been the arms race, more crowded than ever by the entry of Venezuela with its own A-bomb.

But there had also been visitors from interstellar space. Before the moon bases had been developed beyond the level of extraterrestrial summer camps, before man had gone to Mars in person, the stars had come to see him. And brought hope.

The old argument: we have scarcely begun to crawl in space, but look how far we have come in killability. Before we can send our own carcasses—and not some electronic gimmick, some glorified and hopped-up selfie camera—in person to Mars, we are able to sterilize the globe. If we can keep from blowing our collective brains out for just a little longer, we might even reach the Kuiper belt, chilly outpost of the sun's domain.

But to go beyond Pluto and reach the stars would require time; much time. To survive long enough to graduate from the solar system surely would require that we find the magic formula for peace; the therapy to prevent Terracide.

And, similarly, wouldn't visitors from extrasolar systems have found the key to *pacem in terris*; or, rather, *extraterris*?

Scant surprise, then, that *everybody* was ecstatic over the arrival of live and kicking, unbombed and unirradiated neighbors from Out There. Those who had advocated a hard line in foreign policy, consequently being villified as warmongers, were happiest of all, for it is a hard and lonely thing to advocate a necessary evil.

Immediately, all parties concerned got down to work on each other's languages. They learned ours before we learned theirs, naturally. They had more teachers than we did. When said language exchange had been reasonably well accomplished, and all the "hello there" rituals had been suffered through, the first questions from our side was, in essence, "How can eight point nine billion—and more on the way—highly belligerent people coexist on the same eight thousand-mile-diameter life raft without one or more groups of passengers capsizing the shaky thing and drowning one and all?"

The answer, again in essence, was: "We would have to study your history and culture in depth to determine what factors are responsible for any differences between our civilization and yours with respect to war or anything else, and the time required would be prohibitive; would put us so far behind schedule that our home planets would be concerned. Why not let us ferry experts of your planet to our planets and let them study our civilizations at their leisure? When they have determined the causes of differences in our civilizations, we will return them to Earth."

It made sense. If a group of people, all with the same IQ, were placed on an island as children and allowed to grow up with no contact with the outside world, would they ever develop the concept of intelligence? Could a man who grew up on a flat plain conceive of either mountains or valleys without seeing them? If the aliens had never slaughtered each other *en masse*, would it ever occur to them that there was anything unusual about the peaceful state of affairs, any more than we think it unusual that a man can't fly by wiggling his ears? If that man who had grown up on a plain ever wanted to learn all the various techniques involved in mountain climbing, he would have to go to where the mountains are.

Which was why I, Howard M. Nelson, Esq., Ph.D. in political science, and wearer of a white shirt that happened to look violet at the moment, happened to be on a purring spaceship hurtling through space at several hundred times the speed of light.

My mother didn't raise her boy to be a spaceman, I thought. I didn't look the part. An astronaut is as near to physical perfection as flesh born of mere man and woman can be, has the reflexes of a cougar with hypertension, has stamina enough to get out and carry the ship back home, should the rockets fail. This was common knowledge—so common that it had passed into the exalted category of things that "everyone knows." Yet here I was, receding hairline, advancing waistline and all, flying farther and faster than any of the smiling young spacefarers of Projects Mercury, Gemini, Apollo, *et al.*

Aside from some mild panic at takeoff, which had been overwhelmed by the greater fear that I would show the panic and make a fool of myself, all had gone well until yesterday. I had been talking to Arthon, the pilot and entire crew of the ship, and he had hit me between the eyes with an umpteen hundred megaton firecracker—one of the ones that my little thirty-seven light year jaunt could cover, hopefully, with cobwebs.

"There is so much that we can learn from you," I had said. "It's a shame that there is no way we can repay you."

"*The reverse is that which is true*," he had replied. "That which we can learn from you is greater than that which you can learn from us."

Feeling as if a gallon of ice water had been poured into my BVDs, I had said, "Oh, gee. Yeah, sure. Uh." We he-men always have a little trouble speaking our minds; especially when hit with brain-scrambling firecrackers like the aforementioned.

"Pardon? Perhaps I have not the mastery of your language which I thought was mine," Arthon had said, his features clouded with very human concern.

By now, I had re-erected the façade behind which we humans, masters of Earth, spend our lives hiding. "But you are so much more advanced than we, what can we possibly teach you?"

"You underestimate your people and in a way that is unjust, Howard," he replied, smiling a very human smile. "As for what that is known by you that can benefit us"—sorrow flowed across his face and spilled over into his voice—"I think that that will be left as a surprise for the time which will be that of arrival."

Judging from his new mood, the surprise would be as cheery as an unexpected visit by Jack the Ripper.

Now, some twenty-four hours later and about thirty minutes from arrival, I was in a very calm state of hysteria. Dammit, why had Arthon looked like Gloom & Doom, Inc. when he told me that there was much that we Earthside primitives could teach his side—which consisted of some fifty-odd inhabited planets in a loose federation.

Arthon had been very chummy during the trip. He looked very human except for his light blue fur and prehensile tail. He was more human on the inside than the administrators back at my university. I had thought that we were becoming fast friends, as the Rover Boys would say. . . . Maybe he was going to have to throw me to the lions when we arrived and he was regretting it.

But what could *they* learn from *us*?

Maybe we had followed up pathways of discovery that they had neglected. The American Indians were around for a long time without inventing the wheel.

Suppose they developed their space drive without ever developing atomic power.

Arthon had said that the drive had no moving parts. I didn't have the mathematical background to understand how it worked, he said, but he could easily show me how to make one. If it was that simple, could the extrasolarites, as I called them, have hit upon the drive by accident and still be, with the exception of the drive, in a more primitive state of technological development than humans? Then they wouln't have the wherewithal to bump each other off and woudn't need any magic formula for peace. Arthon's planet was out to get the know-how for nuclear power and lick the other planets in the federation. *That* was what his people could learn from me!

Nope—because Earth had been discovered by a *fleet* of extrasolarites; one ship from each planet in the federation. And each ship had taken back one (1) Earthling to its home planet; so no planet would have an advantage over any other. Moreover, each Earthling taken was just like me—an ultra-departmentalized specialist in the social sciences whose total knowledge of atomic power consisted of: "Well, there're some bombs that have uranium in them and some that have hydrogen and the ones with hydrogen make bigger bangs and the bombs cause fallout, yup, yup, yup."

My 10-year-old son was a bug about science and electronics. They could have found out more about atomic power by snatching him than by carting me off.

What if, instead of the planets of the Federation fighting among themselves, they have ganged up and go around looking for other planets to clobber?

Nope—in that case, why did they contact us instead of just going back home with the news of fresh prey? And, if they wanted to size us up as to what kind of a fight we would give them, why were they taking social scientists back with them instead of military experts?

My train of thought was derailed by Arthon's entrance. "Howard, the time which will be that of the breaking out of pseudospace will be ten minutes from this time," he informed me. "Would that which you want be to see it?"

"Lead on, MacDuff," I said. The misquote fit my mood.

I went with him down the corridor, which was throbbing with the engine's pussy-noise galore, and followed him into the control room. We sat down in deep-cushioned seats, both with slots for a prehensile tail, and looked through the viewscreen at the rippling violet shell that surrounded the ship.

"You promised me a surprise," I reminded him.

"At this time the surprise would be that which I could only tell you. In five minutes, it will be that which can be seen with those eyes which are your own." He paused. "It is afraid that I am, Howard, that honest is not what we have been with you."

Little crawling bits of fear were in my spinal column, as numerous as ants in an anthill. "How is that?"

"You are hoping that the secret of peace is something which can be obtained from us, are you not?"

"Yes. We were expecting a rain of death from the skies any day. Then you came and we, well . . . had hope again."

"For how long had this rain of death from your skies been something that you had expected?"

"What?"

"Let me ask again the question in another shape. How long has atomic power been with you humans?"

My heart sank. "Well, uh, since 1945."

"And how many times has a war seen the use of atomic weapons?"

"Well, twice. Both times in the same year—1945."

"So, you have not used the weaons of which you have great fear for almost as long as you have had them."

"Well . .. yes." I frowned.

"Atomic power was our discovery over three hundred of your years ago."

"And you haven't wiped yourselves out? Now I know that you must have the key to peace, Arthon!" (But, still, something was calling the short hairs on the back of my neck to military attention.)

"The terribleness of nuclear weapons has not the final greatness that you think it does, Howard. There are perfect defenses against them. There are energy fields which are such that a fission bomb will not explode within them. There are other such fields for fusion bombs and antimatter bombs."

"Then you've survived because you have defenses against atomic weapons. You can give them to us and there will be no atomic war."

"Understanding is that which you do not yet have, Howard. There are weapons which have a deadliness far greater than those I have named. There are biological weapons. There are X-ray lasers. The knowledge is ours which can convert a sunspot into a laser and incinerate the sunlit half of a planet. And defenses are ours which nullify those weapons. And others that are more terrible."

"To have survived such dangers proves that you have the key to peace that I seek."

"As I have said, Howard, honest is not what we have been with you. We have misled your people. Happiness was ours when we saw that to study us was your wish and so we gladly took you and your fellows to the planets which were ours, because there is that which we must learn from you."

He paused. My tongue was looking for a hole to crawl into and hide.

"As you once told me, and exactly as you told me, 'A common characteristic equally shared by a group is not evident to the group as a characteristic until they encounter another group which has the characteristic to a different degree.' As you said, 'A colony of people, all having the same IQ, would have no awareness of intelligence as a variable.' True would be what this statement would be even if the colony were one of geniuses, would it not, Howard?"

He had amazed me by quoting me verbatim, pedantic professorial phrasing and all. He must have a photographic memory. "Yes, Arthon," I answered.

"Earth is a colony of geniuses, Howard. In the years which have been those of your development of atomic weapons, you have used only two bombs, both small ones. In my planet's number of years that were the same, we used hundreds, many of them more powerful than any that are yours now. Your population is expanding so fast as to be that which is a problem to you. Our population is now one tenth of that which it was when we discovered atomic energy. The time of our discovery was more than three of your centuries back. The number of planets which are those in our federation, as you call it, is shrinking. Eighty-seven planets which once were among those which are members are lifeless balls rolling through space now."

The violet curtain parted and we began the approach to Arthon's planet on slow drive. My white shirt was no longer violet, but I ignored it. I was looking at the ugly craters on the planet's surface, which were plainly visible, even at this distance, like planetary smallpox scars. I could easily see the black areas where nothing green grew.

A tear, running ahead to act as scout for the main body, crept out of Arthon's left eye.

"The job of keeping the peace is that which your humans think you have done poorly," he said in a voice soft as a crumbling dream. "Teach us how to do a job that is as poor. Please!"

HORNETS' NEST

by Lloyd Biggle, Jr.

Humanity's first starship narrowly avoided making contact with aliens—which was fortunate for the human race's survival.

※ ※ ※

LLOYD BIGGLE, JR. *(1923-2002) was wounded in World War II and permanently disabled, in spite of which he resumed his education, finally earning a Ph.D. from the University of Michigan. He subsequently taught at the same university, and also Eastern Michigan University in the 1950s. After he published his first short story, "Gypped," in the July 1956* Galaxy, *he went on to write two dozen novels and hundreds of short stories. He wrote both science fiction and mystery novels and stories, combining both genres in his Jan Darzek series about a private detective in the future, which began with his 1963 novel* All the Colors of Darkness. *His academic field was musicology, which often showed up in some of his stories, most notably in his frequently reprinted novelet "The Tunesmith." I read "Hornets' Nest" when it appeared in* If *in 1959, and it has stuck with me over the succeeding decades. If you'll pardon a digression, in the early 1980s, a science fiction writer announced at a convention that a woman wanted recordings of SF stories that she could duplicate for the blind. I remembered "Hornets' Nest" and recorded it, and a couple of other favorite but less than famous stories on a cassette, and sent it to the address. It came back a*

month later, marked, "Moved—No Forwarding Address." I think of that
experience whenever I find myself having idealistic impulses and need
to suppress them with a dose of reality. At least, I can bring the story
back into print without being thwarted this time.

THEY SAT IN THE CAPTAIN'S QUARTERS, relaxed in the easy
silence of close friendship as they absently sipped drinks and watched
the monitor of the ship's scanner screen. There was Captain Miles
Front, big, formidable-looking, a healthy and robust forty-five. There
was Clyde Paulson, his brilliant young navigator. There was the
expedition's chief scientist, Doctor John Walter, a pleasant-looking,
balding man of indeterminate age.

It was Paulson who broke the silence. "I have an important
mission of my own," he said.

They regarded him with amused skepticism, and he grinned
good-naturedly.

"An ancestor of mine, my great-great-great—how many
generations has it been now? Anyway, old Grandfather Paulson left
Earth in some kind of disgrace. The details have been forgotten, down
through the years, but the legend has been passed along as a family
joke. I don't know whether he joined the colonists to run away, or
whether that was someone's idea of a good way to get rid of him.
Anyway, it's kind of a pledge to the family's honor that the first one to
get back to Earth will check up and see whether Grandfather Paulson
has been exonerated, or pardoned, or acquitted, or whatever. That's
my mission. Not that it will make any difference to Grandfather
Paulson one way or the other."

"So that's why you were so eager to make this trip," the captain
said. "You needn't have bothered. A lot of chance you will have to rake
up a scandal that old!"

"I thought it was a pretty good excuse," said Paulson.

Doctor Walter pointed at a boldly glimmering star. "You're sure
that's the one?"

Paulson grinned, and Captain Front chuckled dryly.

"Disappointed to find it looks just like another star?" the captain said.

"Maybe," Walter said dreamily. "This is a different kind of mission for me. It's a pilgrimage. There are maddening blank spaces in the information the colonists brought with them about this solar system. I hope to fill in some of those. I'd like to fill all of them in."

"You may be able to," the captain said. "Remember that Earth's scientists haven't been standing still all this time. They must have progressed beyond the point they'd reached when the colonists left. Perhaps they'll have everything you want waiting for you."

Walter shrugged and the captain chuckled again, and said to Paulson, "I've disappointed him. He doesn't want to find the answers on file. He wants to dig them out for himself."

Doctor Walter said to the captain, "What's your mission?"

"To get us there and back. And frankly—" he turned to look at the lone, flickering star—"there are angles to this thing that bother me. It's just possible that our mother planet might not be at all glad to see us."

"It should greet us with open arms," Walter said. "The population problem was serious when the colonists left. It will be critical by now. We can use the people, and Earth should be able to spare as many as we want. Our science is bound to be ahead of Earth's in many respects, and we know they can't match our starships, or we would have heard from them before now. Ships that bring out new colonists can take essential raw materials back to Earth. Cooperation will benefit all of us."

"It should," the captain said, "But we don't know how Earth will look at it. When the original colonists left, there was supposed to be a new ship every couple of years. Nothing has been heard from Earth since. It looks as if Earth simply wrote us off and forgot about us. Now that we've built our own civilization, and maybe done far better than Earth expected, we might not be welcomed back. Earth might be jealous. Or it might have a guilty conscience. It *should* have."

"Faulty navigation," Paulson suggested.

"An occasional ship might go astray. Not all of them. No. The thing has me worried. That's why I want to hit Pluto Base and planet-hop our way in. Give Earth notice that we're coming, and a chance to get used to the idea before we arrive."

Doctor Walter brightened. "Pluto Base. I wonder if they ever found a tenth planet."

Clyde Paulson laid out a perfect interception course for Pluto, and he was still grinning with satisfaction when they brought the ship down. The captain rotated the scanner and looked broodingly at the frigid, airless landscape.

"Is this Pluto Base or isn't it?" he growled.

"It is," Paulson said confidently.

"They're taking their time about sending out a reception committee. They should have picked us up hours ago. Some security system!"

They waited, straining their eyes to pick out details. Doctor Walter came into the control room. He glanced at the screen and exclaimed, "Why, there's nothing there!"

"Pluto Base is underground," the captain said, rotating the scanner again. "Or at least it was. I imagine it still is."

"Stop!" Paulson shouted. "Over there on that hill—wouldn't that be the base entrance?"

The captain threw in the magnification unit.

"It could be," Doctor Walter said.

"It is," the captain said. "And the airlock is open."

They landed, watched, saw nothing more and entered.

They went cautiously through the empty corridors. Equipment was there. Supplies were there. Machinery was in operating condition. All signs indicated a hasty departure.

"They left just before lunch," Doctor Walter said in the mess room. "The food is still here, laid out for them."

"All we'd have to do" Captain Front said, "is close the airlock, start the air machines and take over. The supplies would last us indefinitely. I can understand that they might find reasons to abandon this base, but why would they pull out and leave all this stuff?"

"The transmitters are in working condition," a communications officer said. "It'd be easy to start the power station. Shall we call Earth and ask them?"

The captain said, "Now that I think of it, we haven't picked up any signals from Earth, have we?"

There was an uneasy silence. The captain looked around at the faces that peered grotesquely at him through spacesuit faceplates.

"Then we won't call Earth," he said, "until we're certain just what might be there to answer us."

They spiraled slowly in toward the sun, probing, exploring, searching, constantly alert and cautious. They touched Neptune and Uranus and such moons as looked promising. They touched a half-dozen of the moons of Saturn. The bases, where they found them, were desolate and abandoned.

Not until they reached the moons of Jupiter did they find the first dusty remnants of human bodies.

"Whatever it was," Doctor Walter said, "it happened quickly."

"Attack?" the captain asked.

"I can't believe it. An attack can take people by surprise but they're not too surprised to know what's happening. Some of them would take defensive measures. Most of them would act for their own safety. These people were stricken down in the everyday routine of living."

"Disease? Plague?"

"It wouldn't strike everyone at the same instant. This did."

"We might as well go on," the captain said. "If it's necessary, we can hit any of these places again on the way out."

From that moment they all knew. No one talked about it. No one even hinted at the cold fear that twisted within him. The communications men continued to search vainly for signals. The scientists carried on their observations. The ship's officers rotated the scanner toward a far-off corner of emptiness and strained to see a fleck of light that would be Earth when they came closer. And they all knew what they would find there.

On Mars, it was no longer desolate bases. It was annihilated cities except that stone and mortar and steel were untouched. The people had been struck down as unsuspectingly as if a remote deity had suddenly decided upon doomsday. The flimsy atmosphere domes had lost their air and the buildings stood in excellent preservation, a futile monument to a wasted dream.

And then there was Earth. Rolling green hills, majestic cities, awesome natural wonders, all familiar, like a long-forgotten love. Majestic cities of the dead. Towns and villages and hamlets and solitary dwelling of the dead.

They had known what they would find, and they found it, and still were stunned.

"It hit the whole solar system," Doctor Walter said, snapping his fingers, "just like that."

Paulson objected. "There weren't any bodies at the outer bases. Those people had a chance to get away—or at least to try."

The captain nodded. "I have a hunch that Venus and Mercury were caught. If so, that means it struck the solar system out as far as Jupiter's moons. Something from the sun?"

Walter pondered the suggestions, and shook his head. "Heat would have left traces. So would any kind of radiation I know of that could do this. How long has it been? We should be able to pick up the exact date."

They landed at New Washington. The specialists, the experts, went grimly to work. The archeologist who had come to probe eagerly some faded secrets of Earth's ancient peoples found himself with the problem of an extinct interplanetary civilization. The botanist could only wonder at the survival of abundant flora when all fauna had perished. The bacteriologist, the chemist, the physicists, the military intelligence officer masquerading as a diplomat, all pondered the possible source of the catastrophe.

Clyde Paulson, unwanted by the scientists and unneeded by his ship, found his way into the military records section and gazed disheartened at the mountainous files of films.

"Well," he said, "since I've got nothing better to do . . ."

He searched the index references, found Paulsons in quantity, but no mention of his dishonored ancestor.

"Odd," he said, "He couldn't have been such a scoundrel that they destroyed his records."

He prowled through the building, sampling the priceless military secrets of a lost civilization, getting himself lost, becoming more frustrated by the hour. He sat down to analyze his problem.

"Permanent records," he mused. "Those would be records that are complete. In other words, when a man's service was terminated, they filmed his records and put them in the permanent file. There would be another file for those on active service. Which means that old Grandfather Paulson was still considered on active service when it happened. Which is odd, because he left with the colonists. Could that mean the colonists . . ."

Impossible. A shipload of colonists wouldn't kill off the civilization that mothered it, and then leave for the stars in search of breathing room—even if it had the power.

He continued his search, and eventually he found active records of the military services. They were crudely kept files containing paper documents and records and even these were only abstracts of service records. He comprehended, at length, that the complete records were kept with the man at his point of service. What a prodigious amount of effort to devote to such a simple matter as record keeping!

"Paulson, Paul," the file said. "Space Navy. Serial Number 0329 B9472 A8974."

Paulson took the file and carried it out into the fresh air, to a plot of tangled grass where there were no bleached bones to dishearten him. He settled down to read of the bright development of a promising military career that had ended in disgrace.

Paul Paulson had held the rank of captain in the Space Navy. He was a pilot of the highest qualifications. He had served with distinction on a number of dangerous missions. His last assignment had been the Space Navy Base on Callisto, Jupiter Command. The record concluded with the notation of a court-martial on a charge of insubordination, and the terse verdict: *Guilty.*

Accompanying the file was a smaller folder, labeled, "Summary of Court-Martial Proceedings Against Paul Paulson." The contents of the folder had been withdrawn for study, a notation informed him. H opened it and found a single sheet of paper that had been overlooked or unwanted.

Paulson said to the captain, "Have they found anything?"

"They found one thing. This happened just about two Earth months after the colonists left Pluto Base. I remember something in the old records about their communications with Earth breaking down sooner than they'd expected. Now we know why. It looks as if the human race missed extermination by an eyelash. What have you been up to?"

"I found a personnel file on Grandfather Paulson. I suppose no one will object to my taking it."

"None of the natives I've met will object. Have you vindicated the old man?"

"He received a court-martial for insubordination. That would be no disgrace in our family. Funny thing, though: the trial summary is missing, except for one statement by Grandfather Paulson. Interested?"

"Let's have it."

Captain Front took the paper and read. "To whom it may concern: It is true that I have refused to obey the orders of the Scientific Mission, in spite of the fact that my commanding officer ordered me to do so. It is true that I made a serious attempt to break the neck of the Scientific Mission's chairman, Doctor Harold Dolittle. It is also true that I sincerely regret this attempt.

"I hold nothing personal against Doctor Dolittle. Scientists have been playing at exterminating the human race for centuries and it's probably only an accident that one of them hasn't succeeded before now. And since Doctor Dolittle actually has succeeded, breaking his neck would not help the situation. It was bound to happen sooner or later, anyway.

"When I was a kid back in Minnesota, there was a boy on our street named Fitzharris Holloway. We all called him Fizz and he wasn't a bad kid except that he was just too curious to live. Let a bunch of us stand around a puddle and it would always be Fizz who would drop a big rock and splash mud all over our Sunday clothes and get the lot of us whipped. He'd drop it just to see what would happen. The average mentality could figure that out without the experiment, but Fizz's mentality wasn't average. It was scientific. He had to see for himself. Let us find a hornets' nest and it would be Fizz who had to punch a stick into it. He'd get stung, of course, but so would the rest of us.

"You've heard that old gag about throwing an egg into an electric fan? Almost everyone has, I guess, and been satisfied just to hear it. But Fizz had to see for himself. He got egg splashed all over himself and his ma's new dress, and he wore a pillow to his meals for the next three days.

"They'll never forget Fizz at old Central High School. The scars he left in that chemistry laboratory will last as long as the building. All the teacher had to say was, 'Don't do this.' And there would be Fizz out in the lab trying it out.

"I figure now that Fizz was just a natural-born scientist. Most of us are curious about things as children—curious within limits, that is—but we outgrow it. A scientist never outgrows it, and the law of averages gives us a certain number of irresponsible scientists. Fizz met his end in a bar one night, when he dropped a lighted cigarette into the bulging front of a woman's dress. She picked up a bottle and broke it over his head, and the jury called it justifiable homicide. If all natural-born scientists had run squarely into the consequences of their curiosity at such an early age, the human race might be no further along than the Bronze Age, but at least it would have a future.

"I attempted to resign my Space Navy commission when I first learned that I was to assist Doctor Dolittle in his experiments. Contrary to normal procedure, my resignation was not accepted. I am now requesting permission to resign and join the star colonists. They have an opening for a reserve pilot and will favorably consider my application. I believe the risks of star colonization to be considerably less than those of remaining in this solar system. Doctor Dolittle has been poking at a hornets' nest, and the more light-years away I am when the hornets come out, the better I'll like it.

"Respectfully yours, Captain Paul Paulson."

★ ★ ★

Captain Front stroked his cheek thoughtfully. "So they let him go. And then, two months after the colonists left, this happened. What sort of experiments was this Scientific Mission carrying on?"

"The only thing I could find was Grandfather's statement."

"I wonder if they were conducting some kind of solar experiments. I never thought of the sun as being a hornets' nest. What comes out when you poke a sun?"

"Grandfather was attached to the Jupiter Base Command, on Callisto. We might find more information there. Any chance of hitting Callisto again on the way out?"

"We'll see what we find here. If this looks like a likely clue, we'll have to follow it up. So far, there haven't been any other clues. Let's see what Walter says about this."

Vainly they searched such mute records as Earth had to offer. They sifted the bones of the Venus colonists and looked in at Mercury Base, where death had interrupted the lonely vigil of a small group of scientists and soldiers. Then they turned back. Mars again, then an asteroid base, and then Callisto.

And the complete file on Captain Paul Paulson.

Paulson searched further and found the records of the Scientific Mission. He carried an armload of document to Captain Front.

"Found any answers?" the captain asked.

"Not all of them," Paulson said, "but enough."

"Solar research?"

"No. Jupiter research."

"Odd," the captain mused. "Whatever happened hit everything from the Jupiter moons through the system clear to Mercury."

"This Doctor Dolittle," Paulson said, "was doing some intensified research that concerned Jupiter. First, he used a series of atomic warheads to test the depth of the atmosphere. Then he wanted someone to pilot a ship on a tight parabolic orbit that would take him closer to Jupiter than any human had ever been before. As an added twist, the ship was to be paralleled closer in by a guided missile that could broadcast instrument readings. Grandfather Paulson was ordered to pilot the ship. He refused. He was tried for insubordination, convicted and sentenced to a prison term."

"But he left with the star colonists."

"Yes, by escaping from confinement. He got out to Pluto Base and stowed away on the starship. Jupiter Command was furious when it found out what had happened. The commandant ordered the starship to turn around and bring him back. The starship was out of the system then and it refused."

"Well, that's an interesting bit of family history, but it doesn't explain what wiped out humanity."

Paulson said grimy, "Doesn't it?"

"Does it?"

"Grandfather Paulson said Doctor Dolittle had been poking at a hornets' nest. He was poking at Jupiter, and it was vigorous poking—he used atomic warheads. Then, when Grandfather refused to pilot Dolittle's ship, Dolittle found another pilot who would. They went into their orbit and made the trip successfully, but they lost their guided missile. Then, a few weeks later, they found it again."

Captain Front said blankly, "They lost it on Jupiter—and then they found it?"

"The missile came shooting back at them," said Paulson. "I gather that it was only a piece of luck that let them capture it, because the mechanism had been altered in a way they called 'astonishing,' and it used an unknown fuel. Its speed was something they couldn't believe. It represented several hundred years' progress for them at one crack, and it gave them the secret of star travel. They went to work on it, and they were too enthused to give much thought to what else might come up from Jupiter."

The captain walked over to a port and looked out at the sky. *"Jupiter?"*

"It must have been hell for something native to Jupiter to take to space travel, but someone—or something—was as mad as a hornet. Atomic warheads wouldn't soothe anyone's feelings."

"So it—or they—headed toward the sun."

"At unbelievable speeds," Paulson said. "Those on the outer

planets either had time to try to escape, or maybe to come to help."

"And all the humanity they could find—how did they do it?"

"I hope we never know. How did they ever get off Jupiter? Not even our starship could manage that. What's the escape velocity?"

"Too much."

"Well, I found the study they made of the missile. It's an advance in mankind's knowledge—at the price of mankind."

"I'll have Walter go over it."

"Where is he?" Paulson asked. "I haven't seen him for days."

The captain stiffened. "My God! He's down on Amalthea, conducting some Jupiter experiments!"

The desolate rock-strewn surface of Amalthea curved sharply away from them to its shallow horizon and the light in the sky was Jupiter. The huge disc of the planet hovered menacingly above them

The churning bands of clouds writhed and struggled like live beings in the throes of mortal agony. Even as they watched, the colors deepened and faded, yellow clouds boiled into the brown of the North Equatorial Belt, and the enigmatic, so-called *red spot* shimmered with a repulsive, grayish pinkness.

"Grandfather must have had come kind of apprehension about it," Paulson said. "Just the sight of it is enough to scare a man to death. I feel as if it were going to gobble me up."

He turned expectantly to Doctor Walter, and the scientist said nothing. Behind the tinted thickness of his faceplate, his eyes bulged and sparkled.

"I feel," Paulson said, "as if I were on a disabled ship that is likely to crash at any second."

The scientist took a step forward—toward Jupiter. "Out, damned spot!" he muttered. "Out, I say!"

Paulson jumped, and came down slowly. "How was that again?"

"Shakespeare," the scientist said.

"I said I feel as if I were on a disabled ship—"

"I heard you. Nonsense. It's true that this little moon is falling toward Jupiter, but it's only an inch and a fraction a year. Fifty million years from now, it'll be a few miles closer. Eventually it'll go all the way but *you* won't be around to worry about it."

"No one will be around to worry about it," Paulson said. "Do you think someone down there will think it's another bombardment when the moon falls, and come up to see who did it?"

Walter said shortly, "I wouldn't know."

"You have to admit that was a stupid way to experiment on an unknown planet. Atomic warheads!"

"Who would have imagined anything could be living down there?" Walter said.

"But what could they learn?"

"I'm sure they had some definite objective. You don't think they did it just for the fun of it, do you?"

Paulson turned, "Your hour's up. Let's get going."

They made long, slow-motion bounds across the crumbling surface. Suddenly Paulson missed Walter, and turned to find him motionless, staring at Jupiter.

"You said an hour was all you wanted," Paulson said sharply. "We're jumping off at midnight, you know, and I only have half the computations made."

"All right," Walter said. "I was just looking."

When they reached the tiny lifeship, Walter turned again, before he entered the airlock. "I'd give a lot to know what's down there. With all the study that Scientific Mission put in, they really found out nothing about the planet."

"I can tell you how to manage it," said Paulson.

"How?"

"Give us about a six-month start. Then fly down and see for yourself. We'll leave you the lifeship."

Walter turned abruptly and entered the airlock.

Paulson followed him. "Sure, it's a fascinating thing," he said. "And I'm glad the planets in our own solar systems run Earth-normal and smaller. Otherwise, some scientist might decide to conduct some experiments. I'm glad Jupiter is light-years away from my home town, but after this I'll never feel easy about it. Who can say that they won't come out again someday, and take to star traveling?"

They took off, and Paulson set course for Callisto Base. A moment later Walter got up and left the control section. When Paulson got curious and went back to look for him, he found the scientist pressing his face against a porthole, staring at Jupiter.

PROTECTED SPECIES

by H. B. Fyfe

When is a first contact not a first contact? When, as John W. Campbell wrote introducing this story in Astounding Science-Fiction *in 1951, one side has "an inadequate understanding of the facts."*

⋈ ⋈ ⋈

HORACE BROWNE FYFE, JR. (1918-1997) seems to have eluded the biographers of science fiction, and I wish I had more information about him. The ponderously formidable Nicholss-Clute encyclopedia mentions only that his first story was "Locked Out" in 1940, his career was interrupted by army service in WWII, and afterwards he wrote a series about the Bureau of Slick Tricks, in which clever humans outwit dim-witted aliens. In 1962 he published his only novel, D-99, which continues in much the same vein as the Slick Tricks series. "The tone is fortunately light," the Nicholss-Clute tome comments. James Gunn's less ponderous New Encyclopedia of Science Fiction *mentions that he was a laboratory assistant and draftsman. Other sources give little more than bibliographical information. Please note, however, that the aforementioned "Locked Out" has the distinction of appearing in the Golden Age* Astounding Science-Fiction, *and dealt ingeniously with the problem of a space pilot on a solo mission who accidently becomes locked out of his ship, with nothing around but hard vacuum. Over a decade later, Fyfe published "Manners of the Age" in* Galaxy, *with a light tone, but also hilariously and ingeniously exploring the possibility of a future when people communicate electronically and hardly ever see each other in person, with resultant behavior that will be familiar to anyone who's observed the temper tantrums, bullying, and flame wars that' are common on the Internet. And it may be "fortunate" that the Bureau of Slick Tricks stories are humorous, but if "Protected Species" is humorous, it's entirely the gallows variety.*

THE YELLOW STAR, of which Torang was the second planet, shone hotly down on the group of men viewing the half-built dam from the heights above. At a range of eighty million miles, the effect was quite Terran, the star being somewhat smaller than Sol.

For Jeff Otis, fresh from a hop through space from the extra-bright star that was the other component of the binary system, the heat was enervating. The shorts and light shirt supplied him by the planet coordinator were soaked with perspiration. He mopped his forehead and turned to his host.

"Very nice job, Finchley," he complimented. "It's easy to see you have things well in hand here."

Finchley grinned sparingly. He had a broad, hard, flat face with tight lips and mere slits of blue eyes. Otis had been trying ever since the previous morning to catch a revealing expression on it.

He was uneasily aware that his own features were too frank and open for an inspector of colonial installations. For one thing, he had too many lines and hollows in his face, a result of being chronically underweight from space-hopping among the sixteen planets of the binary system.

Otis noticed that Finchley's aides were eying him furtively.

"Yes, Finchley," he repeated to break the little silence, "you're doing very well on the hydroelectric end. When are you going to show me the capital city you're laying out?"

"We can fly over there now," answered Finchley. "We have tentative boundaries laid out below those pre-colony ruins we saw from the 'copter."

"Oh, yes. You know, I meant to remark as we flew over that they looked a good deal like similar remnants on some of the other planets."

He caught himself as Finchley's thin lips tightened a trifle more. The coordinator was obviously trying to be patient and polite to an official from whom he hoped to get a good report, but Otis could see he would much rather be going about his business of building up the colony.

He could hardly blame Finchley, he decided. It was the fifth planetary system Terrans had found in their expansion into space, and there would be bigger jobs ahead for a man with a record of successful accomplishments. Civilization was reaching out to the stars at last. Otis supposed that he, too, was some sort of pioneer, although he usually was too busy to feel like one.

"Well, I'll show you some photos later," he said. "Right now, we— Say, why all that jet-burning down there?"

In the gorge below, men had dropped their tools and seemed to be charging toward a common focal point. Excited yells carried thinly up the cliffs.

"Ape hunt, probably," guessed one of Finchley's engineers.

"Ape?" asked Otis, surprised.

"Not exactly," corrected Finchley patiently. "That's common slang for what we mention in reports as Torangs. They look a little like big, skinny, gray apes, but they're the only life large enough to name after the planet."

Otis stared down into the gorge. Most of the running men had given up and were straggling back to their work. Two or three, brandishing pistols, continued running and disappeared around a bend.

"Never catch him now," commented Finchley's pilot.

"Do you just let them go running off whenever they feel like it?" Otis inquired.

Finchley met his curious gaze stolidly. "I'm in favor of anything that will break the monotony, Mr. Otis. We have a problem of morale, you know. This planet is a key colony, and I like to keep the work going smoothly."

"Yes, I suppose there isn't much for recreation yet."

"Exactly. I don't see the sport in it myself but I let them. We're up to schedule."

"Ahead, if anything," Otis placated him. "Well, now, about the city?"

Finchley led the way to the helicopter. The pilot and Otis waited while he had a final word with his engineers, then they all climbed in and were off.

Later, hovering over the network of crude roads being leveled by Finchley's bulldozers, Otis admitted aloud that the location was well chosen. It lay along a long, narrow bay that thrust in from the distant ocean to gather the waters of the same river that was being dammed some miles upstream.

"Those cliffs over there," Finchley pointed out, "were raised up since the end of whatever civilization used to be here—so my geologist tells me. We can fly back that way, and you can see how the ancient city was once at the head of the bay."

The pilot climbed and headed over the cliffs. Otis saw that these formed the edge of a plateau. At one point, their continuity was marred by a deep gouge.

"Where the river ran thousands of years ago," Finchley explained.

They reached a point from which the outlines of the ruined city were easily discerned. From the air, Otis knew, they were undoubtedly plainer than if he had been among them.

"Must have been a pretty large place," he remarked. "Any idea what sort of beings built it or what happened to them?"

"Haven't had time for that yet," Finchley said. "Some boys from the exploration staff poke around in there every so often. Best current theory seems to be that it belonged to the Torangs."

"The *animals* they were hunting before?" asked Otis.

"Might be. Can't say for sure, but the diggers found signs the city took more of a punch than just an earthquake. Claim they found too much evidence of fires, exploded missiles, and warfare in general—other places as well as here. So . . . we've been guessing the Torangs are degenerate descendants of the survivors of some interplanetary brawl."

Otis considered that. "Sounds plausible," he admitted, "but you ought to do something to make sure you are right."

"Why?"

"If it *is* the case, you'll have to stop your men from hunting them; degenerated or not, the Colonial Commission has regulations about contact with any local inhabitants."

Finchley turned his head to scowl at Otis, and controlled himself with an obvious effort. "Those *apes*," he demanded.

"Well, how can you tell"? Ever try to contact them?"

"Yes! At first, that is; before we figured them for animals."

"And?"

"Couldn't get near one." Finchley declared heatedly. "If they had any sort of half-intelligent culture, wouldn't they let us make *some* sort of contact?"

"Offhand," admitted Otis, "I should think so. How about setting down a few minutes? I'd like a look at the ruins."

Finchley glared at his wristwatch, but directed the pilot to land at a cleared spot. The young man brought them down neatly and the two officials alighted.

Otis, glancing around, saw where the archaeologists had been digging. They had left their implements stacked casually at the site— the air was dry up here and who was there to steal a shovel?

He left Finchley and strolled around a mound of dirt that had been cleared away from an entrance to one of the buildings. The latter had been built of stone, or at least faced with it. A peep into the dim excavation led him to believe there had been a steel framework, but the whole affair had been collapsed as if by an explosion.

He walked a little way further and reached a section of presumably taller buildings where the stone ruins thrust above the sandy surface. After he had wandered through one or two arched openings that seemed to have been windows, he understood why the explorers had chosen to dig for their information. If any covering or decoration had ever graced the walls, it had long since been weathered off. As for ceiling or roof, nothing remained.

"Must have been a highly developed civilization just the same," he muttered.

A movement at one of the shadowed openings to his right caught his eye. He did not remember noticing Finchley leave the helicopter to follow him, but he was glad of a guide.

"Don't you think so?" he added.

He turned his head, but Finchley was not there. In fact, now that Otis was aware of his surroundings, he could hear the voices of the other two mumbling distantly back by the aircraft.

"Seeing things!" he grumbled, and started through the ancient window.

Some instinct stopped him half a foot outside.

Come on, Jeff, he told himself, *don't be silly! What could be there? Ghosts?*

On the other hand, he realized, there were times when it was just as well to rely upon instinct—at least until you figured out the origin of the strange feeling. Any spaceman would agree to that. The man who developed an animal sixth sense was the man who lived longest on alien planets.

He thought he must have paused a full minute or more, during which he had heard not the slightest sound except the mutter of voices to the rear. He peered into the chamber, which was about twenty feet square and well if not brightly lit by reflected light.

Nothing was to be seen, but when he found himself turning his head stealthily to peer over his shoulder, he decided that the queer sensation along the back of his neck meant something.

Wait, now, he thought swiftly. *I didn't see quite the whole room.*

The flooring was heaped with wind-bared rubble that would not show footprints. He felt much more comfortable to notice himself thinking in that vein.

At least, I'm not imagining ghosts, he thought.

Bending forward the necessary foot, he thrust his head through the opening and darted a quick look to left, then to the right along the wall. As he turned right, his glance was met directly by a pair of very wide-set black eyes which shifted inward slightly as they got his range.

The Torang about matched his own six-foot-two height, mainly because of elongated, gibbonlike limbs and a similarly crouching stance. Arms and legs, covered with short, curly, gray fur, had the same general proportions as human limbs, but looked half-again too long for a trunk that seemed to be ribbed all the way down. Shoulder and hip joints were compactly lean, rather as if the Torang had developed on a world of lesser gravity than that of the human.

It was the face that made Otis stare. The mouth was toothless and probably constructed more for sucking than for chewing. But the eyes! They projected like ends of a dumbbell from each side of the narrow skull where the ears should have been, and focused with obvious mobility. Peering closer, Otis saw tiny ears below the eyes, almost hidden in the curling fur of the neck.

He realized abruptly that his own eyes felt as if they were bulging out, although he could not remember having changed his expression of casual curiosity. His back was getting stiff also. He straightened up carefully.

"Uh . . . hello," he murmured, feeling unutterably silly but conscious of some impulse to compromise between a tone of greeting for another human being and one of pacification to an animal.

The Torang moved then, swiftly but unhurriedly. In fact, Otis later decided, deliberately. One of the long arms swept downward to the rubble-strewn ground.

The next instant, Otis jerked his head back out of the opening as a stone whizzed past in front of his nose.

"Hey!" he protested involuntarily.

There was a scrabbling sound from within, as of animal claws churning to a fast start among the pebbles. Recovering his balance, Otis charged recklessly through the entrance.

"I don't know why," he admitted to Finchley a few minutes later. "If I stopped to think how I might have had my skull bashed in coming through, I guess I'd have just backed off and yelled for you."

Finchley nodded, but his narrow gaze seemed faintly approving for the first time since they had met.

"He was gone, of course," Otis continued. "I barely caught a glimpse of his rump vanishing through another window."

"Yeah, they're pretty fast," put in Finchley's pilot. "In the time we've been here, the boys haven't taken more than half a dozen. Got a stuffed one over at headquarters though."

"Hm-m-m," murmured Otis thoughtfully.

From their other remarks, he learned that he had not noticed everything, even though face to face with the creature. Finchley's mentioning the three digits of the hands or feet, for instance, came as a surprise.

Otis was silent most of the flight back to headquarters. Once there, he disappeared with a perfunctory excuse toward the rooms assigned him.

That evening, at a dinner which Finchley had made as attractive as was possible in a comparatively raw and new colony, Otis was noticeably sociable. The coordinator was gratified.

"Looks as if they finally sent us a regular guy," he remarked behind his hand to one of his assistants. "Round up a couple of the prettier secretaries to keep him happy."

"I understand he nearly laid hands on a Torang up at the diggings," said the other.

"Yep, ran right at it barehanded. Came as close to bagging it as anybody could, I suppose."

"Maybe it's just as well he didn't," commented the assistant. "They're big enough to mess up an unarmed man some."

Otis, meanwhile and for the rest of the evening, was assiduously busy making acquaintances. So engrossed was he in turning every new conversation to the Torangs and asking seemingly casual questions about the little known of their habits and possible past, that he hardly noticed receiving any special attentions. As a visiting inspector, he was used to attempts to entertain and distract him.

The next morning, he caught Finchley at his office in the sprawling one-story structure of concrete and glass that was colonial headquarters.

After accepting a chair across the desk from the coordinator, Otis told him his conclusions. Finchley's narrow eyes opened a trifle when he heard the details. His wide, hard-muscled face became slightly pink.

"Oh, for—! I mean, Otis, why must you make something big out of it? The men very seldom bag one anyway!"

"Perhaps because they're so rare," answered Otis calmly. "How do we know they're not intelligent life? Maybe if you were hanging on in the ruins of your ancestors' civilization, reduced to a primitive state, *you'd* be just as wary of a bunch of loud Terrans moving in!"

Finchley shrugged. He looked vaguely uncomfortable, as if debating whether Otis or some disgruntled sportsman from his husky construction crews would be easier to handle.

"Think of the overall picture a minute," Otis urged. "We're pushing out into space at last, after centuries of dreams and struggles. With all the misery we've seen in various colonial systems at home, we've tried to plan these ventures so as to avoid old mistakes."

Finchley nodded grudgingly. Otis could see that his mind was on the progress charts of his many projects.

"It stands to reason," the inspector went on, "that someday we'll find a planet with intelligent life. We're still new in space, but as we probe farther out, it's bound to happen. That's why the Commission drew up rules about native life forms. Or have you read that part of the code lately?"

Finchley shifted from side to side in his chair.

"Now, look!" he protested. "Don't go making *me* out a hardboiled vandal with nothing in mind but exterminating everything that moves on all Torang. I don't go out hunting the apes!"

"I know, I know," Otis soothed him. "But before the Colonial Commission will sanction any destruction of indigenous life, we'll have to show—*besides* that it's not intelligent—that it exists in sufficient numbers to avoid extinction."

"What do you expect me to do about it?"

Otis regarded him with some sympathy. Finchley was the hard-bitten type that the Commission needed to oversee the first breaking-in of a colony on a strange planet, but he was not unreasonable. He merely wanted to be left alone to handle the tough job facing him.

"Announce a ban on hunting Torangs," Otis said. "There must be something else they can go after."

"Oh, yes," admitted Finchley. "There are swarms of little rabbit-things and other vermin running through the brush. But, I don't know—"

"It's standard practice," Otis reminded him. "We have many a protected species even back on Terra that would be extinct by now, only for the game laws."

In the end, they agreed that Finchley would do his honest best to enforce a ban provided Otis obtained a formal order from the headquarters of the system. The inspector went from the office straight to the communications center, where he filed a long report for the chief coordinator's office in the other part of the binary system.

It took some hours for the reply to reach Torang. When it came that afternoon, he went looking for Finchley.

He found the coordinator inspecting a newly finished canning factory on the coast, elated at the completion of one more link in making the colony self-sustaining.

"Here it is," said Otis, waving the message copy. "Signed by the chief himself. 'As of this date, the apelike beings known as Torangs, indigenous to planet number and so forth, are to be considered a rare and protected species under regulations and so forth et cetera.' "

"Good enough," answered Finchley with an amiable shrug. "Give it here, and I'll have it put on the public address system and the bulletin boards."

Otis returned satisfied to the helicopter that had brought him out from headquarters.

"Back, sir?" asked the pilot.

"Yes . . . *no!* Just for fun, take me out to the old city. I never did get a good look the other day, and I'd like to before I leave."

They flew over the plains between the sea and the upjutting cliffs. In the distance, Otis caught a glimpse of the rising dam he had been shown the day before. This colony would go well, he reflected, as long as he checked up on details like preserving native life forms.

Eventually, the pilot landed at the same spot he had been taken on his previous visit to the ancient ruins. Someone else was on the scene today. Otis saw a pair of men he took to be archaeologists.

"I'll just wander around a bit," he told the pilot.

He noticed the two men looking at him from where they stood

by the shovels and other equipment, so he paused to say hello. As he thought, they had been digging in the ruins.

"Taking some measurements in fact," said the sunburned blond introduced as Hoffman. "Trying to get a line on what sort of things built the place."

"Oh?" said Otis, interested. "What's the latest theory?"

"Not so much different from us," Hoffman told the inspector while his partner left them to pick up another load of artifacts.

"Judging from the size of the rooms, height of doorways, and such stuff as stairways," he went on, "they were pretty much our size. So far, of course, it's only a rough estimate."

"Could be ancestors of the Torangs, eh?" asked Otis.

"Very possible, sir," answered Hoffman, with a promptness that suggested it was his own view. "But we haven't dug up enough to guess at the type of culture they had, or draw any conclusions as to their psychology or social customs."

Otis nodded, thinking that he ought to mention the young fellow's name to Finchley before he left Torang. He excused himself as the other man returned with a box of some sort of scraps the pair had unearthed, and strolled between the outlines of the untouched buildings.

In a few minutes, he came to the section of higher structures where he had encountered the Torang the previous day.

"Wonder if I should look in the same spot?" he muttered aloud. "No . . . that would be the *last* place the thing would return to . . . unless it had a lair thereabouts—"

He stopped to get his bearings, then shrugged and walked around a mound of rubble toward what he believed to be the proper building.

Pretty sure this was it, he mused. *Yes, shadows around that window arch look the same . . . same time of day—*

He halted, almost guiltily, and looked back to make sure no one was observing his futile return to the scene of his little adventure. After all, an inspector of colonial installations was not supposed to run around ghost hunting like a small boy.

Finding himself alone, he stepped briskly through the crumbling arch—*and froze in his tracks.*

"I am honored to know you," said the Torang in a mild, rather buzzing voice. "We thought you possibly would return here."

Otis gaped. The black eyes projecting from the sides of the narrow head tracked him up and down, giving him the unpleasant sensation of being measured for an artillery salvo.

"I am known as Jal-Ganyr," said the Torang. "Unless I am given incorrect data, you are known as Jeff-Otis. That is so."

The last statement was made with almost no inflection, but some still-functioning corner of Otis' mind interpreted it as a question. He sucked in a deep breath, suddenly conscious of having forgotten to breathe for a moment.

"I didn't know . . . yes, that is so . . . I didn't know you Torangs could speak Terran. Or anything else. How—?"

He hesitated as a million questions boiled up in his mind to be asked. Jal-Ganyr absently stroked the gray fur of his chest with his three-fingered left hand, squatting patiently on a flat rock. Otis felt somehow that he had been allowed to waste time mumbling only by grace of disciplined politeness.

"I am not of the Torangs," said Jal-Ganyr in his wheezing voice. "I am of the Myrbs. You would possibly say Myrbii. I have not been informed."

"You mean that is your name for yourselves?" asked Otis.

Jal-Ganyr seemed to consider, his mobile eyes swiveling inward to scan the Terran's face.

"More than that," he said at last, when he had thought it over. "I mean I am of the race originating at Myrb, not of this planet."

"Before we go any further," insisted Otis, "tell me, at least, how you learned our language!"

Jal-Ganyr made a fleeting gesture. His "face" was unreadable to the Terran, but Otis had the impression he had received the equivalent of a smile and a shrug.

"As to that," said the Myrb, "I possibly learned it before you did. We have observed you a very long time. You would unbelieve how long."

"But then—" Otis paused. That must mean before the colonists had landed on this planet. He was half-afraid it might mean before they had reached this sun system. He put aside the thought and asked, "But then, why do you live like this among the ruins? Why wait till now? If you had communicated, you could have had our help rebuilding . . ."

He let his voice trail off, wondering what sounded wrong. Jal-Ganyr rolled his eyes about leisurely, as if disdaining the surrounding ruins. Again, he seemed to consider all the implications of Otis' questions.

"We picked up your message to your chief," he answered at last. "We decided time is to communicate with one of you. We have no interest in rebuilding," he added. "We have concealed quarters for ourselves."

Otis found that his lips were dry from his unconsciously having let his mouth hang open. He moistened them with the tip of his tongue, and relaxed enough to lean against the wall.

"You mean my getting the ruling to proclaim you a protected species?" he asked. "You have instruments to intercept such signals?"

"I do. We have," said Jal-Ganyr simply. "It has been decided that you have expanded far enough into space to make necessary we contact a few of the thoughtful among you. It will possibly make easier in the future for our observers."

Otis wondered how much of that was irony. He felt himself flushing at the memory of the "stuffed specimen" at headquarters, and was peculiarly relieved that he had not gone to see it.

I've had the luck, he told himself. *I'm the one to discover the first known intelligent beings beyond Sol!*

Aloud, he said, "We expected to meet someone like you eventually. But why have you chosen me?"

The question sounded vain, he realized, but it brought unexpected results.

"Your message. You made in a little way the same decision we made in a big way. We deduce that you are one to understand our regret and shame at what happened between our races . . . long ago."

"Between—?"

"Yes. For a long time, we thought you were all gone. We are pleased to see you returning to some of your old planets."

Otis stared blankly. Some instinct must have enabled the Myrb to interpret his bewildered expression. He apologized briefly. "I possibly forgot to explain the ruins." Again, Jal-Ganyr's eyes swiveled slowly about.

"They are not ours," he said mildly. "They are yours."

THE CAGE

by A. Bertram Chandler

The humans knew that they had made contact with rational aliens, but the aliens did not return the favor. For the humans, that was humiliating, exasperating—and deadly.

✖ ✖ ✖

Arthur Bertram Chandler *(1912-1984) was a prolific writer, publishing over 40 books and 200 shorter works, for which he won four Ditmar Awards. He is best known for his long-running series about the exploits of Captain (among other ranks) John Grimes, who has often been called science fiction's equivalent of Horatio Hornblower, but his writing started much earlier, with stories appearing in* Astounding Science-Fiction, *the leading SF magazine of the decade, during what has been called its Golden Age. His first story, "This Means War!", appeared in the May 1944 issue. The following year,* ASF *published "Giant Killer" probably his most popular work of less than novel length. (Unfortunately, I can't describe the story without ruining it for anyone who hasn't read it yet.) A lifelong seaman in the English, Australian, and New Zealand merchant marine, Chandler often worked his nautical experience into his stories, particularly in the John Grimes saga. That's something that's not in evidence in "The Cage," which Chandler once wrote was probably his* second *most popular short story. Deservedly so, I hope the reader will agree.*

IMPRISONMENT is always a humiliating experience, no matter how philosophical the prisoner. Imprisonment by one's own kind is bad enough—but one can, at least, talk to one's captors, one can make one's wants understood; one can, on occasion, appeal to them man to man.

Imprisonment is doubly humiliating when one's captors, in all honesty, treat one as a lower animal.

The party from the survey ship could, perhaps, be excused for failing to recognize the survivors from the interstellar liner *Lode Star* as rational beings. At least two hundred days had passed since their landing on the planet without a name—an unintentional landing made when *Lode Star*'s Ehrenhaft generators, driven far in excess of their normal capacity by a breakdown of the electronic regulator, had flung her far from the regular shipping lanes to an unexplored region of Space. *Lode Star* had landed safely enough; but shortly thereafter (troubles never come singly) her Pile had got out of control and her Captain had ordered his first mate to evacuate the passengers and such crew members not needed to cope with the emergency, and to get them as far from the ship as possible.

Hawkins and his charges were well clear when there was a flare of released energy, a not very violent explosion. The survivors wanted to turn to watch, but Hawkins drove them on with curses and, at times, blows. Luckily they were up wind from the ship and so escaped the fall-out.

When the fireworks seemed to be over Hawkins, accompanied by Dr. Boyle, the ship's surgeon, returned to the scene of the disaster. The two men, wary of radioactivity, were cautious and stayed a safe distance from the shallow, still-smoking crater that marked where the ship had been. It was all too obvious to them that the captain, together with his officers and technicians, were now no more than an infinitesimal part of the incandescent cloud that had mushroomed up into the low overcast.

Thereafter, the fifty-odd men and women, the survivors of *Lode*

Star, had degenerated. It hadn't been a fast process—Hawkins and Boyle, aided by a committee of the more responsible passengers, had fought a stout rearguard action. But it had been a hopeless sort of fight. The climate was against them, for a start. Hot it was, always in the neighborhood of 85° Fahrenheit. And it was wet—a thin, warm drizzle falling all the time. The air seemed to abound with the spores of fungi—luckily these did not attack living skin but throve on dead organic matter, on clothing. They throve to an only slightly lesser degree on metals and on the synthetic fabrics that many of the castaways wore.

Danger, outside danger, would have helped to maintain morale. But there were no dangerous animals. There were only little smooth-skinned things, not unlike frogs, that hopped through the sodden undergrowth, and, in the numerous rivers, fishlike creatures ranging in size from the shark to the tadpole, and all of them possessing the bellicosity of the latter.

Food had been no problem after the first few hungry hours. Volunteers had tried a large, succulent fungus growing on the boles of the huge fernlike trees. They had pronounced it good. After a lapse of five hours they had neither died nor even complained of abdominal pains. That fungus was to become the staple diet of the castaways. In the weeks that followed other fungi had been found, and berries, and roots—all of them edible. They provided a welcome variety.

Fire—in spite of the all-pervading heat—was the blessing most missed by the castaways. With it they could have supplemented their diet by catching and cooking the little frog-things of the rain forest, the fishes of the streams. Some of the hardier spirits did eat these animals raw, but they were frowned upon by most of the other members of the community. Too, fire would have helped to drive back the darkness of the long nights, would, by its real warmth and light, have dispelled the illusion of cold produced by the ceaseless dripping of water from every leaf and frond.

When they fled from the ship, most of the survivors had possessed pocket lighters—but the lighters had been lost when the pockets, together with the clothing surrounding them, had disintegrated. In any case, all attempts to start a fire in the days when there were still pocket lighters had failed; there was not, Hawkins swore, a single dry spot on the whole accursed planet. Now the making of fire was quite impossible: even if there had been present an expert on the rubbing together of two dry sticks he could have found no material with which to work.

They made their permanent settlement on the crest of a low hill. (There were, so far as they could discover, no mountains.) It was less thickly wooded there than the surrounding plains, and the ground was less marshy underfoot. They succeeded in wrenching fronds from the fernlike trees and built for themselves crude shelters—more for the sake of privacy than for any comfort that they afforded. They clung, with a certain desperation, to the governmental forms of the worlds that they had left, and elected themselves a council. Boyle, the ship's surgeon, was their chief. Hawkins, rather to his surprise, was returned as a council member by a majority of only two votes— on thinking it over he realized that many of the passengers must still bear a grudge against the ship's executive staff for their present predicament.

The first council meeting was held in a hut—if so it could be called—especially constructed for the purpose. The council members squatted in a rough circle. Boyle, the president, got slowly to his feet. Hawkins grinned wryly as he compared the surgeon's nudity with the pomposity that he seemed to have assumed with his elected rank, as he compared the man's dignity with the unkempt appearance presented by his uncut, uncombed gray hair, his uncombed and straggling gray beard.

"Ladies and gentlemen," began Boyle.

Hawkins looked around him at the naked, pallid bodies, at the stringy, lusterless hair, the long, dirty fingernails of the men and the unpainted lips of the women. He thought, *I don't suppose I look much like an officer and a gentleman myself.*

"Ladies and gentlemen," said Boyle, "we have been, as you know, elected to represent the human community upon this planet. I suggest that at this, our first meeting, we discuss our chances of survival— not as individuals, but as a race—"

"I'd like to ask Mr. Hawkins what our chances are of being picked up," shouted one of the two women members, a dried-up, spinsterish creature with prominent ribs and vertebrae.

"Slim," said Hawkins. "As you know, no communication is possible with other ships, or with planet stations when the Interstellar Drive is operating. When we snapped out of the Drive and came in for our landing we sent out a distress call—but we couldn't say where we were. Furthermore, we don't know that the call was received—"

"Miss Taylor," said Boyle huffily, "Mr. Hawkins, I would remind you that I am the duly elected president of this council. There will be time for a general discussion later.

"As most of you may already have assumed, the age of this planet, biologically speaking, corresponds roughly with that of Earth during the Carboniferous Era. As we already know, no species yet exists to challenge our supremacy. By the time such a species does emerge—something analogous to the giant lizards of Earth's Triassic Era—we should be well established—"

"*We* shall be dead!" called one of the men.

"We shall be dead," agreed the doctor, "but our descendants will be very much alive. We have to decide how to give them as good a start as possible. Language we shall bequeath to them—"

"Never mind the language, Doc," called the other woman member. She was a small blonde, slim, with a hard face. "It's just this question of descendants that I'm here to look after. I represent the women of childbearing age—there are, as you must know, fifteen of us here. So far the girls have been very, very careful. We have reason to be. Can you, as a medical man, guarantee—bearing in mind that you have no drugs, no instruments—safe deliveries? Can you guarantee that our children will have a good chance of survival?"

Boyle dropped his pomposity like a worn-out garment.

"I'll be frank," he said. "I have not, as you, Miss Hart, have pointed out, either drugs or instruments. But I can assure you, Miss Hart, that your chances of a safe delivery are far better than they would have been on Earth during, say, the eighteenth century. And I'll tell you why. On this planet, so far as we know (and we have been here long enough now to find out the hard way), there exist no microorganisms harmful to Man. Did such organisms exist, the bodies of those of us still surviving would be, by this time, mere masses of suppuration. Most of us, of course, would have died of septicemia long ago. And that, I think, answers *both* your questions."

"I haven't finished yet," she said. "Here's another point. There are fifty-three of us here, men and women. There are ten married couples—so we'll count them out. That leaves thirty-three people, of whom twenty are men. Twenty men to thirteen (aren't we girls always unlucky?) women. All of us aren't young—but we're all of us women. What sort of marriage set-up do we have? Monogamy? Polyandry?"

"Monogamy, of course," said a tall, thin man sharply. He was the only one of those present who wore clothing—if so it could be called. The disintegrating fronds lashed around his waist with a strand of vine did little to serve any useful purpose.

"All right, then," said the girl. "Monogamy. I'd rather prefer it that way myself. But I warn you that if that's the way we play it there's going to be trouble. And in any murder involving passion and jealousy the woman is as liable to be a victim as either of the men—and I don't want *that*."

"What do you propose, then, Miss Hart?" asked Boyle.

"Just this, Doc. When it comes to our matings we leave love out of it. If two men want to marry the same woman, then let them fight it out. The best man gets the girl—and keeps her."

"Natural selection . . ." murmured the surgeon. "I'm in favor—but we must put it to the vote."

At the crest of the low hill was a shallow depression, a natural arena. Round the rim sat the castaways—all but four of them. One of the four was Dr. Boyle. He had discovered that his duties as president embraced those of a referee; it had been held that he was best competent to judge when one of the contestants was liable to suffer permanent damage. Another of the four was the girl Mary Hart. She had found a serrated twig with which to comb her long hair, she had contrived a wreath of yellow flowers with which to crown the victor. Was it, wondered Hawkins as he sat with the other council members, a hankering after an Earthly wedding ceremony, or was it a harking back to something older and darker?

"A pity that these blasted molds got our watches," said the fat man on Hawkins' right. "If we had any means of telling the time we could have rounds, make a proper prizefight of it."

Hawkins nodded. He looked at the four in the center of the arena—at the strutting, barbaric woman, at the pompous old man, at the two dark-bearded young men with their glistening white bodies. He knew them both—Fennet had been a senior cadet of the ill-fated *Lode Star;* Clemens, at least seven years Fennet's senior, was a passenger, had been a prospector on the frontier worlds.

"If we had anything to bet with," said the fat man happily, "I'd lay it on Clemens. That cadet of yours hasn't a snowball's chance in hell. He's been brought up to fight clean—Clemens has been brought up to fight dirty."

"Fennet's in better condition," said Hawkins. "He's been taking exercise, while Clemens has just been lying around sleeping and eating. Look at the paunch on him!"

"There's nothing wrong with good, healthy flesh and muscle," said the fat man, patting his own paunch.

"No gouging, no biting!" called the doctor. "And may the best man win!"

He stepped back smartly away from the contestants, stood with the Hart woman.

There was an air of embarrassment about the pair of them as they stood there, each with his fists hanging at his sides.

Each seemed to be regretting that matters had come to such a pass.

"Go *on!*" screamed Mary Hart at last. "Don't you want me? You'll live to a ripe old age here—and it'll be lonely with no woman!"

"They can always wait around until your daughters grow up, Mary!" shouted one of her friends.

"If I ever have any daughters!" she called. "I shan't at this rate!"

"Go on!" shouted the crowd. "Go on!"

Fennet made a start. He stepped forward almost diffidently, dabbed with his right fist at Clemens' unprotected face. It wasn't a hard blow, but it must have been painful. Clemens put his hand up to his nose, brought it away and stared at the bright blood staining it. He growled, lumbered forward with arms open to hug and crush. The cadet danced back, scoring twice more with his right.

"Why doesn't he *hit* him?" demanded the fat man.

"And break every bone in his fist? They aren't wearing gloves, you know," said Hawkins.

Fennet decided to make a stand. He stood firm, his feet slightly apart, and brought his right into play once more. This time he left his opponent's face alone, went for his belly instead. Hawkins was surprised to see that the prospector was taking the blows with apparent equanimity—he must be, he decided, much tougher in actuality than in appearance.

The cadet sidestepped smartly . . . and slipped on the wet grass. Clemens fell heavily on to his opponent; Hawkins could hear the *whoosh* as the air was forced from the lad's lungs. The prospector's thick arms encircled Fennet's body—and Fennet's knee came up viciously to Clemens' groin. The prospector squealed, but hung on grimly. One of his hands was around Fennet's throat now, and the other one, its fingers viciously hooked, was clawing for the cadet's eyes.

"No gouging!" Boyle was screaming. "No gouging!"

He dropped down to his knees, caught Clemens' thick wrist with both his hands.

Something made Hawkins look up then. It may have been a sound, although this is doubtful; the spectators were behaving like boxing fans at a prizefight. They could hardly be blamed—this was the first piece of real excitement that had come their way since the loss of the ship. It may have been a sound that made Hawkins look up, it may have been the sixth sense possessed by all good spacemen. What he saw made him cry out.

Hovering above the arena was a helicopter. There was something about the design of it, a subtle oddness that told Hawkins that this was no Earthy machine. Suddenly, from its smooth, shining belly dropped a net, seemingly of dull metal. It enveloped the struggling figures on the ground, trapped the doctor and Mary Hart.

Hawkins shouted again—a wordless cry. He jumped to his feet, ran to the assistance of his ensnared companions. The net seemed to be alive. It twisted itself around his wrists, bound his ankles. Others of the castaways rushed to aid Hawkins.

"Keep away!" he shouted. "Scatter!"

The low drone of the helicopter's rotors rose in pitch. The machine lifted. In an incredibly short space of time the arena was to the first mate's eyes no more than a pale green saucer in which little white ants scurried aimlessly. Then the flying machine was above and through the base of the low clouds, and there was nothing to be seen but drifting whiteness.

When, at last, it made its descent Hawkins was not surprised to see the silvery tower of a great spaceship standing among the low trees on a level plateau.

The world to which they were taken would have been a marked improvement on the world they had left had it not been for the mistaken kindness of their captors. The cage in which the three men were housed duplicated, with remarkable fidelity, the climatic conditions of the planet upon which *Lode Star* had been lost. It was glassed in, and from sprinklers in its roof fell a steady drizzle of warm water. A couple of dispirited tree ferns provided little shelter from the depressing precipitation. Twice a day a hatch at the back of the cage, which was made of a sort of concrete, opened, and slabs of a fungus remarkably similar to that on which they had been subsisting were thrown in. There was a hole in the floor of the cage; this the prisoners rightly assumed was for sanitary purposes.

On either side of them were other cages. In one of them was Mary Hart—alone. She could gesture to them, wave to them, and that was all. The cage on the other side held a beast built on the same general lines as a lobster, but with a strong hint of squid. Across the broad roadway they could see other cages, but could not see what they housed.

Hawkins, Boyle and Fennet sat on the damp floor and stared through the thick glass and the bars at the beings outside who stared at them.

"If only they were humanoid," sighed the doctor. "If only they were the same shape as we are we might make a start towards convincing them that we, too, are intelligent beings."

"They aren't the same shape," said Hawkins. "And we, were the situations reversed, would take some convincing that three six-legged beer barrels were men and brothers . . . Try Pythagoras' Theorem again," he said to the cadet.

Without enthusiasm the youth broke fronds from the nearest tree fern. He broke them into smaller pieces, then on the mossy floor laid them out in the design of a right-angled triangle with squares constructed on all three sides. The natives—a large one, one slightly smaller and a little one—regarded him incuriously with their flat, dull eyes. The large one put the tip of a tentacle into a pocket—the things wore clothing—and pulled out a brightly colored packet, handed it to the little one. The little one tore off the wrapping, started stuffing pieces of some bright blue confection into the slot on its upper side that, obviously, served it as a mouth.

"I wish they were allowed to feed the animals," sighed Hawkins. "I'm sick of that damned fungus."

"Let's recapitulate," said the doctor. "After all, we've nothing else to do. We were taken from our camp by the helicopter—six of us. We were taken to the survey ship—a vessel that seemed in no way superior to our own interstellar ships. You assure us, Hawkins, that the ship used the Ehrenhaft Drive or something so near to it as to be its twin brother. . . ."

"Correct," agreed Hawkins.

"On the ship we're kept in separate cages. There's no ill treatment, we're fed and watered at frequent intervals. We land on this strange planet, but we see nothing of it. We're hustled out of cages like so many cattle into a covered van. We know that we're being driven *somewhere,* that's all. The van stops, the door opens and a couple of these animated beer barrels poke in poles with smaller editions of those fancy nets on the end of them. They catch Clemens and Miss Taylor, drag them out. We never see them again. The rest of us spend the night and the following day and night in individual cages. The next day we're taken to this . . . zoo . . ."

"Do you think they were vivisected?" asked Fennet. "I never liked Clemens, but. . ."

"I'm afraid they were," said Boyle. "Our captors must have learned of the difference between the sexes by it. Unluckily there's no way of determining intelligence by vivisection—"

"The filthy brutes!" shouted the cadet.

"Easy, son," counseled Hawkins. "You can't blame them, you know. We've vivisected animals a lot more like us than we are to these things."

"The problem," the doctor went on, "is to convince these things—as you call them, Hawkins—that we are rational beings like themselves. How would they define a rational being? How would *we* define a rational being?"

"Somebody who knows Pythagoras' Theorem," said the cadet sulkily.

"I read somewhere," said Hawkins, "that the history of Man is the history of the fire-making, tool-using animal . . ."

"Then make fire," suggested the doctor. "Make us some tools, and use them."

"Don't be silly. You know that there's not an artifact among the bunch of us. No false teeth even—not even a metal filling. Even so . . ." He paused. "When I was a youngster there was, among the cadets in the interstellar ships, a revival of the old arts and crafts. We considered ourselves in a direct fine of descent from the old windjammer sailormen, so we learned how to splice rope and wire, how to make sennit and fancy knots and all the rest of it. Then one of us hit on the idea of basketmaking. We were in a passenger ship, and we used to make our baskets secretly, daub them with violent colors and then sell them to passengers as genuine souvenirs from the Lost Planet of Arcturus VI. There was a most distressing scene when the Old Man and the mate found out . . ."

"What are you driving at?" asked the doctor.

"Just this. We will demonstrate our manual dexterity by the weaving of baskets—I'll teach you how."

"It might work. . . ." said Boyle slowly. "It might just work. . . . On the other hand, don't forget that certain birds and animals do the same sort of thing. On Earth there's the beaver, who builds quite cunning dams. There's the bower bird, who makes a bower for his mate as part of the courtship ritual . . ."

The head keeper must have known of creatures whose courting habits resembled those of the Terran bower bird. After three days of feverish basketmaking, which consumed all the bedding and stripped the tree ferns, Mary Hart was taken from her cage and put in with the three men. After she had got over her hysterical pleasure at having somebody to talk to again she was rather indignant.

It was good, thought Hawkins drowsily, to have Mary with them. A few more days of solitary confinement must surely have driven the girl crazy. Even so, having Mary in the same cage had its drawbacks. He had to keep a watchful eye on young Fennet. He even had to keep a watchful eye on Boyle—the old goat!

Mary screamed.

Hawkins jerked into complete wakefulness. He could see the pale form of Mary—on this world it was never completely dark at night—and, on the other side of the cage, the forms of Fennet and Boyle. He got hastily to his feet, stumbled to the girl's side.

"What is it?" he asked.

"I . . . I don't know . . . Something small, with sharp claws . . . It ran over me . . ."

"Oh," said Hawkins, "that was only Joe."

"*Joe?*" she demanded.

"I don't know exactly what he—or she—is," said the man.

"I think he's definitely *he*," said the doctor.

"What is Joe?" she asked again.

"He must be the local equivalent to a mouse," said the doctor, "although he looks nothing like one. He comes up through the floor somewhere to look for scraps of food. We're trying to tame him—"

"You encourage the brute?" she screamed. "I demand that you do something about him—at once! Poison him, or trap him. Now!"

"Tomorrow," said Hawkins.

"Now!" she screamed.

"Tomorrow," said Hawkins firmly.

The capture of Joe proved to be easy. Two flat baskets, hinged like the valves of an oyster shell, made the trap. There was bait inside—a large piece of the fungus. There was a cunningly arranged upright that would fall at the least tug at the bait. Hawkins, lying sleepless on his damp bed, heard the tiny click and thud that told him that the trap had been sprung. He heard Joe's indignant chitterings, heard the tiny claws scrabbling at the stout basketwork.

Mary Hart was asleep. He shook her.

"We've caught him," he said.

"Then kill him," she answered drowsily.

But Joe was not killed. The three men were rather attached to him. With the coming of daylight they transferred him to a cage that Hawkins had fashioned. Even the girl relented when she saw the harmless ball of multi-colored fur bouncing indignantly up and down in its prison. She insisted on feeding the little animal, exclaimed gleefully when the thin tentacles reached out and took the fragment of fungus from her fingers.

For three days they made much of their pet. On the fourth day, beings whom they took to be keepers entered the cage with their nets, immobilized the occupants, and carried off Joe and Hawkins.

"I'm afraid it's hopeless," Boyle said. "He's gone the same way . . ."

"They'll have him stuffed and mounted in some museum," said Fennet glumly.

"No," said the girl. "They couldn't!"

"They could," said the doctor.

Abruptly the hatch at the back of the cage opened.

Before the three humans could retreat to the scant protection supplied by a corner a voice called, "It's all right, come on out!"

Hawkins walked into the cage. He was shaved, and the beginnings of a healthy tan had darkened the pallor of his skin. He was wearing a pair of trunks fashioned from some bright red material.

"Come on out," he said again. "Our hosts have apologized very sincerely, and they have more suitable accommodation prepared for us. Then, as soon as they have a ship ready, we're to go to pick up the other survivors."

"Not so fast," said Boyle. "Put us in the picture, will you? What made them realize that we were rational beings?"

Hawkins' face darkened.

"Only rational beings," he said, "put other beings in cages."

SHADOW WORLD

by Clifford D. Simak

The survey mission had reported the planet as idyllic, uninhabited, and perfect for a human colony. But when the construction crew arrived, there were bizarre creatures waiting for them who seemed unthreatening, very curious—and completely inexplicable. If the planet was too good to be true, maybe the same was true of the shadow-creatures.

⚹ ⚹ ⚹

CLIFFORD D. SIMAK (1904-1988) published his first SF story, "The World of the Red Sun" in 1931, and went on to become one of the star writers during John W. Campbell's Golden Age of Science Fiction in the 1940s, notably in the series of stories which he eventually combined into his classic novel, City. *Other standout novels include* Time and Again, Ring Around the Sun, Time is the Simplest Thing, *and the Hugo-winning* Way Station. *Altogether, Simak won three Hugo Awards, a Nebula Award, and was the third recipient of the Grand Master Award of the Science Fiction Writers of America for lifetime achievement. He also received the Bram Stoker Award for lifetime achievement from the Horror Writers Association. He was noted for stories written with a pastoral feeling, though he could also turn out a chilling horror story, such as "Good Night, Mr. James," which was made into an episode of the original* Outer Limits. *His day job was newspaperman, joining the staff of the* Minneapolis Star and Tribune *in 1939, becoming its news editor in 1949, and retiring in 1976. He once wrote that "My favorite recreation is fishing (the lazy way, lying in a boat and letting them come to me)."*

I ROLLED OUT EARLY to put in an hour or so of work on my sector model before Greasy got breakfast slopped together. When I came out of my tent, Benny, my Shadow, was waiting for me. Some of the other Shadows also were standing around, waiting for their humans, and the whole thing, if one stopped to think of it, was absolutely crazy. Except that no one ever stopped to think of it; we were used to it by now.

Greasy had the cookshack stove fired up and smoke was curling from the chimney. I could hear him singing lustily amid the clatter of his pans. This was his noisy time. During the entire morning, he was noisy and obnoxious, but toward the middle of the afternoon, he turned mousy quiet. That was when he began to take a really dangerous chance and hit the peeper.

There were laws which made it very rough on anyone who had a peeper. Mack Baldwin, the project superintendent, would have raised merry hell if he had known that Greasy had one. But I was the only one who knew it. I had found out by accident and not even Greasy knew I knew and I had kept my mouth shut.

I said hello to Benny, but he didn't answer me. He never answered me; he had no mouth to answer with. I don't suppose he even heard me, for he had no ears. Those Shadows were a screwy lot. They had no mouths and they had no ears and they hadn't any noses.

But they did have an eye, placed in the middle of the face, about where the nose would have been if they'd had noses. And that eye made up for the lack of ears and mouth and nose.

It was about three inches in diameter and, strictly speaking, it wasn't built exactly like an eye; it had no iris or no pupil, but was a pool of light and shadow that kept shifting all around so it never looked the same. Sometimes it looked like a bowl of goop that was slightly on the spoiled side, and at other times it was hard and shining like a camera lens, and there were other times when it looked sad and lonely, like a mournful hound dog's eyes.

They were a weird lot for sure, those Shadows. They looked mostly like a rag doll before any one had gotten around to painting in the features. They were humanoid and they were strong and active and I had suspected from the very first that they weren't stupid. There was some division of opinion on that latter point and a lot of the boys still thought of them as howling savages. Except they didn't howl—they had no mouths to howl with. No mouths to howl or eat with, no nose to smell or breathe with, and no ears to hear with.

Just on bare statistics, one would have put them down as plain impossible, but they got along all right. They got along just fine.

They wore no clothes. On the point of modesty, there was no need of any. They were as bare of sexual characteristics as they were of facial features. They were just a gang of rag dolls with massive eyes in the middle of their faces.

But they did wear what might have been a decoration or a simple piece of jewelry or a badge of Shadowhood. They wore a narrow belt, from which was hung a bag or sack in which they carried a collection of trinkets that jingled when they walked. No one had ever seen what was in those sacks. Cross straps from the belt ran over the shoulders, making the whole business into a simple harness, and at the juncture of the straps upon their chest was mounted a huge jewel. Intricately carved, the jewel sparkled like a diamond, and it might have been a diamond, but no one knew if it was or not. No one ever got close enough to see. Make a motion toward that jewel and the Shadow disappeared.

That's right. Disappeared.

I said hello to Benny and he naturally didn't answer and I walked around the table and began working on the model. Benny stood close behind me and watched me as I worked. He seemed to have a lot of interest in that model. He had a lot of interest in everything I did. He went everywhere I went. He was, after all, my Shadow.

There was a poem that started out: *I have a little shadow . . .* I had thought about it often, but couldn't recall who the poet was or how the rest of it went. It was an old, old poem and I remembered I had read it when I was a kid. I could close my eyes and see the picture that went with the words, the brightly colored picture of a kid in his pajamas, going up a stairs with a candle in his hand and the shadow of him on the wall beyond the stairs.

I took some satisfaction in Benny's interest in the sector model, although I was aware his interest probably didn't mean a thing. He might have been just as interested if I'd been counting beans.

I was proud of that model and I spent more time on it than I had any right to. I had my name, Robert Emmett Drake, spelled out in full on the plaster base and the whole thing was a bit more ambitious than I originally had intended.

I had let my enthusiasm run away with me and that was not too hard to understand. It wasn't every day that a conservationist got a chance to engineer from scratch an absolutely virgin Earth-type planet. The layout was only one small sector of the initial project, but it included almost all the factors involved in the entire tract and I had put in the works—the dams and roads, the power sites and the mill sites, the timber management and the water-conservation features and all the rest of it.

I had just settled down to work when a commotion broke out down at the cookshack. I could hear Greasy cussing and the sound of thudding whacks. The door of the shack burst open and a Shadow came bounding out with Greasy just a leap behind him. Greasy had a frying pan and he was using it effectively, with a nifty backhand technique that was beautiful to see. He was laying it on the Shadow with every leap he took and he was yelling maledictions that were enough to curl one's hair.

The Shadow legged it across the camp with Greasy close behind. Watching them, I thought how it was a funny thing that a Shadow would up and disappear if you made a motion toward its jewel, but would stay and take the kind of treatment Greasy was handing out with that frying pan.

When they came abreast of my model table, Greasy gave up the chase. He was not in the best of condition.

He stood beside the table and put both fists belligerently on his hips, so that the frying pan, which he still clutched, stood out at a right angle from his body.

"I won't allow that stinker in the shack," he told me, wheezing and gasping. "It's bad enough to have him hanging around outside and looking in the windows. It's bad enough falling over him every time I turn around. I will not have him snooping in the kitchen; he's got his fingers into everything he sees. If I was Mack, I'd put the lug on all of them. I'd run them so fast, so far, that it would take them—"

"Mack's got other things to worry about," I told him rather sharply. "The project is way behind schedule, with all the breakdowns we've been having."

"Sabotage," Greasy corrected me. "That's what it is. You can bet your bottom dollar on that. It's them Shadows, I tell you, sabotaging the machines. If it was left to me, I'd run them clear out of the country."

"It's their country," I protested. "They were here before we came."

"It's a big planet," Greasy said. "There are other parts of it they could live in."

"But they have got a right here. This planet is their home."

"They ain't got no homes," said Greasy.

He turned around abruptly and walked back toward the shack. His Shadow, which had been standing off to one side all the time, hurried to catch up with him. It didn't look as if it had minded the pounding he had given it. But you could never tell what a Shadow was thinking. Their thoughts don't show on them.

What Greasy had said about their not having any homes was a bit unfair. What he meant, of course, was that they had no village, that they were just a sort of carefree bunch of gypsies, but to me the planet was their home and they had a right to go any place they wanted on it and use any part of it they wished. It should make no difference that they settled down on no particular spot, that they had no villages and possibly no shelters or that they raised no crops.

Come to think of it, there was no reason why they should raise crops, for they had no mouths to eat with, and if they didn't eat, how could they keep on living and if . . .

You see how it went. That was the reason it didn't pay to think too much about the Shadows. Once you started trying to get them figured out, you got all tangled up.

I sneaked a quick look sidewise to see how Benny might be taking this business of Greasy beating up his pal, but Benny was just the same as ever. He was all rag doll.

Men began to drift out of the tents and the Shadows galloped over to rejoin their humans, and everywhere a man might go, his Shadow tagged behind him.

The project center lay there on its hilltop, and from where I stood beside my sector table, I could see it laid out like a blueprint come to life.

Over there, the beginning of the excavation for the administration building, and there the gleaming stakes for the shopping center, and beyond the shopping center, the ragged, first-turned furrows that in time would become a street flanked by neat rows of houses.

It didn't look much like a brave beginning on a brand-new world, but in a little while it would. It would even now, if we'd not run into so much hard luck. And whether that hard luck could be traced to the Shadows or to something else, it was a thing that must be faced and somehow straightened out.

For this was important. Here was a world on which Man would not repeat the ancient, sad mistakes that he had made on Earth. On this, one of the few Earth-like planets found so far, Man would not waste the valuable resources which he had let go down the drain on the old home planet. He'd make planned use of the water and the soil, of the timber and the minerals, and he'd be careful to put back as much as he took out. This planet would not be robbed and gutted as Earth had been. It would be used intelligently and operated like a well-run business.

I felt good, just standing there, looking out across the valley and the plains toward the distant mountains, thinking what a fine home this would be for mankind.

The camp was becoming lively now. Out in front of the tents, the men were washing up for breakfast and there was a lot of friendly shouting and a fair amount of horseplay. I heard considerable cussing down in the equipment pool and I knew exactly what was going on.

The machines, or at least a part of them, had gone daffy again and half the morning would be wasted getting them repaired. It certainly was a funny deal, I thought, how those machines got out of kilter every blessed night.

After a while, Greasy rang the breakfast bell and everyone dropped everything and made a dash for it and their Shadows hustled along behind them.

I was closer to the cookshack than most of them and I am no slouch at sprinting, so I got one of the better seats at the big outdoor table. My place was just outside the cookshack door, where I'd get first whack at seconds when Greasy lugged them out. I went past Greasy on the run and he was grumbling and muttering the way he always was at chow, although sometimes I thought that was just a pose to hide his satisfaction at knowing his cooking still was fit to eat.

I got a seat next to Mack, and a second later Rick Thorne, one of the equipment operators, grabbed the place on the other side of me. Across from me was Stan Carr, a biologist, and just down the table, on the other side, was Judson Knight, our ecologist.

We wasted no time in small talk; we dived into the wheat cakes and the side pork and the fried potatoes. There is nothing in all the Universe like the morning air of Stella IV to hone an edge on the appetite.

Finally we had enough of the edge off so we would waste time being civil.

"It's the same old story again this morning," Thorne said bitterly to Mack. "More than half the equipment is all gummed up. It'll take hours to get it moving."

He morosely shoveled food into his mouth and chewed with unnecessary savagery. He shot an angry glance at Carr across the table. "Why don't you get it figured out?" he asked.

"Me?" said Carr, in some astonishment. "Why should I be the one to get it figured out? I don't know anything about machines and I don't want to know. They're stupid contraptions at best."

"You know what I mean," said Thorne. "The machines are not to blame. They don't gum up themselves. It's the Shadows and you're a biologist and them Shadows are your business and—"

"I have other things to do," said Carr. "I have this earthworm problem to work out, and as soon as that is done, Bob here wants me to run some habit-patterns on a dozen different rodents."

"I wish you would," I said. "I have a hunch some of those little rascals may cause us a lot of trouble once we try our hand at crops. I'd like to know ahead of time what makes the critters tick."

That was the way it went, I thought. No matter how many factors you might consider, there were always more of them popping up from under rocks and bushes. It seemed somehow that a man never quite got through the list.

"It wouldn't be so bad," Thorne complained, "if the Shadows would leave us alone and let us fix the damage after they've done their dirty work. But not them. They breathe down our necks while we're making the repairs, and they've got their faces buried in those engines clear up to their shoulders, and every time you move, you bump into one of them. Someday," he said fiercely, "I'm going to take a monkey wrench and clear some space around me."

"They're worried about what you're doing to their machines," said Carr. "The Shadows have taken over those machines just like they've adopted us."

"That's what you think," Thorne said.

"Maybe they're trying to find out about the machines," Carr declared. "Maybe they gum them up so that, when you go to fix them, they can look things over. They haven't missed a single part of any machine so far. You were telling me the other day it's a different thing wrong every time."

Knight said, solemn as an owl: "I've been doing a lot of thinking about this situation."

"Oh, you have," said Thorne, and the way he said it, you could see he figured that what Knight might think would cut no ice.

"I've been seeking out some motive," Knight told him. "Because if the Shadows are the ones who are doing it, they'd have to have a motive. Don't you think so, Mack?"

"Yeah, I guess so," said Mack.

"For some reason," Knight went on, "those Shadows seem to like us. They showed up as soon as we set down and they've stayed with us ever since. The way they act, they'd like us to stay on and maybe they're wrecking the machines so we'll have to stay."

"Or drive us away," Thorne answered.

"That's all right," said Carr, "but why should they want us to stay? What exactly is it they like about us? If we could only get that one on the line, we might be able to do some bargaining with them."

"Well, I wouldn't know," Knight admitted. "There might be a lot of different reasons."

"Name just three of them," Thorne challenged him nastily.

"Gladly," said Knight, and he said it as if he were slipping a knife into the left side of Thorne's gizzard. "They may be getting something from us, only don't ask me what it is. Or they may be building us up to put the bite on us for something that's important. Or they may be figuring on reforming us, although just what's in us they object to, I can't faintly imagine. Or they may worship us. Or maybe it's just love."

"Is that all?" asked Thorne.

"Just a start," said Knight. "They may be studying us and they may need more time to get us puzzled out. They may be prodding us to get some reactions from us—"

"Studying us!" yelled Thorne, outraged. "They're just lousy savages!"

"I don't think they are," Knight replied.

"They don't wear any clothes," Thorne thundered, slamming the table with his fist. "They don't have any tools. They don't have a village. They don't know how to build a hut. They don't have any government. They can't even talk or hear."

I was disgusted with Thorne.

"Well, we got that settled," I said. "Let's go back to work."

I got up off the bench, but I hadn't gone more than a step or two before a man came pounding down from the radio hut, waving a piece of paper in his hand. It was Jack Pollard, our communications man, who also doubled in brass as an electronics expert.

"Mack!" he was hollering. "Hey, Mack!"

Mack lumbered to his feet.

Pollard handed him the paper. "It was coming in when Greasy

blew the horn," he gasped. "I was having trouble getting it. Relayed a long way out."

Mack read the paper and his face turned hard and red.

"What's the matter, Mack?" I wanted to know.

"There's an inspector coming out," he said, and he choked on each and every word. He was all burned up. And maybe scared as well.

"Is it likely to be bad?"

"He'll probably can the lot of us," said Mack.

"But he can't do that!"

"That's what you think. We're six weeks behind schedule and this project is hotter than a pile. Earth's politicians have made a lot of promises, and if those promises don't pay off, there'll be hell to pay. Unless we can do something and do it fast, they'll bounce us out of here and send a new gang in."

"But considering everything, we haven't done so badly," Carr said mildly.

"Don't get me wrong," Mack told him. "The new gang will do no better, but there has to be some action for the record and we're the ones who'll get it in the neck. If we could lick this breakdown business, we might have a chance. If we could say to that inspector: 'Sure, we've had a spot of trouble, but we have it licked and now we're doing fine—"if we could say that to him, then we might save our hides."

"You think it's the Shadows, Mack?" asked Knight.

Mack reached up and scratched his head. "Must be them. Can't think of anything else."

Somebody shouted from another table: "Of course it's them damn Shadows!"

The men were getting up from their seats and crowding around.

Mack held up his hands. "You guys get back to work. If any of you got some good ideas, come up to the tent and we'll talk them over."

They started jabbering at him.

"Ideas!" Mack roared. "I said *ideas!* Anyone that comes up without a good idea, I'll dock him for being off the job."

They quieted down a little.

"And another thing," said Mack. "No rough stuff on the Shadows.

Just go along the way we always have. I'll fire the man who strongarms them."

He said to me: "Let's go."

I followed him, and Knight and Carr fell in beside me. Thorne didn't come. I had expected that he would.

Inside Mack's tent, we sat down at a table littered with blueprints and spec sheets and papers scribbled with figures and offhand diagrams.

"I suppose," said Carr, "that it has to be the Shadows."

"Some gravitational peculiarity?" suggested Knight. "Some strange atmospheric condition? Some space-warping quality?"

"Maybe," said Mack. "It all sounds a bit far-fetched, but I'm ready to grab any straw you shove at me."

"One thing that puzzles me," I put in, "is that the survey crew didn't mention Shadows. Survey believed the planet was uninhabited by any sort of intelligence. It found no signs of culture. And that was good, because it meant the project wouldn't get all tangled up with legalities over primal rights. And yet the minute we landed, the Shadows came galloping to meet us, almost as if they'd spotted us a long way off and were waiting for us to touch down."

"Another funny thing," said Carr, "is how they paired off with us— one Shadow to every man. Like they had it all planned out. Like they'd married us or something."

"What are you getting at?" growled Mack.

I said: "Where were the Shadows, Mack, when the survey gang was here? Can we be absolutely sure they're native to this planet?"

"If they aren't native," demanded Mack, "how did they get here? They have no machines. They haven't even got tools."

"There's another thing about that survey report," said Knight, "that I've been wondering about. The rest of you have read it—"

We nodded. We had not only read it, we had studied and digested it. We'd lived with it day and night on the long trip out to Stella IV.

"The survey report told about some cone-shaped things," said Knight. "All sitting in a row, as if they might be boundary markers. But they never saw them except from a long way off. They had no idea what they were. They just wrote them off as something that had no real significance."

"They wrote off a lot of things as having no significance," said Carr.

"We aren't getting anywhere," Mack complained. "All we do is talk."

"If we could talk to the Shadows," said Knight, "we might be getting somewhere."

"But we can't!" argued Mack. "We tried to talk to them and we couldn't raise a ripple. We tried sign language and we tried pantomime and we filled reams of paper with diagrams and drawings and we got exactly nowhere. Jack rigged up that electronic communicator and he tried it on them and they just sat and looked at us, all bright and sympathetic, with that one big eye of theirs, and that was all there was. We even tried telepathy—"

"You're wrong there, Mack," said Carr. "We didn't try telepathy, because we don't know a thing about it. All we did was sit in a circle, holding hands with them and thinking hard at them. And of course it was no good. They probably thought it was just a game."

"Look," pleaded Mack, "that inspector will be here in ten days or so. We have to think of something. Let's get down to cases."

"If we could run the Shadows off somehow," said Knight. "If we could scare them away—"

"You know how to scare a Shadow?" Mack asked, "You got any idea what they might be afraid of?"

Knight shook his head.

"Our first job," said Carr, "is to find out what a Shadow is like. We have to learn what kind of animal he is. He's a funny kind, we know. He doesn't have a mouth or nose or ears . . ."

"He's impossible," Mack said. "There ain't no such animal."

"He's alive," said Carr, "and doing very well. We have to find out how he gets his food, how he communicates, what tolerances he may have, what his responses are to various kinds of stimuli. We can't do a thing about the Shadows until we have some idea of what we're dealing with."

Knight agreed with him. "We should have started weeks ago. We made a stab at it, of course, but our hearts were never in it. We were too anxious to get started on the project."

Mack said bitterly: "Fat lot of good it did us."

"Before you can examine one, you have to have a subject," I answered Knight. "Seems to me we should try to figure out how to catch a Shadow. Make a sudden move toward one and he disappears."

But even as I said it, I knew that was not entirely right. I remembered how Greasy had chased his Shadow from the cookshack, lamming him with the frying pan.

And I remembered something else and I had a hunch and got a big idea, but I was scared to say anything about it. I didn't even, for the moment, dare to let on to myself I had it.

"We'd have to take one by surprise somehow and knock him out before he had a chance to disappear," Carr said. "And it has to be a sure way, for if we try it once and fail we've put the Shadows on their guard and we'll never have another chance."

Mack warned, "No rough stuff. You can't go using violence until you know your critter. You don't do any killing until you have some idea how efficiently the thing that you are killing can up and kill you back."

"No rough stuff," Carr agreed. "If a Shadow can bollix up the innards of some of those big earthmovers, I wouldn't like to see what he could do to a human body."

"It's got to be fast and sure," said Knight, "and we can't even start until we know it is. If you hit one on the head with a baseball bat, would the bat bounce or would you crush the Shadow's skull? That's about the way it would be with everything we could think of at the moment."

Carr nodded. "That's right. We can't use gas, because a Shadow doesn't breathe."

"He might breathe through his pores," said Knight.

"Sure, but we'd have to know before we tried using gas. We might jab a hypo into one, but what would you use in the hypo? First you'd have to find something that would knock a Shadow out. You might try hypnotism—"

"I'd doubt hypnotism," said Knight.

"How about Doc?" I asked. "If we could knock out a Shadow, would Doc give him a going over? If I know Doc, he'd raise a lot of hell. Claim the Shadow was an intelligent being and that it would be in violation of medical ethics to examine one without first getting its consent."

"You get one," Mack promised grimly, "and I'll handle Doc."

"He'll do a lot of screaming."

"I'll handle Doc," repeated Mack. "This inspector is going to be here in a week or so—"

"We wouldn't have to have it *all* cleared up," said Knight. "If we could show the inspector that we had a good lead, that we were progressing, he might play ball with us."

I was seated with my back to the entrance of the tent and I heard someone fumbling with the canvas.

Mack said: "Come in, Greasy. Got something on your mind?"

Greasy walked in and came up to the table. He had the bottom of his apron tucked into his trouser band, the way he always did when he wasn't working, and he held something in his hand. He tossed it on the table.

It was one of the bags that the Shadows carried at their belts!

We all sucked in our breath and Mack's hair fairly stood on end.

"Where did you get this?" he demanded.

"Off my Shadow, when he wasn't looking."

"When he wasn't looking!"

"Well, you see, it was this way, Mack. That Shadow is always into things. I stumble over him everywhere I go. And this morning he had his head halfway into the dishwasher and that bag was hanging on his belt, so I grabbed up a butcher knife and just whacked it off."

As Mack got up and pulled himself to his full height, you could see it was hard for him to keep his hands off Greasy.

"So that was all you did," he said in a low, dangerous voice.

"Sure," said Greasy. "There was nothing hard about it."

"All you've done is spill the beans to them! All you've done is made it almost impossible—"

"Maybe not," Knight interrupted in a hurry.

"Now that the damage has been done," said Carr, "we might as well have a look. Maybe there's a clue inside that bag."

"I can't open it," grumbled Greasy. "I tried every way I know. There's no way to open it."

"And while you were trying to open it," asked Mack, "what was the Shadow doing?"

"He didn't even notice. He had his head inside that washer. He's as stupid as—"

"Don't say that! I don't want anyone thinking a Shadow's stupid. Maybe they are, but there's no sense believing it until we're sure."

Knight had picked up the bag and was turning it around and around in his hand. Whatever was inside was jingling as he turned and twisted it.

"Greasy's right," he said. "I don't see any way to get it open."

"You get out of here!" Mack roared at Greasy. "Get back to your work. Don't you ever make another move toward any of the Shadows."

Greasy turned around and left, but he was no more than out of the tent when he gave a yelp that was enough to raise your scalp.

I almost knocked the table over getting out of there to see what was going on.

What was happening was no more than plain solemn justice.

Greasy was running for all he was worth, and behind him was the Shadow with a frying pan, and every jump that Greasy took, the Shadow let him have it, and was every bit as good with that frying pan as Greasy was.

Greasy was weaving and circling, trying to head back for the cookshack, but each time the Shadow got him headed off and went on chasing him.

Everyone had stopped work to watch. Some of them were yelling advice to Greasy and some of the others were cheering on the Shadow. I'd have liked to stay and watch, but I knew that if I was going to put my hunch into execution, I'd never have a better chance to do it.

So I turned and walked swiftly down the street to my own tent and ducked inside and got a specimen bag and came out again.

I saw that Greasy was heading for the equipment pool and that the Shadow still was one long stride behind. Its arm was holding up well, for the frying pan never missed a lick.

★★★

I ran down to the cookshack and, at the door, I stopped and looked back. Greasy was shinnying up the derrick of a shovel and the Shadow was standing at the bottom, waving the frying pan as though daring him to come down and take it like a man. Everyone else was running toward the scene of action and there was no one, I was sure, who had noticed me.

So I opened the cookshack door and stepped inside.

The dishwasher was chugging away and everything was peaceable and quiet.

I was afraid I might have trouble finding what I was looking for, but I found it in the third place I looked—underneath the mattress on Greasy's bunk.

I pulled the peeper out and slipped it in the bag and got out of there as fast as I could go.

Stopping at my tent, I tossed the bag into a corner and threw some old clothes over it and then went out again.

The commotion had ended. The Shadow was walking back toward the cookshack, with the pan tucked underneath its arm, and Greasy was climbing down off the shovel. The men were all gathered around the shovel, making a lot of noise, and I figured that it would take a long, long time for Greasy to live down what had happened. Although, I realized, he had it coming to him.

I went back into Mack's tent and found the others there. All three of them were standing beside the table, looking down at what lay there upon the surface.

The bag had disappeared and had left behind a little pile of trinkets. Looking at the pile, I could see that they were miniatures of frying pans and kettles and all the other utensils that Greasy worked with. And there, half protruding out of the pile, was a little statuette of Greasy.

I reached out a hand and picked up the statuette. There was no mistaking it—it was Greasy to a T. It was made of some sort of stone, as if it might have been a carving, and was delicate beyond all belief. Squinting closely, I could even see the lines on Greasy's face.

"The bag just went away," said Knight. "It was lying here when we dashed out, and when we came back, it was gone and all this junk was lying on the table."

"I don't understand," Carr said.

And he was right. None of us did.

"I don't like it," Mack said slowly.

I didn't like it, either. It raised too many questions in my head and some of them were resolving into some miserable suspicions.

"They're making models of our stuff," said Knight. "Even down to the cups and spoons."

"I wouldn't mind that so much," Carr said. "It's the model of Greasy that gives me the jitters."

"Now let's sit down," Mack told us, "and not go off on any tangents. This is exactly the sort of thing we could have expected."

"What do you mean?" I prompted.

"What do we do when we find an alien culture? We do just what the Shadows are doing. Different way, but the same objective. We try to find out all we can about this alien culture. And don't you ever forget that, to the Shadows, we're not only an alien culture, but an *invading* alien culture. So if they had any sense at all, they'd make it their business to find out as much about us as they could in the shortest time."

That made sense, of course. But this making of models seemed to be carrying it beyond what was necessary.

And if they had made models of Greasy's cups and spoons, of the dishwasher and the coffee pot, then they had other models, too. They had models of the earthmovers and the shovels and the dozers and all the rest of it And if they had a model of Greasy, they had models of Mack and Thorne and Carr and all the rest of the crew, including me.

Just how faithful would those models be? How much deeper would they go than mere external appearances?

I tried to stop thinking of it, for I was doing little more than scaring myself stiff.

But I couldn't stop. I went right on thinking.

They had been gumming up equipment so that the mechanics had to rip the machines all apart to get them going once again. There seemed no reason in the world why the Shadows should be doing that, except to find out what the innards of those machines were like. I wondered if the models of the equipment might not be faithful not only so far as the outward appearance might go, but faithful as well on the most intricate construction of the entire machine.

And if that was true, was that faithfulness also carried out in the Greasy statuette? Did it have a heart and lungs, blood vessels and brain and nerve? Might it not also have the very essence of Greasy's character, the kind of animal he was, what his thoughts and ethics might be?

I don't know if, at that very moment, the others were thinking the same thing, but the looks on their faces argued that they might have been.

Mack put out a finger and stirred the contents of the pile, scattering the miniatures all about the tabletop.

Then his hand darted out and picked up something and his face went red with anger.

Knight asked: "What is it, Mack?"

"A peeper!" said Mack, his words rasping in his throat. "There's a model of a peeper!"

All of us sat and stared and I could feel the cold sweat breaking out on me.

"If Greasy has a peeper," Mack said woodenly, "I'll break his scrawny neck."

"Take it easy, Mack," said Carr.

"You know what a peeper is?"

"Sure, I know what a peeper is."

"You ever see what a peeper does to a man who used one?"

"No, I never did."

"I have." Mack threw the peeper model back on the table and turned and went out of the tent. The rest of us followed him.

Greasy was coming down the street, with some of the men following along behind, kidding him about the Shadow treeing him.

Mack put his hands on his hips and waited.

Greasy got almost to us.

"Greasy!" said Mack.

"Yes, Mack."

"You hiding out a peeper?"

Greasy blinked, but he never hesitated. "No, sir," he said, lying like a trooper. "I wouldn't rightly know one if somebody should point it out to me. I've heard of them, of course."

"I'll make a bargain with you," said Mack. "If you have one, just hand it over to me and I'll bust it up and fine you a full month's wages and that's the last that we'll say about it. But if you lie to me and we find you have one hidden out, I'll can you off the job."

I held my breath. I didn't like what was going on and I thought what a lousy break it was that something like this should happen just when I had swiped the peeper. Although I was fairly sure that no one had seen me sneak into the cookshack—at least I didn't think they had.

Greasy was stubborn. He shook his head. "I haven't got one, Mack."

Mack's face got hard. "All right. We'll go down and see."

He headed for the cookshack and Knight and Carr went along with him, but I headed for my tent.

It would be just like Mack, when he didn't find the peeper in the cookshack, to search the entire camp. If I wanted to stay out of trouble, I knew, I'd better be zipping out of camp and take the peeper with me.

Benny was squatted outside the tent, waiting for me. He helped me get the roller out and then I took the specimen bag with the peeper in it and stuffed it in the roller's carrying bag.

I got on the roller and Benny jumped on the carrier behind me and sat there showing off, balancing himself—like a kid riding a bicycle with no hands.

"You hang on," I told him sharply. "If you fall off this time, I won't stop to pick you up."

I am sure he didn't hear me, but however that may be, he put his arms around my waist and we were off in a cloud of dust.

Until you've ridden on a roller, you haven't really lived. It's like a roller coaster running on the level. But it is fairly safe and it gets you there. It's just two big rubber doughnuts with an engine and a seat and it could climb a barn if you gave it half a chance. It's too rambunctious for civilized driving, but it is just the ticket for an alien planet.

We set off across the plain toward the distant foothills. It was a fine day, but for that matter, every day was fine on Stella IV. It was an ideal planet, Earth-like, with good weather nearly all the time, crammed with natural resources, free of vicious animal life or deadly virus—a planet that virtually pleaded for someone to come and live on it.

And in time there'd be people here. Once the administration center was erected, the neat rows of houses had been built, once the shopping center had been installed, the dams built, the power plant completed—then there would be people. And in the years to come, sector by sector, project community by community, the human race would spread across the planet's face. But it would spread in an orderly progression.

Here there would be no ornery misfits slamming out on their own, willy-nilly, into the frontier land of wild dream and sudden death; no speculators, no strike-it-rich, no go-for-broke. Here there would be no frontier, but a systematic taking over. And here, for once, a planet would be treated right.

But there was more to it than that, I told myself.

If Man was to keep going into space, he would have to accept the responsibility of making proper use of the natural resources that he found there. Just because there might be a lot of them was no excuse for wasting them. We were no longer children and we couldn't gut every world as we had gutted Earth.

By the time an intelligence advances to a point where it can conquer space, it must have grown up. And now it was time for the human race to prove that it was adult. We couldn't go ravaging out into the Galaxy like a horde of greedy children.

Here on this planet, it seemed to me, was one of the many proving grounds on which the race of Man must stand and show its worth.

Yet if we were to get the job done, if we were to prove anything at all, there was another problem that first must be met and solved. If it was the Shadows that were causing all our trouble, then somehow we must put a stop to it. And not merely put a stop to it, but understand the Shadows and their motives. For how can anybody fight a thing, I asked myself, that he doesn't understand?

And to understand the Shadows, we'd agreed back in the tent, we had to know what kind of critters they might be. And before we could find that out, we had to grab off one for examination. And that first grab had to be perfect, for if we tried and failed, if we put them on their guard, there'd be no second chance.

But the peeper, I told myself, might give us at least one free try. If I tried the peeper and it didn't work, no one would be the wiser. It would be a failure that would go unnoticed.

Benny and I crossed the plain on the roller and headed into the foothills. I made for a place that I called the Orchard, not because it was a formal orchard, but because there were a lot of fruit-bearing trees in the area. As soon as I got around to it, I was planning to run tests to see if any of the fruit might be fit for human food.

We reached the Orchard and I parked the roller and looked around. I saw immediately that something had happened. When I had been there just a week or so before, the trees had been loaded with fruit and it seemed to be nearly ripe, but now it all was gone.

I peered underneath the trees to see if the fruit had fallen off and it hadn't. It looked for all the world as if someone had come in and picked it.

I wondered if the Shadows had done the picking, but even as I thought it, I knew it couldn't be. The Shadows didn't eat

I didn't get the peeper out right away, but sat down beneath a tree and sort of caught my breath and did a little thinking.

From where I sat, I could see the camp and I wondered what Mack had done when he hadn't found the peeper. I could imagine he'd be in a towering rage. And I could imagine Greasy, considerably relieved, but wondering just the same what had happened to the peeper and perhaps rubbing it into Mack a little how he had been wrong.

I got the feeling that maybe it would be just as well if I stayed away a while. At least until mid-afternoon. By that time, perhaps, Mack would have cooled off a little.

And I thought about the Shadows.

Lousy savages, Thorne had said. Yet they were far from savages. They were perfect gentlemen (or ladies, God knows which they were, if either) and your genuine savage is no gentleman on a number of very fundamental points. The Shadows were clean in body, healthy and well mannered. They had a certain cultural poise. They were, more than anything else, like a group of civilized campers, but unencumbered by the usual camp equipment.

They were giving us a going over—there could be no doubt of that. They were learning all they could of us and why did they want to know? What use could they make of pots and pans and earthmovers and all the other things?

Or were they merely taking our measure before they clobbered us?

And there were all the other questions, too.

Where did they hang out?

How did they disappear, and when they disappeared, where did they go?

How did they eat and breathe?

How did they communicate?

Come right down to it, I admitted to myself, the Shadows undoubtedly knew a great deal more about us than we knew about them. Because when you tried to chalk up what we knew about them, it came out to almost exactly nothing.

I sat under the tree for a while longer, with the thoughts spinning in my head and not adding up. Then I got to my feet and went over to the roller and got out the peeper.

It was the first time I'd ever had one in my hands and I was interested and slightly apprehensive. For a peeper was nothing one should monkey with.

It was a simple thing to look at—like a lopsided pair of binoculars, with a lot of selector knobs on each side and on the top of it.

You looked into it and you twisted the knobs until you had what you wanted and then there was a picture. You stepped into the picture and you lived the life you found there—the sort of life you picked by the setting of the knobs. And there were many lives to pick from, for there were millions of combinations that could be set up on the knobs and the factors ranged from the lightest kind of frippery to the most abysmal horror.

The peeper was outlawed, naturally—it was worse than alcoholism, worse than dope, the most insidious vice that had ever hit mankind. It threw psychic hooks deep into the soul and tugged forevermore. When a man acquired the habit, and it was easy to acquire, there was no getting over it. He'd spend the rest of his life trying to sort out his life from all the fantasied ones, getting further and further from reality all the while, till nothing was real any more.

I squatted down beside the roller and tried to make some sense out of the knobs. There were thirty-nine of them, each numbered from one to thirty-nine, and I wondered what the numbering meant.

Benny came over and hunkered down beside me, with one shoulder touching mine, and watched what I was doing.

I pondered over the numbering, but pondering did no good. There was only one way to find out what I was looking for. So I set all the knobs back to zero on the graduated scales, then twisted No. 1 up a notch or two.

I knew that was not the way to work a peeper. In actual operation, one would set a number of the knobs at different settings, mixing in the factors in different proportions to make up the kind of life that one might want to sample. But I wasn't after a life. What I wanted to find out was what factor each of the knobs controlled.

So I set No. 1 up a notch or two and lifted the peeper and fitted it to my face and I was back again in the meadow of my boyhood—a meadow that was green as no meadow ever was before, with a sky as blue as old-time watered silk and with a brook and butterflies.

And more than that—a meadow that lay in a day that would never end, a place that knew no time, and a sunlight that was the bright glow of boyish happiness.

I knew exactly how the grass would feel beneath bare feet and I could remember how the sunlight would bounce off the wind-ripples of the brook. It was the hardest thing I ever did in my entire life, but I snatched the peeper from my eyes.

I squatted there, with the peeper cradled in my lap. My hands were unsteady, longing to lift the peeper so I could look once again at that scene out of a long-lost boyhood, but I made myself not do it.

No. 1 was not the knob I wanted, so I turned it back to zero and, since No. 1 was about as far away as one could imagine from what I was looking for, I turned knob 39 up a notch or two.

I lifted the peeper halfway to my face and then I turned plain scared. I put it down again until I could get a good grip on my courage. Then I lifted it once more and stuck my face straight into a horror that reached out and tried to drag me in.

I can't describe it. Even now, I cannot recall one isolated fragment of what I really saw. Rather than seeing, it was pure impression and raw emotion—a sort of surrealistic representation of all that is loathsome and repellent, and yet somehow retaining a hypnotic fascination that forbade retreat.

Shaken, I snatched the peeper from my face and sat frozen. For a moment, my mind was an utter blank, with stray wisps of horror streaming through it.

Then the wisps gradually cleared away and I was squatting once again on the hillside with the Shadow hunkered down beside me, his shoulder touching mine.

It was a terrible thing, I thought, an act no human could bring himself to do, even to a Shadow. Just turned up a notch or two, it was terrifying; turned on full power, it would twist one's brain.

Benny reached out a hand to take the peeper from me. I jerked it away from him. But he kept on pawing for it and that gave me time to think.

This, I told myself, was exactly the way I had wanted it to be. All that was different was that Benny, by his nosiness, was making it easy for me to do the very thing I'd planned.

I thought of all that depended on our getting us a Shadow to examine. And I thought about my job and how it would bust my heart if the inspector should come out and fire us and send in another crew.

There just weren't planets lying around every day in the week to be engineered. I might never get another chance.

So I put out my thumb and shoved knob 39 to its final notch and let Benny have the peeper.

And even as I gave it to him, I wondered if it would really work or if I'd just had a pipe-dream. It might not work, I thought, for it was a human mechanism, designed for human use, keyed to the human nervous system and response.

Then I knew that I was wrong, that the peeper did not operate by virtue of its machinery alone, but by the reaction of the brain and the body of its user—that it was no more than a trigger mechanism to set loose the greatness and the beauty and the horror that lay within the user's brain. And horror, while it might take a different shape and form, appear in a different guise, was horror for a Shadow as well as for a human.

Benny lifted the peeper to that great single eye of his and thrust his head forward to fit into the viewer. Then I saw his body jerk and stiffen and I caught him as he toppled and eased him to the ground.

I stood there above him and felt the triumph and the pride—and perhaps a little pity, too—that it should be necessary to do a thing like this to a guy like Benny. To play a trick like this on my Shadow who had sat, just moments ago, with his shoulder touching mine.

I knelt down and turned him over. He didn't seem so heavy and I was glad of that, because I'd have to get him on the roller and then make a dash for camp, going as fast as I could gun the roller, because there was no telling how long Benny would stay knocked out.

I picked up the peeper and stuck it back into the roller's bag, then hunted for some rope or wire to tie Benny on so he would not fall off.

I don't know if I heard a noise or not. I'm half inclined to think that there wasn't any noise—that it was some sort of built-in alarm system that made me turn around.

Benny was sagging in upon himself and I had a moment of wild panic, thinking that he might be dead, that the shock of the horror that leaped out of the peeper at him had been too much for him to stand.

And I remembered what Mack had said: "Never kill a thing until you have figured out just how efficiently it may up and kill you back."

If Benny was dead, then we might have all hell exploding in our laps.

If he was dead, though, he sure was acting funny. He was sinking in and splitting at a lot of different places, and he was turning to what looked like dust, but wasn't dust, and there wasn't any Benny. There was just the harness with the bag and the jewel and then there wasn't any bag, but a handful of trinkets lying on the ground where the bag had been.

And there was something else.

There still was Benny's eye. The eye was a part of a cone that been in Benny's head.

I recalled how the survey party had seen other cones like that. But had not been able to get close to them.

I was too scared to move. I stood and looked and there were a lot of goose pimples rising on my hide.

For Benny was no alien. Benny was no more than the proxy of some other alien that we had never seen and could not even guess at.

All sorts of conjectures went tumbling through my brain, but they were no more than panic-pictures, and they flipped off and on so fast, I couldn't settle on any one of them.

But one thing was clear as day—the cleverness of this alien for which the Shadows were the front.

Too clever to confront us with anything that was more remotely human in its shape—a thing for which we could feel pity or contempt or perhaps exasperation, but something that would never rouse a fear within us. A pitiful little figure that was a caricature of our shape and one that so stupid that it couldn't even talk. And one that was sufficiently alien to keep us puzzled and stump us on so many basic points that we would, at last, give up in sheer bewilderment any attempts that we might make to get it puzzled out.

I threw a quick glance over my shoulder and kept my shoulders hunched, and if anything had moved, I'd have run like a frightened rabbit. But nothing moved. Nothing even rustled. There was nothing to be afraid of except the thoughts within my head.

But I felt a frantic urge to get out of there and I went down on my hands and knees and began to gather what was left of Benny.

I scooped up the pile of trinkets and the jewel and dumped them in the bag along with the peeper. Then I went back and picked up the cone, with the one eye looking at me, but I could see that the eye was dead. The cone was slippery and it didn't feel like metal, but it was heavy and hard to get a good grip on and I had quite a time with it. But I finally got it in the bag and started out for camp.

I went like a bat winging out of hell. Fear was roosting on one shoulder and I kept that roller wheeling.

I swung into camp and headed for Mack's tent, but before I got there, I found what looked like the entire project crew working at the craziest sort of contraption one would ever hope to see. It was a mass of gears and cams and wheels and chains and whatnot, and it sprawled over what, back home, would have been a good-sized lot, and there was no reason I could figure for building anything like that.

I saw Thorne standing off to one side and superintending the work, yelling first at this one and then at someone else, and I could see that he was enjoying himself. Thorne was that kind of bossy jerk.

I stopped the roller beside him and balanced it with one leg.

"What's going on?" I asked him.

"We're giving them something to get doped out," he said. "We're going to drive them crazy."

"Them? You mean the Shadows?"

"They want information, don't they?" Thorne demanded. "They've been underfoot day and night, always in the way, so now we give them something to keep them occupied."

"But what does it do?"

Thorne spat derisively. "Nothing. That's the beauty of it."

"Well," I said, "I suppose you know what you're doing. Does Mack know what's going on?"

"Mack and Carr and Knight are the big brains that thought it up," said Thorne. "I'm just carrying out orders."

I went on to Mack's tent and parked the roller there and I knew that Mack was inside, for I heard a lot of arguing.

I took the carrier bag and marched inside the tent and pushed my way up to the table and, up-ending the sack, emptied the whole thing on the tabletop.

And I plumb forgot about the peeper being in there with all the other stuff.

There was nothing I could do about it. The peeper lay naked on the table and there was a terrible silence and I could see that in another second Mack would blow his jets.

He sucked in his breath to roar, but I beat him to it.

"Shut up, Mack!" I snapped. "I don't want to hear a word from you!"

I must have caught him by surprise, for he let his breath out slowly, looking at me funny while he did it, and Carr and Knight were just slightly frozen in position. The tent was deathly quiet.

"That was Benny," I said, motioning at the tabletop. "That is all that's left of him. A look in the peeper did it."

Carr came a bit unfrozen. "But the peeper! We looked everywhere—"

"I knew Greasy had it and I stole it when I got a hunch. Remember, we were talking about how to catch a Shadow—"

"I'm going to bring charges against you!" howled Mack. "I'm going to make an example out of you! I'm going to—"

"You're going to shut up," I said at him. "You're going to stay quiet and listen or I'll heave you out of here tin cup over appetite."

"Please!" begged Knight. "Please, gentlemen, let's act civilized."

And that was a hot one—him calling us gentlemen.

"It seems to me," said Carr, "that the matter of the peeper is somewhat immaterial if Bob has turned it to some useful purpose."

"Let's all sit down," Knight urged, "and maybe count to ten. Then Bob can tell us what is on his mind."

It was a good suggestion. We all sat down and I told them what had happened. They sat there listening, looking at all that junk on the table and especially at the cone, for it was lying on its side at one end of the table, where it had rolled, and it was looking at us with that dead and fishy eye.

"Those Shadows," I finished up, "aren't alive at all. They're just some sort of spy rig that something else is sending out. All we need to do is lure the Shadows off, one by one, and let them look into the peeper with knob 39 set full and—"

"It's no permanent solution," said Knight. "Fast as we destroyed them, there'd be other ones sent out."

I shook my head. "I don't think so. No matter how good that alien race may be, they can't control those Shadows just by mental contact. My bet is that there are machines involved, and when we destroy a Shadow, it would be my hunch that we knock out a machine. And if we knock out enough of them, we'll give those other people so much headache that they may come out in the open and we can dicker with them."

"I'm afraid you're wrong," Knight answered. "This other race keeps hidden, I'd say, for some compelling reason. Maybe they have developed an underground civilization and never venture on the surface because it's a hostile environment to them. But maybe they keep track of what is doing on the surface by means of these cones of theirs. And when we showed up, they rigged the cones to look like something slightly human, something they felt sure we would accept, and sent them out to get a good close look."

Mack put up his hands and rubbed them back and forth across his head. "I don't like this hiding business. I like things out in the open where I can take a swipe at them and they can take a swipe at me. I'd have liked it a whole lot better if the Shadows had really been the aliens."

"I don't go for your underground race," Carr said to Knight. "It doesn't seem to me you could produce such a civilization if you lived underground. You'd be shut away from all the phenomena of nature. You wouldn't—"

"All right," snapped Knight, "what's *your* idea?"

"They might have matter transmission—in fact, we know they do—whether by machine or mind, and that would mean that they'd never have to travel on the surface of the planet, but could transfer from place to place in the matter of a second. But they still would need to know what was going on, so they'd have their eyes and ears like a TV radar system—"

"You jokers are just talking round in circles," objected Mack. "You don't know what the score is."

"I suppose you do," Knight retorted.

"No, I don't," said Mack. "But I'm honest enough to say straight out I don't."

"I think Carr and Knight are too involved," I said. "These aliens might be hiding only until they find out what we're like—whether they can trust us or if it would be better to run us off the planet."

"Well," said Knight, "no matter how you figure it, you've got to admit that they probably know practically all there is to know about us—our technology and our purpose and what kind of animals we are and they probably have picked up our language."

"They know too much," said Mack. "I'm getting scared."

There was a scrabbling at the flap and Thorne stuck in his head.

"Say, Mack," he said, "I got a good idea. How about setting up some guns in that contraption out there? When the Shadows crowd around —"

"No guns," Knight said firmly. "No rockets. No electrical traps. You do just what we told you. Produce all the useless motion you can. Get it as involved and as flashy as possible. But let it go at that."

Thorne withdrew sulkily.

Knight explained to me: "We don't expect it to last too long, but it may keep them occupied for a week or so while we get some work done. When it begins to wear off, we'll fix up something else."

It was all right, I suppose, but it didn't sound too hot to me. At the best, it bought a little time and nothing more. It bought a little time, that is, if we could fool the Shadows. Somehow, I wasn't sure that we could fool them much. Ten to one, they'd spot the contraption as a phony the minute it was set in motion.

Mack got up and walked around the table. He lifted the cone and tucked it beneath one arm.

"I'll take this down to the shop," he said. "Maybe the boys can find out what it is."

"I can tell you now," said Carr. "It's what the aliens use to control the Shadows. Remember the cones the survey people saw? This is one of them. My guess is that it's some kind of a signal device that can transmit data back to base, wherever that might be."

"No matter," Mack said. "Well cut into it and see what we can find."

"And the peeper?" I asked.

"I'll take care of that."

I reached out a hand and picked it up. "No, you won't. You're just the kind of bigot who would take it out and smash it."

"It's illegal," Mack declared.

Carr sided with me. "Not any more. It's a tool now—a weapon that we can use."

I handed it to Carr. "You take care of it. Put it in a good safe place. We may need it again before all this is over."

I gathered the junk that had been in Benny's bag and picked up the jewel and dropped it into a pocket of my coat.

Mack went out with the cone underneath his arm. The rest of us drifted outside the tent and stood there, just a little footloose now that the excitement was all over.

"He'll have Greasy's hide," worried Knight.

"I'll talk to him," Carr said. "I'll make him see that Greasy may have done us a service by sneaking the thing out here."

"I suppose," I said, "I should tell Greasy what happened to the peeper."

Knight shook his head. "Let him sweat a while. It will do him good."

Back in my tent, I tried to do some paper work, but I couldn't get my mind to settle down on it. I guess I was excited and I'm afraid that I missed Benny and I was tangled up with wondering just what the situation was, so far as the Shadows were concerned.

We had named them well, all right, for they were little more than shadows—meant to shadow us. But even knowing they were just camouflaged spy rigs, I still found it hard not to think of them as something that was alive.

They were no more than cones, of course, and the cones probably were no more than observation units for those hidden people who hung out somewhere on the planet. For thousands of years, perhaps, the cones had been watching while this race stayed in hiding somewhere. But maybe more than watching. Maybe the cones were harvesters and planters—perhaps hunters and trappers—bringing back the plunder of the wilds to their hidden masters. More than likely, it had been the cones that had picked all the Orchard fruit.

And if there was a culture here, if another race had primal rights upon the planet, then what did that do to the claims that Earth might make? Did it mean we might be forced to relinquish this planet, after all—one of the few Earthlike planets found in years of exploration?

I sat at my desk and thought about the planning and the work and the money that had gone into this project, which, even so, was no more than a driblet compared to what eventually would be spent to make this into another Earth.

Even on this project center, we'd made no more than an initial start. In a few more weeks, the ships would begin bringing in the steel mill and that in itself was a tremendous task—to bring it in, assemble it, mine the ore to get it going and finally to put it into operation. But simpler and easier, infinitely so, than freighting out from Earth all the steel that would be needed to build this project alone.

We couldn't let it go down the drain. After all the years, after all the planning and the work, in face of Earth's great need for more living space, we could not give up Stella IV. And yet we could not deny primal rights. If these beings, when they finally showed themselves, would say that they didn't want us here, then there would be no choice. We would simply have to clear out.

But before they threw us out, of course, they would steal us blind. Much of what we had would undoubtedly be of little value to them, but there would be some of it that they could use. No race can fail to enrich itself and its culture by contact with another. And the contact that these aliens had established was a completely one-sided bargain—the exchange flowed only in their direction.

They were, I told myself, just a bunch of cosmic sharpers.

I took the junk that had been in Benny's bag out of my pocket and spread it on the desk and began to sort it out. There was the sector model and the roller and the desk and my little row of books and the pocket chess set and all the other stuff that belonged to me.

There was all the stuff but me.

Greasy's Shadow had carried a statuette of Greasy, but I found none of me and I was a little sore at Benny. He could have gone to the extra effort to have made a statuette of me.

I rolled the things around on the desk top with a finger and wondered once again just how deeply they went. Might they not be patterns rather than just models? Perhaps, I told myself, letting my imagination run away with me, perhaps each of these little models carried in some sort of code a complete analysis and description of whatever the article might be. A human, making a survey or an analysis, would write a sheaf of notes, would capture the subject matter in a page or two of symbols. Maybe these little models were the equivalent of a human notebook, the aliens' way of writing.

And I wondered how they wrote, how they made the models, but there wasn't any answer.

I gave up trying to work and went out of the tent and climbed up the little rise to where Thorne and the men were building their flytrap for the Shadows.

They had put a lot of work and ingenuity into it and it made no sense at all—which, after all, was exactly what it was meant to do.

If we could get the Shadows busy enough trying to figure out what this new contraption was, maybe they'd leave us alone long enough to get some work done.

Thorne and his crew had gotten half a dozen replacement motors out of the shop and had installed those to be used as power. Apparently they had used almost all the spare equipment parts they could find, for there were shafts and gears and cams and all sorts of other things all linked together in a mindless pattern. And here and there they had set up what looked like control boards, except, of course, that they controlled absolutely nothing, but were jammed with flashers and all sorts of other gimmicks until they looked like Christmas trees.

I stood around and watched until Greasy rang the dinner bell, then ran a foot race with all the others to get to the tables.

There was a lot of loud talk and joking, but no one wasted too much time eating. They bolted their food and hurried back to the flytrap.

★★★

Just before sunset, they set it going and it was the screwiest mass of meaningless motion that anyone had ever seen. Shafts were spinning madly and a million gears, it seemed, were meshing, and cams were wobbling with their smooth, irregular strokes, and pistons were going up and down and up and down.

It was all polished bright and it worked slicker than a whistle and it was producing nothing except motion, but it had a lot of fascination—even for a human. I found myself standing rooted in one spot, marveling at the smoothness and precision and the remorseless non-purpose of the weird contraption.

And all the time the fake control boards were sparkling and flashing with the lamps popping on and off, in little jagged runs and series, and you got dizzy watching them, trying to make some pattern out of them.

The Shadows had been standing around and gaping ever since work had started on the trap, but now they crowded closer and stood in a tight and solemn ring around the thing and they never moved.

I turned around and Mack was just behind me. He was rubbing his hands in satisfaction and his face was all lit up with smiles.

"Pretty slick," he said.

I agreed with him, but I had some doubts that I could not quite express.

"We'll string up some lights," said Mack, "so they can see it day and night and then we'll have them pegged for good."

"You think they'll stay with it?" I asked. "They won't catch on?"

"Not a chance."

I went down to my tent and poured myself a good stiff drink, then sat down in a chair in front of the tent.

Some of the men were stringing cable and others were rigging up some batteries of lights and down in the cookshack I could hear Greasy singing, but the song was sad. I felt sorry for Greasy.

Mack might be right, I admitted to myself. We might have built a trap that would cook the Shadows' goose. If nothing else, the sheer fascination of all that motion might keep them stuck there. It had a hypnotic effect even for a human and one could never gauge what effect it might have on an alien mind. Despite the evident technology of the aliens, it was entirely possible that their machine technology might have developed along some divergent line, so that the spinning wheel and the plunging piston and the smooth fluid gleam of metal was new to them.

I tried to imagine a machine technology that would require no motion, but such a thing was entirely inconceivable to me. And for that very reason, I thought, the idea of all this motion might be just as inconceivable to an alien intellect.

The stars came out while I sat there and no one wandered over to gab and that was fine. I was just as satisfied to be left alone.

After a time, I went into the tent, had another drink and decided to go to bed.

I took off my coat and slung it on the desk. When it hit, there was a thump, and as soon as I heard that thump, I knew what it was. I had dropped Benny's jewel into the pocket of the coat and had then forgotten it.

I fished into the pocket and got out the jewel, fearing all the while that I had broken it. And there was something wrong with it—it had somehow come apart. The jewel face had come loose from the rest of it and I saw that the jewel was no more than a cover for a box-shaped receptacle.

I put it on the desk and swung the jewel face open and there, inside the receptacle, I found myself.

The statuette was nestled inside a weird piece of mechanism and it was as fine a piece of work as Greasy's statuette.

It gave me a flush of pride and satisfaction. Benny, after all, had not forgotten me!

I sat for a long time looking at the statuette, trying to puzzle out the mechanism. I had a good look at the jewel and I finally figured out what it was all about.

The jewel was no jewel at all; it was a camera. Except that instead of taking two-dimensional pictures, it worked in three dimensions. And that, of course, was how the Shadows made the models. Or maybe they were patterns rather than just models.

I finished undressing and got into bed and lay on the cot, staring at the canvas, and the pieces all began to fall together and it was beautiful. Beautiful, that is, for the aliens. It made us look like a bunch of saps.

The cones had gone out and watched the survey party and had not let it get close to them, but they had been ready for us when we came. They'd disguised the cones to look like something that we wouldn't be afraid of, something perhaps that we could even laugh at it. And that was the safest kind of disguise that anyone could assume—something that the victim might think was mildly funny. For no one gets too upset about what a clown might do.

But the Shadows had been loaded and they'd let us have it and apparently, by the time we woke up, they had us pegged and labeled.

And what would they do now? Still stay behind their log, still keep watching us, and suck us dry of everything that we had to offer?

And when they were ready, when they'd gotten all they wanted or all they felt that they could get, they'd come out and finish us.

I was somewhat scared and angry and felt considerably like a fool and it was frustrating just to think about.

Mack might kid himself that he had solved the problem with his flytrap out there, but there was still a job to do. Somehow or other, we had to track down these hiding aliens and break up their little game.

Somewhere along the way, I went to sleep, and suddenly someone was shaking me and yelling for me to get out.

I came half upright and saw that it was Carr who had been shaking me. He was practically gibbering. He kept pointing outside and babbling something about a funny cloud and I couldn't get much more out of him.

So I shucked into my trousers and my shoes and went out with him and headed for the hilltop at a run. Dawn was just breaking and the Shadows still were clustered around the flytrap and a crowd of men had gathered just beyond the flytrap and were looking toward the east.

We pushed our way through the crowd up to the front and there was the cloud that Carr had been jabbering about, but it was a good deal closer now and was sailing across the plains, slowly and majestically, and flying above it was a little silver sphere that flashed and glittered in the first rays of the sun.

The cloud looked, more than anything, like a mass of junk. I could see what looked like a derrick sticking out of it and here and there what seemed to be a wheel. I tried to figure out what it might be, but I couldn't, and all the time it was moving closer to us.

Mack was at my left and I spoke to him, but he didn't answer me. He was just like Benny—he couldn't answer me. He looked hypnotized.

The closer that cloud came, the more fantastic it was and the more unbelievable. For there was no question now that it was a mass of machinery, just like the equipment we had. There were tractors and earthmovers and shovels and dozers and all the other stuff, and in between these bigger pieces was all sorts of little stuff.

In another five minutes, it was hovering almost over us and then slowly it began to lower. While we watched, it came down to the ground, gently, almost without a bump, even though there were a couple or three acres of it. Besides the big equipment, there were tents and cups and spoons and tables and chairs and benches and a case or two of whisky and some surveying equipment—there was, it seemed to me, almost exactly all the items there were in the camp.

When it had all sat down, the little silver sphere came down, too, and floated slowly toward us. It stopped a little way away from us and Mack walked out toward it and I followed Mack. Out of the corner of my eye, I saw that Carr and Knight were walking forward, too.

We stopped four or five feet from it and now we saw that the sphere was some sort of protective suit. Inside it sat a pale little humanoid. Not human, but at least with two legs and arms and a single head. He had antennae sprouting from his forehead and his ears were long and pointed and he had no hair at all.

He let the sphere set down on the ground and we got a little closer and squatted down so we would be on a level with him.

He jerked a thumb backward over his shoulder, pointing at the mass of equipment he'd brought.

"Is pay." he announced in a shrill, high, piping voice.

We didn't answer right away. We did some gulping first.

"Is pay for what?" Knight finally managed to ask him.

"For fun," the creature said.

"I don't understand," said Mack.

"We make one of everything. We not know what you want, so we make one of all. Unfortunate, two lots are missing. Accident, perhaps."

"The models," I said to the others. "That's what he's talking about. The models were patterns and the models from Greasy's Shadow and from Benny—"

"Not all," the creature said. "The rest be right along."

"Now wait a minute," said Carr. "Let us get this straight. You are paying us. Paying us for what? Exactly what did we do for you?"

Mack blurted out: "How did you make this stuff?"

"One question at a time," I pleaded.

"Machines can make," the creature said. "Knowing how, machines can make anything. Very good machines."

"But why?" asked Carr again. "Why did you make it for us?"

"For fun," the creature explained patiently. "For laugh. For watch. Is a big word I cannot—"

"Entertainment?" I offered.

"That is right," the creature said. "Entertainment is the word. We have lot of time for entertainment. We stay home, watch our entertainment screen. We get tired of it. We seek for something new. You something new. Give us much interesting. We try to pay you for it."

"Good Lord!" exclaimed Knight. "I begin to get it now. We were a big news event and so they sent out all those cones to cover us. Mack, did you saw into that cone last night?"

"We did," said Mack. "As near as we could figure, it was a TV sender. Not like ours, of course—there would be differences. But we figured it for a data-sending rig,"

I turned back to the alien in his shiny sphere. "Listen carefully," I said. "Let's get down to business. You are willing to keep on paying if we provide you entertainment?"

"Gladly," said the creature. "You keep us entertained, we give you what you want."

"Instead of one of everything, you will make us many of one thing?"

"You show it to us," the creature said. "You let us know how many."

"Steel?" asked Mack. "You can make us steel?"

"No recognize this steel. Show us. How made, how big, how shaped. We make."

"If we keep you entertained?"

"That right." the creature said.

"Deal?" I asked.

"Deal," the creature said.

"From now on? No stopping?"

"As long as you keep us happy."

"That may take some doing," Mack told me.

"No, it won't," I said.

"You're crazy!" Mack yelped. "They'll never let us have them!"

"Yes, they will," I answered. "Earth will do anything to cinch this planet. And don't you see, with this sort of swap, we'll beat the cost. All Earth has to do is send out one sample of everything we need. One sample will do the trick. One I-beam and they'll make a million of them. It's the best deal Earth has ever made."

"We do our part," the creature assured us happily. "Long as you do yours."

"I'll get that order right off now," I said to Mack. "I'll write it up and have Jack send it out."

I stood up and headed back toward camp.

"Rest of it," the creature said, motioning over his shoulder.

I swung around and looked.

There was another mass of stuff coming in, keeping fairly low. And this time it was men—a solid press of men.

"Hey!" cried Mack. "You can't do that! That just isn't right!"

I didn't need to look. I knew exactly what had happened. The aliens had duplicated not only our equipment, but the men as well. In that crowd of men were the duplicates of every one of us—everyone, that is, except myself and Greasy.

Horrified as I might have been, outraged as any human would be, I couldn't help but think of some of the situations that might arise.

Imagine two Macks insisting on bossing the operation! Picture two Thornes trying to get along together!

I didn't hang around. I left Mack and the rest of them to explain why men should not be duplicated. In my tent, I sat down and wrote an imperative, high-priority, *must-deliver* order for five hundred peepers.